★

I crossed over Cabrillo in front of my building. I was almost to the line of parked cars when one of them, up the street from me, accelerated from the curb and made a run at me. Without thinking, I made a dive for the hood of the parked car in front of me. I was barely airborne when the car got to me. I almost made it clear.

The car clipped my lower leg and spun me into the gutter between the parked cars. My head slammed against the curb, and as I instinctively rolled under one of the cars for protection, the black cloud descended.

★

"Exceptional suspense..."

—*The Sunday Oklahoman*

Also available from Worldwide Mystery by
RON ELY

NIGHT SHADOWS

EAST BEACH

RON ELY

WORLDWIDE.

TORONTO • NEW YORK • LONDON
AMSTERDAM • PARIS • SYDNEY • HAMBURG
STOCKHOLM • ATHENS • TOKYO • MILAN
MADRID • WARSAW • BUDAPEST • AUCKLAND

EAST BEACH

A Worldwide Mystery/February 1997

This edition is reprinted by arrangement with
Simon & Schuster, Inc.

ISBN 0-373-26227-2

As always, this is for Kirsten, Kaitland and Cameron.
And for the one who takes care of us all—Valerie.

ONE

JUST ANOTHER lousy day in paradise.

It was a trite phrase the locals of Santa Barbara and every other sunny resort town in the world repeated to one another on those days when the sand, the sea, the sun, and the palm trees all did their picture-postcard best. As much as I fought it, that hackneyed expression still jumped into my mind, but so far I had managed never to utter it to another human being.

It's what I was thinking when I leaned onto my terrace railing to see if the beach had cleared out some. There were days when the sunbathers stayed on into the evenings, not wanting to let go of whatever it was that had made the day special. I remembered such days, with those vague, unfinished feelings about them. You never knew if it was the sun or the girl or maybe just a feeling in the air that made you want to prolong them, take them into the night. Those were the times when the present and the future lined up the right way and the past wasn't big enough to butt in. You lived a little longer, though, and a little harder, and the voice of the past became too loud to ignore. It squelched the future and, with it, such days.

With the beach clear, I put on my old-fashioned cotton sweats and went down for my evening run. I ignored the elevator and opted for the three flights of stairs that let me out on the east side of the building. I passed in front of the art gallery and got a wave from Claudile, who ran the place, and for the umpteenth time ran through a quick fantasy about her. I threaded my way through Tony's Beachside parking lot, which covered the half-block set-back between my place and Cabrillo Boulevard. Once across Cabrillo, I took up my dogtrot toward the shoreline, where the sand was firmer. I turned east and jogged into a steady rhythm, at a pace a little faster than rising bread.

It was a daily thing with me, running. Running or walking or doing something outside, alone, where the mind had its own kind of release. I usually had the affairs of the world pretty well settled by the time I staggered back to my lofty digs. I hit the heavy bag, too, and swam in my lap pool, which was along the west terrace, and still did the Canadian Air Force calisthenics that had been a fifteen-minute hit twenty years ago, but there was nothing that could take the place of roadwork. Of course nobody called it roadwork anymore. It was called jogging or running or extended heel-and-toe, open course, cardiovascular cross-training, or some such nonsense, but it came out the same to me as when I did five miles every morning with Griffith and Moore, Megaton Mike and Sailor, Preacher Jack, and all the rest of the Main Street Gym fighters who were of my vintage. That had been a long time ago. But it still felt the same in the lungs, the legs, and the heart. It was only in the head that it was different.

A couple of miles later I was nearing East Beach with its permanent volleyball sites, where two-man teams were still competing for nighttime bragging rights at Pismo's. I had strayed into Pismo's a couple of times and knew how important those rights were. Pismo's was a local bar that catered to the beach crowd, especially the beach volleyballers and, to a lesser degree, the surfers. This attracted the girls, and that made the cycle, which was self-perpetuating. The winners of the day were the heroes of the night. The spoils were female. It was something even a slow learner like me could grasp quickly.

I ran on past the saves and setups and spikes toward the jut of cliff a few hundred yards farther on that marked my turnaround point. I sprinted the last fifty, made my turn wide, and took my route back in the higher, softer sand. It didn't take long for it to hurt. I pumped hard in the soft stuff until my legs and lungs began to beg. I struggled out of my own deep footprints up toward the sidewalk that ran above the beach and paralleled Cabrillo Boulevard.

Under the trees above the beach line were a series of tables and barbecue grills that had always attracted my interest. The shade and the proximity to the sand and sea spoke to me of other summer sun days and the way they had melted into soft, warm evenings. For many reasons the memory of them connected to something in the pit of my stomach.

Without realizing it, I had slowed to a walk. My short reverie was broken by the sounds of the traffic along Cabrillo and the volleyballers on the beach. One particular game had attracted a small, loud crowd. I angled in that direction. From what I could see the two teams were well matched and the points long. The two men on each team worked of one mind. Each man had grace and power, and though I knew how difficult it was to move, much less jump, in the sand, they made it look easy.

As I settled to a stop in a small open space in the crowd, I could begin to detect a difference in the quality of the players. There was one who was better than the others, much better. He was a better athlete, and he was smarter. He was the crowd favorite as well. He was shorter than I by maybe an inch or two, which still made him on the tall side. He was lean, but muscle lean. There was no fat, and it was clear from the way he moved that those muscles had spring in them.

His sets were perfect, close to the net and just high enough for his partner to time his jumps. He turned the imperfect sets of his partner into points and made some astounding diving saves. Before I was ready for it, the game ended. I watched another moment as he enjoyed his victory, and took measure of his style. He was long on arrogance and short on humility. Par for the course in today's acceptance of the in-your-face hotshot, I thought, and turned to go.

"Jake?" I heard, before I felt the tug at my sleeve.

I tried to keep my eyes up around the face someplace, but there was this naked body down there tugging at my restraint. It wasn't naked, really—it had some string draped over a couple of spots— but skin was what registered on the eye. Skin that was smooth and tanned and very much alive. It curved and bulged, too, in ways that made skin-magazine purveyors rich. She moved and things jiggled and bounced, and it took great resolve for me to keep my eyes from feasting.

It was a moment before I was able to adjust to it all. I had never seen her without her clothes before. She was a uniformed waitress at a place where I had breakfast once or twice a week, whose attention I had sought mainly for coffee refills. I was beginning to think of that as an oversight.

"Hi, Julie," I said with my eyes straight on hers. "So this is where you spend your afternoons, huh?"

She grinned impishly as if we shared a secret. "Sometimes. I didn't know you were a beach chronic. Or are you? What is this stuff you've got on, anyway?"

"Sweats. I've been taking a run."

"Sweats?" She laughed at either my terminology or my appearance. Then with gleeful interest she asked, "You live around here?"

I pointed and said, "Right up there. Not too far."

"Well, mystery man, I find that very interesting." She leaned her large bosoms into me as she pulled my arm to her. "Are you going to invite me over for a drink sometime?"

I could see then that she had already had a bit to drink or smoke. Her eyes were fixed and slow to move. Her grin was too steady.

"Sure," I said.

"Sure," she said mocking me. "I think you're afraid of me, mystery man. When? Give me a time and I'll be there."

I studied her face and ignored the soft pressure against my arm. It was almost a plain face, longish but with good features. The mouth was wide and the dark brown eyes were slightly close together. The black hair was cut short, which was probably a mistake. I could imagine that in repose the face might appear unattractive. It was her spirit and nature that lent a prettiness to her appearance.

What I was having trouble with was her interest in me. From what I could see of her she did not need to chase after some guy twice her age. I decided to quit the stall and call the bet. "Okay," I said. "Come on, you're invited right now."

Her eyes still had a dreamy quality even as they took on some new light. "Now? I can't now, Jake. I have something I have to do before seven."

"Okay," I said with a nod.

"No really, Jake, I do. Every Saturday. It's something I started in college. It's sort of a ritual with me."

"In college, huh?" I said with what must have been an element of surprise.

"UCSB," she responded with the same tease in her voice as before. "There's more to me than meets the eye."

I was about to say that what met the eye was considerable, when I felt a presence close in on us. Actually, I saw him from my peripheral vision, but there was a force I could feel as well. Her head swiveled back sharply, and she instantly released my arm. I tuned to face the volleyballer I had admired a few moments earlier. He pulled Julie to him in an easy, possessive manner.

My first impression was of an animal. A graceful, feral animal on the verge of attack. His eyes were intense fires that belonged more to a leopard than to a man. The man looked at me and only at me.

I felt what was coming. I was about to hear a version of the kind of taunt practiced by slow-witted bullies, "What are you looking at, dogmeat?" Or the stupid verbal gauntlet of the street, "You got a problem, pal?"

I set myself for the line and waited, and took in as much of the man staring at me as I could. He was maybe thirty, with "street smart" written all over him. He had tattoos on both arms, a scar across his chin, and a nose like mine, broken more than once. The only consolation my observations brought me was the thought that someone might have scored a clean hit on him. I watched closely for his first move and measured him for mine.

His smile was quick and surprising. It came so suddenly, and out of such a menacing face, it took a moment for it to fit. It was real, though, and the voice had some of the smile in it.

He said, "I'm Collin. Hi." The accent was Australian. The hand he extended was iron.

Julie bounced and jiggled, which made Collin raise his eyebrows at me and nod down at her with a sly grin. She said, "Oh, Collin, this is Jake. I don't know Jake's last name, but last names don't matter. So Collin, Jake. Jake, Collin."

We finished our handshake with nods and smiles. I didn't offer my last name and neither did he offer his. It was a curious moment, that, when we let go hands and held eyes for that extra beat. I was reading him, and he was recognizing me. I saw it happen. I saw him suddenly know who I was like someone might recognize a film star. I was certainly no one he had ever met or heard about, but he knew me.

Collin's name was called by one in the group just then leaving the beach. He turned to them and waved and called out his response, handling it much as a celebrity might. To Julie he said, "You comin' with me, Jule?"

"I'll see you later, Collin, at Pismo's," she answered.

"Right, your Saturday thing. I know," he responded cheerfully. He faced me again with that smile in place and said, "You comin' to Pismo's, blue? My shout."

"Thanks," I said, "but not tonight."

"Right," he said. "See ya. Later, Jule."

She watched him go with obvious interest. When she could feel me watching her watch him, she said, "Jealous?"

I laughed and said, "You bet. He's some stud."

"So are you," she said with a heavy dose of tease.

"Blue?" I asked with a raised brow.

"He uses it like 'chum' or 'pal.' It's an Australian thing, I guess. It's like when he says it's his shout, he means he's picking up the tab. Which he does most of the time. He lives pretty high for a public servant." She shrugged.

"Did you graduate?" I asked, getting us back onto the subject of *her*.

She shook her head. "Only in partying. I'm twenty credits short."

I let it drop. It was clear that she wasn't ready to go back and finish it out. I doubted that she wanted to face the real choices of career and life that graduation carried with it. Also, the reputation of the University of California at Santa Barbara was not built on academics. UCSB and its attendant village of Isla Vista were well known for the party atmosphere, which often became wild and out of control. It was easy to imagine how a girl like Julie, barely into her twenties, could find the mixed signals from such an atmosphere confusing.

"Why not Pismo's?" she asked suddenly. "I'll pick you up."

"You already have a date," I said.

"Collin?" She laughed. "I don't have anything serious with him."

"Pismo's is not exactly my kind of place," I said lamely.

"I'd like to see what is," she answered. "Can I call you later and maybe we'll have a late cappuccino? At your kind of place?"

"Look, Julie," I said, "I'm not saying that you don't charm the hell out of me, but I'm not what you're looking for, believe me. Why don't we drop it, okay?"

"No," she answered in a very direct way. "What are you afraid of? Are you afraid that I'll strip naked and force myself on you?"

I grinned at her. "Something like that."

She grinned back. "You don't like that idea?" She moved soft bosoms against me, and I felt her leg touch mine. I was more positive than ever that she was high on something.

"Let's just say I put a greater premium on the consequences."

Her eyes sparked with inner intelligence as she considered what I had said. She nodded her head as if some decision had been made. "Are you going home now? Are you heading that way?" she said and pointed in the same direction I had indicated earlier.

I nodded, and she said, "Wait a minute till I get my stuff. I'll walk with you to the parking lot."

She quickly gathered her things from the sand. She stuffed them all into a large beach bag, except for a thermos that she held up toward me. "Margaritas," she said. "Want one?"

"No," I replied, somehow relieved that the slight intoxication I sensed in her was from something legal.

She took my arm again as we walked toward the parking area. She squeezed it against her in an obvious way and looked up at my face for reaction. "You're very solid," she said. "You stay in good shape, don't you?"

"Have to," I replied. "Just to fight off all the soft, beautiful young girls that try to take advantage of me."

She stopped at a black open-topped Jeep Wrangler. "I bet that's not far from the truth. Can I give you a lift home?"

"Nope, I'm out for a run. Thanks anyway."

She turned and put her hands up on my shoulders. "Can't I at least call you?" she asked in a little-girl pout. She moved her upper body toward me, taking my eyes to her. It was clear she was enjoying her game with me.

"Sure, call," I said, and gave her my number. "And just so you know, the name is Jake Sands."

She pulled her head back as if to see me better. She squinted at me in mock seriousness and said, "You're not married, are you?"

"No."

"Divorced?"

"My family is all deceased," I said.

She looked inside me then, as if reading all the things I had left unsaid. The thing that happened with her face and eyes was as pure a look of empathy as I had ever seen. It was the kind of thing that can't be faked, and it made me like her for all it said about her. She was smart, but more important, she was kind.

She put that look away before doing a very slow lean in and giving me a soft, open-lipped kiss. She gave me plenty of time to see it coming. "Oh, yes," she said, with a good long look at me afterwards. "I'll call you tonight. That's a promise. You've been the object of many a fantasy for me, mystery man. I think it's time to know the truth."

She repeated my number once aloud and, with much bouncing and jiggling, jumped into her car.

The satin undulations were still alive in my mind when she passed out of view down Cabrillo Boulevard with a honk and a wave. I picked up my trot again and had a fresh sweat going by the time I hit my three flights of stairs. I pumped up them hard enough to make breathing an unnatural thing to do. Once upstairs, I leaned out on my terrace railing, letting my cardiovascular system return to normal.

I could see all of it, perched as I was on top of my own three stories set back off Cabrillo—a wraparound view of Santa Barbara and the Santa Ynez Mountains on one side and the pier, marina, East Beach, and the Channel Islands on the other. Since my penthouse aerie was the only residential dwelling thereabouts, I had no neighbors to worry about. I had one floor, of warehouse space between me and the ground floor, which was occupied by my commercial tenants: a dive shop, a rare-books store, a trendy boutique, and Claudile's art gallery. I figured that right there I had a microcosm of what was at the heart of Santa Barbara—the ocean, the arts, what was currently chic, and fine dining if I added in Tony's Beachside, a top-notch restaurant that took up the corner facing Cabrillo just west of my building. Two of my ground-floor shops fronted onto his parking lot, which he was kind enough to let me and my tenants share. It was a nice arrangement, all things considered, and as long as my tenants did well and paid their rents, I had my taxes and mortgage covered; so, at the moment, all was right with the world. My breathing settled as I cooled, and by the time I stripped and dove into the lap pool, my life had returned to its original setting.

I sat out on the oceanside terrace in a robe and watched the last light leave the sky. I brought a dinner of grilled chicken and stir-fried vegetables out and chased them with a glass of minted tea. I would have preferred a local chardonnay, but I was still a half step away from allowing myself wine with meals. I had been over the edge once and never wanted that nightmare again. Time was backfilling for me. I could even think about Trinia and Josh sometimes without the overwhelming sadness that had broken me down before. I could think about the woman I had known as Katherine, too, as what she had been rather than what I had wanted her to be. I was becoming less a prisoner to the specter of my own past.

I leaned back in the soft breezes from the sea and let my mind empty. There was nothing to do, nothing to think, nothing but that little breeze which played against my skin. I relived a little of my encounter with Julie and replayed the feeling of her soft rich body as I nodded off.

At some point I went to my bed, and when I awoke the next morning it was to a fresh, bright day. It was a day filled with chores and an unwelcome lunch at a local club with Tim Brandt, a lawyer from Los Angeles, who was doing his best to lure me back to work. I left him with a "no" that I knew he took as a "maybe," but then that was to be expected because he was, after all, a lawyer. I returned to the beach and mingled for the rest of the afternoon with the Sunday afternoon tourists who strolled Cabrillo Boulevard where the local artists and artisans showed their works along that street's oceanside belt of sidewalk and grass. It was a mindless way to spend time, but I was anonymous and free. That was, at times, a compelling combination.

At the end of the day I cleared my own decks to enjoy the sunset hour and, for the first time since the night before, remembered my encounter with the voluptuous Julie and her boyfriend Collin. A full day later I could still feel the press of her body against me. Her lips were still an easy memory. She had not called, but then I had not really expected she would. She had teased me for her own amusement, and I had let her for my own. I put it all aside and packed it into that part of my brain reserved for whimsy. I did not think long on it, nor did I attach any significance to her broken promise. Not that it would have made any difference if I had. Julie was already dead.

TWO

I HAD LUNCH the next day with Jason. His place, Meddler's, was closed on Mondays, so he liked to get away from Malibu for the day to clear his head. Meddler's was a restaurant with a supper-club format right out of the late forties. It had a roving piano player and a torch singer. It also had private rooms upstairs where Jason Meddler maintained an office, a private apartment where we fought our weekly chess battles, and a club room where cards were played for some very big stakes.

I didn't think of myself as a lunch person. Jason was. He got a special pleasure out of persuading me to join him, and the more I groused about it the better he liked it, so I complained a lot. The older I got, the more lunches I seemed to have.

I had to admit there were plenty of good lunch places available in Santa Barbara. The terrace at the El Encanto Hotel was one of them. The El Encanto Hotel sat uphill from the famous old mission. It had a great view looking down over a portion of the city out toward the ocean and the islands beyond. I got there a few minutes early, but I could see the specially equipped Rolls already in the parking lot. I turned my car over to the attendant and said, "Put it in the shade, will you?"

"Sure thing, chief," he responded, eyeing my Porsche 928 like a speed-crazed teenager.

Chief? What ever happened to "sir"? I wondered. I made my way through the lobby, a small motel-like affair that belied the quality of the place, and saw Jason at an end table with his wheel-chair facing away from the view. That figured, since he saw enough of the ocean from his own windows overlooking the beach in Malibu. I could smell his cigar as soon as I set foot out on the terrace. The other diners, all elegantly attired in light shades of linen and silk, and mostly female, were much too so-phisticated to wrinkle their noses in his direction, but I was sure they had opinions on second-hand cigar smoke.

Jason and I shook hands, which was a thing he always did, and I settled into a chair across from him with the captain scurrying forward to help. I accepted the menu and waited while the waiter fussed with my napkin and the busboy filled my water glass and tonged butter onto a dish. I ordered coffee, while Jason swirled the ice around the last of the Glenlivet at the bottom of his glass. "Another of the same," the gesture said.

"I've been sitting here trying to figure out why I like this place so much," he said.

"It's because they let you smoke those old ropes out here. Not many places left, are there?"

"Old ropes? You'll have Cuban lobbyists at your door for that, but you could have a point about the terrace here." He pondered my comment while he studied the end of his cigar. "One of the truly great pleasures in life."

"For the smoker, possibly," I said pointedly and left it there. It was an old argument we had going about secondary smoke and that sort of thing. I took a glance around at our fellow diners and was sure I noticed some olfactory attention being paid. Fortunately, I could feel the breeze shifting to take the smoke away from the terrace. I breathed the fresh air in emphasis.

"I've found a new gambit," he said suddenly. His passion for chess was never-ending. "It's a Karkov move that sets up the middle game perfectly."

"Queen's pawn, knight's pawn, bishop's pawn with a run to the side, right?" I answered.

"Nope," he responded proudly. "But I'll give you a chance to see it as soon as you feel up to it."

"Maybe Thursday," I said. "Isn't it still illegal to import Cuban cigars?"

He nodded and sipped his Glenlivet. After a puff on his cigar he said, "You did right by moving up here. This place has got it all. As a kid, I used to walk down below the Bay Club and look up at those people sitting outside on that shaded terrace having lunch and drinking fancy drinks. I used to wonder what it felt like to live in that way. Well, this is it. It's what Santa Barbara is to me. The whole place here is like the Bay Club."

"Yeah, too much so sometimes, I think." I periodically had a sour attitude toward Santa Barbara. I didn't know why.

"Your problem is one of assimilation. You have to take up tennis or golf, or maybe croquet or polo. Hell, they do all that highbrow outdoor stuff here." He had that glint in his eye which told me he was enjoying himself. He knew I had a general dislike for such games. He heard my prolonged harangue when, several years back, *Sports Illustrated* named a golfer Athlete of the Decade.

"You left out surfing and beach volleyball," I said. "By the way, you seen any beach volleyball lately?"

He shook his head. "You have, I take it?"

"It's not volleyball like I remember it as a kid."

"Ain't it the truth?" he said with a shake of his head. "Nothing's like I remember it as a kid. I don't recognize any of the sports I played, do you? I mean, basketball, football, you name it, it's all faster and tougher." He shook his head again. "But so is everything else in life, isn't it?"

"Maybe it just seems that way," I said. "Like the house you grew up in seems smaller than you remember it?"

We both ordered fish with salads under the guidance of a quickly appearing waiter. Jason accepted another Glenlivet over ice as if he were doing the waiter a favor.

"Yessir, Jake, this place gets into your blood real fast. I might just come up here myself one of these days, when I retire, like you." He gave the last a little twist, trying to get a rise out of me. I didn't respond, so he went on. "I saw where one of your fellow retirees just picked himself up a bundle on the lottery. I forget how many millions he won. Forty, I think."

"Forty million?" I said, wondering how that person must feel. "Someone from here?"

"Yeah, it was in the Sunday paper. Some lucky Santa Barbaran who probably didn't need it. He hasn't come forward yet, so he can't be all that needy, now can he?"

"What do you mean he hasn't come forward? How do they know he's from here?" There was a logic I was missing.

"They know where the winning ticket was bought. They just

don't know who bought it. The rich get richer, I guess. You ever bought a ticket?''

"Nope," I answered. "Have you?"

He gave me a rueful smile. "I have enough trouble with cards.''

Our food arrived, and Jason turned his chair a bit, facing toward the view while we ate. As old friends do, we ate in silence feeling no need to small-talk. The voices from the other tables on the terrace were quiet and civilized. The short bursts of laughter were muted and polite. I felt warmed by such consideration and lapsed into a short introspection. I reflected, for the most part, on my friendship with Jason, which went back well into the dark ages. He had saved my life once in another time a couple of centuries ago, and I had saved his during that same epoch. I hadn't been able to save his legs, though. I had done the next best thing. I had taken a blood revenge when I didn't think Jason was going to make it. "A life for a life," I had figured at the time. As it turned out, Jason recovered all but the use of his legs, so the terrorist overpaid. The odd part about it was that, sometimes, I found it hard to remember Jason without the wheelchair. But that was Jason. He could make anything work. It was the closest bond I had, now that Trinia and Josh were gone. Their names fluttered before me as reminders of misery. My mind locked on their faces and voices. It was that easy and that fast. A few months earlier the melancholy would have crept in on me like a migraine. Jason must have noticed.

"Jake," he said suddenly, "Tim Brandt said he came up here yesterday and met with you and offered you a good recovery. Why the dickens don't you do it? For you it's like reaching down and picking up money off the floor.''

"Give it up, Jason," I said. "I'm not doing that anymore. I'm out of the game. Period.''

"Okay, okay," he said, holding up his hands in surrender. "But you've got to do something. I know that you had to take a mortgage to make the trade out of that Coco Palms house into the building you've got now. Good move, I think, but what happens if one of your tenants falls out or a couple of them go? What then? You don't have such deep pockets, amigo.''

"I'll worry about it then," I said.

"Look, Jake, I know you. You have to do something."

"Why?" I asked.

"Why? What do you mean, why? You're twenty years too young to retire. You can't just not work."

"You can't use a double negative either, but you always do," I said, lightening the exchange.

"What about joining the Paladin Group?" He put that gently on the table between us. "Lew asked me to talk to you about it."

"Tell Lewis no," I answered. "I don't have it anymore, Jason. It's that simple."

"Say what?" he said in a broad imitative style that forced me to smile. "You say that after what you did on the Burley thing?"

I shrugged and fought down the impulse to touch the scars on my shoulder that were thanks to the "Burley thing." There were a couple left on the inside, too, that were a little slow in healing over. I couldn't forget that it was Jason who had introduced me to the woman who called herself Katherine Burley and that it was she who had made some of the scars both inside and out. I didn't think about it much in the daytime. It was one of those things that lived mostly in the shadows that come with night.

"Yeah," I answered. "Especially after the Burley thing."

"Everything working okay?" he asked with a slight change of gears. He pointed to my collarbone. "Still having pain there?"

I shook it off. "No, it's all healed. Lay off, okay?"

He grinned and accepted it. "I worry, is all," he said.

"I know," I answered.

We had espresso and dessert and argued about silly, meaningless things for well over another hour. After we shook hands and I watched his Rolls down the drive, my own car arrived from its spot under the trees.

"Here ya go," the bouncy attendant said.

At least he didn't say, "chief," I thought as I handed him a tip. I turned down the radio and returned it to a more moderate station, aware of where the attendant had spent his idle moments for the last couple of hours. I fastened the seat belt and put the car in gear.

"See ya, chief," he said as I pulled away.

In my rearview I could see him smile and wave. It suddenly struck me that I had received a stamp of approval. I put my hand out and waved back as I left a little rubber making my transfer to the street. The thumb he raised into the air let me know I had been right.

"Loosen up, chief," I said aloud to myself. "It's a different world out there. Damned different."

THE NEXT DAY Jason called just after my morning workout.

"I know you're going to think this is all my doing, but Jake, as God is my witness, I swear this came in from Lew just the way I'm giving it to you. If you don't believe me, you call Lew and check it out with him, okay?" He paused to give me a chance to speak if I wanted. I didn't. "Lew wants a favor."

Lew Vance headed the best private intelligence/security organization on the West Coast. It was called the Paladin Group and did jobs all over the world. Lew was a longtime friend of Jason's and mine, and we had helped him get the Paladin Group started years ago.

"The Burley thing was a favor, remember?" I slung it in below the belt. He audibly flinched but took it. I rubbed at the barely healed scars around my collarbone and said, "So how now, brown cow?"

"Say again?"

"Let's have it," I said, not entirely trusting Jason on it.

"Lew called this morning and asked if you would run a visual for him on a guy up your way. He's got a client named Parkland, a lawyer type, who's doing a deal of some sort with the guy and needs to know if the layout is the real thing."

"The layout?" I asked.

"A horse ranch up near Lake Cachuma. It's ten minutes up San Marcos Pass from you."

"This sounds like one of your plots, Jason."

"See, I knew you'd be suspicious. I told Lew that, but this is on the square. All he wants you to do is give a look-see for horses and trainers and things like that. When you have time."

"When I have time, huh?" I gave it as much sarcasm as I could muster. "Why didn't Lew call me himself?"

"He didn't want it to be a big deal. He knew if he called you, you'd do it whether you wanted to or not, and he wanted you to have an easy out if you needed it. He's just trying to save sending a man up there for a day on expenses for nothing more than a lookover." He paused for effect. "I'll come up and do it if you don't want to."

"Details?"

"Guy's name is Gable. Place is called the Four Gables. That's all there is. A drive by should do it. Just verify that it is a working operation," he said, with a slight lift from knowing I was hooked.

"Okay," I said, "but I'll give it to you, and you pass it to Lew. I don't want him thinking that I'm interested in taking on any jobs. Got it?"

"Right," he said too agreeably.

"This is just a favor," I insisted.

"Right," he answered with a voice just short of gleeful.

THE TRAFFIC WAS LIGHT on highway 154—the San Marcos Pass, as it was called by the locals—and I was able to take the constant curves at the speed limit without any slower cars in front of me. That wasn't good enough for the yahoo behind me. He moved right up on my tail to let me know that he was not happy with my mph. I moved it up a little, but still he played tag with my rear bumper. All kinds of thoughts passed through my head, like hitting my brakes hard or slowing to a snail's pace, but I was an old hand at California driving and was somewhat inured to the idiots who sometimes got driver's licenses. As we crested the hill, the road became less winding, and I sped up a little more, hoping to get more space between me and my shadow. It didn't work that way. He stayed tight to me.

I saw the Four Gables ranch sign ahead and slowed, forgetting for the moment about the Towncar sucking on my tailpipe. I drove well past and pulled to the side before I realized my companion had slipped away. I did a quick look back and saw the silver Lincoln speeding up the long tree-lined drive leading to the main house of the Four Gables.

I made a U-turn and found a cozy spot to the side of the road opposite the Four Gables that allowed me to observe without being observed. It was quite a place. Beyond the tall double row of eucalyptus trees that led to the main residence there were perfect, white-fenced pastures ornamented with grazing Thoroughbreds. I took it all in with a slight twinge of envy and watched someone come out of the main house to meet the simpleton who unloaded from the Towncar. I wanted a closer look, so I rummaged in the console between the small rear seats for my camera and lenses. I attached a 600-mm lens to my old Nikon FM and focused on the two men as they approached each other. They shook hands in a formal way, which led me to believe they might be meeting for the first time. I heard another car approaching from the Santa Barbara side of the 154. As it turned in to the driveway, I quickly put my camera on it and snapped away.

I spent the rest of the morning and the early part of the afternoon watching the various activities at the Four Gables. As a matter of course, I automatically photographed and noted all the vehicles I saw enter or leave the property, but as far as I could tell the Four Gables was legit. Maybe a bit too much traffic, I thought, so when I gave my verbal report to Jason that night I suggested the Paladin Group check out Gable's friends. I gave him the list of plates I had copied down.

"I'll bring the photos with me when I see you later in the week. I want to see how you do with your new gambit."

He perked up considerably. "Make it Thursday, if you can, or Friday. I killed the Count with it this morning. He didn't know what hit him."

"He hasn't known that for some time," I answered. "See you Thursday, maybe."

The Count tended the long bar at Meddler's. He always spoke with a definite accent, but each night it was slightly different. He was Russian one night and Austrian another. I sometimes wondered if he himself knew what he was. One thing he was not was a good chess player. I was looking forward to Thursday.

THE FOLLOWING MORNING, Wednesday, I went to Goleta. Goleta was considered a poor relation to Santa Barbara proper, even though it was hard to distinguish the boundary line between the two. I was a creature of habit, and Wednesdays were Barron's and haircut days, and both were in Goleta. Barron's was the coffee shop where Julie worked, and as I pulled into the parking lot I couldn't help but remember how she had looked on the beach. I noticed the CLOSED sign, which struck me as odd because Barron's was one of those early-to-late chain houses that truckers and travelers depended on. I checked my Promaster and noted the hour was well past eight.

I put it aside with the thought that perhaps they were doing an inventory or a deep cleaning or something or other that such places did on a periodic basis. I adjusted my plans quickly and headed for my barber, a fellow named Al, who ran a little shop in the Fairview Mall. The shop had a barber pole and was about as fancy as fried eggs. Supposedly it was only in the last year that he got a blow-dryer, but I'd still never seen him use it. He used a straight razor to shave the fringe hair and sprinkled talcum afterwards. He tweezed and clipped the wild hairs of his aging male customers as part of his basic service.

Cluttering the walls of the shop were plaques and citations from civic groups, along with his license and school banners from all the local teams. He knew his customers by name. All, that is, except me. He called me "sir," and I kept it that way, but then I was the only one of his regulars who tipped him. I got there just after he opened, and took a seat and a *Sports Illustrated* to wait.

The conversation around me that morning was for the most part about the big lottery hit from last Saturday night. I glanced through the *News Press* trying to catch up. It seemed that whoever had won it had bought the ticket locally but had not as yet stepped forward to collect. End of story. Beginning of speculation.

"You suppose the guy lost his ticket?" one fellow offered. That thought was too awful to contemplate, even for Al.

"I bet he's checking it all out with a lawyer before he comes forward," Al offered. "I know I would."

"Maybe he's wanted for something," another customer said.

"He's probably another one of those illegals tryin' to figure a way to get it all over the border without payin' U.S. taxes on it." The one who said it looked around waiting, I suppose, for applause. He settled for a few nods.

"You know," Al interceded, taking back the floor, "it's probably just some guy who forgot to check his ticket. I do that all the time. Lois is always yelling at me to watch the eight o'clock show and check the tickets. Sometimes I do, and sometimes I don't. Lois does, though. She don't let nothing slip."

Some guy who had heard enough of it said, "Raiders didn't do dick last year. Think this year's draft will make any difference?"

"The Raiders? How about the Rams? At least the Raiders have got a quarterback that'll take a hit."

"You got that right, Jimmy. He was sacked more'n anybody in the league."

"Bull," Jimmy countered.

I felt a soft smile grow inside as I leaned back and listened. I drifted into a semi-conscious state, letting the wave of argument and discussion break around me. When my turn came I settled into the chair as quietly as I could, not wanting to break the cocoon I had slipped into. "Short," was all I said to Al, and I closed my eyes to listen.

"Sir?" Al shook me gently. "Sir? You're all done, sir."

I opened my eyes to realize I had fallen completely asleep. There was silence around me as the others stared in my direction. I wondered if I had snored. I sat up straight and slowly got to my feet. The silence followed me. I handed over money to Al while all the others watched. I tipped a little bigger than usual.

"Thank you, sir," Al said politely and formally.

I stepped to the door and looked back at Al. I said, "You ever think maybe it's a woman?"

Al said, "Sir?"

"That lottery winner. Might be a woman."

The silence was something I could feel all the way to my car. My radical idea had ruined my chance of ever making it into the inner circle at Al's Barber Shop.

I WAS TRYING TO decide where to have breakfast when I passed Barron's again. I glanced toward it and noticed some activity inside. The same cars were in the parking lot that had been there on my first stop. Something was not right. I pulled in.

The CLOSED sign was still up, but I ignored it and went to the door. I pulled, and it opened. I stopped just inside and waited as the woman I recognized as the hostess left a small group of employees and approached me in zombielike fashion.

"I'm sorry, sir, but we're closed," she said. Then she broke momentarily from her trance as she recognized me. She almost smiled. "Oh, I know you. You're one of our regulars. It's a terrible day for us here."

I scanned the room quickly. Most of the employees were seated at one large table. There were two men I didn't recognize at another table talking to one of the waitresses. They turned in my direction, and I could read "cop" in blazing neon right across their foreheads.

"Trouble, huh?" I said with a short nod at the two cops. "I hope no one was hurt." I was thinking then that they had been robbed. Nothing else figured to me at the moment.

The hostess shook her head, swallowing back some teariness.

"Julie, the girl who usually waits on you?" the hostess said and paused for my acknowledgment. I held my breath and gave it. She continued. "They found her body this morning. She was killed."

"She was killed?" I repeated, not quite grasping it. "How? Was it an accident?"

"The police say no. They said she had been beaten up and strangled. It was so bad, they had a problem identifying her. They've been here since early this morning questioning all of us. It's such an awful thing. I can't believe it yet. None of us can."

"You're sure it was Julie?"

"Oh, yes, they took Carrie to see her, for the identification, you know. She and Carrie were best friends. Carrie won't be coming back in today, but I guess we won't be open anyway, so it doesn't matter."

She was in that state of shock where she didn't know what she was saying or to whom. I decided to get as much as I could before she woke up or before one of the cops began to show more interest in me.

"When did it happen?" I asked.

The hostess raised her eyes to me for the first time. "I don't know," she said. "I assumed it must have been last night, but I don't know. I should ask that, shouldn't I?"

"Was Julie at work yesterday?" I asked.

She shook her head.

"The day before?"

Again she shook her head.

"Was she scheduled to work those days?" I asked, pressing a little harder.

The hostess nodded in an absent sort of way.

"And Julie didn't call in sick or anything of that nature?"

"No," the hostess finally said. "That's odd, isn't it? I should tell the police that, shouldn't I?"

One of the policemen was turning his full attention to me. I could see his mind taking in my size and general appearance. I wanted to get away from there before he got a close-up look at the crisscrossed scars across the bridge of my nose or noticed some of the other dents that were not laugh lines.

"I'd better go now," he said. "I'm sorry it was Julie."

"Yes," she replied as I pushed at the door. "I'm sorry it was Julie, too. She was special, you know. This will kill her folks."

I moved rapidly to the car and pulled out of the parking lot as the curious detective stepped out to follow me. I pretended not to see his signal to stop and turned out into the light traffic of Calle Real. I let a truck hide my rear license plate from him. His body language was a bit on the nasty side as I lost sight of him in my rearview.

It was only then, or maybe a few blocks later, that I actually thought about it. Julie. I had not known her, really. She had been a waitress who poured me coffee and smiled and made my Wednesday mornings a little brighter. I knew her about like I knew the other waitresses I didn't know. The hostess had said she was special. She was young and she was vibrant, I knew that much. She was kind, too, I thought. It was in her eyes, always. Yes, she had been special.

"This will kill her folks," the hostess had said. I thought about Julie as I had last seen her: bikini-clad, suntanned, playing at being naughty, and rich with the adventure of a future before her. No more. I wondered how her parents would remember her, how they had last seen her. Would it kill them, or would they live the rest of their lives empty and ridden with hate or guilt or both?

I said her name aloud into the wind passing in my window. It came back to me not as "Julie" but as "Jule." Where had I heard that? Jule. Jule. It was what her father might have called her. Or a lover.

THREE

Jason was on his game. I, on the other hand, was struggling for concentration. He was using his knights sparingly and well, which was unusual for him, since he generally overused them, so taken was he with their complex movements. I had managed a stalemate in the first game and was barely holding on in the second. We played without a clock, which made for some prolonged deliberations between moves. It was in those long intervals that our individual quirks surfaced. When Jason was losing, he usually rubbed the underside of his chin with the backs of the fingernails of one hand and twirled his scotch with the other hand. When he was winning he would whistle low and tunelessly between his teeth. It drove me up a wall.

"It's getting late, Jason," I said, trying to prod him into making his move.

"My, my, aren't we edgy tonight," he said without looking up and with a resumption of his little whistle.

I swallowed back any further exchange and waited. It was an old pattern with us. On my good nights, during my contemplations, I would evidently snap my fingernails, which Jason could not bear. Such habits were not intentional, but neither of us did much to curtail them. There was some fun in getting under the other's skin. Therefore, we each fought to hide our irritations. It was more or less what my trainer from years ago, Cannonball Brown, used to tell me when I was just starting to learn to fight. "Never let the other guy see you're hurt or tired. You win most fights inside the other guy's head."

Jason finally made his move and leaned back in satisfaction. I could see why. He had a neat little trap set on my queen. Three moves later I resigned.

"I'd like to believe I did this with my superior play, but I have to acknowledge that you're a bit off your game, chum. What's up?'' Jason wheeled himself to his bar to add a splash of Glenlivet to his glass.

"Nothing's up. It just takes so damn long between moves I forgot what I'm doing.'' I said it with the show of rancor I felt it deserved.

Jason put his head back in a deep, spontaneous laugh. At my expense, of course. "I love it when you're a bad sport,'' he said. "That really makes it sweet.'' He continued to grin but looked at me with that look I knew from all our years as "Tell me.''

"A girl I knew was killed a few days ago,'' I said. "The paper today said it happened Saturday night. I saw her Saturday. It's just something I've been thinking about, is all.''

"You know her well?'' he asked.

I shook my head. "That irritating whistle of yours got me thinking about habits, though. She did something on Saturdays that was habitual. I was wondering if it figured.''

"Was I whistling?'' he asked in surprised innocence. "What did she do on Saturdays?''

"I don't know,'' I answered. "Something she'd done for years, though.''

"Who was she? Anyone I'd know?''

Again I shook my head. "A waitress at a chain house called Barron's.''

"So how are you in this?'' he asked, with more than a casual look up over the rim of his glass.

"I'm not. She was young and probably one of the good ones. I don't know. It seems like a tragedy.'' I got to my feet. "It's late.''

"Did you bring me that stuff for Lew?'' he asked as he wheeled himself ahead of me to the door.

"The photos and a time-and-description sheet on the arrivals. I dropped it on your desk on the way in,'' I answered and nodded toward the packet.

He grinned. "How'd it feel?'' he asked.

"How'd what feel?''

"Being back at it?'' he said. "Out there doing something again?''

"For God's sake, Jason, will you knock it off?" I said, letting my irritation show.

"There's a big difference in you, amigo, when you're involved in something. In that last little thing you got mixed up in, it wasn't just Katherine Burley, or whatever her name was, that had you turned on. It was the Leeds murder and all the dark corners you began to look into that got you going. You acted ten years younger while that whole thing was happening. Didn't you feel it? Didn't you feel some of it again when you were out at Gable's place?"

"Feel what out at Gable's place? Number one, all I did was sit in my car for a couple of hours and watch people come and go, so I wasn't out there 'doing something again.' Number two, I'm not going to go back to work. Period."

He accepted it with a shrug. We shook hands. He said, "How about next week?"

"You're on," I said.

"Let me know what you turn up on that girl. What's her name again?"

"Julie Price," I answered. "I'm not going to turn up anything, Jase. I'm not involved in it. Now don't start on that, okay?"

"Start what?" He sold innocence about like today's overpaid sports stars sold humility.

"Good night," I said from an attitude filled with exasperation.

"Adios, amigo," he replied and watched me to the stairs.

I heard the door close at my back, but just before it did I heard that irritating little whistle begin again. I wondered if that supercilious grin of his made the whistle more difficult to do.

I GOT HOME in time to watch the late news on a local channel. The coanchors were a mismatch. He was stiff and humorless, and she was too pleasant about people starving in Somalia.

From a semidoze I saw a couple being followed by a determined reporter as they approached the front of the Sheraton Hotel. They looked haggard and deeply saddened. I knew who they were instantly and sat up to listen.

"Mr. and Mrs. Price, is there anything new in your daughter's case? Do the police have any leads yet?"

The man stopped and shook his head, looking lost and slightly afraid. His wife pulled at his arm. The reporter shot another question quickly.

"Is there anything you would like to say to the public about Julie or about the way the police are handling things? Anything?"

The man hesitated, with a look around as if he were trying to identify his surroundings. He looked at his wife before he said, "She was a good girl. Someone knows something, and they should come forward. Please."

Tears welled up in his eyes, and his wife moved between him and the reporter and pushed him along. The reporter turned to the camera and said, "Well, Barb and Dave, you can see that the Prices have been hit pretty hard by this. The police don't seem to have anything new on it either, so it's pretty much as we reported it yesterday."

I tuned out the inanities that passed between the on-site reporter and Barb and Dave, while I watched the couple in the background. The man was shattered completely, and the woman was not much better off.

Their image haunted me through the night, and though I slept, it seemed as if I had not. I awoke in the morning with the odd feeling that I knew those people as one might know a neighbor or distant relative. I couldn't shake the sense of sadness they'd projected. It was especially acute when, on my evening run, I passed the volleyball courts on East Beach. I ran past hard, not wanting to remember too much about Julie as I had last seen her.

THE LOCAL PAPERS carried stories about Julie's parents for the next couple of days. Because Julie's body had been found on an empty parcel of land called Pelican Point, the paper was calling it the Pelican Point murder. A caption to a picture of the couple I had seen on television read, "Pelican Point murder victim's parents speak out." They hit the human-interest angle a little too hard for my taste. There was no new information to be gleaned from their stories, other than the fact that the Prices lived in a northern California town called Lodi and that Julie was their only child. One particular quote struck a chord with me. It was in response to a tactless question asked by the reporter.

"How are you coping with losing your daughter in such a brutal manner?" the reporter asked.

I could imagine the look of astonishment that must have crossed the faces of the Prices. The answer quoted in the paper was attributed to him, but I felt sure he spoke for them both.

"Coping? You don't cope with such a thing," he was quoted as saying. "You don't survive the loss of a child no matter how it happens. Only thing I could hope for now is a little revenge, but life for Milna and me is the same as over. You wouldn't know about that, though."

The Prices had probably walked away at that point, since nothing more was quoted. It was amazing that he had bothered to answer such a question, but his answer did bring the tragedy home to the reader, or at least to me.

The Pelican Point murder case ran out of steam and disappeared from the pages of the newspaper in a very few days. I had to guess that the Prices had left town and the case had come to a dead end. Of course, there was a big story to replace it. The forty-million-dollar lottery winner had come forward.

I read the headline over my coffee at Barron's. Oddly enough, I went there without any intention of doing so. I was in the parking lot before I realized where I had so automatically and unconsciously driven. I went inside and took the table I most often used when Julie had been alive. The hostess offered coffee, which I took, and a paper left behind by another customer, which I also took.

The headline read LOTTERY WINNER COMES FORWARD. The story went on to tell of a claim that the winning ticket was being held by a small group of investors. Their spokesman was a man named Parkland, who declined to give the names of the other members of the small syndicate since they were, as he stated, "a business entity who wishes to remain anonymous." Parkland himself was identified as a lawyer from the Los Angeles area. That was when the tumblers inside my brain clicked, and my interest picked up.

Parkland went on to state that they had legally verified the ticket as a winner but were not yet ready to submit it to the lottery board for the official claim. The group was "at this time looking at the tax ramifications before establishing the form in which the claim would be made." He was coming forward now because he needed the board's help in making the determinations, and he wanted to be sure to meet all the time requirements. The story was accompanied by a picture of a convenience store owner who, by virtue of the fact he had sold the winning ticket, was also to be handsomely rewarded by the state.

I was well committed to the story when the waitress made a small sound beside me to get my attention. "Did you wish to order something?" she asked. She looked at me with a sad straight face.

"Oh, sorry, I was reading about this lottery thing," I said and quickly reached for the menu I had put aside.

"Yeah," she said with a slanted smile, "they probably bought a few thousand tickets. There are a lot of syndicates doing that now for all the big ones."

I suddenly had a feeling about her. I knew her, or thought I did. "You're Julie's friend, aren't you?" I asked and did a quick rummage through my memory bank. "Carrie, isn't it?"

She nodded and said, "And you're the mystery man. Julie used to talk about you a lot. That's why I sort of stole you from the other waitress. This isn't my station."

"Good," I said with what I figured would pass for a smile, "because I'm not hungry. I'll just have coffee. What do you mean she talked about me? I didn't really know Julie other than from the times I came in here."

"No, I know that. I mean she used to speculate on you. Fantasize, you know?" There was a tiny gleam of fun in her eyes, though they still read sad to me. "You were always alone and came in on Wednesdays, I think it was, and had this look, you know, of having lived a lot, you know?"

"You and Julie were close friends, I take it?"

She nodded. "Ever since she came to work here. We shared a duplex."

She was pretty. I put her in the mid-twenties. She was tall and very tanned, with dark gleaming hair and eyes that were almost black. Her lips were full and painted with fresh red lipstick. I wondered if she had done that before coming to talk to me. I

could smell her perfume, which made me think it was also fresh.
It was of a lemon scent. I would have chosen attar of roses for
her.

"I'm Jake," I said.

She immediately put out her hand. We shook hands very formally. Hers was smooth and long-fingered. The nails were short
but neatly trimmed. She gave my hand a squeeze before she let
it go. "Carrie," she said.

"You were roommates?" I asked.

"Not really," she answered. "It's a duplex. She had one side,
I have the other."

I nodded. She felt she needed to say more and continued. "It's
near the beach, in the Mesa area. I lived there already and told
Julie about it when the other side became vacant. It was real nice
that way, because we had each other there to talk to if we wanted,
and then when we needed privacy, you know, we had our own
place. It was nice, you know, living next to each other like that.
We kept keys to each other's places and kept an eye out for each
other. It was nice."

The sadness had crept back.

"Carrie, what was it that Julie always did on Saturdays? Do
you know?" I asked.

She cocked her head in the same quizzical way of a child. "On
Saturdays? What do you mean?"

"There was something she did every Saturday. It was habit
with her. Saturday evenings, maybe?" I groped with it, not knowing enough to make a clear-cut question.

She appeared to give it real thought before answering "I can't
think of anything she did like a habit. She went to Pismo's on
Saturdays a lot, but not always. She was going on the Saturday
they said she was killed. I know, because she called me real
excited about it and wanted me to meet her there."

She paused long enough for me to form a picture of Julie as I
had last seen her. She had invited me to Pismo's also. I wondered
if she had ever made it.

"Did you meet her there that night?" I asked.

"Oh, no," she answered. "I didn't even get the message until
Sunday. She was real spontaneous, you know, like she did things

on the spur of the moment most of the time. She was real hard to predict, you know?"

"I got the impression it was part ritual with her. I seem to remember that she even referred to it as ritual. It might have been religious in nature. Can you think of anything like that?" I felt she had the answer if I could only press the right button.

She made a sound that could have been a chuckle if there had been humor in it. "Julie was not religious. I mean she didn't go to church ever that I knew of."

"Maybe it was a synagogue. She would have gone to services on Saturdays in that event."

"I don't think so. That is, I don't think she went to any kind of services, Jewish or any other kind. She wasn't like that, you know. She was, you know, a free spirit," she said with more sadness creeping in.

I let it drop. I didn't know why I was pressing the point anyway. It was none of my business. I sipped the coffee, which had turned cold.

"You want some more coffee?" she asked, a waitress again.

"No, thank you," I replied, once more the customer. "I need to be going. It was nice talking to you, Carrie."

"Her parents have sort of, you know, put me in charge of her things. I even have to pack them up from her side of the dupe before the rent is up. I guess they don't want to have to face it and all. If you want to call me ever, you know, about Julie or something, I'm in the book. My last name is Berry," she said with a weak smile.

I nodded as I rose, trying to determine if she was making some play I wasn't getting. Her face was set in a sad smile, which said nothing more to me than her words had. Her face didn't change even as I sent her a last small wave from the door.

I pulled into traffic thinking about her name and imagining there must have been some tough moments growing up with a moniker like Carrie Berry.

FOUR

THE WATER WAS deep blue, the sky orange. A hard vista to ignore. I kept one eye on it while I prepared a green sauce for the poached salmon. There was nothing tricky about it as long as I kept the right proportions of parsley, chives, onion, tarragon, and garlic. I mixed that into the wine vinegar and olive oil, added some Düsseldorf mustard, and topped it all with grated hard-boiled egg. I tore some romaine and threw in some sage croutons with a Caesar dressing. Supper.

I carried my creations out to the terrace along with a tall glass of iced coffee and let myself enjoy the last lights of an exceptional day. It had been classic Santa Barbara weather from dawn to dusk without the glitches of wind or fog. All my petty complaints about the place disappeared into a desire to live in such days forever.

It was a Saturday on the verge of becoming a Saturday night. The heat of the day was holding firm, and I felt a sense of relief that I was not on the ground floor without the benefit of the small upper-level breeze. I relaxed back in the comfort of the chaise with a full stomach, watching the last orange tones leave the sky.

I had once heard it said that the center of a man's pleasures grow ever upward as he grows older. I did not necessarily smile at the fact that I was spending so much attention on the affairs of my stomach. I patted it then, less in satisfaction than in the awareness that it was not as lean as it once had been, nor was I as quick and ready to move, but I was in a denial mode that night. I roused myself from my comfortable chair as if the movement to the terrace railing was all I needed to turn back the years.

It was full dark before I showered and dressed for going out. Without a conscious destination in mind, I went out chasing my youth or running from my encroaching years, whichever the case might be. Or so I thought. The real truth of it was lodged in a restive corner of my mind. Things troubled me sometimes that stayed beneath the surface, moving me to act in ways strange to my conscious mind-set. I had learned to let it happen.

I peeked in briefly at Tony's Beachside. Tony had already left for the day. If I knew Tony Scolari, he was not sitting at home watching TV sitcoms. Unlike me, Tony needed company. That was the main reason he was making out three separate alimony checks each month. He was a modern man with all the modern crises of identity the new age brought with it. I liked Tony and enjoyed his style, but I pitied him, too. One day he'll wake up and be old, and the worst part of it is, he won't have seen it coming.

I wandered an hour or so, enjoying the old town of Santa Barbara. I could do that because the street beggars tended to back off from me once they got a good look. The streetwise see with eyes the insulated mainstream of society do not. They recognize a danger to them at a much earlier stage. I did not pretend to be sympathetic to their cause.

Somewhere around eleven I came to my inevitable destination. I had been headed for Pismo's from the beginning, most likely, without knowing it. I was not surprised. In fact, I was relieved.

I had known places like Pismo's all over the world. The in spots for a passing parade of in people. It was when the in people were out, or the in people moved out, that such places turned into empty caverns overnight. The "what's in, what's out" concept always reminded me of those sidewalk cafes in Rome that lined the Via Veneto. All alike, all serving the same food, all positioned in roughly the same locale, but at any given time, one of them would suddenly be in, with people standing waiting for tables, while the places across from them and even immediately adjacent to them would have all their tables empty, their waiters standing watching the business next door. It was a kind of madness I never understood, and I never knew how all the people knew when to change places. It was as if a notice had been posted.

There was no question that Pismo's was riding the crest of its in wave. The noise was at the hurt level, with people crushing themselves into a squirming sea of bodies dancing in the spaces between tables. I edged my way through to the only opening at the bar I could see. It was at the end against the wall, which

proved to be a good vantage point for the rest of the room. I was
glad I had worn chinos and a pullover. A jacket might have
brought a hush to the place. A tie would have caused apoplexy.

I knew no one and no one knew me. The bartender, however,
seemed to think he knew me. He thought I was someone named
Buddy.

"Hey, buddy, what'll it be?" he asked in his best surly macho
manner.

I let him think I mistook him for someone named Pal.

"I don't know, pal. Maybe a plain soda."

He sneered and delivered my order with a gruff, "Two bucks."

"Does that include tip?" I asked innocently.

"No lip, pal, just give with the two bucks," he answered back.

"I thought *I* was buddy and *you* were pal," I said, sliding the
two dollar bills to him with a look into his eyes. "Keep the
change."

He took an extra beat before he decided that no reply was his
best move. I watched him retreat away from me down the bar.
He had not helped my night, and I had not helped his. Why?

"Buck's an ass," a strong female voice declared.

She was sitting on the stool closest to me. She was with a male
friend and had sat facing him before. When she turned toward
me, I could see a bright, pretty face. I nodded in agreement, assuming that Buck was the bartender.

"He thinks if you're not swilling booze, you shouldn't be in
here," she continued. "Have you ever tried these flavored mineral
waters? They're really good."

She indicated the bottle by her glass. It was shaped like something a genie might pop out of. It had a picture of cherries on it.
The fellow with her gave me a sort of shrug, then glanced away
toward the sea of flesh. I nodded to her in my most agreeable
fashion.

"I'll try it next time," I said.

She leaned slightly to me. "I loved that bit about the tip. You
really scalded him with that one."

"What am I hearing? Not England?" I left it dangling as a
question. At the same time, I was thinking, bar talk, an easy thing
to slip back into.

She laughed and shook her head. "Most definitely not. Down under. I'm long time away, but I'm still Aussie to the core."

I smiled and nodded in a polite way that could end it and allow her to easily turn back to her companion. She did not. Instead she looked even more intently at me.

"What kind of sport did all that to you?" she asked bluntly.

"You mean the nose?" I asked somewhat defensively.

"The nose isn't so bad," she continued candidly. "I was looking more at those nicks around the eyebrows and along the jaw there. You didn't play Australian football, did you?"

"Nope. That's too rough for me," I offered.

"I doubt that," she replied. "That's what scared Buck off, I'd bet. He's a natural bully, that one."

Something had tugged at me from the moment she first spoke. It finally hit home.

"I met another Australian here a few days ago, playing volleyball. Do you have a colony here?" I asked.

"There are a few of us about. Now if he was a bad or mediocre player, it was either Rod or Tony," she said with a finger pointing to vague areas across the room. "If he was super, it was only one. Collin." She did not point into the room with Collin.

"Yes, it was Collin," I said, happy that she had supplied the name.

"I thought as much," she said with a strange smile. "Most people remember meeting Collin."

"I don't see him in here tonight," I ventured.

"He's been among the missing for a few days," she replied. "You can tell by all the long faces on the young girls."

For the first time I noted that she was not herself a young girl. She was most likely in her early thirties, but her lilt and energy gave the impression of a younger person.

"I met him with Julie Price, the girl who was killed a couple of weeks ago," I said as simply as possible. "Did you know her?"

"I knew Julie," she answered without hesitation. "She was great. I tried to warn her off Collin, but you know Julie, she was full of adventure."

"What do you mean, warn her off?"

"Collin can be a bit rough on the ladies. Men, too, for that matter, those who dare stand in his way. There's more than one boyfriend or husband who's come up with a broken head for coming in at the wrong moment. Collin's gratifications always come first."

I remembered my first impression of him before he turned on the charm. I asked, "He's violent?"

She answered softly, "Brutal."

I was slightly bewildered by what I had just heard. I was still trying to put it in perspective when her companion returned his attention to us.

"You gonna give me a lift home or what?" he asked, not unpleasantly.

She smiled in an odd way at him and said, "We were just discussing Collin. I described him as brutal. Would you agree?"

It was a cruel thing she had done, for I could see instantly that the man had been one of Collin's victims. His eyes took on the fright of some flash memory from within. He unconsciously rubbed his shoulder.

"He's none of my concern," he said sharply. "Yes or no on the ride?"

"Yes," she said and stood. She was tall and slender in an athletic way. Her hand came forward as she said, "Angela Borne."

I stood and shook the offered hand. "Jake Sands. Just one last thing. Is there any way you would know if Julie was in here two weeks ago? It was a Saturday like tonight."

She answered right away. "I was here, but Julie wasn't. She never showed. I had two new suits for her she'd ordered from the week before."

She seemed to study me for a moment before she said, "You can find me at Angela's Bikinis and Things on State Street. Come take me to lunch someday and we'll continue this little dialogue. Okay, mate?" She gave the last an exaggerated Aussie twist.

Sometimes I believed in fate. Sometimes there was no other explanation for the way things happened. I suspected that fate had led me to Pismo's that night. And perhaps it was fate that I met Angela Borne.

IT WAS WELL AFTER midnight when I got home. There were a couple of messages on the machine from Jason, which I played back through the intercom while I brushed my teeth. He was miffed because I had been ducking him. He always knew.

It was this Julie thing. I didn't want to admit an involvement in it, yet I couldn't let it go. Jason would probably have said that I had been suckered in by the sight of the parents. Price's statement about revenge and not surviving the loss of a child was compelling, I had to admit, but that wasn't it. There was something about it that was all wrong. It should have been simple. A girl was beaten to death. Someone did it. Case closed.

Jason answered on the second ring. His world was a late-night one. Phone calls at one or two in the morning were commonplace to him. It was the ones before noon that rankled him.

"Where the hell have you been, compadre? What are you doing that you're hiding from old Jase, huh?" His good humor was not always so evident.

"What are you in such a good mood about? You win someone's farm tonight?" I countered.

I heard him puff on his cigar and chuckle. I could imagine the small rings of smoke he was sending up. I could also imagine the Baccarat double old-fashioned beside him with a half finger of deep amber still remaining.

"Give," he said.

"It's that girl. That Julie. I can't shake this feeling that a big piece of it is missing," I said.

"You mean like, Who done it?"

"She was supposed to call me that night. She didn't. She was happy and up and on her way to do something she had done every Saturday, she said, since she had started college at UCSB. She was going to a place called Pismo's that night. She didn't make it, yet she called her girlfriend and told her to meet her there."

My pause let him in. "So?" he said. "Now don't get me wrong, I'm pleased you're doing something, but I don't see a payday in this thing."

I ignored his comment. "I think what's bothering me is this Saturday ritual of hers. I somehow feel it had something to do with her not calling me, and her call to her girlfriend, and her death.''

''Why was she going to call you?'' I could hear in his voice a change of attitude. He was taking me seriously about it finally.

''We were going to meet for a cappuccino, I think she said,'' I answered.

''And why do you think the call to the girlfriend is significant?'' he asked, getting on track.

''The girlfriend said she was excited. As it plays for me, something must have occurred during her Saturday thing, or maybe after that, that sort of buzzed her up. Maybe good, maybe bad, but it made her forget all about me and probably put her in harm's way.''

''Have you checked the synagogues?'' he asked.

''Yes,'' I answered quickly, feeling his mind engage. ''No link there.''

''What's in Isla Vista that's not in the rest of the area?'' he shot at me suddenly.

''You've lost me,'' I had to admit.

''You said it was something she had done since starting at UCSB. That's in Isla Vista.''

His message was clear. I was a dope. I wasn't so sure he was wrong.

''Yeah,'' I said, mulling it. ''I'll check it out. What else hits you?''

He thought for a moment. ''Okay,'' he said finally, ''define 'excited' for me.''

I was, all at once, feeling very slow witted. ''I get your point.''

''Chess?'' he asked.

''Maybe midweek,'' I answered.

''Night,'' he said.

''Night,'' I answered back into a dead phone.

CARRIE BERRY WAS, as she had said, in the book. She was not, however, home the first few times I called her. No answering machine picked up. That didn't mean there wasn't one, I told myself. It was late Sunday before she answered.

After I explained who I was, she seemed fairly glad to hear

from me. "I hope you don't mind, Carrie, but I wonder if you could tell me a little more about that last message you received from Julie. The one where she wanted you to meet her at Pismo's?"

"Like what?" she asked.

"You said she was excited. How was she excited? Was she exuberant, terrified, what?"

"Gee, I don't know," she said, giving it some weight. "I think she was up, you know, happy. But now that you ask, I'm not so sure."

"How did you get the message?"

"My answering machine," she answered after a brief pause.

I took a deep breath. "Is there any chance that message is still on the machine?"

"Maybe," she said. "Just a minute, I'll check."

That was a long minute. I could hear messages playing in the background. Carrie Berry got a lot of calls. That was good, because if Julie's call had come in behind several others, chances were good that it had not been recorded over. I suddenly heard a screeching, almost hysterical voice, which was shut off immediately. Carrie came back to the phone.

"Yes, I still have it. What should I do with it? Do you think the police would want it?" she asked.

"No," I answered quickly. "Not yet. Could I come by and hear that message myself, Carrie?"

"I'm sorry, but I have a date tonight," she said. "but I'll be sure and not tape over it. I'm off tomorrow."

"Good, tomorrow," I accepted quickly. "Midmorning?"

She agreed and gave me a cheery "bye-bye." It seemed she had recovered nicely from the death of her best friend.

FIVE

I FINISHED UP my workout with a final hard round on the heavy bag. At two minutes I was punched out, with leaden arms and burning lungs. I flurried combinations into the swaying pocket of the bag, trying not to count off the remaining sixty seconds in my head. Deep from the past came Cannonball's voice saying, "He's as tired as you are. Keep in there. Make him think you're fresh."

The kitchen timer I used for my workouts sounded its weak *cha-ching* as I reached the bottom of my reserves to finish a double-hook, right, upper, right-hook combination. The bag swung in gentle mockery while I gasped for breath and gushed sweat from every pore. I took the minute rest before taking to the slant board for two sets of fifty quick-pace sit-ups. When I finally slipped into the lap pool for a cool-down swim, I could feel the last vestiges of old wounds giving way to the mending process. My wind was coming back, and my arms and shoulders were gaining strength each day.

I pulled the Porsche out into the light Cabrillo Boulevard traffic at a few minutes to ten. All the radio stations were getting in their end-of-the-hour news summaries, which I did not care to hear, so I reached into my collection of CDs and grabbed one blind. I was passing the marina when the sweet mix of horns and strings enveloped me. Speakers, high and low, front and rear, spilled magical sounds into the space around me. They were transporting sounds, the stuff romantic dreams fed on.

In the mid-fifties the late Jackie Gleason, known primarily as a comedic actor, put out some remarkable instrumentals. It was rich, melancholy music. Late-night DJs played it for lovers in secluded lanes and lonely people anywhere. It cut a deep, sentimental swath. It softened the edges of hard desire. It made love a gentle thing.

The first bars of "Shangri-La" drifted in around me as I pulled to a stop in front of the duplex that Julie had shared with Carrie Berry. At another time I might have sat and listened to the end of the song, but not at that time and not there. I felt an unexplainable discomfort as I approached Carrie's front door.

She was freshly scrubbed, dressed in leotard bottoms and a baggy T-shirt with the message "Get Your Tail in Vail" and no makeup. The hair was pulled back, the lips were fresh red, and the perfume was the same citrus extract she'd worn at Barron's. Her expression was not entirely welcoming. The tiny lines of uncertainty were working around her eyes.

"Are you a policeman?" she blurted out after our exchange of hellos.

"No," I answered.

I didn't offer more, and for some reason she decided not to ask more. She wrestled with it, but after a moment her face relaxed, and she shrugged.

"I guess it can't do any harm to let you hear this tape," she said and led me into her kitchen.

The answering machine on the counter was a newer AT&T model. I sat at one of the stools while she pushed the playback button. The machine produced a male voice in midmessage. He was awkward and the humor he was attempting was failing miserably. There was something familiar about the voice, but no one came immediately to mind. She looked up at me with an expression of "What can you do?" as the poor fellow stumbled into his sign-off of "Stay sanitary." He was followed by another male voice, which was deep and mechanical, stating the date and time. That machine voice stamp came as an unexpected bonus. Carrie nodded, indicating Julie was next.

"Carrie, Carrie, Carrie-Carrie-CARRIE," the voice shrieked. "Where are you, girlfriend? Where can you be? You have to be there. Pick up if you are." There was a short pause. "No? Where could you be? You're there, I know you're there. Do you have company? This is an emergency, girlfriend! A call for assistance! Still not picking up? Okay, no problem, I'll get somebody, but the very minute you play this back, come to Pismo's. I'll wait for you there, okay? No, no, call first. Call me at Pismo's, got it? I can't wait. Oooh, you won't believe it. I want to do this with you there. Carrie Berry-Berry, you won't believe it. Pismo's, got it? I should be there in half an hour from now, and now it's, oh I don't know, nine, I guess..." The message, which was punctuated with wild, almost hysterical laughing sounds, ended abruptly as if she couldn't waste time on a sign-off. I had never heard anything quite like it. The mechanical male voice followed. It announced, "Saturday, nine forty-two p.m."

She hit the stop button. "Again?" I requested. She complied. We listened to the bizarre message three more times. It took that long for me to assimilate what I had heard. Even then I wasn't sure of it.

"I said she was excited," Carrie said. "She was up, I'd say. Definitely happy."

I smiled at that. I said, "She was beyond any happy I've ever heard. Did she do that often, that shrieking, laughing, hysterical stuff?"

"Never," Carrie answered. "I've never heard Julie do that. She was cool, you know, reserved. She worked at that, at underplaying everything, you know."

"Why would she think you'd be home on a Saturday night?" I asked.

"Because I told her I was going to be," she said. "I'm going for my real estate license and I thought then that I'd be, you know, here all night studying."

"But you weren't?" I coaxed.

"Not all night," she answered coyly. She stretched her arms up, pulling the thin fabric of "Get Your Tail in Vail" tightly across the unbound mounds beneath. She watched me watch.

"Was it you she was after that night?" she asked, keeping her arms up with her hands clasped behind her head.

"Can you explain that?"

"It was, wasn't it?" She grinned. "When I last saw her, it was about eight or so, and she was rushing off, but she said something about not being back till late, or maybe morning if she was lucky." She put a lot of innuendo into the last part of it. Her upper torso accentuated the sexy connotation. Her smile said she had a trump card yet to play. "She borrowed one of my tops, a sexy one. We shared clothes a lot because we were, you know, proportioned sort of the same, if you know what I .mean.''

I knew what she meant. I could see it quite clearly.

"When you identified Julie's body, was she still wearing your blouse?" I asked with an edge to my voice.

Her face lost its smile. Her arms came down. I could see her temperature drop. She said, "Yes. I don't like to think about that.''

"No, I guess not," I said. "But just one other thing about that. Do you know if there was a list of personal items found with Julie's body?''

"There weren't any. No purse, keys, nothing. That's what they told the Prices. It's probably like they say. Somebody followed her to rob her. She fought, and they killed her and took her things,'' Carrie said in a solemn monotone.

"Followed her from where?" I asked.

She looked at me with sad eyes, which somehow made me feel better about her. She said, "I don't know.''

I wrote down my number for her. "If you think of anything that might have to do with her Saturday habit, would you call me?''

"Sure," she agreed and followed me out to my car. "Neat," she said when she saw it. "Great color.''

The deep tone of the oak green worked on the 928 like on no other car. I could never understand why, or why women responded to the color so well. The car responded instantly to the turn of the key with its low, guttural purr. Carrie leaned in at the sound of the music and cocked her head in response to the lush, sentimental strain.

"Muzak?" she asked, referring to the supplier of elevator music.

"Gleason," I answered, biting back a harsh defensive reply.

She smiled. "Do you have Glenn Miller?''

"And Sinatra and Nat King Cole," I replied.

"My dad would love you," she said with a small skip back.

I let her have her little moment before making a nice slow departure. She watched me away, probably thinking how quaint a man I was. For my part I was wondering how people these days developed love relationships listening to heavy metal or rap. It seemed to me that Ice T doing "Cop Killer" was a poor substitute for Sinatra singing anything. Or Gleason.

THE SHORT DRIVE from Carrie's was pleasant. Palm trees silhouetted against a pastel sky brought high expectations as I headed toward the ocean and the colorful sign proclaiming the entrance to Isla Vista. I turned off the music, put down my windows, and prepared my mind to accept and record everything I saw. I figured I would sort it out later, since I had no idea what I was looking for. After passing a row of unremarkable fraternity houses, I entered the commercial section on a street called Embarcadero Del Mar. It quickly U'd into a name change and a parallel run back the other way, making it a block between the two streets. At the middle of the U it became Embarcadero Del Norte. The only difference I could detect in the two was that Del Mar was given more to the larger places like food stores, service stations, and a couple of large pizza places. Del Norte seemed to cater more to the small front shops where you could find espresso or subway sandwiches. None of it was attractive. Isla Vista was, to the eye, a small, rather shabby place for a college town. It was not charming and quaint, as some eastern college towns were. Its only saving grace lay in the way it sat between the ocean and the mountains in a temperate climate, promoting an outdoor lifestyle.

I saw one of its problems early on as I drove by an assemblage of local gendarmes; one was highway patrol, and the other two were from the sheriff's department. I pulled over to watch as they dealt with two shabbily dressed young men who were supporting a young, equally scruffy female creature between them. It was clear she could not walk, so they literally dragged her away from their brush with John Law and proceeded down the block to a run-down apartment house. They dragged the poor girl up to the second floor, where they tossed her inside and followed before closing the door on my curiosity. I backed up next to one of the sheriffs who sat in his car writing his report.

"Excuse me, officer," I said from the interior of my own car, "I was just wondering about that young woman who was being dragged by the two men."

He measured me quickly as the concerned citizen I was and answered politely. "Transients. Drunk as skunks, not hurting anybody but themselves at this point." He shook his head. "We got a bunch like that here. They aren't all so harmless."

I nodded my thanks and took a different perspective on Isla Vista. Its reputation for wild, uncontrolled partying at Easter and Halloween tended to draw all types, I supposed. Some just never knew when the party was over.

I checked out the cross streets, finding only one thing there that was in any way unique. A rustic wood-frame structure housing a coffee shop, a sandwich place, and a beer bar filled a half block of one of the cross streets. On the wall facing the street were hundreds of messages left tacked in place by any and all who cared to do so. You could find bicycles for sale or roommates wanted. It was all on that wall.

I walked around the town a couple of times. Since it was summer, fewer college students were on the streets than there would be in the fall, but what struck me were the number of seedy characters hanging around. I spotted more than one guy who I read to be bad news. I began to see a possibility here in Julie's death if, in fact, she had come to Isla Vista that night, as Jason assumed.

One small store was separated from all the others. It was called Escobar's Keg. It sold beer by the six-pack, case, and keg, along with wine in all its forms. It was also a general convenience store. It was remarkable for one thing more, which made me smile and take a memory plunge. The front of the shop was adorned with pink flamingos. There were two permanently attached to the concrete in front of the store. Others were painted on the store's front window. I knew instantly that Escobar was a Cuban who had come here probably by way of Miami. It was a while since I had been to Miami, and I wondered if the homes in the predominantly Cuban section there still featured pink flamingos like Escobar's on their front lawns. No matter, because Escobar was certainly keeping the tradition alive in Isla Vista.

The store was also closed. A large sign was pasted to the inside of the window that read: 2, 3, 10, 18, 28, 31 YOU ARE A WINNER. ME TOO! GRACIAS, GRACIAS, GRACIAS. ADIOS UNTIL THE 11TH.

Escobar had three more days of sun and sand or whatever he was
off enjoying before the Keg would reopen its doors. The numbers
meant nothing to me, but they were certainly cause for Escobar's
celebration.

I left Isla Vista with the distinct feeling that it was a wrong
turn. Whatever it was that Julie started doing on her Saturdays,
it did not figure to have been done in Isla Vista. There was nothing there that I could see that would lure anyone back.

I felt the shabbiness of the place clinging to me. Its human
grime had worked into my pores in the short time I had been
there. It wasn't that what I saw was so bad. It was that it was
supposed to be so much better than that. A college town should
be a safe haven for the sons and daughters the trusting parents
send there. It should be uplifting, inspiring, stimulating to the
imagination. It should be a place of hope and future. It should
promote the dialogues that only begin at two in the morning
around tables littered with coffee cups and books. It should not
allow the mumbling incoherency of drunks on its streets at two
in the afternoon.

It took several miles of Gleason to dissipate the anger and to
make me feel clean again.

SIX

JASON CALLED ME the next morning wanting to see me. He said he'd pick me up at eleven. I knew something must be up because Jason didn't like to get going much before noon.

I had already had my workout, so with nothing but a little time to kill, I took a walk down Cabrillo. I stopped at the cinnamon-roll place, planning to have just a small coffee, but that was before I got close enough to pick up the scent. If I were the suspicious type, I'd think they turned the fans out toward the street when they baked those rolls to lure people in. They got me. I waved off the melted butter but took the extra icing. After all, I had worked out hard that morning.

I sat with a large coffee and my roll at an end table outside the little stand, watching the lazy movement of the ocean while I thought over the Julie thing. I thought briefly about Carrie and Isla Vista. I didn't understand Carrie and I didn't like Isla Vista. I thought a little about the encounter I had had with Angela Borne in Pismo's and what she had said about the volleyballer Collin. I still wanted to talk to him if I could, which probably meant at least one more trip to Pismo's.

My thoughts began to drift in a vague, unfocused way. Without realizing it I found myself watching a young couple who had pulled their vehicle to a stop across the street to take a quick look at their tourist map. It was clear the map was her idea. He, like all men everywhere, was showing some reluctance to look at it. It was strange how men charged forward thinking some ancient gene would lead us to our destinations without any help from gas station attendants or maps. Women, on the other hand, asked every person they saw for directions.

It took me another moment to recognize a real source of interest. What had drawn my attention in the first place was something my subconscious eye had picked up. It was the vehicle itself. This one was maroon where hers had been black, but it was the same

kind of car. It was an open-topped Jeep Wrangler, like the one
Julie had driven away in the last time I saw her. It hadn't been
at the duplex when I saw Carrie. Where was it now? I wondered.

That thought plagued me as I wandered back up Cabrillo. It
wasn't at the duplex. Why? It wasn't mentioned at all in any of
the newspaper reports, so it most likely was not at the scene where
they found Julie. I continued to chew on this until Jason's Rolls
pulled up.

"You'll have to guide me," he said immediately after shaking
hands. "I've never seen Gable's place." That was his way of
telling me where we were going. The why would come later.

"Take State Street out. It's easy," I replied and belted myself
into the luxurious seat.

Jason's useless legs were no hindrance to his ability to drive.
Special equipment made it a snap for him. He was a good driver
with only one flaw. He tended to talk a lot when he drove, and
he tended to look at the person he talked to.

"Jason," I complained. "Will you look at the road?"

He continued on as if I had not spoken. His occasional glances
forward were comforting, but far from what I would have liked.

"I knew if I told you Lew wanted another look in on Gable
you'd hit the ceiling, so I figured you might take it better if I
came with you," he was saying. "According to Lew, something
has really freaked out his client Parkland. This time Lew wants
to verify Gable's presence at the ranch. Think we can do that?"

"We?"

"Just like old times, isn't it?" he said with a huge grin.

"Do *we* know what he looks like?" I hit the "we" with a
sledge.

"Yes we do, thanks to your photos," he replied. He nodded
to the briefcase in the space between our seats. "One of those
people you photographed was identified as Gable. It's the enlargement."

I looked at the picture of Gable. The enlargement was grainy
and slightly out of focus, which gave me a fleeting embarrassment. It was, however, more than adequate for our purpose.

The briefcase contained Lew's follow-ups on the cars I had
reported and photographed. I read the reports automatically and

without much real interest. Three of the cars had been rentals, two of those from L.A. airport, the third from San Francisco. The two other cars were privately owned, one by a man in Orange County, the other by a private L.A. corporation.

It was the notation at the bottom of the last page that I found most interesting. It said the report was to be sent on a hand-carry basis to Mr. Michael Parkland at his home address, 948 Mapleton, in the Hancock Park area of Los Angeles. Parkland was identified as a corporate attorney with the law firm of Barns and Petrie, where he could be reached on an as-needed basis during business hours. Billing was to remain private, and all correspondence was to be directed to the Hancock Park address.

"So what's grabbed you, amigo?" Jason said.

"This Parkland? Who is he?"

He shrugged. "What does it say?"

"It says lawyer. Corporate. Barns and Petrie."

"Well," he said. "There you have it. So what?"

"So why doesn't the report or the billing go to Barns and Petrie?"

"It's a private matter, I guess," he said. "It's Lew's baby, not ours. Let him worry about that."

We were approaching the Four Gables ranch. I alerted Jason to the fact and put away the Paladin Group reports. Jason drove past once then circled back to park in roughly the same place I had when I was there before.

Immediately, it looked different. There was much less activity around the place. There were fewer horses in the pastures than I remembered, and it seemed there was less movement around the stables. Jason's look to me was saying, "Now what?"

"We're going to have to go in," I said. "We'll play it like we're old friends of Parkland's just passing through."

"Sounds good enough to me," he said as he turned the Rolls into the long eucalyptus-lined driveway. It was quite a place, Four Gables, with perfectly cross-fenced pastures reminiscent of the elegant Kentucky horse farms. The main house was a white Colonial and big enough to raise Jason's eyebrows while he parked the Rolls in front of it. I had one foot on the polished stone steps leading up to the house when a man approached from the side, moving with the authority of one in charge.

I stepped down toward him with a hearty hello and my hastily prepared story. He seemed to buy it without hesitation but shook his head and said, "I'm sorry, sir, but Mr. Gable is not here at the ranch now. I'd be happy to show you around, if you'd like to see the place. I'm Mimms, the ranch foreman."

"Well, thank you for that, but we were hoping to see Mr. Gable. Would you happen to know where he is now?" I said cheerfully.

"No, sir, I don't," he answered, his face taking on a serious expression. "It's got us a little bit worried, too, because he didn't show up for the auction."

Jason's back stiffened. "Auction?"

"Yessir," he said, with a lean down to peer in at Jason. "We sent practically all of our stock down to the auction in Phoenix."

Jason asked, "What are all those?" He indicated the horses in the pastures and the few visible in the stables.

"Boarders, sir." He looked around and for the first time, I could see the bewilderment on his face. "It was a pretty sudden thing. I can tell you he had some fine stock that went on the block."

"They've already sold?" I asked.

"Yessir."

"And Mr. Gable wasn't there for it? Who handled it?" Jason asked.

"Our head trainer. Seems real odd to us, though, that Mr. Gable never did show up," he said.

"Have you tried to reach him at the places he regularly goes?" I asked.

"He's usually here or on his boat. We called his boat several times, but there's no answer." He was a man who obviously was beginning to perceive a problem growing up around him. It was clear that he was anxiously hoping Gable would return.

I fixed my eyes with one last look around before opening the door of the Rolls. I said, "Thank you, Mr. Mimms, for your time. We'll stop by at a later date and try to catch Mr. Gable when he comes back."

We both waved to Mimms, who watched us all the way to the road. We were well on our way back over the pass when Jason finally said, "Son of a bitch, what do you make of that? Sounds like he's cut out, doesn't it?"

"Not necessarily," I said. "It looks to me like he's trying to raise money. Maybe he has to keep his head down for some reason until he comes up with it."

"Could be," he said, with a tug at his lower lip. "Could be. And he could have been sitting there watching us from behind those curtains, too, you know?"

"No," I said. "I'm not sneaking into that house. Don't even ask."

Jason responded with a look as if I'd just accused him of genocide. "You've become terribly paranoid and suspicious lately, do you realize that?"

I smiled it off. We rode in silence for a few miles before Jason's mind changed course. He asked, "How's it going on that girl's death you were checking out? You still doing that?"

"Sort of," I replied. "Not much there. Nothing that I can see that would have taken her to Isla Vista, and I did find out that she was very excited, on-the-up side that night."

"You check out the boyfriend yet? What's his name?"

"Collin. I'm looking for him."

"Aussie, you said?"

"Yeah, and plays it."

"It's hard for me to think of an Aussie going wrong. I don't think I've ever met one I didn't like."

"You and Will Rogers," I said.

"You described him, but I've forgotten most of it. Tell me about him again."

I pulled up the image of Collin and recited from what I remembered. "Tall, athletic as hell, handsome but tough looking, a broken nose that helps temper the too perfect looks, tattoos, mean eyes that turn friendly with a blink."

"Tattoos? Both arms?" he asked.

"Yeah, both arms," I replied. "One on each, I think."

"Jungle tattoos," he said with his eyes straight ahead.

"I thought of that, but with him being Australian, I didn't figure him to have spent any time in the pen here in the States. But maybe that's something they do down under as well.''

He nodded and let it settle. His fingers were dancing on the steering wheel. I knew he was dying for a cigar, but I would let him wait until he had the car all to himself.

''Vera wants to come up and have dinner with you at the Port House,'' he said out of nowhere. ''You should call her.''

I felt the chagrin he intended I feel. ''I will.''

''Maybe I'll come, too, and bring the whole group. You up for that?'' He glanced my way.

''Sure,'' I answered quickly to get his eyes back on the State Street traffic.

''I used to love the Port House. Is it still a good restaurant?''

We were at State and Cabrillo at that point. We were looking straight down the pier at the Port House restaurant perched midway down. Jason's eyes were softened as he remembered something from some pocket of the past. His eyes were locked on the gray building down the pier. I wondered if the last time he had eaten in that restaurant he had walked to it on two good legs.

''A tourist trap,'' I answered. ''You set it up with Vera. But just the two of you. We'll have everybody else up some other time.''

He returned to the present with a nod as he turned left onto Cabrillo Boulevard, where he pulled to a stop at my building. I got out and shook his extended hand.

''Thanks,'' he said and shot a thumb back in the direction of Tony's Beachside. ''How's Tony doing?''

''Good,'' I said. ''Same old Tony.''

''We'll eat there sometime, too,'' he said around the cigar he was preparing for ignition. ''My hunch on this Collin guy is that he did time, here or down under. I'd bet it.''

''What do *you* know?'' I countered. ''You still bet the Dodgers?''

He puffed the cigar to life before granting me his last scowl and putting the car in motion. ''With friends like you,'' he said as he pulled away, ''thank God for good cigars.''

ANGELA'S BIKINIS and Things was one of those small lower–State Street shops that I would have never seen if I had not been looking for it. I even walked past it once and had to go back to it, which was not such an unusual occurrence for me, since I was given to preoccupation.

Angela Borne greeted me with a casual warmth I had more or less expected. What got me was how much better she looked in the light of day than she had looked in Pismo's. She was not a beauty, but she sparkled with a kind of female energy. She had slender shoulders, bust, waist, and hips, but the package read all woman. I liked looking at her, and it was clear she liked being looked at.

"I saw you walk by. I thought you were going somewhere else," she said.

"I'm just lucky I remembered where I was going before I'd walked another three blocks," I replied.

"Well, I'm hungry," she said as she came around the corner and led me to the door.

"What do you do, close shop?" I asked, noting that she was alone in the store.

She nodded, turned the sign, and locked the door. She took my arm in a familiar sort of way and said, "Lead on, Macduff."

We walked up a couple of blocks to the busiest coffee shop in town, Little Audrey's. There was one empty booth along a wall of booths that ran from State to the back of the place. It looked like a half block of booths to me, and they were all filled. The waitress brought our sandwiches and coffee with an absence of nonsense and a lot of efficiency. That was probably why they did such good business.

Our conversation stayed on the safe, dull side while we ate. I waited until the busboy cleared the plates and poured fresh coffee before turning it up a notch. I said, "I'd like to talk to Collin. Do you know where I could find him?"

"At the moment, no," she replied.

"No ideas on it?"

She smiled in a grim way. "No. I'm not in his immediate circle."

"But you were once?"

"I'm not a masochist. I don't like pain of any kind. Besides, I'm too old for Collin."

"I'd say you're younger than he is," I offered.

"And you'd be right, but he likes them very young. He likes to bounce the young ones. Hurt them a little and train them to his desires. I have my own standards of pleasure."

I noticed that she had not answered my question, but I left it alone. I watched her slender fingers, which rotated the cup in a very deliberate pattern of short quarter turns. The handle moved by twice before she picked it up to drink.

"Do you know if he's ever been to prison?" I asked.

"Collin?" she said in a stall, and then added too quickly, "No, of course not."

"What kind of a job does he have? I remember Julie said something about him being a public servant or something?"

She laughed. "I don't think so. He works at something, I guess, but he has a lot of time off. Days at a time."

"Stewards and pilots for airlines have time off like that." I said it offering a possibility. She gave it one of her shrugs.

"By the way, what's his last name?" I asked, remembering that Julie had not given it.

"I believe it's Fraser."

"Collin Fraser," I said aloud, trying it for my ear. He did not look like a Collin Fraser. The name more easily evoked an image of some British actor who specialized in playing fops.

"Can I tell you something, Jake?" Her eyes were back on her cup, which was making its rotations again. "You shouldn't chase after Collin Fraser, because he might catch you." She raised her eyes to me then.

"He sounds like a very bad number all right," I said as seriously as I could. "That fellow with you the other night. He had some kind of problem with Collin?"

"That's Robert. He used to be engaged to my ex-partner. Then Collin came into the picture. Robert caught them together, and Collin put him in the hospital. That was the end of the engagement, and not long after that, Terri sold out to me and left." She quickened the movements of the cup. "That happened months ago, but Robert is still terrified of Collin. I've tried to tell Robert that Collin has no interest in him, but he won't believe me. I had to swear that Collin would not be in Pismo's before Robert would go there with me that night.''

"It was that bad, huh? Did Robert go to the police?'' I asked.

She shook her head. Suddenly she said, "Julie was a good egg. I liked her.''

She took a sip of coffee, and I looked at the strange pattern of rings left by the quarter turns of the cup.

"She seemed to be,'' I agreed. I had other questions, but I was not getting what I thought I would from Angela.

We moved to other topics and by the time I returned her to her shop, she was in a flirtatious mood again.

"Do you ever accept dinner invitations to ladies' homes?'' she asked with lids lowered in a parody of seductiveness.

I laughed and responded in big quick nods in my own parody of eagerness. "I eat a lot, though.''

"Give me your number,'' she said and pushed a pad toward me. "I'm a gourmet cook in training. If you don't mind taking a chance, I might call you some night to try one of my concoctions.''

"Deal,'' I said. "Anytime.''

My walk home was a contemplative one. I had the strange feeling I had been given a warning, delivered by a messenger, directly from the source.

SEVEN

SOMEWHERE AROUND three o'clock in the morning I came slightly up out of a restless sleep thinking about the lawyer Parkland. I wondered if Gable was part of Parkland's lottery syndicate. I wondered only briefly because sleep returned like a slow, warm wave and swept my thoughts aside.

I forgot to mention it to Jason when we spoke later that morning. He had Vera on the line with us—conferencing, he called it—while we made arrangements for dinner that night at the Port House.

"You've been very bad," Vera said, as only Vera could say things. "I expect to hear some good, original excuses from you, dear boy, for not visiting me in the last two months."

"Time gets away from me, Vera," I said, intending to say more, but she cut me off.

"And none of that drivel about how you hate L.A.," she said, letting me know the old lines wouldn't work. "Brentwood is not L.A. At least my part of Brentwood isn't. So work on your alibis, dearest Jake. We'll see you at seven. And we'll make it just the three of us, you and Jason and me, like old times."

It was a wonder to me how talking to Vera still made me feel as young and green as the day I had first met her and, of course, Henry. When Henry had been alive she was always fussing with things in the background while we talked. Her comments, when she had time to make them, had been succinct and pertinent, but she had been too busy with dinner and such for prolonged conversations. Now that she was older, and with Henry gone, she seemed to fill both their spaces. She still fussed, but now she talked, as Henry had. I looked forward to the evening.

After speaking with Jason and Vera I felt a need to get out of my own surroundings for a while. Anyway, there was something I needed to do. It was one of those mental itches that started in the back of my mind and got worse the longer I left it unscratched. I drove west along Ocean Avenue with the windows down, listening to the mix of ocean, wind, and Kenny G, who joined me from a New Age station out of L.A. I liked Kenny G. I wondered if Carrie Berry thought of that sensual silver sound of his as elevator music, too.

I passed by Pelican Point once before stopping. There was no sign of the yellow police tape that had marked the place for a week or so after Julie's body had been found. After parking on Ocean Avenue, I studied the area a few moments before walking to the spot where her body had lain. It was about two hundred feet in from the road, in dense brush next to a little-used trail.

I spent half an hour looking around for any small thing the police might have missed. I was not likely to find anything, I knew, but it also gave me a chance to get a feeling for the area. It was isolated, hidden from the road, and clearly not the sort of place Julie, or anyone, for that matter, might have had reason to come to willingly. It was possible to conceive of some nefarious schemes that might require someone to meet in such a locale in the dark of night, but none that a young woman like Julie might involve herself with.

I returned to the road and looked around. Several hundred yards to the east was a neighborhood of small, closely planted residences. Across was an intersecting road that dead-ended at the spot where I stood. It bisected a large open area with some houses set some distance back. I knew that to the west, at what would probably measure a half mile or so away, and not visible from my position was the entrance to a public beach. I walked in that direction.

There were two signs at the turn-in to the parking areas. One identified the beach as Johnson Beach, and the other was for the restaurant on the sand called the Pelican's Perch. The parking lot closest to the beach and the restaurant was filled. The upper lot was nearly half full. I had seen it when both lots were full, and both sides of the road outside as well. I rated it as an average summer day at Johnson Beach. About like the day the two hikers found Julie's body.

I wandered down the ocean, not looking for anything specific, still merely trying to gain some feeling for the place. The sight of sunbathers and the occasional whiff of sun lotion brought fragmented images from the past. My mind wandered, and at one point I even found myself wondering what that ingredient was in suntan lotion which made it smell that way. I thought of it as the scent of Coppertone, but they all smelled basically the same. And why, I wondered, was that scent to be found in nothing other than sun lotions?

That was primarily what I was thinking, but I was looking at a vehicle parked close to the outdoor phones by the restaurant. I was still mulling suntan lotion as I approached the black open-topped Jeep Wrangler.

Reason told me that there had to be hundreds if not thousands of cars like Julie's, and any number of people who frequented Johnson Beach might own one. But it wasn't a car like Julie's. I knew better. From the moment I first saw it, I knew. It was Julie's car.

The registration slip in the glove compartment verified it. I looked quickly over the rest of the car. Nothing, initially, seemed out of place or worth noting as a clue to Julie's death. It was when I began to look more carefully that I noticed the keys in the ignition. I was amazed. How many days and nights had the car sat open and unguarded with the keys in the ignition? Minutes like that in L.A. and the car would be gone.

Unless. Unless the car wouldn't start. Unless the battery was dead or there was no gas. Or unless someone had just recently driven it there.

I made a careful visual survey of the area. From what I could see, no one was watching the car or in any way showing an interest in me. Then I studied the position of the car. It was parked in front of the phones. It was near the restaurant but not in front of it. I considered the fact that, at night, she could have parked closer if she had wanted. Also she was not so far away from the restaurant that she was seeking privacy. So, to my mind, that left the phones. I wondered if she had called Carrie from there.

I looked carefully at the angle of the key. It seemed to be in the on position. That meant nothing to me unless I knew something more. I used a small scrap of paper to turn the radio switch. The nasal wail of hard-core country jumped out at me. It seemed an odd choice for Julie, but then I knew very little about her, really. I let it play until I heard the announcer give the call letters, KCAW. K Country and Western? I mused as I pondered my next move.

The battery had enough juice for the radio, but would it start the car? By touching only the rim of the key I turned it slightly more to the right. The starter growled to life right away and continued for as long as I held the key engaging it. The gas gauge did not move from its position below the empty mark. Okay, I thought, two possibilities. She came here out of gas or someone drained the gas from the car once it was here.

I wanted to be sure to get as much from the car as I could before leaving it for the police to find. I did another complete visual, looking for details. The light switch was not pulled out, the radio had been turned off but was last tuned to KCAW, the gearshift was in neutral, the key was in the on position, and, more important, it was left in the car. The front tires were turned slightly to the right and were resting hard against the curb, and Julie's purse, which had not been found with the body, was not anywhere in the car.

I spent a good half hour with the car before I walked away, as casually as possible, toward the Pelican's Perch. It had a large outdoor terrace, with tables that were half occupied. A low concrete wall separated the terrace from the beach. It gave one the feeling of actually being on the sand itself, which was nice if that's what one had come to enjoy. There was a well-appointed interior room if one had not. It was also at beach level, with large windows allowing a wonderful view from almost any table in the room. I chose a seat at the bar and ordered an iced coffee.

I tried to clear from my mind the bits and pieces I had just picked up. I wanted a clean shot at it later when I was ready to assemble it. The bulk of it was there somewhere, I figured, so at the moment, I was looking for extras. I started with the guy tending bar. He was friendly but busy getting his place ready for the late afternoon and early evening trade. He then nodded to a waitress seated by a window at the back of the room.

"She's the only one here who works Saturday nights," he said.

"There's a whole different group that works weekends. Except for her."

I thanked him, tipped him, and took my coffee for a walk to her table.

"Excuse me," I said. "I don't want to bother you, but if you have a moment, I'd like to ask you a couple of questions."

She had nice eyes, which I'd caught on the way back from a dream somewhere. "About what?" she asked.

"About a Saturday night a short time back," I said, leaving it ambiguous.

She looked a little uncertain as she nodded and said, "Okay. You can sit if you want."

Seated across from her, I could see the fresh good looks that California girls were famous for. She was college age or maybe a little younger. I could no longer tell. The freckles across her nose testified to an absence of makeup. The sparkling clear eyes, to an absence of drugs. My snap first judgment was that I was in the company of a "nice girl." It felt good.

"My name is Jake, and I don't know if you can help me or not. I haven't been here at the Pelican's Perch in the evenings, but it doesn't strike me as a place where single people hang out. Right or wrong?" I asked it with a slight lift at the end to give it a harmless note.

She smiled and said, "Right."

I nodded and gave the place a good looking-over. "I guess this is going to sound a bit odd to you, but I'm wondering if you would notice if a single person did come in here. Would it stand out to you?"

"I don't know," she answered honestly. "We do get single people in for dinner or for a drink, but it's not one of those places where single people come to meet other single people."

"No, I didn't think so." I looked for a way to approach it. "Most of your nighttime trade is local, isn't it? Repeat customers?"

"Yes. Mostly from Coco Palms, which is just up the road from us."

That was something I knew very well. Until a short time ago

I had lived in Coco Palms. I had never eaten at the Pelican's Perch, however.

"So, if someone came in alone who was not a regular, you might have noticed them?" I coaxed. "Is that safe to say?"

She gave me a cocked head and a grin. "Are you a lawyer or something?"

"Not guilty," I said with raised palms. "I'm simply trying to determine if a friend of mine might have stopped in here on Saturday night a couple of weeks ago. She would have probably been pretty up. Happy. She might have had a drink and waited around for a short time."

"Oh, I know who you mean. Yes, I do remember her. Real happy. Kinda pretty with a real, well, a real body," she said, stumbling with it. She put her hands out, slightly cupped with her palms in. The gesture could have meant arthritis or bosoms. It meant bosoms, and that meant she had seen Julie.

"Can you tell me about her?" I asked.

She gave a small shake to her head. "There's nothing really to tell. She was dressed really sexy and was like you say, really up, almost like she was high on something, only I don't think she was. I think she was just riding high on some really good thing happening in her life. She sat right there at the bar and ordered something from the bartender and left in a real short time. Once or twice she made a squealing noise like she was about to explode with some great news or something. She left a huge tip on the bar, I know that. She was waiting for someone, but I never saw who it was. I didn't see her leave, but I know she wasn't here more than ten minutes or so."

"Do you remember the woman who was killed at the point?" I asked, taking a calculated chance.

"Yes," she said slowly, suddenly more alert.

"Could that have happened the same week my friend was in?" I could tell no one had been in to question them on it.

"Yes, I think it was," she answered, obviously not making the connection. I had not thought she would, because the picture that had been in the paper was an old one where Julie had long straight hair. It had looked nothing like the pretty, vivacious young woman the waitress had seen that Saturday night.

"Well, her story checks," I said, tossing a red herring at her. "My buddy will be glad to know that."

"I thought it was something like that," she said slyly. "Are you sure it's not your own wife you're checking on?"

"Not me. I'm not cut out for the old ball and chain."

I put a bill on the table in front of her. "Thanks," I said. I left quickly while her attention was on the ten.

I walked up the other side of the lot from the Wrangler toward Ocean Avenue. I could see that the road coming in from Coco Palms was very much uphill. Fortunately the half mile or so back to my car was downhill. I was thankful for small blessings.

I SPOTTED Vera's white limo in front of the Port House restaurant as soon as I set foot on the pier. They were early and I was on time, but still I stepped up my pace.

They were seated on either side of a table by a window when I joined them. The handshake with Jason and the kiss to Vera's cheek accomplished, I sat between them facing the view of the water and the lights of the shoreline beyond. I could see that they were both slightly uncomfortable with the chairs of the tables next to ours pressed against their backs. The view did little to make up for it.

A waiter arrived with Jason's Glenlivet and Vera's Jack Daniel's. The cup of coffee was obviously for me. I met the smiles from Jason and Vera and raised my cup in salute. They did likewise with their drinks, which, as much as anything else, marked their similarities and their differences.

"It's so different," Vera said. "I know the original place burned down, but it's like going to Paris and finding Maxim's has been rebuilt as a McDonald's."

"It's for tourists now," I said with a small look around.

Vera made a grunting sound. "It may come as a surprise to the new owners, but all tourists do not appreciate being packed in like sardines and given poor food and large bills for it. You should complain."

I shrugged. "I don't care."

Jason said, "You don't have any ghosts here, amigo."

Vera leaned toward me and put her hand on my arm. "You

should have seen it as it was when Henry and I came here. I think it was owned then by the old-time movie star Ronald Colman. Or maybe he had owned it before, I can't remember, but it was wonderful. Very romantic, with decent food, French service, and a wandering violinist if I remember correctly.''

Jason's head had turned toward the view. Vera caught it about the same time I did. A silence, uncommon at our gatherings, settled in upon us.

Jason filled the silence but remained facing the window. ''It looks the same from here,'' he said. ''The view hasn't changed.'' He turned to us then with an odd smile on his face. ''Only the company.''

That was Jason. He had run through his tough memories and was done with it. Vera wanted to be sure.

''Have you kept up with her, Jason? Do you know what happened with her?''

''Yeah, remarried, children,'' he said simply. ''Three boys, one with a child of his own. I had a narrow escape there, didn't I?''

Her name was Donna, and she had taken off when Jason was injured. She left when the doctor confirmed the spinal damage. Jason was still in the hospital when he received the divorce papers.

''She sure loved this place,'' he said and added with a wry smile, ''but then, she thought the Ramada Inn was a world-class hotel.''

We laughed. The ghosts were chased away.

We talked and argued a bit through appetizers and entrees. Vera switched to champagne, I to espresso, and Jason ordered another Glenlivet.

''You haven't said a word, not a word, about yourself,'' Vera accused in my direction. ''You can be the Sphinx with your empty-headed little girlfriends, but I want some hard facts. What are you doing with yourself, my dear Jake? Are you ever going to go back to the work you did before?''

''No, Vera. I'm finished with all that.''

''See?'' Jason said, verifying my suspicions that they talked about me on a regular basis.

''Then what?'' she asked.

"Golf, tennis, polo," I responded with an accusing look at Jason. "I'll learn the games of the idle rich."

She laughed her whiskey laugh at the image it provoked. "Crap," she said, resorting to her favorite word.

"Anything new on that Price killing?" Jason asked at last, assuaging his guilt by coming to my rescue.

"I think so," I said. I did a brief fill-in for Vera before I told them both about what I had found that afternoon.

"Something's wrong there," Jason reasoned. "Surely the police searched the vicinity when the body was found. They must have had a notice out on the car. And cars don't sit in lots for that length of time without someone reporting it."

"On the other hand the beach parking lot is not all that close to the place the body was found," I countered. "They might have done a quick survey of the area, but the car would have been easy to miss if they weren't looking for it specifically. A notice on the car would have been effective if the car was on the street. And it just could be that if someone did note the car had been there for a while, they did not take the time to report it."

"Go on," Vera prodded. "What has finding the car told you?"

They waited while I assembled it in my head.

"The car was out of gear and out of gas, the key was in the ignition in the on position, the wheel was crimped to the right, and the tires were pressed against the curb," I said in quick reprise for them. "My best guess is that for some reason, probably because of her excited state, she didn't remember she was low on gas. She ran out suddenly somewhere between Coco Palms and Johnson Beach, I'd guess. I say that because Johnson Beach is downhill from Coco Palms. She must have thought fast enough to put the car in neutral and coast the rest of the way into the parking lot. She left the key on so her steering wouldn't lock out on her. Then the car was stopped against the curb at the angle she used to coast in. She couldn't back it up and straighten it out because she never got it started again."

I stopped to allow their comments. None was offered, so I continued. "She probably used the pay phone to call someone for help. I think she might have made more than one call. It could be that the first person she called was her girlfriend Carrie. I need to hear the message tape again to be sure. But it was the other person or persons she called that I want to know about. One of her calls got her killed, I believe.''

"You don't know where she had been?" Jason asked.

"Not yet," I answered.

"So you are busy," Vera concluded. "According to Jason you're locked inside a melancholy cocoon and won't rejoin the rest of the world. I can see that's not the case."

"Jason exaggerates," I said. "And my melancholy is no longer a problem. It comes in tiny moments that I can handle very nicely."

"I worry when you don't keep in touch," she punched back into the opening I had left. "I was especially worried about all that business in Coco Palms and that lovely Katherine. You seem to have recovered nicely, though."

I had prearranged the payment of the check, which irked Jason no end. He was one of the few people I knew who took great pleasure in picking up dinner checks. He complained about it to the waiter, the hostess, and most of all to Vera, who had seen the scene played both ways in the years she had known us. We made our exit from the restaurant into a warm night with almost no breeze. Vera commented on the stars, which she never got to see in the Los Angeles area.

"The Port House is crossed off my list for good. We'll try the San Ysidro Ranch next time I come up, or has that become a Burger King?" she said as she accepted my kiss to her cheek.

"Nope, it's still top-notch," I replied.

"Santa Barbara is a paradise, Jake. You've made a good move."

"Shangri-La," I corrected.

It clicked in her quick mind. "Ah, yes, your music," she said and disappeared into the dark interior of the car.

I shook hands with Jason, suddenly remembering Parkland.

"By the way," I said. "I've been thinking about that lawyer Parkland. He's the guy that came forward representing that group that won the forty-million-dollar lottery. Did you know that?"

Jason did a fast take. "No, I missed that. Why didn't you mention it before?"

I grinned. "I'm mentioning it now. I was thinking that maybe Gable is part of the group. Maybe so are all those fellows who visited Gable the day I staked him out."

"Could be," he said, losing interest fast. "Oh, by the way, Lew said to say 'thanks.' I know he's got a present for you, too, to show his appreciation. It's probably an automatic-focus camera," he slid in low and dirty, as a dig about the soft focus on the picture of Gable I had taken.

I gave him the sneer he expected. They offered, but I declined the short ride to my building and waved to them as they turned onto Cabrillo heading back to the starless skies of L.A.

I walked at a leisurely pace. I smelled the air and leaned on the wooden railing of the pier for a while, looking at the ocean with the lights of the shore in the background. I was getting well, physically and emotionally. It was nice to have a shoulder that worked reasonably well again and a mind that didn't vapor-lock on lost dreams at unexpected moments.

I sauntered along the beachside walkway, which in the daytime was filled with roller-bladers and bicyclists. At night it belonged to the walkers who ambled, strolled, or strutted the walkway in accordance with their own purposes. My saunter fit right in with those who came to look at the moon over the ocean and do a little dreaming.

I crossed over Cabrillo in front of my building. I was almost to the line of parked cars when one of them, up the street from me, accelerated from the curb and made a run at me. Without thinking, I made a dive for the hood of the parked car in front of me. I was barely airborne when the car got to me. I almost made it clear.

The car clipped my lower leg and spun me into the gutter between the parked cars. My head slammed against the curb, and as I instinctively rolled under one of the cars for protection, the black cloud descended.

EIGHT

I KNEW WHAT A concussion felt like. I had had enough of them. That dizzy, sick feeling was unmistakable. I pulled myself up to a sitting position on the curb and let the first wave of nausea pass.

After a few moments, I was able to try my leg, which was beginning to throb from the knee down. It took the weight, but the ankle was swelling so fast my shoe was beginning to bite into the skin. It made me wonder how long I had been out under the car.

I got a few looks from the people who passed by. They were enjoying a nice warm evening, and I was a drunk who was spoiling their image of the place. I wound my way to my building through Tony's parking lot, using the cars for support. For the first time since I had lived there, I was grateful for the elevator. I practically fell into it and pushed the up button.

After filling two plastic bags with ice, I used an Ace bandage to tape one to my ankle and held the other to my temple. I was fairly sure nothing was broken in the leg and from past experience knew the headache would subside in a couple of days. All things considered, I was lucky.

It was hard to imagine that someone had done it on purpose. I wasn't a danger to anyone. Or was I?

I kept telling myself that it was most likely someone who had had too much to drink and didn't even see me. I kept telling myself that, but I kept not buying it. It felt intentional. It was timed too right. There was even a correction by the driver there at the end to get as much of me as he did. Otherwise, I was clear.

I hadn't seen the driver, nor had I gotten much of a look at the car. I had heard it, though. I would not forget its loose, throaty sound.

I kept the ice on for three intervals of twenty minutes each, separated by five-minute breaks so the nerves wouldn't suffer any additional trauma. I would have done more, but I was ready to sleep. I had determined that my concussion was minor and sleep would not become coma, or I didn't care at that moment, so I slept.

I slept beyond noon of the next day. It was no doubt good for me, since the headache was manageable and the leg was bruised but functional.

Exercise was out and I was hungry, so I went to Tony's.

"Hey, pal," Tony said when he saw me. "You don't look so good."

"I got dinged by a drive-by last night," I told him once we were seated. "Right out here on Cabrillo. Check with your parking guys, will you, if they saw anything?"

"What time?" he asked, all business.

"I don't know exactly. Ten or eleven."

"Sit tight," he said. "I'll see."

He was back half a cup of coffee later. He slid into the booth opposite me and leaned in.

"Toots, the guy that runs the late shift for me says he saw something. Says he was taking a smoke on the Jardin Street side when he heard this car peel out on Cabrillo. He thought he heard some kind of crack or something, and then he heard the car take the corner in a skid. He only glommed a quickie, but he says it was a light-colored car. No make, no driver, that's all he got."

"Thanks, Tony," I said. "Keep your ears open, okay? I'd like to talk to the fellow who clipped me."

Tony's face took on a new light. "I guess if there was anybody I wouldn't want to be at this moment, it's the guy who clipped you." He grinned. "You into something that's making somebody nervous, or is this an accident we're talking here?"

I shrugged it off. "Accident, most likely."

Tony's eyes shot to the door where two halter-topped beach bunnies stood waiting to be seated.

"You want company, paesan?" he asked without taking his eyes from the door.

I followed his gaze and got his meaning.

"No, thanks, Tony. I've got things to do."

"Me too, I hope," he said rising from the table. "You understand."

"Yeah, good luck," I said. What I understood was Tony.

THAT AFTERNOON I made an anonymous call reporting an abandoned vehicle, putting the police on to the Wrangler. I also placed a call to Carrie. She didn't answer and neither did her machine.

I soaked in my pool awhile and spent the rest of the afternoon napping in a chaise on the terrace. I awoke from time to time in the midst of a jumble of thoughts. I would have probably continued that pattern into the night had the phone not rung.

It was Angela Borne.

"You sound a bit strange. Are you quite all right?" she asked with something akin to concern in her voice.

"You know those old men who sleep in the afternoon sun, sitting up on park benches?" I asked.

"Yes," she replied tentatively.

"Well, I've become one of them. Only I stay home and do it."

"So you were sleeping, eh?"

"That's the quick way of saying it."

"And outside in the sun?"

"Yes," I answered. "And I'm not even ashamed of it."

She laughed again. "Do you think you could stay awake through dinner if I cooked it for you?"

My first instinct was to decline. I was still hurting. But I was curious about where she lived and how. I said yes. She gave me the address and told me, "eightish." "I hope you like lamb," she added.

LATE THAT AFTERNOON and again in the early evening I made attempts to reach Carrie, with no success. I dressed in pleated denims and a Sea Island cotton short-sleeve shirt that suited the warm evening. Shoes were a problem. My ankle was swollen the size of a grapefruit, and my foot had taken on some extra bulk as well. I rummaged until I found a pair of open-weave leather slippers I had bought one weekend in Acapulco. The no-sock look wasn't always my style in Santa Barbara, but Angela Borne didn't know that. I was simply interested in avoiding any questions about my injuries.

She lived in a small cottage near the railroad tracks in Montecito. It was brightly lit, with all the windows open. There was a driveway next to the cottage, but no garage. A tan Celica was parked where the driveway ended, just beyond the back corner of the house. Angela met me at the door in T-shirt and shorts, barefoot.

"Don't you look nice," she said, ushering me inside. "You smell good, too."

I wondered if she would have told me if I had not.

She accepted the wine bottle I handed her, noted the vintage with raised brows, and said, "Very nice. Thank you, kind sir. Have you ever had Australian wine? I've a bottle open."

"Not for me, thank you," I said.

"No? Then what may I get you? Something harder, maybe?"

I asked for iced tea, which brought a question to her eyes she left unasked. She led me outside to the porch, where she had set up a table, and raised her wine to touch my tea glass. "Cin cin," she said.

"This is nice," I responded with a look around the small, private place.

"I hope you say the same for my carre d'agneau persillé."

"I never met one I didn't like," I said.

"Parsleyed rack of lamb," she interpreted. "Also grilled tomatoes with garlic and rosemary, and noodles with nutmeg."

She left for a moment and returned with large white plates. The food was carefully positioned in moderate portions in the center. "Voilà," she said.

"I'm impressed," I said after tasting it. "Really impressed. I didn't expect you to be so good."

"You mean you thought I was just someone who hung out in Pismo's chatting up strangers."

"Well, you have to admit that Pismo's and this are slightly different worlds," I said. I indicated the food, the cottage, and all of it.

"And you?" she said. "You were only in Pismo's seeking information?"

"I'm still seeking information," I said definitely.

She seemed suddenly skittish. It was enough so that I noticed. "Then you haven't dropped your interest in Julie?"

"In Julie? No, not in Julie. But you mean in Collin, don't you?"

"Well, yes, him too."

Her eyes were having trouble staying on me. I couldn't put my finger on what it was I was getting from her.

"Not even a little bit," I said. "Matter of fact, I get more interested in Collin by the day."

We had a silence that put an end to the subject.

"Do you like music?" she asked and was up before I could answer. A speaker on the porch began to issue sound just as she returned. "Okay?"

It was short of hard rock, so I gave it my nod of approval.

"What I really like," I said, meaning it, "is this meal. I don't understand how you can work all day and then have time to cook like this."

"This was easy," she said. "Next time I'll really put you to the test with sauces. That's what takes the time. This is nothing."

We kept our conversation on neutral ground through the rest of dinner. We finished the meal with fruit and cheese and some talk about how all the cities of the world were beginning to look alike. She was saying, "Except for the signs on the buildings, there's no difference between downtown Tokyo and Los Angeles or Cairo and Chicago. Even the cultures of the people are blending. It's taken the fun out of traveling. Cities no longer have a distinctiveness about them."

I was watching her hands. She was making those same quarter turns with her glass. The rings she made on the glass top of the table were the same as the ones she'd made on the table in Little Audrey's the other day.

"Saigon does," I said.

"Give it a decade," she gave back quickly. "What's it called now? Ho Chi Minh City?"

"Saigon," I said stubbornly. "It will always be Saigon to me."

"Care to move to the swing?" she offered, already up and leading me to it.

I hadn't been on a porch swing for many years. It felt good.

"I won't break this, will I?"

"No," she assured me and curled up on her end of it, facing me. Her legs, and fine legs they were, too, were pulled up touching me.

"Can we talk more about Collin?" I asked.

"Of course we can talk about him," she answered. "But don't you think there are better topics?"

"I want to see him," I said. "There are questions I feel only he can answer."

"That's not smart, Jake."

"Why not?"

"Because he's a very dangerous man," she answered solemnly. "And most people call me Angie."

"Okay, Angie," I responded, inwardly smiling at her effort to deflect me. "I'll drop it if you'll just tell me as much as you can about him and Julie. What was their relationship?"

"She was a girl," she said with a short laugh. "Or didn't you notice?"

"So you're saying it was nothing special?"

"Right."

"And what is Collin? It appears that he's a beach bum. A volleyball player," I said, making it sound as deprecating as possible.

"Oh, make no mistake about it. He's much more than that," she said vehemently. "Don't underestimate Collin."

"Did you ever go out with him?"

"Go out?"

"Were you and Collin ever lovers?"

"No," she said. "Never. I thought I'd answered that before."

"That's right, you did," I agreed. "Do you know where he lives?"

"Vaguely. I know approximately where, but I've never actually been there myself. Now, please, let's drop it."

"Done," I complied.

She pressed slightly toward me. Her legs were gaining more of my attention. She rested fingers lightly upon my arm.

"I want to know about you," she said. "And these." She leaned closer and touched a scar on my jaw and one at my eyebrow. She left the hand to rest on my shoulder.

"I was a careless child," I answered.

"And the nose?" she prompted.

"There were a lot of doors in the house where I grew up."

"And you were always bumping into them," she finished for me.

"Something like that," I said.

"Don't you work?"

"Not right now. I'm on a sort of prolonged vacation."

"From?"

"I recovered things, usually of great value, that couldn't be recovered by any other means," I said. For clarification I added, "Hidden assets, that sort of thing."

"And you were never married?"

"I had a family, but I lost them," I replied in such a way as to end it.

"I'm sorry," she said, without seeking more on it.

A sudden rumbling, crashing, grinding sound shattered the stillness of our night. I straightened back against the swing, almost toppling us. I looked in all directions, trying to identify what I was hearing.

Angie began to laugh at my startled expression and reaction. "It's a train," she said, barely able to get the words out. The more she looked at me the more she laughed.

As the train drew nearer and passed close enough to actually be seen, I settled down and began to laugh with her. She was weak from the laughing and collapsed forward onto me. There we sat and laughed together, she more than I, while the train passed by. As the train's sound diminished into the distance, she turned over with her head in my lap, still unable to stop her laughter.

"You should have seen your face," she said a couple of times, which only brought the giggles on more.

As she settled and I settled, we found ourselves looking at each other. It was slightly awkward, but it was nice. She put her hand up to my face and said, "I'm glad to see that you can laugh."

I said, "Well, you certainly can laugh. There's no question about that."

"It's not too ladylike, is it?"

"On you it is," I replied gallantly.

She eased herself up to me for an even closer look. I held her that way until she made it a kiss.

I was surprised because I hadn't seen it coming. The little hints had not been there, or if they had been, in my concussed state I hadn't seen them.

She leaned back, holding my face between her hands to study me in earnest. "I don't know why that happened," she said, expressing my thoughts exactly. "I didn't know I wanted to do that."

I grinned. "I didn't either, but it was nice."

She moved away and said, "It'll be nice to see if it happens again next time."

She was a class act. I got to my feet and took her hands.

"Maybe I'll cook for you next time," I said.

"That's a deal," she accepted and then kissed me for real.

She waved from the door as I backed out of her narrow driveway. I couldn't help but wonder if hers were the only eyes that had been on me that evening.

It was a feeling that had started with her fidgeting. It had lodged at the back of my neck and stayed there. I wasn't entirely comfortable with Angela Borne. It was also possible that I had developed some mild paranoia after my incident the night before.

The car that pulled in behind me as I turned out of Angela's street didn't help the feeling any. It stayed well back, but it took the same turns I did. I decided that maybe it wasn't a good idea to go straight home. Anyway, I had a lot on my mind, and could use a longer drive. I took the on ramp to the 101 freeway heading south. If someone wanted to follow me, they were going to have a hell of a drive.

I left the 101 at Oxnard and took the coast. It was empty and winding, and I turned the Porsche loose. Long after I knew there was no one on my tail, I still headed south toward Malibu.

OVER THE ENTRANCE was neon blue script that said "Meddler's." Upon entering, I was greeted instantly by Sebastian Kuhl, who ran the place for Jason. Sebastian was a huge man who extended his ham hock of a hand to me in welcome. I had seen that same hand hold a drunk aloft on his way out the door.

"Jake, what a surprise," he said. "Are you meeting Jason?"

"No, I'm slumming. This is my first stop."

His hearty laugh was genuine but predictable. He fed me straight lines and I amused him. That was part of our relationship.

"Would you like a table? Dinner?" he asked.

"I ate at McDonald's," I said because he expected me to. "I'll sit at the bar."

He smiled and patted me off in that direction. He looked like the late Orson Welles, or what Orson Welles would have looked like with a cauliflower ear.

My stool was at the end of the long bar, where no one but me ever sat because it was too far away from the center of things. That was what I liked about it. The Count, a fellow I had come to appreciate as a man who could play a joke on the world and keep it going, approached me with one of his many foreign accents and a cup of coffee.

"Ees varee late forrr you, myee frrreend," he said in a mixed European dialect.

"Funny, you don't look Japanese," I said.

He gave me the smile as he sidled away toward his paying customers. I took one sip of the good coffee before I heard the first bars of "Tangerine." I looked into the main room and saw Eddie at the roving piano give me a little nod. Lorna didn't nod but sang the song to me.

Too quickly the song was ended. I waved my thanks as they made a slick transition into a modern ballad. They were good, and part of the reason people kept coming back to Meddler's.

I heard the elevator door behind me, and a moment later I heard Jason's voice. "So you're slumming, huh, amigo?"

"That was supposed to be a secret," I said without looking at him.

He wheeled himself to the small table set up in the alcove on the other side of the elevator. I followed with my coffee. He had his drink with him but no cigar. He never smoked downstairs. Seated as we were, we could see all of the bar area and a good part of the main dining room. We could hear Eddie and Lorna very well.

"I heard 'Tangerine' and figured you'd come in," he said.

"So you buzzed Sebastian and he spilled the beans," I added.

"I'm pleased to see you, but why? Something up?"

"Just restless," I said, not wanting to tell him about the incident with the car.

"Well, I've got a piece of news for you, if you haven't heard it already." He let that sink in before continuing. "About Parkland? The lawyer client of Lew's we did the check on Gable for? You haven't heard?" I shook my head. "He's dead."

"Dead?"

"I just heard it on the late news. The news reader said Parkland had been killed in an apparent robbery attempt." Jason refused to call the television anchors newspeople or reporters. He always called them readers or robots.

"So he was murdered?" I was trying to tag it in some way that opened up possibilities. "Any details?"

"Not really," he answered. "The news-at-eleven robot just said robbery was becoming a very common problem in that area." Jason added with a sardonic twist, "Hancock Park ain't what it used to be."

"Any reason to think it wasn't a robbery?" I asked.

"I guess not," he said. "Lew didn't seem to think anything about it. He was here playing some cards and saw the news with me. Bastard was on a streak tonight. Beat me for eleven hundred."

"You'll win it back bluffing a pair of deuces," I predicted.

He raised the one eyebrow. "Do you mean with or against?"

I ignored his question and looked at my watch. "Time for me to go."

He handed me a package from the side pocket of his chair. "Lew brought this for you."

I took it and opened it as I walked. Jason wheeled along with me out to the car, watching as I pulled away the wrapping. It was an eight-by-ten enlargement of a snapshot taken several years ago, in a solid-silver frame. It brought an ache but made me smile at the same time. It was a picture of Trinia, Josh, and me that had been taken at Lew's Malibu beach home. The happiness in our faces was unmistakable. There was Josh wearing the new glasses we had just found out he needed. There was Trinia just beginning to show her new pregnancy she was so proud of. There was I so secure that what we had would last forever. That picture had been taken two months before they were killed.

"Lew has had that picture for you for a long time. He wasn't sure if he should give it to you now or not," he said.

"Tell Lew thanks," I said. "It was the last picture taken of us all together. It means a lot to me."

We shook hands and I started to get into the car when he said, "I guess you're not going to tell me about the ankle and the bump on the head, huh?"

I was always amazed at his powers of observation. That was probably what made him a good card player.

"Last night a crazy driver bounced me into the gutter right after I left you and Vera. A drunk probably. It's nothing."

"A drunk, huh?"

I nodded. "See you soon," I said.

"Look both ways, amigo. You might have a hunter out there," he said.

"You're paranoid," I replied as I slipped behind the wheel.

He grinned and answered, "I'm not the one who drove sixty miles to lose a tail."

Somehow he always knew. I pulled away without a look back, not wanting to give him the satisfaction of knowing I had even heard his comment. But then, he would know that, too.

NINE

A COUPLE OF DAYS after the incident with the car I was feeling much better. My vision had sharpened and the ankle was almost down to its normal size. No headaches, and my luck was holding in other ways as well. It was midafternoon when Carrie finally answered her phone. It seemed her mood swung slightly to the up side after I identified myself. I couldn't tell if it was real or not.

"I need to hear that tape again," I said. "Do you still have it?"

"Yes. I haven't touched it. I didn't know what to do with it," she said. "Is it important? I don't know about those things."

"I can tell you more when I hear it again," I said.

"I'm not going to be here tonight until late. You can come by then if you want, about eleven."

"That's fine," I accepted. "There's one more thing I wonder if you could tell me, Carrie. Was there anyone else Julie thought of as a close friend?"

"You mean like me?" she asked.

"Yes, from work or the university or a place where she used to hang out."

"No," she responded definitely. "All her other close friends were from college, but they all graduated and moved away. She wrote them and all, but I'm really the only one she had here in town."

"Was there any one place she frequented? Maybe a place she went when she was off work?"

"Oh, sure. The beach. She was a volleyball nut. She was an East Beach regular. That'd be the only place else where she had friends, but that's mostly guys. The girls that hang around that group aren't exactly pals, if you know what I mean?"

I thought I did. I asked, "Competition?"

"Yeah," she said, "but she had a bod that put her way ahead in that department."

I remembered.

"See you at eleven," I said.

It kept coming back to the beach and Pismo's. Collin Fraser was the ideal person to talk to about that. For some reason, I still felt he could tell me more about Julie than anyone else could.

When I dressed for my run a few minutes later, I opted for shorts and a T-shirt. That was as close as I could come to fitting in with the volleyball crowd, but it was worth a try.

All the courts were filled when I got to the volleyball section of East Beach. There was no sign of Collin as I wandered around the edges of some of the other games. I could see there were plenty of girls, both watching and playing, and from my point of view it appeared that several of them could have been competition for anyone in the bod department. I found a fairly decent vantage point near the center of the action where the two-man teams were competing. I sat down to watch and in a very short time became enthralled with the sport. It was a great tactical game that required real athleticism. My eye picked out the better players and studied their movement and form.

After watching for half an hour, I wandered to some of the outer games where the four-man teams were competing. That seemed more my style. There were also some players who were closer to my age group in the four-man game. I found what appeared to be a group waiting to play, and joined them.

"How do I get in a game around here?" I asked of one of the more agreeable-looking types.

"We have an open spot," he said without hesitation. "You can take Benny's place. He's got to go." He looked down the way and called out to a short man who was in the process of putting on his shirt. "It's okay, Benny, we got someone."

Benny looked up to give us half a beat of indifference. "I'm Troy," the agreeable one said, extending his hand. He turned to the two men beside him and introduced them. "Terry, and Tom. They call us the three Ts."

"Jake," I said with a nod at all three men. "Look, Troy, don't expect much. I haven't played for some time."

Some of his good humor faded, but he said, "You'll pick it back up fast. You look like you're in good shape."

He didn't say "for a man of your age," for which I was grateful. He did, however, edge slightly closer to his two friends.

I was beginning to wonder what craziness had infected me when Troy motioned to me. "We're up."

I took the court with them, filled the empty corner, and tried to do what they were doing. It was a warm-up drill I had observed others doing. They were popping the ball up in simulations of sets in a rotating fashion toward the net. I fumbled my way through the rotation once, barely, before committing my first error. As the warm-up moved to the second phase, which was a volleying exchange with our opponents, I could feel my partners' confidence waning. By the time we actually started to play, they'd seen enough to lose all hope.

It was an inauspicious debut into the world of beach volleyball. In watching I had gained no idea of the difficulties of the game. What volleyball I had played had been from my days in the Marine Corps. We had usually played on hard-packed dirt or grass. We had occasionally played in mud during my time in Quang Tri, but very seldom had we ever played on sand. It was a different game. The soft sand footing made timing a movement to hit a ball much harder. I scrambled and flailed and dove and slammed to the best of my ability, but in the beginning it was to no avail. It took some time for me to get my eye. The timing came in slow measures. My serve was underhand, weak, and too often in the net. I came to know the meaning of the word "dork." It came as no surprise that we lost the game and our right to the court.

What did come as a surprise was Terry saying, "Jake, you in for another game?"

I said, "Sure, if you guys can put up with me."

The three Ts gave each other a look but gave me the nod.

"We'll be up again quick. This team isn't as good as we are," Troy said. He was still civil but far less agreeable than when I had first met him. I didn't blame him.

In all we played four full games. We won none of them, but we did play well eventually. I finally got the hang of it. I was tall enough to be dangerous at the net once I was able to time my jumps. I spiked a few away for kills, which put the three Ts into hysterical celebrations. I made a few saves, digging some out of the sand, and even got a point or two on my serve.

When the day was over, I agreed to meet my team the next day for more of the same. Benny would be out of action for a few days, they said, and I could fill in. Some of Troy's agreeability had returned, and Tom and Terry actually shook my hand.

I checked out the other courts on my way up to Cabrillo Boulevard. The two-man and two-woman teams were the elite, and that area was where the beach bunnies, the girls who didn't play volleyball, hung out, both literally and figuratively. I looked for Collin, but still there was no sign of him. I started to dogtrot my way home, but legs and lungs protested, so I settled for a nice walk back, dreaming of the pool and steam all the way.

I was five minutes early arriving at Carrie's and sat in my car out front listening to the wind-down of the hour on KCAW. I had been turning to that station often of late, trying to get some clue as to why Julie's radio had been tuned to it. Some of it wasn't bad, I had to admit, as I listened to the end of a Garth Brooks song. Country had come a long way from the days when Roy Acuff topped its charts.

Carrie met me at the door in a robe with her hair done up as if she had just come out of the bath. Her skin looked fresh and clean, her eyes looked a little dreamy.

"Come in, mystery man," she said, taking it up where Julie had left off. I followed her slightly oversold hip movement into the kitchen. She turned barefoot and small against me. "Oh," she said as if startled. "God, you're big. I forgot how tall you are."

I backed away without comment as she readied the machine for play. "Drink?" she offered.

"No thanks," I declined.

She fixed slightly hooded eyes upon me and offered, "Smoke?"

I knew what she meant, because I had smelled the distinctive sweetness as soon as I had entered.

"Nope," I declined again. "Not my thing."

"Ever tried it?" she asked with the leer of a pusher.

"Yeah," I replied, "but I didn't inhale."

She didn't get it, but it didn't matter. She pushed the button, and Julie's voice was taking all my attention.

After playing it through a couple of times more I was certain Julie had been calling Carrie to come help her. It could have fit into my scenario without much of a stretch. She had said, "This is an emergency, girlfriend! A call for assistance!" She could have been joking, and her state of excitement was so high it was difficult to read her voice on it, but I chose to believe it was the real thing. It was in the rest of her message that most of my questions arose.

"Why was she so insistent that you meet her at Pismo's, do you think?" I asked.

"I don't know. She did that sometimes if she met someone really sharp, you know?"

"Did she have friends who lived in Coco Palms?" I asked.

"Wow, Coco Palms," she said. "You're turning it all over, aren't you? The Shermans were who she knew, but not like friends or anything. She house-sat for them a few months ago while they were in Europe. They paid her."

"Did she ever visit them?" I asked.

"No. She hardly knew them. She drove through Coco Palms a lot, though. She went there to dream, she said. She loved to look at the mansions and imagine living in one of them one day. I would drive her sometimes, and we would talk about how it would be to live like that, you know?"

"Coco Palms isn't open to the public. How did she get by the security guards at the gates?" I asked.

"She had the pass thing from the Shermans."

"You mean the blue entry decal for her windshield?" I had not seen one on the Wrangler.

"Right, only she didn't put it on her car. Sometimes she drove my car or hers or somebody else's. She kept it in her purse and just put it up there when she was going in, you know?" She gave me a bored, little-girl look. "You sure you won't have a drink? Or maybe something else? Something white and nice?"

I shook my head and pushed on, afraid she was about to close down on me. "What kind of music did she listen to?"

"You mean did she like elevator music?" she asked with an impish gleam.

I grinned my good-sport grin. "I mean did she like any particular kind of music that you knew of?"

She put her head back to issue a small hoot of derision. "You sure didn't know Julie, did you, mystery man? She was heavy metal. The beat was the thing with Julie, you know?"

She turned away from me and picked up a half-empty glass of wine. She topped it off from a bottle of red and leaned back against the counter. Her lids had dropped a little more, and it was clear that whatever she had smoked had found her mellow button.

"Can I see her place?" I asked. I fully expected her to say no.

Instead she asked, "What is this thing with you? This is sort of creepy, if you want to know what I think."

I answered honestly. "I can't really say, Carrie. I feel there's something missing, and I'm looking. That's all there is to it."

It was clear she did not understand, but she was a girl who was used to not understanding much of what went on in life around her. "To each his own," she said with a shrug.

"So, may I?" I reminded.

She thought about it before saying, "I guess so. The police have been all over it, and her folks, so it probably won't hurt for you to see it."

She pushed herself away from the counter, took a key from a drawer, and padded barefoot out one back door to the other. She led me inside through a small service area into the kitchen, where she turned on the light.

"It's like mine, see? Only reversed."

I did see. It was identical to Carrie's. I could tell immediately that it would reveal little on the surface. I glanced around the kitchen, trying to get a mental foothold.

"No answering machine?" I asked.

Carrie said no from close behind my ear. She moved by me, brushing me with her body as she did so, to the door leading out of the kitchen. She leaned against it and stared, openly putting her eyes all over me. I looked away, but not before I noted the smile playing around her lips.

I first disregarded, then took notice of a large framed piece of poster board attached to the pantry door. The board was covered with small orange-colored squares of paper. It caught my interest as I got close enough to see they were ticket stubs or receipts. I couldn't determine which, but they were all identical.

Without looking behind me I said, "What is all this?"

"Her dream board. Her lottery tickets."

"All these?"

"Not one a winner."

"There must be a couple of hundred here," I said.

"She played it every week, and for a long time. She was convinced she was going to win."

Once I knew what they were I took a slightly more careful interest in them. I had never played the lottery, so I had no ability to quickly assess what I was seeing. I could tell, however, that she had them carefully arranged and glued to the posterboard in chronological order. The last ticket on the board was dated from the week before Julie was killed. The first one dated back four years. It amazed me to think of all the years she had bought those tickets, week in and week out, without ever winning, yet without losing the faith that made her do it. I felt a tiny ache inside that I had not known her better. I was beginning to see that she had been a special kind of person.

"You want to see the rest?" Carrie asked.

I followed as she led me on into the living room, where one end was set up as a dining area. Carrie watched me closely from heavy-lidded eyes and swayed slightly as if some inner music was stirring her.

"Did Julie entertain much?" I asked.

She looked me over again in an insolent, suggestive way. "It depends on what you think of as *much*," she said with a juicy emphasis on the word "much."

I nodded, avoiding more contact with her eyes, and waited until she led me into the hallway. There were two bedrooms, with a bathroom connecting them. First I checked the front bedroom, the more sparsely furnished of the two. The bedroom at the back was larger and more fully furnished.

"Julie's bedroom," Carrie announced in a somewhat sarcastic tone as we entered the larger room.

It brought my eyes to her. She answered me with a sleepy-looking smile. "What you expected?" she asked.

"About," I answered, as I looked at the pictures on the dresser and the general furnishings of the room. The pictures were practically all of Julie and her family. There were group shots and singles of all of them. Her parents were heavily featured in the display. I remembered her father's words, "Julie was a good girl." She probably was.

"You might want to check out the bottom drawer," Carrie said from behind me.

I was not so sure about that. It sounded ominous.

"Don't be shy. It's only pictures." She sat heavily on the bed and leaned back on one arm. I watched her in the mirror while I thought about what I might find. She taunted me with her eyes while she played with the belt of her robe. The robe, I noted, was considerably looser than it had been a few moments earlier.

Reluctantly I opened the bottom drawer. Among some sweaters I found a large softcover binder. I put it down on the one bare space on the dresser and opened it. In the mirror I could see Carrie watching me with that sly, loose grin which had taken up permanent residence on her face.

It was a loose-leaf photo album of the sort that models used. Professional models referred to such albums as their books. This one was of that ilk. The first pictures were composites: a group of several different poses put together on one page. A picture of pictures. There followed a series of head shots and fashion poses in various wardrobes. The last pages were lingerie and swimsuit poses. Carrie evidently knew which pictures I was looking at.

"You like?" she asked.

I admitted the obvious. "She had a fine body."

"You like," she said again, but as a statement.

I leafed back through the book to the pages toward the front. They were the best pictures of Julie and told me the most. They were as good as pictures could have been of her, but she was not the stuff good models are made of. She just did not have the kind of face to have made it big. She was not pretty in the right way. She had wanted it, and tried her best, it was clear to see, but I had known many models from my days in Los Angeles, and there was something, a spark, the successful ones all had that was missing in Julie. What did photograph in her was a soul. Her innocent dream lived in her eyes and brought her alive to me again.

I closed the book and replaced it in the bottom drawer. From the corner of my eye I could see Carrie's position on the bed had become more provocative, the robe even looser. It was very clear she wore nothing beneath the robe. I looked around the walls of the room, anything to keep my eyes away from Carrie.

I spotted the stereo stack with a high-powered amplifier, equalizer, and tuner supporting the best CD and tape players money could buy. It was probably already outdated as I looked at it. I bent down to examine the collection of tapes and CDs. I saw names like Red Hot Chili Peppers, Guns 'N Roses, and U2. I saw no country and western.

"She liked it hot," Carrie said.

"Did you ever hear her listen to country music?" I asked.

"Were you in love with her or something?" Carrie asked in a low voice, ignoring my question.

"No," I said, and looked around as casually as possible. "I hardly knew her."

"Yeah," she said with a sultry edge to her voice. "Her fantasy man. Did you fantasize about her? Did you imagine her body?"

She changed her position and let the robe fall open. She watched me with those taunting, hooded eyes as I looked back at her. She misread me. She shrugged the robe completely free of her shoulders. She leaned back on both arms, moving her body again to that slow, silent beat in her head.

"Like this maybe," she said in a voice almost too low to hear.

I kept my eyes on hers, trying to imagine what could have brought this on. I had the uneasy feeling that it had very little to do with me.

"Our bodies are alike, don't you think?" She moved her legs so they, too, were free of the robe. The motion of her hips became more definite.

"Do you like?" she asked in a voice husky and suggestive.

She was stoned, I knew, but there was something more working on her that had transported her. There was something here, in Julie's place, that had snapped on all her erotic switches.

"You can pretend it's Julie if you want to," she said so quietly I had to strain to hear her. She moved her legs apart. "We're the same. We feel the same. It's Julie. I'm Julie."

Then I knew. I wondered if Julie had ever known.

"I have to go, Carrie," I said with a side step toward the door.

"I'm Julie. You can do what you've always wanted with me."

"Goodnight, Julie," I said.

I let myself out the back door. She did not follow, as I was sure she would not. I was sure, too, she would spend the night in Julie's bed, just as she most likely had done every night since Julie had died.

Goodnight, Julie.

TEN

I WAS STILL AWAKE at dawn, still on the terrace, still thinking about Julie, still in the seat I had taken when I returned home from my experience with Carrie. Much of the night I had floated on clouds of indistinct thought. Other moments, however, brought lucid insights, which I tried to capture and connect to my images of Julie.

She had called someone. I felt reasonably sure that after she had called Carrie she had called someone else. My money was on Pismo's. From what I could tell of Julie's life, her only close associations were centered around the beach and that night spot. I would have given odds that she had called someone at Pismo's to come help her. I had to know who.

I put on coffee to brew and looked out from my kitchen window as the new day's light reflected against the ocean, until it was ready. I took my cup back out to the terrace to lean against the railing and watch the rest of the shoreline awaken. A few walkers appeared on the beach walkway in the slow meanderings of out-of-towners who wanted to see it all. When the sun was a half ball over the mountainous jut that formed the eastern end of the bay, the first of the roller-bladers came forth. They appeared like marauders descending upon the hapless walkers to steal their space and their peace. They glided on silent wheels with an effortless grace that was fun to watch. Then the bicycles and the joggers and the heart-patient walker who looked only at his immediate path and his watch took the stage with a fully risen sun.

I had seen it before, of course, after other sleepless nights, or sleep-filled ones, when I had wanted the day to begin. The odd part of it was that no two dawns looked the same to me. My perspective was altered by the demons inside.

Who had Julie called?

A light workout, a swim, a shower, and breakfast helped me break the hold that question had taken on my mind. Late morning

I walked over to Smiling Jack's, a trendy beach shop on Anacapa, to buy a few pairs of the shorts I had seen most prevalently on the volleyballers. They were loose, midthigh, and didn't come in navy blue. I bought some tank tops as well and watched my two hundred dollars disappear into the coffers of a grinning opportunist who was riding the crest of a wave he had seen coming before anyone else. On the way home I stopped at the All-Sport store and bought a volleyball. In for a penny, in for a pound, was the way I figured it.

While I tossed some bay shrimp into a romaine-based salad, I thought about Carrie. She had been close to the edge when I last saw her, and I wondered about her mental state. I dialed her number and heard her voice greet me from her machine. I hung up without leaving a message, slightly relieved that I had not had to talk with her.

That afternoon I jogged over to East Beach, where the three Ts seemed happy to see me. My iridescent costume from Smiling Jack's had given Claudile a quick laugh as I passed her window, but it was the uniform of the day at the beach. Troy, Tom, and Terry hardly seemed to notice. Of course, it is always hard for guys in luminous pinks and greens to laugh at a fellow because he's in incandescent orange.

It was a good afternoon. We did all right as a team, and I learned a little more about the beach.

"Do any of you fellows know Collin Fraser?" I asked.

"Everybody at East Beach knows Collin," Troy said. "He's numero uno."

"I haven't seen him around here lately," I said.

"Yeah, he's been gone. Somebody said he was playing down at Santa Monica beach, but you never know with Collin," Terry offered. "You know him?"

"I've met him," I said. "Did any of you know Julie Price?"

They exchanged looks. Troy was the one who answered. "I made the mistake of dancing with her over at Pismo's."

"Why a mistake?" I prompted.

"Because later when I was leaving," he said, "Collin followed me out. Terry was with me, he can tell you. I was just going to my car when the guy grabs me."

Terry took it up. "He had him in a choker. Man, it happened so fast we didn't even see him coming."

"Why? What was the deal?" I asked, remembering my first gut instincts when I had met Collin.

"Jeez, he had me. He's strong, that guy. And you should have seen his eyes."

I had seen his eyes. "What was it about?" I persisted.

"Her. Julie. He was pissed because I danced with her. And she wasn't even really with him, was she?" He turned to Terry for support.

"No," Terry said. "There are always a lot of girls around Collin. She was just part of the group, it looked like to us." That's when Tom added something. "Yeah, but you guys know you don't mess with Collin. You don't even get close to messing with Collin. There are some bad stories about him."

"I wasn't messing with him," Troy protested.

"Did she have anyone special she palled around with? Another girl?" I asked.

"No, I don't think so," Troy said. He paused and seemed to think about her. "She was nice," he added. "Really a nice person."

"But she was part of them," Terry interjected. His head nodded in the direction of the two-man teams. "There's a caste system on this beach, and they think they're the elite."

"They can have it," Tom said.

They left it there. I studied the volleyball beach as a whole. It was filled with teams lined up waiting, both male and female. The girls who weren't playing were on towels surrounding the area, getting the sun before the bigger games began in the late afternoon. The two-man team games. I checked out the two-man courts. No Collin.

I played one more game with the three Ts before their friend Benny showed up. They didn't seem particularly happy when I dropped out to give him his spot back.

I moved around the beach a bit, checking out the different teams. It was easy to get into games. Teams were always looking for another player. I felt fairly confident to join in after my indoctrination period with the three Ts. I played with some good teams and some not so good. I had a full day, and when I finally made it home, I was bone tired and suffering from the lack of sleep.

I had a long steam, a hot shower, and a small meal before taking my volleyball into the high-ceilinged hallway for a little work. I spent half an hour practicing one-hand and two-hand pops, never letting the ball hit the floor. I cooled down under another short shower before flopping into bed. The last thing I did was try Carrie's number again from my bedside phone. Our last encounter plagued me and caused me to worry in some unspecified way about her. Her machine answered again, and again I hung up without leaving a message. Sleep was quick to come, and when it began to take me, thoughts of Carrie were pushed aside by a wave of new images from my memory of Collin Fraser's eyes. Intense feral eyes. Animal eyes.

IN THE NEXT FEW DAYS I didn't do much but hang around the beach and play volleyball. I stayed in the four-man area, feeling my way into the strange society of the beach game. I was learning a new sport, getting some good exercise, and I hoped that somewhere along the way I might find out who Julie had trusted well enough to have called the night she died.

It was an easy game to learn but a hard one to become good at. The more I learned about it, the more I admired the players who played the two-man game. I filled in on the four-man teams, but more and more I spent my time watching the twos. Collin Fraser didn't show.

I went to the beach earlier, stayed later, and practiced longer at night, alone, in my hallway. It paid the right dividends. I played better, the other players began to take my presence for granted, and there were even some who sought me out for their teams.

Morning and night, before I went to the beach and when I returned, I called Carrie's number. The machine always answered, and I never left a message.

Before heading toward Malibu on the night of my weekly chess war with Jason, I wandered into Pismo's for a quick glance around. I didn't hang around or loiter at the bar, where the day's winners were holding court. I waved at some familiar faces and kept moving. I made a casual tour, including the back section, where the rear wall was dedicated to the heroes of the beach game and the dart games were played. No sign of Collin Fraser. Angie wasn't around either.

Jason had trouble accepting the image. "Volleyball? You're not serious," he said.

"It's a great game, Jase," I answered. "The beach game takes a fine athlete to play it right."

He watched me as I considered a counter to his check on my king. "Does this mean that you'll be taking up tennis next?" he smirked. "And golf?"

"Not in this lifetime," I answered as I interposed my bishop. Not until then did he see the trap he had fallen into.

"Damn," he muttered when he saw his mistake. "How did you do that?"

"It's like a setup and a spike," I replied.

"Please," he said as he toppled his king in defeat. "I can live without the volleyball jargon. Next you'll be calling me a dude."

I loved beating him, he took it so badly. "That's surfers who call each other dude."

"No, it's not," he said and blew smoke in my direction. "It's all you California beach bums. One more?"

I accepted, and we played another game to the same result. After his second defeat of the night he sullenly wheeled himself to his bar, poured a small drink, and took out a fresh cigar.

"So what's all this volleyball getting you?" he asked, his eyes peering up over the flame he extended to the end of the Cubano.

"Sunburn, aches and pains—and inside."

"I suppose you're referring to the exalted society of the beach bum?" he asked, giving me a light prod.

"That and the Pismo crowd. They're linked. And there's no way I'm ever going to find out anything if I'm not one of them."

"What's in your craw?"

I thought about it. "Curiosity."

He shook his head and puffed his cigar. "You take a good look at how deep you're getting in here, and it appears to be more than curiosity. Have you forgotten the swipe job that car did on you?"

"I'm okay," I said. "In all probability it was an accident. My paranoia is under control."

"Well, mine's not," he grunted. "It never sounded like dead aim to me. It sounded like just what it was, a brushback. Somebody was sending you a message."

"That's what I thought at the time, but I'm less convinced of that now."

"You don't think the volleyball thing is a little silly?" he asked.

"Silly? Would you accept 'foolhardy,' maybe?"

"That too." Then, after a moment, "It wouldn't be that you're just trying to hold back the clock, would it?"

I grinned. "You think I'm going through a middle-age crisis? That could be."

"I don't know what I think, amigo, but I'll tell you what I hope. I hope this Aussie stays gone."

"He won't," I said.

"You seem awfully sure of that. Why?"

"Because he's the king of East Beach. He would never walk away from that. Not from what I saw of him."

The ringing phone caught us both by surprise. Our chess matches were sacrosanct, and Jason cut off his phones. The only line he left open was to Sebastian at the front. And it would only be used if something of vital importance arose. It rang a second time, increasing the sense of foreboding.

He picked up the phone and said, "What's up?"

He listened and I watched. His face grew very still. His eyes narrowed. He asked one question, "When?" He listened more and then said, "Thanks, Sebastian."

He looked at me as he put the phone down with raised eyebrows. "Our friends from the local sheriff's station were here," he said and took a sip of his drink. "They found a body washed up on the beach."

"What beach? Yours?" I asked.

"No, not mine. They were just letting us know about it, and trying to nail down an ID. It was found a couple of hours ago on that rock-strand beach just above Zuma. Some beach walker stumbled over it. Can you imagine that?"

"Off a boat," I said.

He looked at me as if I had suddenly spoken to him in a foreign language. "Off a boat? Why would you say that?"

"The sea tends to bring things to shore there. Wasn't that the beach where Vera used to collect all her driftwood?"

He shook his head and laughed. "You're right. And I still have some of those polished driftwood pieces around here someplace." He toyed with his glass and puffed on his cigar and muttered, "I'll bet you're right. I'll bet they find out it came off a boat."

Jason suddenly looked at me with eyes slightly brightened and said, "Damn, I like your mind."

On my way home I passed the Zuma beach. As I moved north of it I glanced toward that rocky beach area and the line of official vehicles parked on the side of the Pacific Coast Highway. I gave a vague and passing thought to the body that had washed up there. Three possibilities, I thought: suicide, murder, or accident, but luckily not my problem. Or so I thought at the time.

IT WAS LATE when I got home and later still after I had spent an hour or so on the terrace leaning out toward a dark and almost soundless sea. No wind moved it, and no breeze pushed the warm air away. It was a good time for sorting out and thinking through some of what Jason had brought to the surface. Jason was many things to me and for me, but more than anything he was a catalyst for those deeper thoughts that from time to time needed some dredging.

He had caught me with a partial jab when he suggested that I was trying to turn back the clock with my newly found passion for beach volleyball. Some of that was true, I had to admit. It was a good feeling to compete in a new game at a younger man's level. But at the root of it was Julie. I couldn't shake her. I couldn't forget how she had loved her life on that last Saturday of it. I couldn't stop wondering why she had been killed and by whom. I couldn't erase the feeling that she had called someone to come help her who had instead snuffed out her life. Someone from the beach scene. Someone who went to Pismo's. Someone who might do it again to another Julie.

When I thought of another Julie, I thought of Carrie. Her envy or jealousy or raw love for Julie had taken her over the edge. I wondered how long she had struggled to keep her grip on reality. I had seen it slip from her grasp, and my concern for her was that finally her obsession had taken her too far. I worried that she had slipped into a mental abyss that she couldn't climb out of alone.

I picked up the phone and called Carrie's number again. I expected what I got, the answering machine, and hung up with a strong sense of foreboding. Carrie still had some answers to questions I had not yet formed. I wondered who else might have a similar thought. I wondered if Carrie was in danger from more than her own psyche.

I took my musings down to the beach. I waded into the soft lap of gentle tide that came from a wide, dark horizon. There was no moon, and the light from Cabrillo didn't penetrate far beyond the shoreline. The deep breaths I had been needing came more easily there.

The water was breaking just beneath my knees with a calming, cooling effect. Perhaps there were no answers to the vague, uncertain feelings I had formed around Julie's death. My instincts may have been wrong. It was, after all, a police matter. Perhaps it was time I put it aside.

The one unsettling element that remained was the issue of Collin Fraser. For some reason I had given an enormous significance to him. As I thought about it, I realized that he was the bottom line to it all for me. I knew it would not be over until I talked to him again.

That was what it was all about, the volleyball, the excessive training. I was preparing myself to meet him on his own playing field. I had kept it vague before, but with the clarity of those thoughts came a feeling of excitement. So where was Collin Fraser? I wondered. Was he aware that I was waiting or that someone would be? Did he care?

It wasn't until I was already home again and beneath the cool spray of water from the shower that the other thought hit me. Was Collin Fraser still alive?

ELEVEN

THE HOSTESS AT Barron's was the same one who had told me about Julie's death. She was a person who smiled a perfunctory welcome to patrons when they entered, with eyes that looked as if they were focused elsewhere. I glanced around as she led me to a front window booth.

"Carrie working today?" I asked.

She looked at me with some new interest before she asked, "Has that been you calling for her every day?"

"No," I answered quickly and threw back just as fast, "Did he sound like me?"

She put her smile back in place as she put the menu down and said, "No. You're not rude. He has been very rude."

She was gone before I could pursue it further. I ordered from an impatient waitress who had evidently come in that morning as a favor to someone. That became clear when I asked if the bacon was cooked earlier and was reheated when needed. Her look and shrug told me she did not know, did not care, and that I should eat it and die for taking up her time with this question.

I had to wonder if she had used that little shrug on her job interview. Have you ever waited tables before? Shrug. Do you like working with people? Shrug. I had a fantasy of leaving a penny tip, having her nab me at the door and ask, "What kind of tip is this?" Shrug.

Fool that I was, I ordered the bacon and answered my own question. It had first been cooked hours ago, if not days, and had been microwaved to death for my benefit. As I ate around it, I had this acute longing for the Montecito Coffee Mill's good food and excellent service in the person of Peggy Cooley. It was closed for a remodel all summer, and as time wore on I was growing impatient for it to reopen. It was a place that knew how to cater to the early-morning cranks who needed coffee hot, food fresh, and a personality at the other end of the hand that dropped the plate in front of you.

Finally, I stood at the front counter with my check in hand, once again facing the automatic smile of the hostess.

"I miss Julie, don't you?" I said in an effort to shake some recognition out of the woman.

It worked. She took a real look at me then and said, "Yes, I do. You haven't been in lately, have you?"

"No, I've been busy. I was hoping to see Carrie, though. This her day off?"

She shook her head. Her attitude toward me had softened somewhat. "Carrie hasn't been in for several days. She's quit, I think, but nobody seems to know."

"You mean she just stopped coming to work?"

"Yes, I think so. We've had a lot of changes around here lately."

"Yes, I could tell. The food and service were both lousy."

My comment seemed to shock her. "Really? I'm sorry. Would you like to talk to the manager?"

I shook it off. "No, I only came in to see how Carrie was doing."

"The last time I saw her, not too well," the woman said as she rang up my ticket.

"Could you tell me about that?" I asked from something I saw in her eyes.

"She'd had some kind of accident that banged her up pretty good. She was limping, and the right side of her face was swollen and purple. Makeup didn't cover it too well." She handed me my change. "Personally, I think she's been drinking a lot since Julie's death."

"Did she say it was an accident?" I asked.

"Yes," the hostess answered. "Said she fell."

From what I had seen of Carrie she did not strike me as the clumsy type. "And that was the last time you saw her? Was that in here?"

She handed me my change and nodded. "That was five or six days ago. It was the last time she came in to work. She hasn't even been in to pick up her paycheck, I don't think."

I was turned to go when I remembered something she had said earlier. "This guy that's been calling for her? What's that all about? A boyfriend?"

She shrugged. "I don't know. He's very rude and persistent. It's as if he doesn't believe us when we say she's not here. He swore at Janet, the night hostess. Called her some terrible names."

"It takes all kinds," I said, falling back into the comfort of cliché.

"I'm sorry you weren't pleased with your breakfast. I hope you come back," she said.

I turned from the door, about to tell her the truth, that it would be a cold day in hell before I'd ever set foot in another Barron's, but instead I smiled a wimp's smile and said, "I'm sure it will be better next time."

I drove straight to the Mesa area and stopped a few houses short of the duplex. There was no car and no movement of any kind. The place did not look inhabited. I walked by it for a closer look. The shades were drawn on Carrie's side, and I had a brief mental image of her watching me from behind them. That thought was dispelled by a deeper feeling that Carrie was not there at all.

I did not want to attract any attention from the neighbors, so I made a slow walk by and returned to my car without any satisfaction. The feeling of unease, which had begun even before my visit to Barron's, was not helped by what I sensed at the duplex.

On the way home, I turned on the radio, which was still tuned to KCAW, and heard an old Waylon Jennings song about Luckenbach, Texas. I liked it and began to wonder if I was becoming indoctrinated. After the song, the announcer plugged the auto dealer sponsoring the hour and reminded his listeners that the lotto results were brought to us by that same dealer every Saturday night, starting with the draw at eight o'clock.

I HAD A good day at the beach. I lost count of the games I played, but I knew that my team had held the court from two in the afternoon on. I had become a factor in the four-man game.

I felt little of the body ache that had accompanied my first days in beach volleyball. My wind had come back, and some spring was returning to my legs. I was getting into shape.

I sat in my steam room a little longer than usual, letting the day settle away, clearing my mind for what lay ahead. I was not looking forward to what I had planned for the night. Breaking and entering was always a tricky business, but more than anything else, I was afraid of what I might find.

I finally showered and dressed for the evening in lightweight dark clothes. It was too early for what I had to do, with the daylight hanging on to the long summer evening, so I let my subconscious lead me. I exited the 101 freeway at the Storke Road off ramp and turned toward Isla Vista. I still had the nagging feeling that I had overlooked something there.

As I skirted the boundary of the university, I tried to imagine what a young freshman girl might have done on a Saturday night that had become ritual with her for the rest of her life. When I entered the business section of Isla Vista I experienced the same sort of disappointment in the village that I had felt on my earlier visit.

I drove slowly along the main street that U'd back upon itself before tackling the intersecting ones. Nothing brought that little nudge to my mind which I so often depended upon. Nothing even clicked enough to make me take a second look. I studied each place in great detail as I slowly cruised by. I was getting nothing by driving, so I parked and walked.

I looked for possibilities in the coffee shops and sandwich shops, the drugstores and grocery stores, and even in the video and book stores. Still nothing clicked. Nothing even drew a second glance, other than a fairly busy pizza place that had tables in an outside glass-enclosed but unroofed area. I went for a closer look.

The smell of the place sparked my appetite, so I ordered a small Veggie Supreme. I checked out the interior while I waited for my number to be called. It was typical pizza-house decor: simple tables and booths that looked like they'd all been wiped down with the same dirty rag. It said nothing beyond what I might have guessed from the street.

I took my veggie pizza and a drink called Fruit Splendor out to the open-roofed area. I sat facing the street, isolated from the rest of the diners. The pizza was good, but the drink fell well short of splendor. I had nearly finished both when I finally found something that sparked my interest.

I was directly across the street from the small convenience store called Escobar's Keg, which I remembered from my first visit to Isla Vista. The pink flamingos stood silent sentry in front just as before, but unlike before, the store was open. The lights inside made the flamingos painted on the windows come to life. I studied the spectrum of advertising on Escobar's windows. The range was very different brands of beer and sodas to the variety of candy bars available. In between were posters pitching wines and breads and one that said LOTTO.

Click.

I left two pieces of a Veggie Supreme and three quarters of a Fruit Splendor behind as I crossed the street to Escobar's. It was one of those places that smelled faintly of chocolate and produce. The scent of soap powder also lingered in some areas. The back was all glass-doored refrigerator cases that looked oddly modern compared to the rest of the store. It was the kind of place where small accounts were kept in a spiral notebook, or so I imagined.

I picked up some toothpaste and carried it to the counter. The man seated on the stool behind the gum racks watched a small television set that looked new. He was friendly and greeted me with a smile. "Will this be all, señor?"

"I think so," I said.

He nodded and continued to smile from a broad friendly face while he took my money and gave me my change. Then he did an odd thing with my receipt. He stamped it with a marker he had pressed into a pink ink pad before putting it into the bag with my toothpaste. He appeared to be a man who liked people, and I imagined people liked him.

"Thank you," I said, taking the bag, then, as if in afterthought, "I'll bet in a store like this you know a lot of your regular customers by name, don't you?"

"Many," he agreed.

"Would you know if a girl named Julie came in here regularly?"

"Julie?" he said, giving it serious consideration. "No, señor,

I don't know. I know some Julie, yes, I think. But I have many customers who change every year, señor.''

I nodded, recognizing the wisdom of that statement. "She might have come in every Saturday before seven. She'd have been a regular for about four years now. Dark hair, dark eyes.''

"For the lottery, señor?'' he said. I could see he had someone in mind.

"It's possible, yes.''

"Very lovely young lady?'' He held up his hand to the approximate height of Julie, which was about an inch above his own head.

"Yes,'' I said. "That could be.''

"I think you talk about La Rosa, señor,'' he said. "Every Saturday for many years she comes and buys the ticket. She never win, not once, in all those years. Not even the little five-dollar ones, I don't think. Very lovely girl, La Rosa.''

I knew enough Spanish to know that "La Rosa'' meant "the rose,'' but I couldn't connect that to Julie. I asked, "Why do you say 'La Rosa'?''

"Her name, señor,'' he said happily. "Rose. I call her La Rosa. Is the same.''

"You're sure this was her name? Rose?''

"Sí, señor. I think always it is her first name, but perhaps it is the family name, no? Is this the one?''

I was disappointed. "I don't think so. Could you be mistaken about her name?''

He pushed an ink pad to the center of the counter. I saw the cover read "Flamingo'' before he flipped it open to reveal a deep pink color. "I stamp my customer's receipt with my own stamp and my own ink. For each one hundred dollars they get five in free trade. She loves the color and always puts her ring into the pad to mark her tickets. For many years, señor.'' He looked at me expectantly. "The rose ring? I asked her one day about it, and she said it is her name. Rose.''

"I see,'' I said, the disappointment growing. "Would there be anyone else you can think of who might fit the description? Came in on Saturdays, always before seven?''

"La Rosa is the only one,'' he said with a shake to his head.

"The lottery closes at seven forty, but always she hurries in before seven. It is her superstition, señor. She has a strong belief."

I took one last shot. "The girl I'm talking about is dead. She's the one who was found at Pelican Point."

"Ah, no," he said, his hand going to his mouth. "Someone was telling me about the tragedy, but I never thought La Rosa."

"It's most likely not. Has La Rosa been in lately?"

His eyes held a stricken look. "I can't remember, señor. I think so, yes, but I am not so sure."

"Mr. Escobar, does every place that sells lottery tickets have the same Saturday deadline?"

"Sí, it is the law," he said reverently. "You are policía?"

I shook my head. "No, I'm a friend."

His face was crumbling. "It is not La Rosa. She has so much life."

"Possibly not," I said, trying to placate him. "Tell me more about this rose ring, would you?"

"She wears it here." He pointed to the pinky finger of his left hand. "She pushed the ring into my ink pad and then presses it onto the back of her lottery tickets. For luck, she says." He took the pad and showed it to me. "My cousin sends me these ink pads from his factory in Miami. This is their special color. It is quite famous to some, señor."

"Flamingo," I said as I read the cover again.

"My cousin's company, señor, and the color as well."

"Would you know when La Rosa last bought a ticket from you?"

"Ah, no, that is impossible. I have no way to check."

"And the numbers? Would you know what numbers she chose?"

"That too, señor, is impossible. I type them into the machine. It gives back the ticket. There are so many numbers," he said and ended it with a faint shrug.

"Thank you, Señor Escobar," I said. "I hope your La Rosa comes in to see you soon."

"Sí, señor," he said. His face took on a serious look. "You will find the one who did it?"

"I?"

"You are El Cazador, señor," he said. "I have seen the look on a few men in my life. You have the look."

His comment was unnerving, but his eyes trusted me. I decided to trust him back. "I will try," I answered.

The flamingos in front of Escobar's Keg no longer caused me to grin. Because I had met the man who had planted them there, the birds took on a different cast. They now seemed noble and proud to me. I took a look back through the window at Escobar seated on his stool behind the counter with his head tilted slightly forward and his eyes fixed in private thought. He had pegged me as El Cazador. The Hunter.

I PARKED AROUND the corner from the duplex, where I sat in the car for a short time before getting out and strapping on a small belt pack filled with a few vital items. The night was dark enough for me to hide nicely as I took the short walk by the place for a preliminary check. Once I had confirmed the absence of dog walkers or night strollers of any kind, I approached the front of the duplex for a closer look. There was no light and no sound. I made a quick move to the back of the house along Julie's side, which was well hidden from the neighbors' view by a tall wooden fence.

At Carrie's back door I stood quietly for several minutes, letting my ears pick at the sounds around me. I registered the sounds for future comparisons, if it should become necessary, before rummaging in my belt pack for the two-tined pick and the penlight. I put the flashlight in my mouth and knelt down with the lock pick ready before I pulled the screen door open. I did it slowly, reducing the squeak as much as possible.

Even before I turned on the penlight I could see the door was slightly ajar. I froze and listened hard for anything from the interior. After putting the pick away I turned on the penlight and examined the door frame. It had been chewed up by a crowbar, and the door forced without any surreptitious intent. That in itself caused me considerable alarm. I switched off the light.

I envisioned the interior to the best my memory could recall before getting down on my stomach and slowly pushing the door fully open. Again I paused, acclimating all my senses before I moved inside. I made myself ready for anything as I slowly inched into the house on elbows and knees. From somewhere a blinking red light imposed itself upon the darkness of the kitchen. Her answering machine, I thought automatically.

I found the counter and slowly lifted myself up until I could place the penlight on it facing toward the open door leading into the living room. I switched the light on and dropped silently back to the floor, moving several yards away in the process. Nothing happened. No flash and boom, no bounding attack by a screaming maniac. Nothing. I got to my feet and retrieved the light.

I followed the tiny spot beam through the rooms, expecting to smell the stench of death, expecting Carrie's body to suddenly appear in the pale illumination. I looked in every corner of every room. I then checked the closets. I had not expected what I found there.

The closets were empty, cleaned out, as were the dresser drawers and cabinets. I pulled down all the shades and tightly closed the curtains so I could turn on the lights for a better look. All the furniture was there, the beds were made, but there were no personal items of Carrie's left in the place.

I worked my way back through the house into the kitchen. I checked out the refrigerator, where I looked at expiration dates on milk and egg cartons and smelled the contents of various containers. I checked out the drawers and cabinets and looked into the trash container for grocery and other receipts. There was nothing conclusive, but considering the dates on the receipts, the mold on the cottage cheese, and the slightly sour smell of the milk, I found enough to draw some conclusions.

The furniture in the place was rental stuff, according to the contract that had been left behind. The same was true with the television and the appliances. Sometime in the neighborhood of five days ago, as I figured it, Carrie had packed up all her personal belongings and split. I began to get the feeling that this was something Carrie Berry had done before. Maybe she had done it a lot of times before, in a lot of different places.

The blinking red light on the answering machine begged my attention. I had found no contract for an answering machine rental. I didn't even know if they could be rented. I doubted it.

Could she have simply overlooked her answering machine? Not likely. It struck an odd note with me. It bore the marks of a purposeful act. It was set to auto answer, which could have been something she did on her way out the door.

I pushed rewind and waited while the machine whirred its way back to the first message. I was less interested in the message itself than I was in the date and time that the machine plugged on afterwards. The message was from her boss at Barron's and the date was five days ago. That meshed with my ballpark guess on the date she ran. I let the rest of the messages play.

There were several that had that small moment of silence before the click and buzz which indicated a hang-up. I knew that some of those were my calls. I knew that others were not. Some of those were three and four o'clock in the morning calls. There was one call from the Prices giving Carrie the time the movers would be arriving at Julie's and thanking her in advance for letting them in. There were more calls from her boss at work, one call that ended with the brainless sign-off "Stay sanitary," which I had heard on her messages before, and another one that had a very chilling effect.

"Bitch," the voice spat out into the quiet of that little house. "Answer, bitch!" The phone slammed down.

I turned off the playback. I took the message cassette from the machine and stored it safely in my belt pack. That last message had given me a pretty good idea why the answering machine was left behind. Carrie had probably used it to gain some lead time for her run. What I did not have a thought on was from whom and why. Those loomed as big questions to me.

I turned off the lights and slipped out the back door. I stood outside on the small porch listening for a sound that might be out of place. With care I took the few steps to Julie's door and shined the penlight on it. It, too, had been forced, as I expected.

I went inside to find a place completely bared from wall to wall. The movers had definitely gained entry by some means. There was not a stick of furniture left. There was no vestige of Julie remaining in that place. Still I walked through it, not really looking for anything, listening to the sound of my footsteps echoing through the empty rooms.

Something penetrated. A sound crept in from the street. A car started up a short distance away. It revved its engine and rolled to life. I stood rooted to the spot, listening hard as the car gained speed moving quickly away from the duplex and me.

I followed the sound out the back door, along the side of the house to the street. I began to run, following it to the corner. I was too late. The car was gone. But not the sound of it. It was a sound I would remember, guttural and wheezy, as if the exhaust was bypassing the muffler. It was a sound I had already stored away inside my memory from the night that same car had slammed me into a gutter on Cabrillo Boulevard.

TWELVE

ABOUT THREE a.m., I gave up on the idea of sleep. There was too much inside my brain that I could neither sort nor ignore. I got out of bed, heated cold coffee in the microwave, and took my confusion out to the terrace.

Eventually, I wound up in the pool, floating on my back, looking up at the stars. I was still there when the sky began to lighten. I waited until the sun had climbed to a decent level before dialing the number I got from Lodi information.

The man who answered was wide awake. I felt better about that. "Mr. Price?" I asked.

"Who's this?" he asked back.

"My name is Jake Sands, sir. I'm calling from Santa Barbara."

He took a beat before responding. "This is Carl Price. What do you want?"

I had an inkling as to what he might be thinking. "I'm not with the press, sir. I knew your daughter, and I would like to talk to you about a few things, if I may."

There was a slight change in his attitude when he asked, "You knew Julie? How so?"

I took a deep breath and dived in. "I was a customer at Barron's where she worked. I got to know her a little there and at the beach she frequented. I won't pretend to you that I knew her well, but I did know her well enough to know what a fine person she was." I paused to let him absorb what I had said before continuing. "I'm trying to help, on an unofficial basis, to discover what happened and who did it."

"Then you're not with the police?"

"No, sir, I am not. As I said, I am *very* unofficial."

The stress on "very" did it. "Well, I can't say as I'm too happy with what the police have done so far, so I suppose it can't hurt to talk to you."

"The police are pretty good in Santa Barbara, Mr. Price, but I suspect this is something that normal police procedures might have trouble sorting.''

He made a grunting sound in response, then said, ''And I suppose for a fee you can do what they can't.''

''I'm not sure what I can do, but I don't want anything for it. I'm not doing this for money.''

''You find who killed my daughter, mister, I'll give you everything I own. You just give me the son of a bitch when you do.''

His anger was real. Not for the first time did the thought cross my mind that the proper punishment for violent crimes should be left in the hands of the victims.

''I'd like to ask you a couple of questions about Julie and her life in Santa Barbara, if I may,'' I said. ''Did you know her friends? The people she spent time with?''

''Well, she had a lot of friends in college there, but I guess this June most of them left at graduation. She didn't graduate. She dropped out a few months shy. Beats me why she did, but she always had her own way of doing things,'' he said as he organized it in his mind. ''Other than all her school friends—and I don't know if any of them lived there local, you know—there was the girl she shared a duplex with. A girl that worked in the same hash house she did.''

I heard his wife's voice in the background. He put his hand over the mouthpiece, and I got a muffled impression of an ensuing discussion. I waited until I was sure he was back with me.

''Carrie? Is that the girl you're talking about?'' I asked.

''Yeah, that's right,'' he replied with a touch of disgust in his voice. ''Not a real dependable type that one.''

''Have you heard from Carrie lately? In the last few days?''

''Nope,'' he answered. ''Haven't heard word one. She was supposed to let movers into Julie's place four days ago, but she wasn't around to do it. We had to call a locksmith to let 'em in. Had to do it all from here, because we was counting on her to do it for us.''

''Are you sure she knew about it?'' I asked.

''She knew. We told her direct when we first set it up and then left word on her machine the day before they was to be there. She knew."

"And you've heard nothing from her?"

"Not a by-your-leave, a kiss-my-foot, nothing," he stated emphatically.

"Other than Carrie, can you think of anyone else your daughter might have mentioned in the more recent months? A friend she talked to, or went to the movies, had dinner with—anything like that?"

"No, just that Carrie. Hold on a second," he said. I heard him discuss it with his wife. He came back to me with, "Wife said there was somebody else Julie mentioned, fairly recently, and I kinda remember it, too, but neither one of us can recall the name. Is it important?"

"Yes, I think it is," I replied. "Did she ever mention Coco Palms to you? Maybe someone who lived there?"

"Coco Palms," he said, rather wistfully I thought. "We never went to see her that she didn't drive us through all those mansions there. No, she didn't know anybody there except those folks she house-sat for that one time, but she didn't visit them ever, that I know of. She always said she was going to live there someday. Even had one of those big houses all picked out. That was one of her dreams. She was a big dreamer, you know?"

"Did you by any chance talk to her that last day?" I asked carefully.

"Nope," came his pinched reply.

"Was there any reason why she would have been excited about something on that Saturday? Had anything happened, or was anything about to happen that could have affected her emotionally?"

He seemed to be having trouble with my question, and I was about to try to rephrase it when he said, "No. After she was found dead we received a letter she had written and mailed to us that Saturday. There was nothing like that in it."

"Have you received her possessions from the police?"

"A list is all."

I sensed he was tiring of me and my questions. I quickly asked, "Was her bag found? Or her wallet?"

He answered a very short, "No."

"Mr. Price, did you have all her things brought to you there in Lodi? All her personal items, like phone books, bank records, things like that?" I asked.

"Everything in her house, yes," he answered. "Furniture we put out at Milna's sister's, but things like you mentioned we got here in boxes."

"There was a collage of lottery tickets she kept in her kitchen. Do you have that?"

"A what?"

"A framed board with old lottery tickets pasted to it?" I explained.

"We have that." His voice was growing dim.

"Mr. Price, may I come there to look at those lottery tickets, and her phone books, and other personal items?" I asked. "I would especially like to see that last letter Julie wrote."

"You want to come here to Lodi?" He said it as if no one in his right mind, would of his own free will, do such a thing.

"Yessir," I replied. "An hour or so is all I would need."

The muffled conversation between him and his wife took on the tone of argument.

"Can't stop you from coming," he said, "but can't promise you nothing."

"Let me say this to you, Carl," I said cutting through the impersonal formality. "I know what your nights are like. I've been there."

I intended to say more, but for some reason I stopped with that. He was silent for long enough to make me wonder if he was still there. When he did speak it was so low I had to strain to listen.

"When?" he asked.

"Monday?" I suggested.

"What's today?" he asked.

"Saturday," I had replied, not at all surprised that he had lost track of the days. I had lost track of months after Trinia and Josh.

"You come," he said. "I'll see you."

THE DAY WAS turning into one of those hot, still miseries uncommon to Santa Barbara. The beach was filling up from one end to the other. By noon the sand was too hot for bare feet.

I finished up a tough, long workout with five rounds on the heavy bag. I leaned on my terrace railing to catch my breath and let the flow of sweat subside while I untaped my hands and wrists. The comedy below with pale-skinned tourists hopping on one foot and then the other in a lemming's rush to the water said the beach was no place for me.

I heard my name called from below and looked down to see Tony standing beside his car in the parking area.

"Come on down for some lunch," he yelled.

My first impulse was to say no, but Tony Scolari was an upper. I needed an upper. "Half an hour," I called back.

I spent most of it under the cold shower. I dressed in light, loose, white cotton pants and shirt and sockless canvas Top-Siders. Tony met me at the door and led the way to a booth at the back.

"Thank God I'm air-conditioned," he said. "I pity the joints without it on days like this."

Tony's Beachside was on the A list of Santa Barbara. It was part food, part location, but it was most of all Tony. He had a style and verve that made his place work.

"So, pally, tell me something. You playing the big-white-round-ball game? Is what I hear true?" He grinned his big grin.

"Where do you hear these things?" I asked.

"Hey, you know me. I got the ear, Jake. It all comes to me."

"How'd you hear it? How come that made the news?" I asked.

"It's all over town, paesan. They're all talking about this big slammer taking over the game. New top gun in town, the way I hear it."

He broke himself up with that. It struck me funny, too.

"You saw me, right?" I prompted.

He held up his hands. "Hey, the way it looked to me, they should be saying those things."

"It gets clearer all the time, you didn't see very much," I said.

He made a wide circular motion over the table to a waiter who looked in our direction. The waiter gave me a wave of recognition and went to carry out his silent orders.

"No, I was driving by and looked over to check out the action. I got a regular that plays East Beach. Well, you coulda struck me blind. What I saw was you, doing all that diving and crap.'' He shook his head. ''I almost took out a crosswalk full of pedestrians. I woulda put ten to one you'd never go near a wimp game like that.''

''Take my word, it's no wimp game. It's tough,'' I replied. ''The guys that play it well are top-line athletes.''

''C'mon, Jake,'' he scoffed. ''We're talking volleyball here. So, what got you into it? Some chick, I'll bet.''

''Something like that,'' I answered and let it drop while the waiter put down my iced coffee and Tony's red wine. Our conversation remained on hold until our plates were placed before us.

As Tony inspected the piece of veal scaloppine marsala he had just cut, I said, ''What do you mean, one of your regulars? Customer?''

''Customer, sure,'' he answered while chewing and evaluating the veal. ''Always pays in cash.''

''That's surprising,'' I said. ''Most of those guys don't strike me as having the means to be regulars at Tony's Beachside.''

''Okay, you're right. I should have said, the regular guest of a customer.'' He waved his fork in a little circle. ''They got a thing going on the games down there, I think. I'm guessing it's not big money, but it pays the lunches, you know what I mean?''

''What's his name, the player?'' I asked, my curiosity tweaked.

''Hey, Jakey, I know enough people. I don't listen to a guy's name unless he's paying the tab, capisce?''

''I understand,'' I said. ''You ever get in on the action?''

''Me? Nah,'' he responded. ''I kibitz with Barney, but you know me...see no, hear no, speak no. Know what I mean?''

''Barney's the customer?'' I asked. He nodded.

We enjoyed the veal, and the pasta primavera that followed and the salad that followed that. I waved away the glacé kiwi torte, which he took, but accepted the espresso as we talked on about meaningless things and Tony dipped into his bottomless bag of anecdotes.

I had always found Tony to be a great raconteur. His stories were both funny and unique. Our lunch passed quickly with Tony keeping me well beyond my first attempts to leave. After a third espresso, he walked me to the door.

"Thanks for lunch, Tony," I said. "Great as usual."

"Don't mention it," he responded. "Oh, and one other thing, paesan, don't mention what I said about Gable, okay? Things like that sometimes go into the wrong ears, you know what I mean?"

"Gable?" I asked.

"Yeah, the customer, you remember, with the volleyball player whose name I don't get?"

"I thought you said Barney?"

"Barney Gable, sure, that's his name."

"Name rings a bell. Does he own a big horse spread on the valley side of the pass?" I asked.

"I wouldn't know. He plays the ponies, though. That guy'd bet two flies on a wall."

"He comes in here often?"

"Oh yeah, all the time. He brings in all kinds of people. Keeps his boat at the marina and is always coming in before or after taking it out. He's a big party guy. Lotsa chicks, too. My kinda guy." He gave a double click with the side of his mouth.

"Would you say he played it straight or a little loose?"

"Loose," he said emphatically. "Very loose. My read on Barney is that he puts the fix in every chance he gets."

"Interesting," I said. "Try to catch the volleyball player's name next time they're in, okay? I'd like to know who's playing the curve out there."

"Jeez, Jake," he said. "There might be two or three different guys, you know. I might not even remember what he looks like. Probably don't. All you volleyball players look the same to me." He gave me his little laugh to punctuate his little joke, then put up his hands and said, "I'll get it, I'll get it. I'll probably lose a good customer over this."

"Jason asked about you the other day," I said.

"Does he ever come up?" he asked, immediately refocused.

"Sometimes."

"Why don't you bring him in sometime?"

"He's mentioned it. Maybe next time."

We stepped outside and a hot tongue of heat wrapped around us.

"Whoa," Tony said. "Addio, amico, I'm getting back inside my ice palace."

A wise choice, I thought. I had visions of Tony's hair spray melting. He was not the sun-and-wind kind of guy he used to be.

A large truck awaited me at my building. A crew was busily unloading and setting up light scaffolding. The truck's side panels were painted with bright colors identifying it as part of the Rainbow Awning Company.

I recognized Judy from Bob Claiborne's office talking to the crew boss. She nodded as I approached with a quick look back to the snarling man in front of her. He seemed unhappy about something as he shook his head and showed her his wristwatch. "We been here since one."

"To do what?" I asked, joining them.

He played to the space around us to show what an absolute fool he had to deal with. He gave a full one eighty turn of his head, displaying his incredulous expression. His voice took up the cause as he repeated my question back to me. "To do what?" He gave another look to the air around us before he finally answered our question. "To put up the awnings. You people are supposed to have a check for me."

He thrust an invoice at me. The figure was staggering. Then I remembered vaguely the call from Bob Claiborne, the real estate agent whose office handled the management concerns of the building for me. He had told me of the complaints from my tenants about the sun glare in the afternoons. They had asked for some kind of structural relief from it. The solution, according to a high-priced consultant, had been awnings. The argument for awnings had also been that it would improve the appearance of the building. I had agreed. That had been before I knew how expensive awnings were. I put my hands up and backed away.

Judy spoke up quickly. "I have that check for you right here. He's one of the tenants."

The crew boss gave me a quizzical look to which I responded, "I just live here. Up there." I pointed.

He said, "Oh, sorry, I thought you were the owner or something."

I shrugged it off and watched as Judy handed over a check which could have fed a family of twelve for ten years. I knew I would be writing a check to the Surf and Turf Realty in the next few days for that same amount, and I did not feel too good about it. I wasn't cut out to be a landlord.

The crew boss asked Judy, "You want these installed tight or loose?"

"Tight," she said with a small turn to me. I gave a quick nod and she affirmed. "Yes, tight."

Judy left, but I watched for a while to see what all that money I had just spent was paying for. The answer was brightly colored canvas hung tight. I began to feel my spirits sag and decided on a short walk. I wandered to the pier and strolled among the tourists, more or less drifting with the crowd toward the end balusters. I leaned over the railing and looked out as people do at large bodies of water and breathed in the ocean smell. I stayed there for a while and did some thinking about *me*. I had this thing ahead of me called the rest of my life, and I just wasn't sure I wanted to live it as a landlord.

Hours later, the sun had set, new awnings graced my building, and I sat at a sidewalk café table with a great view of the traffic along State Street, still thinking about who I had become. The out-of-towners around me, some lobster red, were squeezing the day and the night for all it had left in it. They were on a high that would carry them into the wee hours. Some would pay dearly in the days ahead, but at that time, in that place, they weren't thinking of the cost. They reminded me of Julie as I had seen her last.

Much later, at an hour when the lobsters were probably winding up their visits to places like Le Club, the Metal Shop, and Pismo's, I was home, outside, and finally finished with my self-examination. I had at last managed to get rid of the dismal image of myself as the prototypical landlord. Finally, too, a small breeze moved the hot stale air around, so the night felt more like paradise.

THIRTEEN

I WAS NOT a good Sunday person. Sundays were often bleak things to me. In the years of Trinia and Josh, Sundays had been rich, happy times. Without them I was a spectator to the day, which belonged to families and couples. I never felt more isolated than when a maître d' raised his eyebrows in silent query and I was forced to answer, "One." The solitary diner was a Sunday misfit, a mute reminder of the half step that separated the haves from the have-nots.

It was easier in a resort town like Santa Barbara. It wasn't like in some small Southwestern town where the main street became a deserted canyon of wind and dust. Here there were people walking, smiling, doing things, and the single could drift in among them and pretend. I tended not to do that, though. I tended more to watch and compare and feel sorry for myself.

All that made traveling on a Sunday more appealing. I knew I wasn't missing out on something. I wasn't wasting a day.

I planned my drive to Lodi using some basic common sense. I took some exercise early and breakfast late. I let the sun get high and angled in from the south before I set forth on my trip north. I drove at a speed fast enough to keep me in the traffic flow yet moderate enough to allow me to see the world I passed. There were times when it was not so bad to be alone.

I stopped in Stockton, which was still a few miles short of Lodi, but I felt I would have more options in motels and restaurants. I did, but I don't know that it made any difference. I saw the same kind of motel when I entered Lodi the next morning, and a Denny's that looked very much like the one I had eaten in the night before. Chez Denny, Trinia called it on a long-ago trip to Orlando, Josh's first look at the wonders of Disney World.

It was hot in Lodi. I had the air-conditioning on the high mark at ten o'clock in the morning on my drive to the Jefferson Street address where the Prices lived. It was the kind of quiet working-man's neighborhood that sported pickup trucks and camper shells in the driveways. The houses were small, the lawns neat, and the streets wide. I parked in front of 813 and took my time walking to the door. I wanted them to get a good look at me from that front window.

Carl Price pulled open the door before I had a chance to locate the bell. He took open and careful measure of me in the same way he must have done to the boys who first showed up on his doorstep to take out Julie. I had a fleeting thought of how Julie must have looked at fifteen or so, and how hard it must have been for him to allow his precious girl to leave on the arm of some walking mass of testosterone with a buzz cut.

His handshake was passive, his eyes permanently sad. He had the large angular kind of frame I thought of as rawboned. He was awkward and uncomfortable as a host but stood aside with the door open to allow me entry. "Come in, Mr. Sands," he said in a very formal way, and in a smoker's voice.

I followed him to a large back room with comfortable chairs and an old console TV. I took the chair he offered and said, "Thank you for seeing me. I know this isn't easy for you."

He nodded and continued to study me. I heard kitchen sounds from a room behind us and assumed Mrs. Price was there.

"You don't look like a fellow my girl would've known," he said candidly for an opener.

"No? How so, Mr. Price?"

"You're not pretty, and you don't look empty headed," he said in reply.

"Thanks for both those observations," I said, smiling at his blunt manner. "But I wasn't her boyfriend."

"Probably a shame you wasn't." He added, "We're close enough in age you should call me Carl."

I nodded and said, "I'm Jake."

He suddenly looked around and called out toward the sounds I had heard. "Millie, bring some coffee, will you?"

It was the kind of thing that could have as easily been said by her to him. It was easy and familiar, that taking the other person for granted in a way that was so good it was to be envied.

"You care for coffee, don't you?" he asked as an afterthought.

"Very much," I replied.

"What do you think of Lodi?"

"It looks like a good place to grow up."

"I think it was," he said as Mrs. Price entered from the kitchen with a tray of coffee and rolls.

I stood, as did he. He said, "This is Milna, my wife. This is Jake Sands, Millie. We're on first names."

She nodded politely and passed us coffee before taking her seat in a straight-backed chair to the side. She did not speak.

"Well, as you can see, Lodi is not like Santa Barbara," he said as he moved a sweet roll in front of me before taking one for himself. He took a large bite and somehow managed to chew and talk and swallow all at the same time, and without making me look away.

"You got a lot of movie stars living there. Our girl was always writing us about seeing some of those people out places." He turned to his wife and said, "Who were some of the ones she saw, Mil?"

She sat very straight and composed, and answered in a strong voice. "Robert Mitchum, Michael Douglas, Kevin Costner," she said and paused to smile. "There were some music people, too, but I don't remember their names."

Carl's eyes took on a soft look as he said in a teasing way, "And who did you see, Mil, that you almost fainted over?"

He grinned at me, pulling me into the tease.

"Oh, Carl, I did not," she said, waving a hand at him. "You make me sound like some starstruck teenager."

"Well, you sure put on a show at the time. Rosie thought we were going to have to carry you back to the car," he said and turned to me. "You know the fellow that played Daniel Boone and Davy Crockett on the TV? Fess Parker?"

I nodded with a look over at Milna. In those few brief moments I could see who they had been before their daughter was brutalized and killed. They would never be that again except in such small interims.

"That was the one," he said. "She always did like him, and I thought she'd die when she saw him walk into a restaurant right there in Santa Barbara. I guess living there you get used to it, huh?"

"I don't recognize that many," I said.

"No, you don't strike me the type that'd care much about that sort of thing."

Then came that lull we had all three been dreading. We sat with nothing to say except the obvious. None of us knew quite how to get to the business at hand. We sipped at the coffee and waited.

Finally I said, "You mentioned you had Julie's personal things brought here to the house?"

He took a quick look at his wife. His eyes apologized.

"They're in her room," he said and stood.

I followed him, leaving Milna alone and sitting ramrod straight in her chair.

He stepped aside and let me enter ahead of him. It was a girl's room to be sure. Pink-flowered paper, filmy sheer curtains, ruffles and lace, all spoke Julie's name. I stood at the foot of the bed and glanced around the small room. It was most probably just as it had been when she left it to go away to college. Another sad day in the life of Carl the father.

He opened the closet and pulled out a large box. "Her books and things," he said. "There's another box with more of the same. There's all kinds of papers and such. We haven't gone through it yet. It's gonna be hard to do that."

"I don't know what I'm looking for here, Carl, so I'll just sift through it all, if that's okay with you?"

He nodded and backed out the door. "We'll be out here if you need us."

I sat on the bed and opened the box. It was an eerie feeling to be examining the personal effects of someone deceased. Something of the person always lingered, bringing a reverence to the process.

The books were a mix of fiction and nonfiction, paperbacks mostly, which said only that she had wide-ranging tastes. One hardcover book made me know Julie to be a soul mate. It was the collected works of Robert Frost. I thumbed the pages, spotting phrases here and there that brought his genius to mind. It was a book that had been much read but well cared for. The inscription on the inside of the cover said, "To Rosie, miles to go. We love you, Mom and Dads."

A book borrowed from a friend named Rose? I wondered enough about it to set the book aside. I was hoping it was a friend who lived in Santa Barbara. I remembered then that Carl had mentioned the name "Rosie" earlier in the context of one of their visits to Santa Barbara. I made a mental note to ask about her.

I finally found the address book. It was an old one with names in other places on the page. It was such a mess I could hardly read it. It would have been impossible to glean much from it without seeking out a specific name. I had been hoping to find a coterie of current friends from it, but that was out of the question.

On a whim I looked in the Fs for Fraser. Even in its abused state I could see there was no listing for a Collin Fraser. I was on the verge of giving it up when I remembered Julie's casual attitude toward last names. I wasn't sure if she had been joking then or not, but I turned to the C pages for a look. It was there. It was listed as "Collin (hunk), AAA, Breakers #14. NP."

I had already broken her code by the time I read the listing on Collin. "Hunk" was clear enough. "AAA" was a rating she gave very few others in her book, which might have related to looks or some talent he possessed. I didn't let myself pursue that any further. "Breakers" was most likely the posh hotel/apartment complex close to East Beach, with "#14" being the apartment number. "NP" I reasoned to mean "no phone."

There was also a diary, which raised my hopes briefly, but it was two years old and empty beyond the middle of February. There was also a directory of modeling agencies with several circled, all located in L.A. The picture of Julie grew with each item, but none of it was what I needed.

Nor was anything the second box yielded. Even though I found some snapshots, papers, letters, and receipts, I wound up replacing it all without satisfaction.

I was sliding the two boxes back into the closet when Carl tapped on the open door. "You want to stay for lunch?" he asked.

"I don't think I better," I said. "Thank you, but I'll need to get on the road soon."

"Finished?" he asked, seeing the two boxes put away.

"Yes," I said, "all except the letter you mentioned. The one Julie wrote her last day?"

He nodded and led me back into the family room we had been in before. Milna was making noises in the kitchen again, and I felt a sense of relief that I did not have to read the letter in her presence. Carl went to an ornate box on top of the television set and took out the letter, which he carried in both hands to me.

It had a broken wax seal on the back. The imprint was too separated to make out, but I noted the color of the wax was of a deep pink. I took out the letter and read it while Carl Price sat looking away from me. I knew he had memorized it and could have followed my eyes with the words locked inside his own memory. I finished the letter and returned it to its envelope. His eyes were hard to meet.

"What'd you expect to get from her letter?" he asked.

"Nothing in particular," I admitted. "I was hoping something might hit me."

"Did it?"

"No. Not what I'd hoped."

"Rosie always wrote good letters. I can't stop reading this one," he said, as he accepted the letter back from me.

"Excuse me? Who's Rosie?"

"Rosie," he said, showing me the letter as if that explained it. It took another moment for him to understand my confusion. "Oh, yes, I see. Julie. I always called her Rosie. That was from the time she was a tot."

"And she called you Dads?" I was visualizing the inscription in the Robert Frost book.

"Dads, yeah," he said with a small nod, as if hearing her say it in his memory. "She got that out of a movie she liked with Spencer Tracy, where he played a dad whose daughter was getting married. She wanted to be a bride for as long as I can remember. As a tyke she always had bride dresses for playing dress-up. Funny, but she must have been all of three or four when she saw that movie on the TV and started that 'Dads' business."

I had to look away before his pain became contagious.

"Was there some special reason you called her Rosie?" I asked.

"That was her name," he said simply. "Julianna Rose Price. Mil never called her anything but Julie and hated it when I called her Rosie. But it was habit, you know, and I think it made Rosie feel kinda special."

I could feel my mind working slowly and carefully through it. There was suddenly a lot to put together.

"Did she have a ring with some kind of rose image on it?" I asked. I held up my left hand pinky finger.

"A signet ring. I gave it to her when she was in junior high school," he said with what must have been another painful look back. "I picked it up at a swap meet. It was real gold, though, and she loved it. She used to seal her letters with it."

We were both silent for a moment. I had a quick thought of Escobar and the way his eyes had smiled when he had said, "La Rosa."

"Carl, I need to see that posterboard with the lottery tickets pasted on it," I said. "Is it here?"

"In the kitchen," he answered with a question in his eyes about it. "Millie wanted it hung like Rosie had it."

Milna Price turned from the sink to stare at us when we entered her sanctum. I waited until she and Carl exchanged looks and she turned back to the sink before I approached the collage of lottery tickets.

It was as I remembered it, tickets arranged in order of date, ranging from four years ago to one week before Julie's death. The last one was slightly loose, so I lifted it to see the back side of it.

"Go ahead. Pull it off if you want. Why she kept them like that, I don't know. Played the same numbers week after week. Never even came close to winning that I knew of. Funny, though. You know how when they don't have a winner from the draw one week the pot goes on to the next week's lottery, and so on? Rosie always thought those big ones were for her. I think she'd have been disappointed if she'd won a little one. She was a big dreamer."

"She always played the same numbers, from the beginning?"

I asked and looked more closely at the tickets. It was true. Every ticket bore the same six numbers.

"Our birthdays, Mr. Sands, the months and days," Milna said without turning to us. "She was very superstitious. She was also very loyal."

"She was a dreamer, Mil," he persisted. "Her favorite show when she was home was that *Rich and Famous* show. She always said that would be her one day."

I moved into a better light to see the back of the ticket I had taken from the board.

"You can keep that if you want," Carl said. "What is this about the lottery tickets?"

I looked around at Milna. She looked frail and helpless. He read me pretty well.

"Let's take a little walk, Jake. Let me show you my part of town."

"I need to be going anyway," I said. "Thank you, Mrs. Price."

She nodded and answered without turning toward me. "You're welcome, Mr. Sands. Come back anytime."

I waited until we had walked a half block or so. "I have a question," I said. "Do you think Julie bought a lottery ticket the day she was killed?"

"She bought a ticket every Saturday," he answered emphatically. "I don't think she ever bought a Wednesday ticket, because she was superstitious to a fault, but she never missed a Saturday. Why are you asking me that?"

"Have you found the ticket?" I asked in place of an answer.

He shook his head. "No. Is it important?"

"Keep looking for it in her things, will you?" I asked, because I didn't know how to answer him.

"I'll try. It's not easy to go into Rosie's things with Milna about. She fought off the tears while you were there, but she cries most of the time now. She's not getting over it. I worry a lot about that. But then I'm not either, I guess. Not really."

I knew what he was talking about, but I didn't tell him about my own personal hell of sixty-one days in an alcoholic oblivion,

a slide into clinical depression, and continuing bouts with melancholy. Instead I said nothing for a while.

The silence between us began to feel like a link. We were
walking in step the way soldiers often did out of habit.

"A few years ago," I finally said, too quietly for any ears but
his, "I lost my wife and son and unborn child. In my mind it was
yesterday."

That was all I intended to say. That was all I wanted to say,
but he looked at me. His eyes sought me out.

I said, "It doesn't go away, Carl. There will be days when you
might not think so much about it, but it doesn't go away."

He asked, "Automobile accident?"

"No," I said. "They were killed by someone trying to get
me."

"That's awful," he said. He looked at me in between shakes
of his head as he digested what I had told him. "Then you know
what we're going through. Not many people know this feeling.
Most people say time will take care of it. Maybe they'd be right
if Rosie had died of cancer or something, but she didn't."

I looked at the houses we passed and wondered if each of them
had a tragedy to tell.

"I keep thinking that if I could get the bastard that stole her
life..." He said it not so much to me as between the two of us.
"I think I could sleep again if I had that."

That was the time to tell him that when I had chased and caught
and finally finished with Clyde Walls, the pain had eased. Only
the ache remained.

I stopped and said, "You could. You will."

His eyes sought the meaning of my words. I could see him
understand as we turned back the way we had come.

At my car I put out my hand and said, "I'll stay in touch with
you, Carl. I'll do what I can to find out who did it."

He took the promise from my eyes as he shook my hand and
said, "I've given up asking myself why you might be doing this,
and I'm not going to ask you that now. Fact is, I'll take all the
help from any source I can get. I just want to say, Mil and me
don't have any money to speak of, I'm on early retirement from
the bottling plant here outside of Lodi, but if you ever need a

little money to find out something or to pay somebody to tell you
something, I'd be willing to pay what I can.''

He did not watch me drive away. He hurried inside, his mind
probably switched quickly to concern for his wife. As I drove I
took the lottery ticket from my pocket to check over again. It was
dated several weeks back and bore the same numbers that had
been on all the other tickets affixed to Julie's board. I turned it
over. I was glad Escobar was not with me to see it. In the lower
left-hand corner, clean and distinct, was the flamingo pink impression of a rose.

La Rosa.

FOURTEEN

IT WAS TOO LATE to return calls when I got home from my trip to Lodi, and I was too tired to listen to the messages, so I let the red message light on the answering machine blink away untended. It was midmorning the next day when I finally did get around to playing back the messages. I felt an immediate rush of guilt as I heard the first one. Angela was calling to see if I was available for a spur-of-the-moment early supper. Her message was marked Sunday noon. Jason had called Sunday night saying only that he had some interesting news. Monday morning Bob Claiborne had called following up on the work his office had ordered done by the Rainbow Awning Company. "So if there are any problems," he droned on, "let Judy here in the office know and she'll have them back out there pronto. There's some other maintenance due on your building, so we'll set that up and let you know. By the way, I hope we didn't blow your cover with the tenants. That's it for now. Stay sanitary."

The next message was from Tony Scolari, left Monday afternoon, but I hardly listened as he left a simple request that I call him. I was still hearing Bob Claiborne with that ridiculous sign-off "Stay sanitary." I had heard it before, and I knew where.

The messages played on with Jason again on the final one. He seldom waited for the beep to sound before starting his messages. It was his way of resisting the age of impersonal communication. He was in midsentence when the machine started recording him. "...Sunday night. So, knowing what a back-fence curiosity you have, I have to assume that you've taken off someplace. I'll just leave this to tease you a little. It's about a dead body...the identity of which you should find very interesting."

He had me sure enough. I called, but his phone rang on unanswered. That most likely meant last night had been a late one and he had cut his phones off for the morning. I tried one other call, to Angela, but got no answer there either. It could wait. At the moment, I was more interested in satisfying my curiosity on another matter. To do that, I needed to make a short visit to a place no more than five minutes away.

Breakers was well known in Santa Barbara. It was trendy and upscale. It was where the young affluent set lived before they met and married others of their stripe. It was both an apartment house and a hotel, with a small bistro-style restaurant where those who "did" lunches sometimes met for their power meals. Out-of-towners who had the means and the resources stayed at Breakers instead of the mainstream hotels because it held a particular status factor. Also, that was where the action was.

I entered the heavily arched entry gate and parked in the visitors' section. I walked around the tennis courts and club—they did allow nonresidents to play on a membership basis—toward the pool area. The architectural style was Spanish Mediterranean with a heavy Moorish influence. The smooth-plastered buildings were snow white with blue tiled roofs.

The Olympic-sized pool was open and ready for business. The blue-and-white striped umbrellas were up, which matched the awnings on all the buildings, which matched the chaise pads and towels laid out for use by the privileged in residence.

A waiter stood by at the cabana. A lifeguard checked the water for purity. A gardener trimmed errant leaves from a line of bell-shaped tangelo trees on the surrounding terrace. It was the kind of thing one expected for the kind of money one had to pay at Breakers.

As I wandered the grounds looking for number fourteen, I could not help but wonder what Collin Fraser did to afford such an address. Breakers was strictly high rent. A security guard, who cruised by in a golf cart with a blue-and-white striped canopy, gave me the eye. I decided on the direct approach.

"Maybe you can help me," I said.

"Yessir," he answered with reserve.

"I'm looking for number fourteen, I think it is. Would that be in the main building or one of these bungalows?"

"The main building numbers start at one hundred, sir." He took a clipboard from the seat beside him and asked, "What is the name of the guest?"

"Fraser," I replied. "Collin Fraser."

It was not clear to me whether he verified the name from the clipboard or from his memory. He said, "That is fourteen, a bungalow. I can take you there."

"That won't be necessary, if you could just direct me," I said.

He pointed to a triplex bungalow, accepted my thanks with a nod, and went on his way. I was sure he had committed my face and form to memory, just in case. I was also rather certain that once out of my view he would probably do a quick check-in with the front desk from that two-way I had spotted in the golf cart.

I pretended to knock at the door of number fourteen. I spent my time there casually looking in through the plantation shutters, trying to spot some sign of life. Daily maid service like the Breakers provided killed off any chance of getting a good read on an interval of absence. I waited an appropriate amount of time before giving it up with an exaggerated shrug.

The main building was a two-story affair that sent two wings in a V out from the main lobby. I walked through it, giving a careful once-over to the mailboxes behind the receptionist. Number fourteen was full.

I had done little more than verify what Julie's notations had told me and verify that Collin Fraser was probably away. She had indicated "no phone," which I took to mean no private phone, as he was surely connected to the main switchboard. Other than that, the most remarkable aspect of it was the fact that Collin Fraser did in fact reside at Breakers. Where did his money come from? What did he do for a living? Where was he?

I wasn't sure Collin Fraser was the answer to anything, but my curiosity about him was growing. The questions about him became more significant.

ANGELA HAD her head down when I entered the store. The entry bell brought her eyes up from some problem, with vestiges of it still playing in her initial look of irritation. Her expression changed quickly when she recognized me. I was flattered that she seemed delighted to see me.

"You live," she said.

"Thank you for the fine evening you provided me, and I'm

ashamed I haven't called," I said. "There are no excuses for it except my bad manners."

"That sounds like something Lord Essex might have said," she replied with lively eyes.

"Lord Essex would have called," I argued. "How are you?"

"Mired in the glop of payables and receivables. I am not a figure person."

I looked around at the bikini displays and said, "Oh, I wouldn't say that."

"Are you here in response to my message?" she asked bluntly.

"In a way, yes. I tried to call you back but got no answer. I was thinking that perhaps we could have dinner together whenever you're free."

"You are very gallant," she said with a deep nod. Then she took a moment to consider me seriously and added, "You really are. When did they stop making men like you?"

"Is that a side step I detect there?"

She laughed. "No, it is not. As a matter of fact the reason I called Sunday was to invite you over for an early supper, but that was before I started on this mess. Now I can't even think of dinner until I get these books in order. I have a nightmare here, Jake. You don't have an accounting background by any chance, do you?"

I shook my head. "I wish I could help."

"You have," she said. "You've lifted my spirits."

She got up from behind the counter and came around to me. "My God," she said, "I forget how big you are until I'm standing next to you."

"Will your books take you long? Weeks?"

She laughed again. "No. A couple of days. Does it bother you if I call you? You can call me, but does it seem too unladylike for me to call? Tell me."

"No," I said, not entirely sure I was telling the truth. "But I will call you. I promise."

As I started to go I said, as if I had just thought of it, "By the way, was it you who mentioned that Collin Fraser lived at Breakers, or was it someone else?"

Her reaction seemed normal enough. She said, "It must have been someone else."

At the door it was her turn to throw a curve. She said, "I hear you're getting quite good at the beach game."

"You and Tony Scolari have the same sense of humor," I replied.

"Who?"

"A friend of mine," I explained. "He teases me about it too."

"I'm not teasing," she said. "I hear you're good enough for the two-man game. That's no joke, chum."

I felt unreasonably pleased by her comment. I stayed puffed up by it most of the way home, or until it dawned on me that someone might be having me for sport through her.

THE TAPE I had taken from Carrie's answering machine was the same size minicassette that my machine used. I inserted it in place of my own tape and rewound it. I played back the messages until I got to the one with the adolescent sign-off, "Stay sanitary." I played it back a couple of times before replacing my own tape and playing back Bob Claiborne's message. The attitudes on the messages were different enough to slightly change the quality of the voice, but the sign-off was identical in tone, attitude, and voice quality. It was Bob Claiborne on both tapes.

I got slightly lost in the ponderings of an association between Claiborne and Carrie. It was from deep left, and I had trouble getting a mental glove on it.

The sound of the phone brought me up to real time. I caught it just as the answering machine began its recorded spiel.

"I hate those damn things," Jason said as soon as I had stopped the machine and made my live presence known. "The guy who invented those and the guy who invented self-service gas stations should be hung from the same tree."

"How do you feel about voice mail?" I asked facetiously.

"Even worse," he answered. "So, I didn't pique your curiosity enough or what?"

"I've been to Lodi," I explained. "I didn't play messages back until this morning. I called, but you had your phones shut off, I would wager. Right?"

"Lodi, California? Why you lucky devil, you. You win this on a game show or something?"

"I went to see the Prices. The parents of the girl who was killed. So what've you got?"

"I got some news last night that I wanted to share with you. They've ID'd that floater, but they're keeping it under wraps until they've been able to talk to the family."

"You're talking about the body that washed up above Zuma?"

"That's the one. Interested?"

"Should I be?"

"It's a name you know."

He loved his games. He would string me out for days if I didn't bend.

"Okay, tell me," I said, giving him his victory.

"I should make you say 'please' after making me deal with your machine, but I'm feeling generous today. Ready?"

I couldn't help but laugh. I knew he was. I could hear it in his voice.

"Yes, I'm ready, and just to make your day complete, *please*. Does that do it for you?"

"Gable," he said with no further stalling.

"Our Gable? The ranch Gable? Parkland's client Gable?"

"Barney James Gable, one and the same."

"Barney Gable," I repeated. "Any family?"

"Well, they call it family, but it's more like ex-family. He's got four ex-wives they're trying to track down, notify, and question on it," he said. "And by the way, amigo, you pulled the brass ring with that boat guess. They're sure he either fell overboard or was tossed out of a boat at sea."

"Which way are they leaning on it? Do you know?" I asked.

"I don't think they know," he answered.

"Any children?"

"None," he said. "Just the ex-wives. Alimony hell."

"Four Gables," I said.

"Say again?" he asked, not getting what I meant.

"His ranch. Four Gables," I repeated. "That's what it was supporting."

He laughed out loud. "So you think Gable had a sense of humor? Not bad."

"Tony knew him," I threw in. "Said he gambled. Big-time is what it sounded like."

"Scolari?" he asked with a hint of disdain.

"Yeah," I answered, ignoring the attitude. "He asked about you. Asked if you were ever coming in. I said you would."

"He still dye his hair?" was his response.

"Dye his hair? Tony?"

"Yeah, look next time. You'll see that funny red color dyed hair gets."

I stifled the laugh. I didn't want him to think I was encouraging him.

"Got anything else on Gable?" I asked.

"Nada," was his reply. Then before we hung up he said, "You know, amigo, I could have played you for a day or two on this. You remember my kindness."

"Sure, Jase, I'll remember," I replied with as much sinister inflection as I could muster.

EAST BEACH was full. There were players stacked up waiting. I got a wave from a group needing a player and nodded to let them know I was in. As I plodded toward them through the hot sand, I checked out the two-man games. No Collin.

Two or three times throughout the rest of the afternoon I had the uneasy feeling that I was being watched. I could never put a face to it. No one ever loomed up out of the players or next-ups or beach bunnies that I could identify, but I trusted that feeling at the back of my neck.

It was not until I was ready to leave the beach at the end of the day that I turned to catch eyes focused on me. One of the players from the two-man game looked at me in an open, forthright way. I recognized him as the left-hander who had been partnered with Collin Fraser.

It wasn't him, I thought. Someone else had watched me and watched me still. It was a feeling that stayed with me all the way home, although I turned to look behind me several times and found no one there.

I believed in those feelings. I had survived too long because of them not to.

THAT NIGHT, before I turned in, I returned Tony's call.

"A slight piece of info that came my way from a gold badge I happen to know from Smogtown," he said. "You remember the guy we were talking about when you were in?"

"Barney Gable. Washed up on the beach at Zuma," I said, scoring a clean hit on his information bubble.

If there was one thing Tony Scolari took pride in it was his insider knowledge on the things that affected his territory and the people he knew. He hated to be scooped.

"You know that?" he asked. "How'd you get it? It's supposed to be hush stuff for now."

"Maybe we know the same L.A. detective," I answered, letting him hear the tease. "What else did he tell you?"

"Nothing. He just asked me if I knew a Barney Gable from up here, and then he told me they'd pulled him out of the water at Zuma. You got more than that?"

"Nope," I replied. "Just something about four ex-wives they're trying to locate."

"Gable had four exes?" he exclaimed with a laugh. "Jeez, I didn't know that. I shoulda given him more respect, poor bastard. So who told you?"

"A friend," I answered noncommittally.

He gave it a moment before he said, "Yeah, and I bet I know the friend, too. Jason. He's not always right, you know."

"He's not?" I said rather stiffly.

Tony laughed. "I know better than to ever say anything bad about Jason to you, Jake. Don't worry. Jeez, you'd think you two were blood kin the way you defend each other."

"Jason can take care of himself," I said.

"You're telling me," he replied with his little chuckle. "So is he ever gonna come in, or not?"

"To your place? Yes, I think so. Maybe next time he's up here. I'll let you know."

"Good," he said. "I'd like to see him. Tell him for me."

"Consider it done," I answered.

After I hung up from Tony, I called Bob Claiborne. He agreed to meet me for breakfast the next morning at Chase's on State Street. I liked it because we could sit outside and because there were no mirrors handy for Bob to stare into. I always found it disconcerting to try to talk to someone whose self-adoring eyes were focused on the glass behind me.

FIFTEEN

THE CHASE WAS an indoor/outdoor restaurant on the street level of the old California Hotel. The hotel had seen better times, but the Chase had picked up a nice modern-day clientele. In the summer most of them wanted the outdoor tables, which looked out on State Street with a partial view of the harbor. I sat facing up State away from the ocean. It was possible to get too much of a good thing.

Bob Claiborne was not late. I was early. I wanted to read the paper and do the crossword before dealing with him, which is exactly how it worked out. He arrived just as I had solved "Danube feeder, ancient mystic, and African fox." For some reason, dating back to the days when Trinia first got me hooked on crosswords, I always wrote "All Done!!!" beneath a puzzle when it was completed. I dotted the final exclamation mark as he pulled out the chair across from me.

After we had exchanged greetings and he had his coffee before him, he did his usual glance around for faces or forms of interest to him. Had there been a mirror handy, he would have gazed at himself, but a close second to that was always the waitress, whatever she looked like. Ours was curvy but no-nonsense and gave him a glare that would have withered anyone else. Bob was oblivious to such responses. He leered undeterred, to her annoyance and to my embarrassment. His eyes had done a complete X ray on her before she finally was able to retreat with our orders.

"Hope I'm not late," he said with a forced robustness I had learned to expect from him. "I've been at the gym making myself gorgeous."

That was one of his lines. It was also one of the most self-revealing things he said or did. He was a real estate man who before that had been a failed actor. His one claim to fame was a stint in a daytime soap. His opinion of himself, that he should be a star, and the industry's were not in sync. After the soap he had a few minor jobs, one-liner affairs, which dwindled into an oblivion that most actors serious about their craft lived with and overcame. He folded after being dropped by two agents in a row and sought his fortune in L.A. real estate. He was good at that. He transferred his life and new career to Santa Barbara, and the rest was history. A clever wife was his most valuable asset. She had come up with the name of his company, Surf and Turf Realty. Many said his success was due to the fact that people related to the informality of the name and sought him out because of it. That might have been part of it, but Bob Claiborne was also a very good salesman.

"Sorry about that little mix-up with the awning guy," he said. "Judy should have been there earlier."

I asked about his wife.

"She's fine," he said in a manner indicating he wished to pass it off quickly. "You know Flossie, always into everything."

"And tennis?" I asked, opening the door to his passion.

"I'm ready for the tour," he replied, as I knew he would. "I was serving and volleying yesterday like a pro."

"Did you win?" I asked cruelly.

"No, but there was a little wind, and I'm not a good wind player," he alibied. "And this guy that I play, Harold Johns, the weather guy on four, he always likes to play at noon. The sun's okay for him, but for me and my toss it's right in my eyes."

"I wanted to meet with you today to ask you about Carrie Berry," I said, bringing it over the plate straight and hard.

He was lucky. The waitress brought our omelets just then. She must have wondered why she had suddenly lost her appeal to him. His eyes remained wide and fixed on the table between us while she put our orders down and poured more coffee.

When she had left I said, "How'd you meet her?" I had fished in streams like this before. I knew a hooked fish when I saw one.

"Judas Priest," he muttered. "I should've known. Did she tell you?"

"Let's start with my question first," I countered. "At Barron's?"

He nodded his head. "Yeah, I was handling a new development

out there in Goleta and dropped in a few times for breakfast. I should have known."

"Did you ever meet Julie? The girl she shared the duplex with?"

He looked up at me for guidance. I kept my face blank.

"Is that what this is all about? That girl's murder? I knew this was going to happen. As soon as I read it in the paper, I knew that somehow I'd be brought into this thing. Judas damn Priest, that's my luck. I only saw her five or six times."

"Julie?" I asked for clarification.

"No, Carrie. I never saw Julie except at Barron's. I gotta admit I was interested in Julie, but she had a way of sloughing me off, you know, so that I could never make any headway with her. Then one day Carrie started asking me about real estate, and I said I'd help her get a license. I took her number and then saw her a few times for lunch."

"For lunch?" I let my skepticism show.

"Yeah, I swear it," he said. "I mean I was trying, I'm not saying that, but it was like she was married or something. I got some very strange vibes from that lady."

"Lunch and real estate lessons?"

"I swear it." He was slightly panicked. "Jake, what is this?"

Instead of answering, I asked, "When was the last time you saw Carrie?"

"It's been quite a while," he said. "I've left some messages, but she hasn't called back."

"Do you know where Carrie is now?" I asked.

"Is she gone? I didn't know she was gone. Is she?"

"Lock, stock, and barrel. Any guesses?"

"Honest, Jake, I don't know anything about her," he said. "If she is gone, then it's probably a good thing for me. She has that great body, but she's kind of strange. She sort of tranced out there the last time I saw her and did some weird things."

"Was that before or after Julie died?"

He looked very nervous. "I'm not sure," he answered. "I think it was after she was dead, but before they had found her body. Carrie was really freaked out or really high on something, I remember. She said some strange things I can't remember now, but talked a lot about Julie. I remember once she even said, 'I'm Julie now.'"

"What day of the week?" I asked, getting that little feeling at the base of my neck.

"I don't know exactly," he answered. "The best I can remember, it was a couple of days after that they found Julie's body. It kinda spooked me at the time."

"And you didn't see Carrie again after that?"

"No, I called a few times but she never called back. I did something else I feel sort of stupid about now, too." He still didn't look at me. "I loaned her two thousand dollars. What do you think I should do, Jake?"

"Ask Flossie," I answered from deep within my disgust for him. "She's always given you the best advice you've ever gotten."

EAST BEACH filled up early with volleyball players scrambling for courts. Summer was winding down, and the beach crowd seemed to want to squeeze it for every drop of sun and fun they could. By early afternoon, when the better players began to arrive, many of the morning group stepped aside and joined the beach bunnies as spectators.

The day had a festive air about it. From the first moment I stepped onto the sand, I could feel the sense of holiday around me. As the day wore on and settled into the midafternoon ritual of play, I could see there was a tournament atmosphere as well. When the better players took the courts, the crowds around the area of the two-man team competitions grew.

I filled in as the fourth man on several different teams and moved around quite a bit. It was very clear to me why beach volleyball could become a habit. I wandered over to the two-man area while I rested between games, to observe a different level from what I was playing.

As I watched the matches from around the fringes of the crowd, I had a sharp memory of the first time I had watched in such a way, and summoned up my last memory of Julie. The feeling of the day was very much the same. The only difference was that Julie and her dreams were gone.

I was finally drawn to one particular match, where the competition was fierce and the play exceptional. The left-hander who had been looking at me the day before and his partner were dominating play. They were both big and fast and made very few mistakes. It was beach volleyball at its best. I joined the swelling crowd around the court perimeter. My intention was to learn, but I became swept up in the play. I was so focused on it, a moment had to pass before I realized the voice at my ear was intended for me.

"A bit of a bummer what happened to our Jule, eh mate?"

Collin's eyes were as I remembered them, fierce and intense. He was almost on a level with me as I turned to face him. His animal energy filled the space between us.

"A tragedy," I responded. "I'm flattered you remember me."

His eyes flickered. "Oh, I'd never forget you, blue."

"Or I you," I answered.

Like the first time we met, there was an exchange of recognition between us. All the things we knew of other men we used then to identify each other.

"You got a partner?" he asked with a nod toward the play we were both observing.

"For the two-man?" I asked back. "No. I'm just watching."

Suddenly that smile of his hit me. He said, "What say we give 'em a go?" He again nodded toward the teams at play.

"Me play with you? Oh, no, I'm not in your league," I answered.

"You're fit and you smack it well," he said. "We'll do okay."

"You've watched me play?" I asked with that strange feeling returning to the base of my neck.

"Righto," he answered with a small smile. "You need a bit of pop on your serve, but you get it in and I'll do the rest."

He turned to watch the teams at play. As their last point was played, he stepped forward onto the sand within the roped boundary.

"Let's go, blue. We're up." He never looked back at me. It was such an act of confidence that I had to admire it. I followed him to the center of the net, where he nodded to the team opposite us. "That's Riggs and Mako." He walked away without speaking my name. I shook their hands and said, "Jake." Last names were obviously of no interest in the strange macrocosm of East Beach. They each seemed to take full measure of me from behind their sunglasses, but I got the feeling that the one called Riggs was especially interested. Maybe he thought I was a ringer Collin had brought in. The thought made me smile, which seemed to shake him. He did a whip turn away and took his place to start play.

For all I had learned in the days I had been playing beach volleyball, I knew instantly it was nothing. From the first moment I was propelled into a maelstrom of play that was several notches up from anything I had experienced. The ball came with speed and spin I had not imagined from watching on the sidelines. Two men covering the territory I had heretofore considered formidable for four was a major adjustment. The open spots I tried to hit to were filled so quickly I began to question my eyesight.

The marvel, however, was Collin. He rotated me constantly to net and covered the rest of the sand with incredible anticipation. It amazed me how he managed to shore up my weaknesses so that we made a contest of it. Somehow, he managed to dig balls out that I had conceded as sure winners. In trying to hold up my end, I reached down for all I had. He took me with him to a level of play I didn't think I would be able to reach. It was intoxicating.

Our fatal flaw was my serve. Riggs and Mako pressed that advantage for easy side-outs. It was too much for any team to overcome, and eventually we went down to a respectable defeat.

"Good on you," he said to our victors, and to me he gave a nod of sanction.

After the customary fist upon fist taps he joined me in the unaccustomed role of team in waiting as Riggs and Mako faced new challengers.

"Not bad for a first go," he said without looking around at me. "We'll have it right in a few tries."

"You want to play with me again?" I asked, letting the surprise show.

"We're mates," he said, as if that answered it.

"You don't have a regular partner?"

"I'm not much on commitment," he said. "Variety is the spice of life," he quoted as if it were a new thought.

We played four more games. When it was time to leave the beach, Collin said, "Comin' to Pismo's, blue?"

"Maybe later," I said.

"Lotta sheilas there, you know?"

I knew enough to know that he was talking about girls. I nodded.

"Won't be the same without Jule, though," he said, and with a cheery smile was swept off in the midst of the group headed then for Pismo's.

Riggs and Mako were not in that group. They were behind me, and I knew that if I turned I would find one or both of them looking in my direction. I did not turn. I kept my head and eyes forward as I left the sand.

I walked home feeling as if I had made a bet that had just been raised.

SIXTEEN

JOSÉ ESCOBAR was closing his store when I got there. It was later than I realized, as I had spent the last few hours mulling the strange mix of ingredients that had attached themselves to Julie's death. The whole thing had been a little nuts from the beginning as far as my involvement was concerned. I recognized that I had wandered this far into it basically on a feeling that Julie had been killed by someone she knew. I continued to feel there was something deep and strange beneath the surface, still waiting there to be discovered.

I did not go to see Escobar with the intention of gaining information but to impart some. I wanted to tell him, face to face, that the girl I had asked about, the dead girl, was the same girl he knew as La Rosa. It seemed kinder, more appropriate for the gentle fondness Escobar had displayed for her. Yet subconsciously I must have been seeking that puzzle piece which would connect the others and make a picture. It had been with Escobar all along.

"El Cazador," he said by way of greeting.

I smiled, accepting his sobriquet for me. There was an irony in it which he could not know. He called me the hunter by virtue of what he saw in me. Years ago I had been part of an antiterrorist unit called the Orion Force. Our mission had been to hunt and kill those who committed gross acts of terrorism against the innocent. Orion was the god in Greek mythology otherwise known as the hunter.

"I come with some bad news, Señor Escobar," I said.

"It was La Rosa," he said for me. "The girl who was killed?"

"Yes," I answered. "I'm sorry."

His face showed an unusual amount of sorrow for a shopkeeper to feel for a customer. He was not a usual shopkeeper. La Rosa had not been a usual customer.

"*Ayee,*" he said in what sounded like a moan. "She was so

beautiful in her soul. She had a smile which made smiles. Do you know?''

I nodded that I knew. ''I've been trying to put together her last few hours on that Saturday. It would be helpful to know whether she came here that night or not. Would you know?''

He shook his head. ''There is no way, señor. I have no records to tell me such a thing. But each Saturday she was here.''

I understood what he was saying. ''When I first saw your store it was closed. You were away on a vacation. Could you have been gone that Saturday?''

I gave him the date as he reached for the calendar behind him. He stopped and turned back to me without the calendar.

''Ah, no,'' he said with wide eyes. ''I was here that Saturday for sure. That was my most lucky day. My customer won the big prize, the forty-million-dollar lottery. That brought me a great reward. I will never forget that date, señor.''

''That ticket was bought here, from you?'' I asked.

''Sí, from me.'' He showed me the computerized ticket dispenser and said, ''From this machine. For that the state paid me two hundred thousand dollars. I will retire soon, and maybe even when things change a little more, I will return to my homeland.''

It sparked an indistinct memory that made me ask, ''What customer? Who bought the ticket? What was the name?''

''The name? I do not know. They never tell me.''

''You don't know who bought it?'' I asked.

''I have no way to know. Only when they collect the prize will the name be known.''

I put up my hands, palms out, to stop time and motion and to freeze all things in place. ''This ticket,'' I said slowly and carefully, ''was a forty-million-dollar winner, and it has not been claimed? Is that what I'm hearing?''

''Sí,'' he answered and gave it the age-old shrug that said, ''It takes all kinds.''

''But wait a minute,'' I said. ''I remember someone claimed it. A lawyer representing a syndicate claimed it.''

''I heard this too, señor,'' he said, ''but they never claim it. They are in the paper to say they win, but they do not claim the prize. Not yet, they don't.''

I reached in my pocket for the lottery ticket I had taken from Julie's board. I extended it to Escobar, backside up, displaying the imprint of the flamingo-colored rose.

"Is that the imprint you remember La Rosa making?" I asked.

He looked at the ticket without touching it and nodded his head.

"Do you remember the numbers of the winning ticket?" I asked.

He looked up at me somewhat bewildered.

I prompted, "The forty-million-dollar winner? Do you have those numbers?"

He smiled a full mouth of teeth at me and nodded. "My friend is a sign painter. He makes sure I don't forget my good fortune," he said. He turned to point to a set of six numbers done in an exaggerated baroque style, framed and hanging behind him on the wall.

I read from the ticket in my hand. "Two, three, ten, eighteen, twenty-eight, and thirty-one."

Escobar said, "Sí," as he looked around from the framed numbers to face me. He saw me with my head down, looking not at the numbers in the frame he had been looking at but at the ones on the ticket in my hand.

"Those numbers are on that ticket?" he asked incredulously.

"Yes," I answered, checking them again against the numbers mounted on the wall. "This is the ticket Julie bought the week before."

He did not get it. He looked at me in confusion. He asked, "The week before? One week earlier she had the numbers? Is this right?"

"And the week before that, and the week before, and on and on all the way back for four years worth of tickets, all with the same six numbers."

He became very serious. His mind was quickly assimilating what I had said.

"Let me ask you a question. Is there any reason you can think of that, if she came here that evening, she would not buy a lottery ticket?" I asked.

He shook his head silently, almost reverently.

"Can you imagine that she would not have played those same

six numbers that she had played every week for four years?'' I asked, pressing on with it.

"No," he uttered in a low voice.

We stared at each other, probably thinking the same thing. Julie Price, La Rosa to Escobar, had bought a lottery ticket worth forty million dollars hours before she was killed.

"When would she have known?" I asked. "What time and how would she have known that she won?"

He had both hands up to his cheeks, fingers rubbing at his eyes, and making his *ayee* sound as he shook his head. "Do you think this is so?" he asked. "Did she really have it? Incredible. I do not know. There are many ways. She could have seen the drawing on TV or heard it on the radio."

"What time?" I asked.

"After eight," he answered. "The drawing is at eight. Channel five, I think, shows it live, and eleven maybe. *Ayee.*"

"How about the radio?" I asked.

"I do not know, señor," he said.

But I knew. I had been playing the station off and on since I had found Julie's Wrangler.

"KCAW," I said aloud.

"Maybe," he agreed.

"I need information about the lottery, its rules, the way it works, all that. Where's the office for it? Where do you call when you need something?" I asked anxiously.

"Ventura. That's the district office."

Suddenly I was out of questions and Escobar was out of noises. We faced each other with the discovery between us. I could guess that he was beginning to realize that his own good fortune would be forever tainted by this incredible turn.

"I'm sure she would have been happy for you," I offered lamely.

"You must find out," he said. "I must know if it was La Rosa's ticket."

I extended my hand to his and shook it. "I will find out," I said. "I promise you."

"Of course," he answered with the faintest of smiles. "El Cazador."

THE COCO PALMS Homeowner Association decal was still on my windshield from my time there as a homeowner. The guard at the gate flashed a light on it and opened the gate to grant me entry. I didn't recognize him and he didn't recognize me. He was new as was the rest of the security force since my time there.

I was entering the front gate on Faring Lane leading into a community where some of the wealthiest people in the country resided. It was slightly past midnight, but the guard's interest in me ended when he saw the blue decal. Perhaps they had over-corrected from the time when Captain Charlie Jessup had run the patrol and knew everything that happened in Coco Palms.

I couldn't help but think of him and all the rest of it as I passed the stone pillars of the gates at number 411. The perfume of the night flooded through the open windows, and I paused, inevitably replaying from memory my last visit there. The sweet aroma of the night flowers made the memories real for a moment, and I let it happen. I thought of Katherine Burley, not as I had last seen her here at 411 Faring when I was leaking blood, but as she was when I first saw her, beautiful and perfect. I ran the memory loop and put it to rest.

I felt a burden lift as I accelerated again down Faring Lane, as if I were erasing the past for good. I took command of my thoughts and refocused on my reason for returning. Julie Price had taken this drive on the night she had died. I had to know why.

There was something gnawing at me, which had grown ever since I had left Escobar's. It had to do with her detour into Coco Palms. It had made no sense to me as it had blocked my passage to sleep many nights in the past, and it made no sense to me as I sought to follow the route she must have taken.

I slowed a bit to take in the scene as it might have appeared to her. The palm trees lining both sides of the road were spot-lighted and majestic. The walls and gates to the estates were grand and imposing. It all must have seemed even more so to her young, dreamer's eyes.

She came to Coco Palms to dream, Carrie had said. She had done it often when she was up and excited about things. She had gone well out of her way to do so that Saturday night. She had been noticeably excited when she called Carrie. My bet was that she had brought her dream through Coco Palms riding on a high, not remembering she needed gas.

I slowed even more as the scenario took shape. She had left her duplex, I thought, wearing Carrie's blouse, in a normal frame of mind. She had driven off in her Wrangler heading most likely to Pismo's or to town, where she had possibly planned to see me. She had turned her radio to KCAW. That was when all her plans had changed.

I stopped my car and felt the rush of comprehension pound in my ears. In one fell swoop it all came together so cleanly I felt a little slow for not having grasped it earlier.

Julie had probably been heading for the 101 freeway when KCAW announced the lottery results. She had most likely slowed as she heard the first of her numbers read. Numbers she knew by heart because she had played the same ones for years. Then she probably came to a complete stop as another number matched. I could imagine the moment of disbelief, the utter shock that must have coursed her system when she heard her final number announced. Then what? Did she scream into the open skies above her?

I started up again, following Faring Lane to Coral Ridge Road and the gates of the back entrance. I was sure now that she had been here and that she had done the same. She had put her car in motion and headed straight for Coco Palms with the incredible thought that her dreams had come true. I passed out the gates with a small nod from the guard, just as she must have done that night. I could understand now, with her excitement bubbling up inside so much, she had not noticed the car beginning to falter. The car had probably been running on fumes when she exited the gates. A mile farther on, at about the point that Coral Ridge Road suddenly changed its name to Ocean Avenue, was where I imagined she had run out of gas completely.

I cut my own engine, then switched the key back to the on position as I coasted in neutral, without power but with steering and lights. I took the slight upgrades using the speed I gained from the downslopes. The only sound other than the wind was the squeal of tires as I took the curves at speed. I pulled into the empty beach parking lot and stopped in front of the pay phones just as I was sure she had done that night. I was stopped exactly where I had found her Wrangler.

I got out to stand by the phones where she must have stood. The headlights from my car cast an eerie light. I looked around to find myself quite alone, with nothing but the crashing sounds from the beach below. I tried to put myself in her place. She had called Carrie. She had been so up, so happy, she did not even care that her first source for help was not there. She tried someone else then. Who would she have called? She had been in a state of excited disbelief. She had needed assistance for her car. She called Carrie and then she called someone else. I repeated it to myself several times, hoping that a name or face would magically fall into place at the end.

What would she have said? How greatly had her excitement bubbled? How careless and happy had she become? Had she been so anxious to share it that she blurted it out on the phone?

I stood there holding the phone in my hand, lit by my own headlamps, listening to the ocean and trying to imagine who she had called and what she had said.

She had, of course, told them she needed a ride or help, but I was beginning to imagine she might have told them something else. She might have, for instance, told them she had just won forty million dollars.

SEVENTEEN

I LISTENED TO KCAW all the way to Ventura. I was beginning to recognize the sounds of a few of the performers like Vince Gill and Billy Ray Cyrus. Not bad. The station played some of the slightly older music as well, and I found myself becoming a fan of Anne Murray. She was most likely considered crossover, but I couldn't become a "good ol' boy" overnight.

The district office of the state lottery was not as impressive as one might imagine for an agency doling out millions of dollars a week. When was it, I wondered, that government offices became such bland, lifeless things? I seemed to remember a time when the grandest edifices in a city were either hotels or government buildings. No more, I thought, as I pushed open an aluminum-framed glass door to a room painted in Navajo white with a floor covered in gray linoleum.

Mrs. Sanchez greeted me with a friendly smile.

"Just a few questions," I said after the amenities, "for clarification on how the whole thing works."

She cleared away a small space on her desk and gave me her full attention. "It's fairly simple. What would you like to know?"

"Are all the drawings on Saturday nights at eight o'clock?"

"Wednesdays and Saturdays," she corrected. "When it started it was just Saturdays, but we added Wednesdays to sell more tickets and to make the pots bigger. However, we've found that many won't play Wednesdays purely out of superstition. My dad's that way. Only buys Saturdays."

"What do I do if I win?" I asked.

"Take it in to get it validated," she said. "Any vendor can do that, then if it's a big one, you bring it here to the district office to turn it in. Then you go celebrate."

"What if I lost the ticket and somebody else picked it up?"

"Did that happen?" she asked, suddenly sorry for me.

"No, no," I assured her. "I'm just wondering."

"Then I'm afraid you'd be very much out of luck. That winning ticket is paid to whoever brings it in, if there's nothing to prove it's not his. Now, what you can do is write your name on the back of it in the place provided for that. That's the safest way. Then nobody but you could cash it out."

"How long do I have to claim a winner?"

"One hundred and eighty days," she said. "But why wait?"

"Exactly," I agreed and matched her smile. "Now is that the amount of time you have for validation or for turning it in?"

"Turning it in. All the validation does is verify that you have a winning ticket, and it tells you how much you've won. Sometimes there are multiple winners, so you don't win the whole pot. It gets split."

"I see," I said. "I can take it to any vendor and get it validated and learn if I'm the sole winner? I don't have to give my name then or anything? Then if my ticket is legit, I bring it in for the payoff? Is that the order of things?"

"Yes," she said with a cautionary note in her voice, "but bear in mind that if it's a large winning you don't walk away with the whole bundle. That's paid over a twenty-year period. Like if you won ten million, you'd get five hundred thousand a year for twenty years."

"Less tax," I said agreeably.

"Right," she nodded definitely. "That's taken out right off the top."

"I may be a little slow, but I'm curious about this validation step," I said.

"Oh, you don't have to do it that way at all," she said quickly. "You can bring it straight into the office here if your numbers match. We can certainly validate it here. We have to, anyway."

"I see," I said, "but if I had the winning numbers and for some reason wasn't ready to declare it, I could take it in and validate it to be sure it was really a winning ticket and at that time I would know exactly how much it was worth? Is that right?"

"Oh, yes," she said. "Your ticket would be put into the machine and read. Then you could be told how much the pot actually was, and how many winners, if any, there were, other than yourself. You would have an exact figure on that anytime after the drawing. Anything else I can do for you?''

"That's about it," I said. "By the way, what would the vendor who sold the ticket get out of it if I won?''

She was very emphatic. "The vendor who sells the ticket gets half a percent of the amount paid on it. It doesn't come out of your winnings. The state pays that." She cocked her head at me. "You haven't played it much, have you?''

"I must be the only person in the state who hasn't," I offered.

"It would seem so," she said. "Come Saturdays, if the pot's built up, there'll sometimes be lines of people all the way out the doors of some vendors. The vendors tell us that when the pot gets real big, they might as well forget about regular business.''

"I've just got one more thing to ask you, and then I'll get out of your way. I heard that a few weeks back there was a very large pot no one claimed. Is that so?''

She sat straighter, looking at me a little more closely. "There was a forty-million-dollar pot that has not been claimed yet, yes," she said cautiously.

"A single winner?'' I asked.

"That's right," she answered. "The ticket was validated but never turned in. It is worth forty million dollars.''

"That's something," I said. "Can you imagine that?''

She smiled ironically. "On my salary I can't imagine it, no.''

"Two million a year?'' I said as if I were just figuring it out. "For twenty years?''

"Less taxes," she prompted. "Don't forget about Bubba in the White House." She wasn't smiling.

Back in my car I mulled over the basics I had picked up on the lottery game. It was essentially as I had reasoned it to be. I put it into some mental order before checking the time and heading for Malibu and lunch with Jason. I was anxious to place the particulars of it before him to get his read.

I gave myself a break from country and tuned into a New Age station that played a lot of solo instrument stuff. The best of the lot was still Kenny G, who made me think of Klemmer, Trinia's favorite, but there were others coming along who sounded pretty good. I cleaned out the mental bins while I drove. It was time to set aside the clutter and get down to the grit of it. I was counting on Jason for that.

The pier at Malibu didn't compare with the ones in Santa Barbara or Santa Monica, but it was quaint and had a history. There was a restaurant there that had worn more different names than Zsa Zsa and Liz combined. I did not even bother to look at what it was currently called. Jason liked it and was waiting for me there, which was enough to get me in its doors.

Jason was at a table by the window overlooking the beach, reading a magazine at arm's length.

"You could see the print a lot better with those glasses you only wear in private," I said, taking a seat across from him.

"I didn't bring 'em," he answered. "At least I admit I need reading glasses."

"Meaning what?"

"Meaning you need them but you're too damned afraid of age to get any."

"That's a little outrageous," I protested. "Because you need glasses doesn't mean that I do. And I'm not afraid of age."

"No, Mr. Volleyball?" he riposted with an arch to his brows. He took a small pink packet from the ceramic dish for sweeteners and tossed it across to me. "Read the small print on that."

I put the packet back in the dish. "You wouldn't know whether I was reading it right or not," I answered.

"Yes, I would," he said with a conspirator's smile. "I've got it memorized. You'd be surprised how much you can get someone to bet on a little reading game."

He was wrong. I wouldn't be surprised at all. I had seen him get sucker bets from some of the smartest people I knew.

By the time we finished our grilled salmons and salads I had brought him up to date on the lottery angle. He thought it out with mumbled questions like, "Same numbers every week, huh?" which required no answer on my part, or a query like, "How long do they have to make the claim?" which did.

"Six months from the date of the drawing," I said.

Finally he sat back in a thoughtful pose, giving voice to his own summation. "The girl buys the same numbers every week for four years. The Saturday her numbers come up, she's killed.

Several days later the lawyer Parkland comes forth as the representative of a group who supposedly have the winning ticket. He gets it validated but does not make the official claim. Then Parkland is killed in a robbery in his home. Is that what we've got?''

"I'd say we've got more. Don't forget Barney Gable.''

His mind was working it fast behind his eyes. "You're thinking that maybe the robbery on Parkland might not have been a robbery, and that Gable didn't just take a late-night drunken tumble into the sea? They connect, you think?''

"I think." I watched the surfers work the waves of the small bay and wondered what it was about that sport that made them such fanatics. "I think that I just might have been on the spot when that little syndicate Parkland said he represented got itself together. I think I got pictures of them all and their license plate numbers. It times out right and it feels right. Now you tear it up.''

He put up his hand and shook his head. "No, no, Jake, I think you're putting a bead on it. Let's work this a little." He also looked out at the surfers a moment before continuing. "I see the first question as 'Who has the ticket now?'—right? If we make the assumption that Parkland had the ticket in his hand, and we are starting first with the assumption that it is Julie's ticket we are talking about, then where did it go from Parkland? Are we thinking alike?''

"Let's take a step back first," I said. "Let's deal with why they didn't claim the money. That's what really doesn't make sense to me.''

He thought about it while we watched the same comical wipe-out by a novice boarder.

"They were still negotiating," he said from a sudden insight. "The deal never finalized.''

"Between?''

"Whoever had the ticket and the group," he said. "They took the ticket to verify it and to validate its worth, and then they sat down to hammer out the particulars of the deal.''

"Maybe," I agreed. "That could well be it. That might be a tough deal to work out, too, when you think about it. The tradeoff is money up front for a twenty-year payout.''

"I'd like to know how often deals like that are made," he said, giving it some thought. "I think I'd rather have hard cash now than a strung-out payment of twenty years. What if it's some old cocker? Hell, he's going to want to get it now. Ten cents on the dollar would do it."

"So what went wrong?" I asked.

He shrugged. "Cold feet?"

"Maybe, but it wouldn't be over the ticket being hot. It wouldn't have been connected to Julie in any way. I'm sure we're the first to do that, so what was it that backed them off?"

"Maybe nothing. Maybe Parkland really did get killed in some random robbery, and with him gone, the deal collapsed."

"And Gable?" I pressed.

"Accident. Coincidence."

"Yeah, maybe," I conceded verbally but not mentally. "You know what I'd like to do? I'd like to get that list of names from the Paladin office. The ones I spotted going into Gable's place. Could you get that?"

"Consider it done," he said quietly.

After a slab of silence in which we watched the novice give up his enthusiasm for his new sport, I said, "Collin came back."

Jason's head snapped to me as if he had been jerked.

"Damn," he said, "I don't feel good about that. Has he seen you?"

"He chose me as a partner in the two-man game," I answered matter-of-factly.

"You're not kidding, are you?" He stared hard at me. "There's trouble there, Jake. I don't know what it is, and I don't know why I feel it, but I do."

"I think that whoever Julie called that night was a part of the beach volleyball scene and a regular at Pismo's. Collin Fraser is my ticket into that world. I need to know what he knows and I need to know what his friends know."

He sat back and viewed me with a look of amused appreciation. "You're pulling this thing together out of nothing, aren't you? What worries me is that you've been out in the open on it a long time now."

"Yep," I agreed. "And I think I've picked up a bird dog. That

car that did the brush job on me showed again when I was checking out the duplex. I forgot to tell you.''

"You saw it?''

"Heard it. It's got a funny sound. I can't describe it, but I
know it when I hear it. It's like a bad chest rale.''

We fought over the check, as usual. The waiter felt more threatened by him than by me, so he took his card. "I'd have left a
bigger tip,'' I told the waiter as we left.

''You mean something more than the dime Mr. Meddler always
leaves me?'' the waiter quipped. I had forgotten they knew each
other.

Jason and I idled on the pier for a while. He liked that. It was
something we used to do a lot, before my life took a nosedive on
me, and I began to look for corners with dark shadows.

We watched some children and some old people. Men and
women fished and smoked and wandered the weathered planks
of the pier with their faces in the sun.

"Is this our future, Jake?'' Jason asked, more of the horizon
than of me. "Will we wind up two old men sitting on the end of
a pier, staring back at our lives across an ageless sea?''

"Considering the alternative,'' I said, "it doesn't sound so
bad.''

CARL PRICE answered after the fourth ring. His voice was hoarse
and weak.

"Carl, this is Jake Sands. Am I catching you at a bad time?''

"Not meaning to sound sarcastic, Jake, but all time is bad for
us these days. You're not interrupting anything, though, that's for
sure. What's on your mind?''

"How's Milna?'' I asked, not liking what I heard in his voice.

"Worse by the day. You know, I think we feed this hurt or
anger, or whatever this thing is, off each other. I think if one of
us could get over Julie's death, the other would, but we're both
so damned lost here.''

"Have you by any chance found that lottery ticket?'' It was a
question I had to ask, although I knew the answer.

"Nope. We've looked all over. Not a trace of it in her things.
You know, I thought about that after you left, and I remembered

her little routine about that ticket." He stopped, catching me with a mental lean forward.

"You mean she had some ritual with it?" I asked.

"You might say so. She always bought the ticket late. She had this idea that they changed the numbers or something according to what people picked. She said they wouldn't have time to do that with the last-minute picks. I don't think she really believed that, you understand, but it formed her pattern early on, and she kept to things once she started them. I think Mil mentioned how stubborn she was. Pardon one minute, please," he said, and said something away from the phone to Milna, which I did not quite make out.

In the background I could hear Milna's voice replying, repeating the word "always" in a very ardent, emphatic manner.

"Yes," he said, returning to me on the phone. "Mil was just saying that she stuck the ticket in her dresser mirror frame." He spoke to her again, saying, "Yes, Mil," and then back to me with, "Always she did that, Mil says. She always put that ticket in the mirror that way after she bought it."

"How long did she leave it there, usually?"

"How long, Mil?" he asked her. He came back to me with, "Sundays she took and pasted it on her board."

"She did that every time, the same way?" I asked.

"Every time," he answered without having to consult his wife. "Like I've told you, Jake, there were some things she was real unchangeable about. The things she built up some superstition about, she was real careful on. Those things she did in the same order and the same way all the time. She wasn't some nut on it, don't get me wrong, but she liked to do it, the same way some people like to never step on a sidewalk crack."

"Who would know that, other than you?" I asked.

"Her roommates at school or anybody who spent that part of a Saturday with her," he answered slowly. "She wasn't quiet about it. She was real playful and fun with it, if you understand. She'd make a big deal out of having to go fix up her lottery shrine before the drawing, that sort of thing. It was part game and part real for her, but she shared it with anybody she knew."

"So it definitely wasn't something she did secretly or privately?"

"No sirree," he answered with some increase in spirit. "What is all this, Jake? Are you onto something?"

"Yes I am, Carl," I answered honestly. I took a deep breath and hoped I was doing the right thing. "I think Julie bought the winning ticket the night she was killed. Those were her numbers that won."

"I don't understand," he said.

"I think Julie knew she had won. It was not a small one, Carl, it was forty million dollars." I paused to let his inner ear hear it. "With what you've told me now, I imagine that someone must have taken that ticket out of her mirror frame."

"Who?"

"I don't know, but that's one thing I'm trying to find out," I answered. "At the moment it probably doesn't mean anything to you, Carl, but that forty million dollars, I think, is rightfully yours and Milna's now."

"I'll be damned," he said. "It was over money, then?"

"Maybe."

"You know something, Jake? You're right, it doesn't mean a damned thing to me. You know what does?"

"Yes, I do," I answered. And I did. So would every other person who had ever lost a loved one to a violent crime. The closest word was "vengeance," but it didn't begin to cover the complex feelings that were especially part of a parent's promise to nurture and protect.

"We're a little closer now, aren't we?" His voice was much more alive than when we had started our conversation.

"Hang in there, Carl, and keep Milna strong. We get closer to finding them with everything we learn."

"Mister, I gotta tell you, that thought is the only thing keeping me alive right now."

I believed him. I said, "I'll keep you informed."

"What would happen if we found that ticket? If you found that ticket?"

"You and Milna would be very rich people."

His voice was the voice every potential murderer should hear. "Give me the one who did it, and the money's all yours."

EIGHTEEN

I FELT STRONG as I jogged to East Beach late in the afternoon. No headaches, no tender ankle, no physical glitches were in my way. The game of car tag I'd played that night on Cabrillo was nothing more than a vehicle sound I had stored away in my memory. The soreness phase from my first experiences with the game of beach volleyball was long past. I had wind and muscle tone back. It was my mind that I had to work on as I approached the line of tautly strung nets. I had to be inscrutable and extensively aware, a receiver, not a transmitter. That was a tall order, considering how anxious I was to nail down some connections to Julie.

I filled in right away with a four-man team and got my eye and timing going. The guys I played with had all seen my two-man debut and regarded me with a deference they had not shown me before. I realized it was not a common practice for the players to switch back and forth between the two-man and the four-man game. I wondered momentarily if by doing so I was killing my chances for being asked back into East Beach's standard of the big time.

My concerns were put to a rest by the sound of my name being called out from a farther court. I looked around to see Collin waving me to him. "C'mon, Jake, over here," he called out. "Jake, we're up."

My earlier moment of uncertainty notwithstanding, I had expected it. I couldn't say why, but somehow I knew that he was going to keep me in the two-man game as his partner. The others knew it and had known it from the time we teamed together. He had presented us as a team, in effect throwing down the gauntlet. He had put a challenge to the pride of the other teams. He was going to prove he could win with anyone, even with me.

So be it, I thought, as I watched him glide in my direction and announced my abdication from the four-man team.

"Feeling fit, blue?" he said. "Partner?"

"Couldn't feel better," I answered. "You?"

"Always." He put his fist forward. I hit down on it and took the return. I was becoming well indoctrinated.

We stepped right onto the open side of a court in the two-man area. The other team was popping the ball up between them in warm-up sets. Collin scooped a ball off the sand and did the same with me. Before I felt completely ready, we were set to play. I caught only the name "Ken" from the casually tossed introductions. That could have been because a slight case of nerves had taken up residence in my stomach.

As the game progressed, I heard Collin say to me several times, "Straight up, straight down." I didn't get it, and there was no time to ask. Riggs and Mako had been a much better team than Ken and his partner, but I was the weak link, and they were able to make key plays against me. We drew a crowd, as Collin always did, and the last few points were long, hard-fought exchanges. It looked for a moment as if we were going to pull it out, but we ran out of time and luck. Ken ended it with a nice shot around my block for the final point.

After we tapped fists with the other team, Collin and I took our place at the sidelines awaiting our turn up again.

"Straight up, straight down?" I asked. "What did you mean?"

"Your blocks, mate. When you go up, go straight up, and when you come down don't drift to one side or the other. I can't know what to cover otherwise." He said it simply.

"Anything else?"

He looked to see if I was serious. He decided I was.

"Okay, blue, just a couple of pointers. When the other team makes a set, watch to see where the set will be, then forget the setter and forget the ball. Watch the striker. Watch his eyes, his jump, his shoulder turn. You can tell what his hit will be and where he's aiming it."

He was right. In our second game against Ken and his partner, I made blocks on balls I would have missed before. I timed a jump in sync with the partner who was approaching to spike a good set close to the net. With hands up, and reaching slightly over the other side of the net, I managed to make a stuff block. I turned around in my moment of glory to see Mako and Riggs both watching me from another court, where they had stopped their play momentarily. Riggs curled his lip into a sneer while Mako gave me a thumbs up. I had arrived in the world of two-man beach volleyball.

We ended the day without a victory, but I felt I had progressed to a point well beyond where I had started a few hours earlier. I could see it reflected in Collin's face when he said, ''If I don't see you at Pismo's, I'll see you tomorrow, then, eh blue?''

''I don't know about Pismo's, but tomorrow sure.''

I was tired when I got home and I lolled in the pool, letting the kinks straighten out. The tiredness I felt was more a result of the nerves brought on by the extra pressure of playing the two-man game. Odd how I had bought into that elitist notion held by others on the beach.

I gave no serious thought about going to Pismo's. I ate lightly and went to bed. Among the thoughts that chased me to sleep was the fanciful wish that Jason could have seen that stuff block.

I HAD BREAKFAST at the Four Seasons Biltmore, where I got decent food, fair service, and down-the-nose looks at my attire for the twenty dollars and change I left behind. I had jogged down the beach to the hotel and took the same route home at a walk. It passed along East Beach, where a few volleyballers were already at it. The condos and hotels along Cabrillo Boulevard were by that time spilling their inhabitants out to the sea. The beach towels already made a colorful patchwork upon the sand.

I jaywalked across Cabrillo to my building, once again admiring its setting with the surround of palms and lush greenery. The new awnings dressed the building well, giving me a slight rush of pride. I was looking up and around and almost bumped into Claudile, who had stepped out of her art gallery into my path.

''Mr. Sands, I have a fax for you,'' she said.

I was not clear on how it had come about exactly, but shortly after I moved into my building, Jason had been up one day complaining that I did not own a fax machine. He eventually discovered that my tenant Claudile had one in her gallery. Jason had made use of it then and on a few occasions since. I had a sneaking suspicion that he periodically sent me fax messages through Claudile just to give my life a slight nudge. Jason was of the opinion that I did not get out enough. He possibly felt it was one of his roles in life to see that I did not miss any opportunities.

"I'm sorry about this," I apologized, as I had done the last time Jason had sent me something.

She smiled. "Don't be. I told Mr. Meddler to use it any time, and I meant it. It's no inconvenience, believe me."

"You're very generous," I said.

She handed me the two pages, which I took with more thanks and more apology. She stopped me as I was backing my way out the door.

"Do you have a minute?" she asked.

"Sure," I said. "Something wrong?"

"No, but I'd like to talk to you a moment, if I may. Do you take coffee, tea?"

"Coffee," I accepted. She led me to a seating arrangement that I knew to be a viewing area for her customers. From a side table she poured coffee for us both. I tried not to stare at her, but she was one of those women who had it all. I imagined that she could have made it big in films if she had wanted. She had old-fashioned, movie-star good looks. She was like Carole Lombard or Frances Farmer to my eye. Jason commented often on her beauty, in his own subtle fashion trying to direct my interest to her. I waved off the sugar and cream, which she took.

"Do you by any chance know who owns this building?" she asked suddenly.

My surprise must have been evident in the way I spilled coffee on myself. I had arranged things very carefully when I bought the building so that none of the tenants would know I owned it. Bob Claiborne's office handled the leases, the rent collections, and the maintenance problems. It was important to me that the secret be kept.

"The Surf and Turf Realty handles my dealing with the building," I said in an effort to deflect her. "I thought they probably handled all of us."

"They do," she said. "Yes, they do, but that's the management company. I'm talking about the owner."

"I think it's a corporation that's on the deed," I said truthfully.

"But who owns the corporation?" she persisted. Then she quickly gave it up. "Oh, well, I guess it doesn't make any difference. I was hoping you knew the owner and could get me a meeting with him. I can't talk to that real estate company. They're very rigid."

"Problem?" I asked.

"My lease is up at the end of the year," she said. "Relocating will be like starting over."

"Why not just renew your lease?"

"Someone else wants the space. Or so I hear."

"You should have priority. You've been here for a while."

"Three years is all. They're going to raise the rent too high for me to make it."

I got to my feet and said, "No, I don't think so. I've heard that the corporation that owns this place is interested in keeping all of us here. Don't get worked up about it. I'll see what I can find out, okay?"

"Thanks," she said. "I didn't mean to drop this in your lap."

"No problem," I replied. I held up the fax pages. "And thanks for these."

"Oh, did that man ever find you the other night?" she asked.

"What man? What night?"

"I believe you were away," she said, thinking about it. "It was one of the nights I stayed late, and your car was gone."

"And the man?"

"I didn't get a good look at him. He was by the door to your stairs and I told him where to find the bell. I also told him I didn't think you were in. He stayed in the dark back there."

"What night do you think that might have been?"

"Either Saturday or Sunday. I stay late both nights trying to catch the tourists. Sunday I think."

I thanked her and went back upstairs. The bird dog was getting bolder.

THE FAX PAGES were copies of the information I had seen earlier, which had been compiled from my Four Gables surveillance reports. There were names and addresses of each of the visitors to Gable's ranch, for which I had supplied only long-lens photos and license plate numbers. There were also a few biographical notes.

The first name on the list was "Abbot, Arthur Alfred. 10 Bridge Road, Seattle, Washington." The bio that followed was standard, superficial stuff.

The second name listed was "Carlson, Brandon. 2013 Crescent Drive, Walnut Creek, California." I read his short bio before going to the next name in alphabetical order, which was "Kohler, Jerome." He lived in San Diego. The fourth listing, "Willis, Arlo K.," resided in Marina Del Rey, California, and from Orange County, California, came the last on the list, "Putwell, James."

The geographical summation was simple. Four of them lived in California, and one lived in Washington. According to the bios they all lived well, wherever they did live, which was the only obvious link I could find from the report. Anything else I was going to have to dig out for myself.

I started with their phone numbers. All but Arlo Willis had listed phone numbers, which I obtained from their local directory services. My first call was to James Putwell from the Irvine Directory in Orange County. His phone was answered by a woman with a very short fuse.

"Don't you understand English?" she said. "'Not here' is not here!"

She slammed the phone down in my ear, leaving me with nothing but to wonder how my simple request to speak to James Putwell prompted such a reaction. My guess was that she had mistaken me for a previous caller who might have also wanted to speak to James Putwell. Or maybe the rich weren't so different after all, and Putwell was just another deadbeat ducking bill collectors.

My next call, to Seattle, went unanswered. The Walnut Creek number was answered, but by an answering service that referred me to a business number that was answered by a woman who informed me that Mr. Carlson was in Europe for an indefinite period of time. On my fourth call I learned that Mr. Jerome Kohler of San Diego was deceased.

The residential listing I had received for Kohler was the Harbor

Club. The male operator who answered the phone was properly somber in imparting the information to me.

"We're not certain how Mr. Kohler died, sir. He was in Mazatlán at the time. It was some sort of incident on the street there, as we understand it," he said. "A random mugging."

"Poor Jerry," I said, hoping to sound like an old friend. "When did this happen?"

"We don't know. It's only this last week we were notified, and our club steward went down to identify and secure his yacht. It could have happened the week before or more. We don't know. They aren't disclosing much about it."

"He was down there on his boat, was he?"

"Yessir."

"Poor Jerry," I said again. "Do you know if anyone was with him? Did his boat have a crew?"

"On this trip apparently not. He seems to have taken this trip on the spur of the moment.'

I took a small gamble. I said, "That doesn't sound at all like Jerry to me."

He responded as I had hoped he would. "No sir. We feel the same way. Also, the man he ordinarily used to captain his boat was not called. It's most strange from that standpoint."

"Is the boat back yet?"

"It's in Mexico, sir. That can be a very difficult process."

"Yes, right," I agreed. "With many hands out."

Once off the phone, I let the information sink in a bit. Taken by itself, of course, it did not mean anything, but considering the fact of Kohler's association with Gable and the additional fact of Gable's demise, it looked rather sinister. I had to caution myself not to be too quick on my assumptions.

I sat with the list for a while studying it and the information on the men it contained. For a clearer impression from it, I took another paper and copied off the names of the men from the list. I added Gable and Parkland to the bottom of the list before putting a mark beside their names and the name of Kohler. It was a graphic demonstration of the circumstances. I had a list of seven names. Three had died recently and within a very short span of time, all of unnatural causes. Those were unnatural odds.

As I dressed for my afternoon on the beach, I thought of the remaining four names on the list. It could be a very lonely place, there among the names of the survivors. Especially if the list of survivors should continue to shrink.

IT HAD BECOME an automatic thing, the clearing out of the mind when I stepped onto the sand. All the excess mental baggage was dumped by the time I saw Collin waving me toward him. I was just another fanatic of the game when I set up under the first ball.

Collin's tutelage brought my net play up to parity with the teams we played. I had brought with me years of experience in reading movement and reacting to it. Collin helped me apply those skills to the beach game we played. He told me where to focus and verbalized the options.

"If you're too late getting up to net to try for the stuff, go for the soft block. Lay back a step and just try to get your hand on the ball. Anything you get up, I'll get a play on. I'll do the same for you, so be ready." He was intense but supportive.

We finally won a game: the last game of the day. We did it in spite of my pitiful underhand serve. As we were walking off the beach Collin said, "Try serving overhand tomorrow, blue. The motion's a lot like throwing. Just get a few in and then we'll work on some spin, eh?" He tossed me his ball.

"I've got one," I said and tossed it back.

"Righto," he responded cheerfully. "A little practice at home, eh?"

"Can't hurt."

A look of discovery broke upon his face. He said, "Don't leave anything to chance, eh blue?"

"Not until it's time to play, I don't."

He laughed, but his expression did not change.

"Work on the toss. Get that right, the serve will come. Toss it out a little in front, about like you'd do if you kept your left arm straight on release," he instructed and was away.

Upon returning home I tried James Putwell in Irvine, Brandon Carlson in Walnut Creek, and Arthur Alfred Abbott in Seattle again. The only answer I got was from Carlson's phone, with the same message referral to the business number.

That night I practiced in my hallway. After a dozen or so misses I began to make fairly good contact. I put up a barrier of chairs to simulate a net. I had enough room to duplicate the length of the court and enough height with my twelve-foot ceilings to accommodate the ball toss. I began to work in earnest. I lost track of time. By midnight I had accomplished the minimum. I was consistently getting the ball over and in. I settled for that and went to bed.

Before I put out the light I dialed Putwell and Abbot again. No answer.

NINETEEN

I HAD NO better luck the next day in reaching Putwell and Abbot. I tried the business number for Carlson again and asked if I could get a location or number on him in Europe. I got a very definite no and did a mental scratch-off of Carlson from the list. I was left with only Putwell and Abbot for phone contact possibilities. Willis was unlisted, but his address in Marina Del Rey, a coastal suburb of Los Angeles just south of Santa Monica, was fairly close by. Ninety miles and ninety minutes would put me there.

Because there was so much I was trying to juggle mentally, I resorted to an old method of data sorting and problem solving I had used in the past. I put up a two-foot-by-four-foot framed corkboard in my library. I stickpinned several items to it, including the lottery ticket and the fax pages. I took the names from the list and wrote each of them on a yellow index card, as I did with the names of Parkland and Gable. I put the names of Julie Price, Collin Fraser, and Carrie Berry on plain white cards. On one side of the board I pinned up the cards with the four names from the list I was yet to contact or get some definitive word on. On the other side of the board I put up the names of the deceased; Julie, Parkland, Gable, and Kohler. I also drew a small map of Julie's last drive as I imagined it and pinned that in the very center. I put a question mark after Carrie's name before tacking it with Collin's card at the bottom center.

I took a last glance at the corkboard before leaving for the beach. It was an image that stayed with me. Even as I reached the sand I could see the effect of the display. I wondered which of the yellow cards would be the next to be moved.

"Got something for you, blue," Collin said without preamble as I joined him by the nets. He tossed a bag to me.

"What's this?"

"See for yourself," he answered. "Time you got with the program, mate."

The bag was from Smiling Jack's, the trendy shop where I had bought my fluorescent beach wardrobe. Inside was a long-billed multicolored cap and a pair of sunglasses. The glasses were mirrored in a purple-green mix of hues and wrapped around the entire eye zone to the temples. On the right hand edge was imprinted "Killer Loop." They were similar to the ones he wore.

"Thanks," I said as I replaced my aviator-style glasses with the new ones. "Dare I ask why?"

He gave me his simple shrug and his answer for everything. "We're mates."

I put on the cap. The bill was turned up in the style I had noticed on some of the others. I felt slightly ridiculous.

"Let's play," he said.

At my turn to serve I unleashed my new weapon. The first two missed, but even so Collin cheered. When we scored our first point on my new serve, he jumped high into the air and whooped.

"You got it, blue. You got the whole game now."

We won our second time around and held the court the rest of the afternoon. Although it was an end court, we had a good crowd watching because of Collin. They seemed to move back and forth between us and the middle court where the best, Riggs and Mako, played.

As usual, at the end of the day, Mako and Riggs still held reign over the middle court. Collin saw me looking in that direction and said, "We'll be there, blue, just keep the faith. And try to hit up and over on your serve. It'll put a little spin that'll make a tougher play for the receiver."

Something was not clear to me. "The first time we played as partners, we played on the middle court. How come?"

"We needed to test against the best," he answered simply. "Pismo's?"

I declined.

"We begin our move back toward the middle tomorrow," he said. He shot me a kidder's grin as he looked me over. "I think you've finally found your look, blue. That's you."

All the way home I replayed the points of the day in my head. I was reluctant to switch my thinking back to the puzzle awaiting me on the corkboard. My focus for the afternoon had been solely

on digs and blocks and kills. The white ball had become everything, and winning of the most importance. I took one glance in
the mirror before stripping for the shower.

Yeah, right, Sands, you've finally found your look.

THE TRAFFIC ON State Street was thin. I had my windows down
because it was unnaturally hot and I had an aversion to putting
my air-conditioning on at nine in the morning. I was on my way
back from breakfast at an upper-State Street café that piped in
classical selections through a good sound system. Shirred eggs
and ''Fantasy and Fugue on Bach'' was enough to sate my appetite for both music and food, so I had the car radio turned off.
With music on I might not have heard it. The sound came from
behind me and to the right. It was the loose, rumbling sound of
the car that had hit me.

I slowed, bringing the other vehicle up beside me. It was a
burgundy Toyota pickup truck driven by a man who seemed to
take no notice of me as I slowed even further to pull in behind
him. I followed at a decent interval, listening to the distinctive
sounds from his engine. I was not mistaken about the sound, but
the truck was darker than the flash I remembered from the night
I had been struck. It also did not jibe with Tony's lot chief Toots'
report on the car being of a light color.

The truck continued down State to Cota, where it took a left.
I stayed with it over to Milpas, where I backed off a good half a
block for fear he would spot me on his tail. I almost missed his
quick turn into a Unocal service station near the freeway. I drove
by the station and parked on the street a hundred feet away. I
walked back in time to see the pickup pulling into one of the
service bays. The driver parked it inside and stepped out. He was
young, mid-twenties, unshaven, and wearing the company uniform in the untidy manner of one who did not consider the corporate image to be important. He was just another example of a
whole generation I could see out there strangling their futures with
attitudes.

He took a good look at me as I stepped into the bay, but there
was no reaction. To him I was another customer, and he didn't
care one way or the other about customers.

"I was wondering if you do smog checks here?" I asked from beneath a large banner reading OFFICIAL SMOG CHECK STATION.

"Not me," he said with a trace of Mexico in his speech.

"Then who?" I put back at him a little on the hard side. "Or is that a secret?"

He gave me his gang look, but what he saw was not so friendly, and his gang wasn't so handy, so he decided to be nicer. "Fella's not here now. It's better if you can make an appointment."

"I'll do that," I said and turned toward his truck. "Your truck there?"

"Yeah," he replied, paying me closer attention all the time. "Somethin' wrong, man?"

"I heard it when you came in. It's got a funny sound," I said.

"Yeah, I got to take 'it in and have it fixed. It's a recall thing, so it ain't gonna cost nothin', but I keep putting it off. I've gotten kinda used to the sound by now."

"A recall?" I asked, not getting it.

"This model engine is the old 20R that had a defect in the exhaust manifolds. Toyota's replacing it as a goodwill thing, not a real recall, but I'm happy because it'd cost a good three hundred to have it done."

"All the trucks have that problem?" I asked.

"No, just the older ones with that motor."

"Would they all sound the same as yours?"

I could see he considered it an odd question, but he answered it anyway. "I guess," he said. "That's how I got onto it, hearing another one that sounded like mine. That was the guy told me about the recall. He was in getting gas."

"Same as yours, huh?"

"No, just the same motor," he said and quickly shifted to business. "You want to make an appointment for that smog check?"

"I'll call. He a regular customer? This guy that told you about the recall?"

He had already made a half turn away from me. "Just some dude that works out at the dojo up the street," he said without facing back to me.

"Dojo?" I asked with a real interest.

He pointed with his head up the street in the direction of my car and ambled into the cubbyhole office of the station. Our interview was obviously ended, leaving me with an unsatisfied feeling.

On the way back to my car I looked for the dojo he had mentioned. About the length of two football fields beyond my car a small sign proclaimed "Martial Arts Studio" in front of a storefront dojo. I was drawn to dojos, the studios in which karate is practiced, much as I was drawn to old fight gyms. I also stopped at high school practice fields to watch football and baseball workouts. Big chunks of my life had filtered through such places, and I enjoyed the occasional sense memories they evoked.

I looked in the window and saw two gi-clad karatekes sparring. The kicks and punches were sharp and accurate, measured to stop a scant inch or so from the opponent's face or body, but delivered with full force. Both men wore black belts binding their gi tops and exhibited the grace and skill of the advanced practitioners such belts signified. The one working with his back to me was the better of the two, giving me the feeling that he might be the instructor, or sensei, of the other. After another moment of watching I could see that was clearly the case.

When the two men changed positions and I could see the face of the instructor, I felt a sudden surge of recognition. I knew the instructor from someplace, but couldn't place him.

I continued to watch as the two men bowed and moved to the mirrored section of the room to perform the routine of choreographed attack-and-defense moves, called kata, which embodied the mental disciplines. While watching the dancelike moves, I let myself remember my own early experiences with Takayoma Kamura, my first sensei, in what we used to call the concrete cell. His dojo had not been a nice studio with a storefront window and quarter-cut oak flooring. It had been a square room of concrete floors and walls without windows. That was where I learned the rudiments of the Japanese form of the art, karate. I, along with some specially selected members of the L.A. SWAT and two local representatives of the FBI and Jason. I was flooded with memories of the concrete cell. Kamura would sometimes place obstacles on the floor at night and make us fight in blindfolds around them.

And there were times we would arrive for our five o'clock morning workout to find the concrete floor wet and slick. It brought the memory of the way Kamura laughed as we learned the hard lessons and glared at us with intense eyes as we became his equals. I walked away from the fancy storefront dojo with my eye fixed inward on Kamura in the concrete cell performing the ancient katas to perfection. Another part of me was still remembering the cold of the concrete on my bare feet.

THAT AFTERNOON I learned another thing about beach volleyball. Placement beat power.

We moved one court closer to the middle courts and one step up in class. After a loss, we took our turn on the sidelines. Collin faced his mirrored glasses to mine.

"If I give you a low set, blue, don't try to power it. They'll be up there like two big birds waiting to stuff it. Soft-lob it or take the angle. Watch me. Oh, yeah, that reminds me. Try to get your sets a little higher." He gave me that grin, which was as infectious as hepatitis.

"And I should look for that from them when they get low sets?"

"Right. Be ready to come down fast with a fallback." He leaned back in a small imitation of the move. "Hey, we've got the brains, and we're the best looking, so we can't lose."

I saw his eyes go more than once to the center nets. Riggs and Mako were holding the center court as usual. I considered the possibility that they had taken it easy on me when I first played on that court against them. It hadn't seemed like it at the time, but as I watched them play at their own level it was obvious. Mako and Riggs were dominant, and Mako was slightly better than Riggs, or so it appeared to my eye. He was not like Collin, who stood out to the untrained eye. With Mako a person had to know the game to know how good he was.

Riggs made a neat kill, and Mako celebrated with a fist pump. The action instantly connected to the karate workout I had observed a few hours earlier. So did the face. Away from the beach volleyball scene I had not identified the black-belted instructor in that storefront dojo as Mako. After making the connection, I could see as I watched him further how he used his training in karate to his advantage in volleyball. When he moved in on a net set for a kill shot his strike was delivered with concentrated power. He exhaled at point of contact with a sharp *kiai*. I did a quick recall on his mode of transport. The only car I had ever seen him drive was a new BMW.

"They're good, blue, but we'll be better," Collin said in my ear.

I heard his words, but I listened more to the subtle reminder that his eyes were watching me as much as mine were him.

When Collin and I played again, we won. The things he told me worked. I began to play with my head in the game for the first time. When I won a point with a soft poke over the blocker's hands, Collin made a fist, pulling it to him with a loud "Yeah!" It was the same motion I had seen Mako perform earlier.

To me, he tapped his index finger upon his temple. "Brains," he mouthed. I wasn't sure whether he was doing it for my benefit or our opponents'. He was pretty good at the head game, too.

We won and held the court. When the day's play was ended I felt none of the fatigue I had felt in the days before. I could have played on and I was sorry to see the last game over.

"Pismo's, blue?" Collin asked.

"Nope, not tonight."

"Do you have a sheila stashed that you rush home to?"

"Sure, and eight children who think I work every day in a bank."

He open-handed me on the back. "We're winners. Come have a brew and let's brag a bit."

"Another day," I said.

He laughed at what he thought was my joke. "You've got something going, blue. I'm going to meet her someday and try to take her away from you."

I didn't doubt for a second that he meant it.

NO ANSWER FROM Abbot in Seattle, but on the fifth ring of the Irvine number Putwell's phone was picked up. I couldn't identify the accent. My closest guess was Filipino, but whatever it was, I had trouble understanding it.

"No here," I got easily enough, but when I went for the deeper stuff like where is he and when will he be back, the voice at the other end responded in what I assumed to be hysterical Tagalog.

I tried some Spanish. The Tagalog response got higher and faster. I tried English again, only louder, as I had witnessed my fellow countrymen doing abroad when the translation books they'd clutched had become too tedious.

"They no here," was shouted at me.

"No one? Is the lady there? The madam? Señora? Missy?" I sounded silly to myself. I must have sounded crazy to my telephone pal.

At last I got, "No here. No more here. No more."

"Moved?"

"No more here."

He hung up on that note. Putwell had moved, maybe, or simply left the instruction to say that he had. There was one other possibility that I did not like to think about. Putwell was dead. That brought my focus back to the corkboard, and I felt a sense of urgency begin to develop about the whole thing. It was as if the other side of the chess clock had been punched and my timer had been activated. I had to talk to one of the guys on that list. If I waited too long, I was beginning to feel, there wasn't going to be anyone left to talk to.

The more I looked at the board, the more I focused on Willis. As much as I hated Los Angeles, it began to look like I was going to have to go down to Marina Del Rey and check him out. I made some quick calculations. An hour and a half drive would put me there at ten or ten thirty. I could eat dinner in Santa Monica and do my look-in on Willis by midnight. If I did not make contact I could stay over and pick up on him with daylight. It began to sound like my only choice.

I threw some things in a sports bag, in case I got stretched out on it a couple of days, took Arlo Willis' address, and hit the road south to L.A. I had trouble keeping my speed down. The feeling the clock was ticking on this thing was too strong.

TWENTY

I COULD HAVE gone down the coast, but I took the freeway instead, because it was usually easier to drive on mental autopilot. I tended to forget about the traffic, though, which was always a factor when going to Los Angeles. Even at nine at night, the traffic stacked up three exits before the 405 freeway interchange. I put the windows down and listened to the sounds of urban sprawl. Traffic, coarse and demanding, was most of it. I took the 405 interchange at a crawl, thanking whatever gods there be for my deliverance from L.A.

Once over the hill the traffic lightened up, so I was up to speed again when I passed my old turnoff at Mulholland Drive. I may have slowed, but I didn't take much of a look. There was nothing there for me to see, only some slightly open wounds. After once seeing the charred remains of what had been my home, I had never been able to revisit the site where Trinia and Josh had died. Sunset Boulevard, however, had a different pull. It reminded me of my convertible days, when it was nothing more than my pathway to the beach. I had to fight the impulse to take the turn at the Sunset exit. The urge to take a quick nostalgic look was very much with me as I drove by that main artery of my past.

Marina Del Rey was just south of Santa Monica and Venice beach. Not that long ago Venice was low rent and loose living. In the sixties it was a hippy haven, but all that changed. People got wise to the facts of a coastline. There's only so much of it. So it all got expensive. Then some folks with vision and dollars dredged out chunks of the area abutting Venice and built a marina. With that came the developers, who knew the tastes of the boating crowd. Marina Del Rey became a hot ticket very fast in the real estate trade. Hot and expensive.

Arlo K. Willis lived quite well, judging by where he lived. I parked across the street from his address, which happened to be the Marina Park Tower, a posh condominium building. It was one of those places where you tended to lower your voice as you entered. I took my time sizing up the place, watching a few cars enter the underground parking garage, where the use of a card was required to open the gate. Not many people arrived at the front entrance of the building. There was no doorman, but I could see a uniformed man inside who figured to be a security guard.

When I felt I knew the place well enough I drove a few blocks away to a large drugstore and bought a package of brightly colored extra-large envelopes. I selected an orange one and wrote the name "Arlo K. Willis" on it before sealing it. I returned to the Marina Park Tower and entered its front circular drive. I let the guard see my car but pulled it forward so he wouldn't have an easy look at my plate. The guard lounged on a stool between the front entrance and the bank of elevators in the elegant lobby, where he seemed to be quite relaxed.

"Hi there," I said. "I'm Mr. Good. I believe you have a package here for me to pick up from Mr. Willis. I would have been here much earlier, but I got held up in traffic."

He gave me a bewildered look and rose from his perch on the stool. "Nobody left a package with me."

"From Mr. Willis," I said, as if he had simply missed the name. "I'm Mr. Good."

"I don't know anything about a package," he declared.

"Well, actually I was supposed to pick it up this afternoon, but I've been tied up at the office. Would you check, please? I'm sure it's clearly marked."

I was counting on the building having a reception area with a room for package deliveries too large for the mailboxes. His eyes went to one of the alcoves beside the elevators.

"Well, I don't know. No one said anything," he muttered.

"This has happened before," I said in a petulant voice. "Mr. Willis should get this straightened out."

That hint of complaint seemed to be enough to spur him to action. He walked, reluctantly, to the alcove at the left of the elevators, with me following close behind. The alcove housed the wall of mailboxes for the building's residents. After a look around, and finding nothing on the floor, the guard took a key from his pocket and entered the door beside the bank of mailboxes. After leaning down to peek into one of the boxes, he returned from the room shaking his head.

"Nothing there," he said

I heaved a large, impatient sigh. "You'd best call him then," I said. "I remember how angry he was the last time."

"Who'd you say again?" he asked.

"Mr. Willis. Arlo K. Willis," I answered.

"Him I know," he responded. "I mean you."

"I'm John Good," I said firmly.

He picked up a house phone and punched in four numbers. He waited, looked at me all the while, before he finally hung up with a shrug. "Not there," he said.

"I'm going to leave him a note," I said angrily. "This is too much, coming all the way over here and not finding the package or him. It's too much."

I went to my car and returned with the bright orange envelope with Willis' name on it.

"Will you see that he gets this, please?" I said, still playing my anger.

"Won't be tonight. Like I said, the box is empty. Mail's been picked up already."

"Tomorrow will be fine," I said, extending the envelope to him. The corners of his mouth turned up in an obvious reaction to the color. "That's all I could find," I explained to his little smirk. "You just see that he gets it." I strode out angrily.

Once out of the drive I pulled a U and parked once more on the opposite side of the street at an angle where I could observe the mailbox alcove. I watched the guard take the orange envelope into the alcove and come out again empty-handed.

It was eleven p.m. and I was hungry. I drove back to Santa Monica, where I stopped at an all-night deli on Wilshire for a sandwich before checking into a motel called the Surfrider. Sleep came quickly in spite of the strange bed, but my five thirty wake-up didn't let me enjoy it long enough.

I was showered, shaved, and at breakfast by six thirty, and parked across from the Marina Park Tower an hour after that. There were a number of items I kept in my car as a matter of practice. Among them were binoculars and a clean thermos. The thermos I had filled with coffee from the restaurant. The binoculars were on the seat beside me, ready for use.

The way I had it figured was that Arlo Willis had gone to ground. It was reasonable to assume that he had heard the news on Kohler by now and a fair certainty that he had been aware of the deaths of both Parkland and Gable. The question that remained for me was, How deep in hiding was he? If he was not too proficient at it or if he was simply obeying some precautionary instincts, then what I was doing would turn him up. It could take a few days, but I was prepared to play it out. If he was dead or in deep hiding, I would know that, too, soon enough.

The early morning passed uneventfully with traffic out of the tower picking up around nine. Just after ten the mail delivery person showed up. I did not pay much attention to the delivery itself, but it served as a demarcation line for me. From that moment on I needed to watch closely for movement from the elevators to the mail alcove. I focused my binoculars, took a drink of coffee, and waited.

I could have been staked out there for days, which I knew, but I got lucky. Just after eleven the elevator doors opened to release a woman with dark hair cut short, wearing large-frame dark glasses. She moved with the slow pace of disinterest. She was thirty-something, chic, and not hard to look at. I watched her through the binoculars until she disappeared around the corner of the alcove. A moment or two later, she reappeared with mail in her hand. I focused on it, easily recognizing the bright orange envelope.

I waited until the elevator doors had closed behind her before starting my car and moving closer to the building's garage driveway. I kept a count going on in my head, which was my way of mentally tracking her progress from the elevator on the lobby level down to the garage level, into the car, and out the garage driveway. I had determined the count by watching others enter the garage and reappear from the lobby elevators, or the same action in reverse. I could visualize her exiting the elevator into the garage, checking her bag for her keys, walking across to her car, opening the door, checking herself in the mirror before starting the car, pulling out, and then driving out the automatic gate. One hundred and twenty-seven seconds. There she was.

The new white Lexus sport coupe was easy to tail. Her steady pace and careful lane changes indicated that she was unaware of my presence behind her. I moved in fairly close for a tail job and stayed with her for the duration of the drive to West Hollywood. She pulled into the driveway of a house just above Sunset Strip on Doheny Road. I cruised on by before parking where I could watch the house. She carried her mail collection inside, entering through the front door, using her key.

A short time later, she came back out wearing workout leotards, but without the orange envelope, as far as I could see. There was an old Hollywood movie maxim, "Stay with the money." It simply meant keep the camera on the star. That orange envelope was the money at the moment, and as far as I knew, it was still in the house. I watched her turn right onto Sunset, but I did not budge from the house and "the money."

She came and went several times during the course of the afternoon. I stayed put, keeping my eye on the house. Shortly after six that evening, during one of her trips away, a Porsche like mine, only a brand-new model, pulled into the driveway. The man who got out was on the plump side, about forty, and losing the black scrags of wire he accepted as hair. I recognized him from the long-lens photos I had taken. He unloaded two bags from the car and was on his way with them to the front door when I caught up with him.

"Hi, Arlo," I said. "Give you a hand?"

His eyes opened to maximum exposure. He came to a dead stop and for a moment I thought he was going to cry.

"I'm a friend, Arlo. I'm here to help," I said in a soft careful voice.

"Oh, God, how did you find me?" he moaned.

"Take it easy. I'm a friend," I repeated. "You're not hearing me. Let's go inside and talk."

He moved as if I had a gun at his temple. He was terrified. I waited while he fumbled with the door, took one of his bags, and followed him inside. He turned on the lights and faced me for the execution.

Pointing to a chair, I said, "Arlo, relax. I've come to talk to you about something. I know you're frightened, but I'm no danger to you."

"Who are you?"

"My name is Jake Sands. I live in Santa Barbara, where Barney Gable lived." I waited to let his reaction to Gable subside. "I need to know some things from you, and one of them is your connection with Barney Gable. What kind of a deal did you have going with him?"

His breathing was coming so fast I was afraid he would hyperventilate. He put his head back and opened his tie. "This is a nightmare," he said. "Can I get a drink? I need a drink."

"Of course," I said. "You do what you want. I'm your guest here."

He gave me a very strange look before stepping to a portable bar set up in the living room. After he had taken a drink from the four fingers of booze he'd poured into a standard highball glass, he faced me.

"No thanks," I replied to his silent query.

He was noticeably more relaxed when he returned to his chair with his drink. "Oh, man," he sighed. "I guess if you'd come to kill me, you'd have done it by now. I about lost it out there, didn't I? Scared the hell out of me when you came up like that."

"I'm interested in Parkland and Gable. Were you and Barney Gable friends?"

"Sort of. I'd been in a couple of small deals with him. I only met Parkland on this one. That's one intro I'd like to buy back."

He smiled slightly, testing the water with me. I smiled in return, responding to his sense of humor.

"Now this was the deal with Gable, Abbot, Carlson, Putwell, and Kohler?" I asked.

"All friends of Gable's."

"I'm assuming that you're in hiding because of the deaths of Parkland, Gable, and Kohler," I said. "Am I right?"

He took a large swig. "As rain," he answered. "I didn't think too much about it when Gable turned up dead, but when I heard about Kohler, man, that was too much."

"How'd you hear about Kohler?" I asked.

"Jim Putwell told me. He was shaky from the time Parkland died. When he heard about Gable he called me and all the others and got us all worrying. He took off even before Kohler was killed. He called me from someplace on the East Coast where he's hiding out. He's even more spooked than I am. He thinks Abbot is dead, too."

"Wait," I said visualizing the corkboard. "Abbot's from Seattle?"

"Yeah," he nodded. "Art was a strange guy, but okay, I guess. He, Kohler, and Gable were boat friends and into some other things that might not have been on the up-and-up." He sipped his drink and appeared to be thinking about what more he should say. "Putwell thinks Abbot and Kohler were trying a scam on this thing. I don't know about that. And for the record, I was never part of their other stuff. The illegal stuff."

"And Carlson?"

"Long gone. He split at the first sign of trouble. He'd been in a couple of shaky limiteds with Gable and me before, but he told me from the beginning he thought this one was trouble. He wanted no part of the deal and said so right away. He was only at one meeting."

"At Gable's horse ranch?" I said.

"Yes, that was the first meeting. There was another one at Parkland's house. This whole thing came from Gable, and I sensed that Parkland wasn't a hundred percent sure about it."

"Tell me about the deal," I said.

"Well, Gable calls me late one night and says he's got something that has to be moved on, like now. He asks me if I've got a million liquid enough to turn to cash right away. I said maybe, and he tells me there is a meeting on it the next day at his place. At the meeting he mentions Parkland, who isn't there, but says that he's the lawyer who's drawing up the deal and will verify its worth. He tells us that we can buy a twenty-year forty-million-dollar payout for five million cash."

He downed the rest of his drink and got up to pour another. He was shaking his head on his way back to his chair. "It was a lottery ticket, it turns out. Barney said nothing about that the first day. He said he just wanted to know who would be in and who would be out, if he could prove the deal was a sure thing.''

"Carlson opted out," I supplied. "Anyone else?"

"Nope. Hell, it sounded pretty good. The investment payback is done in three years, and the rest is gravy. The catch came later. We met at Parkland's house a few days after the first meeting, and that's when we saw the lottery ticket.''

"You saw it. Actually saw it?" I asked.

"Sure. He had it in a plastic sheath and passed it around. He showed us the newspaper announcement of the winning numbers, and they matched with the ticket. None of us knew what to think about it or what questions to ask, but the more we thought about it, the better the deal sounded. It was about as sure a thing as you could get with the state behind it. The only thing we were doubtful about was how to guarantee it was the real ticket. Parkland had the answer and said at the next meeting he would be able to produce the proof, but that was when we had to put up or shut up. He wanted some earnest money on the table that night, but none of us would go for it.''

It was spilling out of him in waves. He couldn't get it out fast enough, it seemed.

"Then two days later, we meet again, and Parkland has this official validation thing with the ticket and a statement by a notary public that she had witnessed the validation. Also he had gone to the press that day and made the validation public. It was about perfect. We each threw in fifty grand to secure an interest. We had a week to deliver the rest.''

"And the catch?" I asked.

"Yeah, well, that's why it wasn't so perfect. We're told later the deal had to be cash, straight up and in front. Nobody wanted to go with that. No records. No tax benefit. It made no sense to put five million out in the cold like that. And it seemed like it might be illegal in some way, even with Parkland setting things up. Then the price dropped to four million and then to three and a half. That's when it fell apart.''

"Who owned the ticket?" I asked.

"I never knew. Gable did, and Parkland, and maybe some of the rest, but I never knew.''

"That may be the luckiest thing that happened to you out of this," I said. "What happened to your fifty thousand?"

"Gone," he answered. "It was cash, given to Parkland, and now Parkland is dead. I've kissed it good-bye."

"Do you think Parkland kept it?"

"No, I think Gable took it. I think Gable and Kohler were trying to screw everybody on this thing. What's got me scared is thinking that somebody who shouldn't be messed with was messed with and thinks I'm part of it. If I knew who it was I'd tell them that I got screwed, too, if it'd do any good."

"And the ticket? Where is it?"

"I don't know. Parkland had it, I do know that, but I think maybe Gable took it back to hold. I didn't know much, really. Just what I've told you."

"How long after this thing folded was Parkland killed?"

"Right after," he answered immediately. "That's what spooked us so much. And then Gable and now Kohler."

I gave him my name and number in Santa Barbara. "If you think of anything more or you think someone is on your tail, call me. If you think you're in danger, go to a police station and call me from there. I'll come, don't worry."

Just then the door opened and the dark-haired woman entered the house. I stood and turned toward her. She dropped two bags of groceries and screamed. Arlo got right over to her and calmed her.

"It's okay, baby. He's a friend. It's okay."

She had trouble getting her breath and started crying. Arlo led her to a chair and eased her down. "Marla, this is Jake. He's a friend."

I said, "Hello, Marla. Sorry I startled you."

To me he said, "Marla is my ex. She's the only one I could think of when I got in trouble. She's been great."

"That should tell you something," I said by way of parting. "Don't forget my number."

By the time I got into my car and turned onto Sunset Boulevard heading toward the ocean, I was wrestling with what I had not said to him. I had not told him how easy it was for me to find him, and how vulnerable he was. I had not told him to get out of town fast and stay there until the coast was clear.

I hoped I would not soon regret what I had not told him.

TWENTY-ONE

I STOPPED AT Meddler's on the way home. While we battled through two games of chess, I told the story as Willis had told it to me.

Jason looked down into the swirl of amber he controlled within the Baccarat double old-fashioned. The slow circles he made with the twelve-year-old Glenlivet was something I had watched him do for so many years it seemed like forever. Some people tugged at their ears when they thought, others rubbed their foreheads or tapped fingers on a table. Jason swished around his scotch.

"The question is, How big did this thing get?" he said finally. "How much was it noised around? There is one biggie to consider, and I'll just throw it in the pot to cook for a minute. Suppose the seller, this guy who originally brought the deal to Gable and Parkland, saw things falling apart and tried to find other interested parties. Let's say he put some feelers out in places like Vegas, for instance. He might not be the one doing the boys in Gable's group. It might be group number two, whoever they might be. Just thinking, that's all." He leaned over and picked up his cigar from the ashtray. After tapping it, he took a small puff of it, with a connoisseur's appraisal of the taste, and added, "Just thinking."

"That would presuppose the ticket never returned to the seller," I said. "I agree with that, but forget a second-group theory. Without the ticket, the seller wouldn't have had anything to show. I think the seller never got his ticket back when the deal fell through, and I also think he never saw any part of the fifty grand each of them coughed up for earnest money. There were five of them, so that would be two hundred and fifty thousand, right? Now what if Gable, or Gable and Kohler, decided to stiff the seller when they saw the deal wasn't going to make it, and take their chances? What if Gable had some reason to believe the seller couldn't make a stink about it if he got jobbed? So he and

Kohler scam their friends and cheat the seller all in one fell swoop.''

"Or maybe they tried to make the seller settle for the two fifty," he amended. "Have any thoughts on where the ticket might be now? You think maybe the seller finally got his ticket back?" he asked.

I said, "Someone has been after Putwell. The first time I called the woman who answered mistook me for a previous caller who evidently had been very insistent about reaching Putwell. She gave me hell and hung up. That makes me think that just maybe the seller has not found the ticket yet. So, if the seller is still looking, then that might mean Kohler didn't have it."

"Kohler is the guy who was bumped in Mazatlán?"

"You want a program with numbers?" I asked.

He ignored my sarcasm with another thoughtful puff on his Cuban rope, which he exhaled in my direction. "You could be complicating someone's life here, Jake. They might begin to view you as more than a nuisance. They might begin to see you as a threat. Just how visible in this thing are you."

"Less than you might suppose," I answered. "I'm not making any big gestures in it. I've asked a few questions around about Julie. That's about it."

"What if this seller starts to think you're after the ticket?"

"I'd like that."

We still sat at the chess table with the remnants of our last game between us. His black king lay toppled in resignation among the few pieces remaining on the board. He looked at the board and shook his head. I could see the chess metaphor coming.

"A lousy gambit, amigo," he said.

"Could be," I allowed.

"I've got a thought on it," he said from a thoughtful pose. "Why not back off for a while? Let time do the work for you. Pretty soon someone is going to have to come forward and lay claim to the forty million, or it's history, right? You know this seller is not going to let that happen, so either he sells it off or he claims it himself. Either way he'll be out in the open."

"Two problems," I said. "Given the ticket and a little time, the seller could build several layers between himself and the eventual claimant. He's smarter now. He's had some time to calculate. He's more dangerous. Also more people might die. I'd hate to see Willis get it. He's a pure innocent in this thing, but the seller may not know that. And the other thing is, that ticket is the rightful property of the Prices. They should have something from Julie.''

He looked at me in that way which was staring under my skin. "So that's it," he said. "I was wondering what had put you in high gear on this."

I got up, stretched, and said, "I've got to go home and get some sleep. This has been a long day of sitting. I don't know how those guys that pull a lot of stakeouts do it. I'd go nuts."

"Maybe the seller is dead, too," he said as he wheeled himself ahead of me to the door. "Maybe there's a wild card."

"Maybe," I agreed as we shook hands.

"You'd better keep a Sig in your belt from now on," he said, referring to my weapon of choice, the Sig Sauer 9-mm.

"Maybe," I said again, not wanting to get into a discussion on it.

"I'll come up for lunch this weekend," he said.

"Good, we'll go to Tony's Beachside," I said with a slight pull on his chain.

It was his turn to say, "Maybe."

I stopped outside the door to his upper private quarters and looked down on what was visible of the main dining room of Meddler's. I said, "Remember Kamura and the concrete cell?"

He grinned and said, "Impossible to forget. I'll bet you just visited a dojo, right?"

"Not exactly," I said. "I watched a few minutes at a window."

"A window? Kamura would have a fit. I suppose they had nice wood flooring and mats and all that junk?"

"And mirrors," I supplied. "Even so, it brought it all back."

"You're a sentimentalist, Jake," he said.

"How much difference did the concrete cell make?" I asked, more for the question than the answer.

He didn't try for the answer. He probably wondered why I cared one way or the other.

"Goodnight," he said.

"Adios," I replied.

I did not take my usual lingering at the long bar downstairs. I gave a wave to Lorna and Eddie at the piano, took a hefty pat on the back from Sebastian, and wasted no time getting the Porsche up to speed on the Pacific Coast Highway, heading toward home and sleep.

THERE WERE some high, thin patches of clouds that did nothing to quell the heat. By late morning the slightly filtered sun had still managed to simmer the condensed air. It was one of those dead-calm days when the heat actually seemed to be rising from the earth. It was the kind of day common to Palm Springs but not to Santa Barbara. After a good workout and a large breakfast, I still had not made up my mind if I liked the day or not.

I made a stop at Bob Claiborne's office on State Street. I passed through an empty outer office to the open door marked "Mr. Claiborne," where I found him in tennis garb primping before a mirror. He was checking both profiles, no doubt wanting to verify that he was still matinee idol stuff in case *The Young and the Restless* should call.

"Contemplating surgery?" I inquired.

"Hey, Jake, you surprised me. I was seeing if I needed to shave again." He moved quickly behind his desk as if seeking its support. "I don't think so, do you?"

"You're always an eight-by-ten glossy to me, Bob," I said. I settled into a chair before continuing. "I've got a couple of things to talk to you about. Maybe you better grab the file on my building."

"Sure, sure," he said and called for Judy through the intercom. When she answered finally, having returned from wherever she had been, he asked her to bring in the file.

While we waited I said, "Do you know who leased that duplex to Carrie and Julie?"

He had a moment of wide-eyed reaction before he let his mind work on it. "I think it was Ruth Durney. I'm pretty sure it was, because I looked it up one time."

I did not ask why. I didn't want to know. My opinion of him was not very high as it was. I said, "I want you to find out from

Ruth Durney what sort of references Carrie gave. I want to know what she put down for prior addresses. I'd also like to know the terms of her lease on the duplex.''

He started to protest when Judy entered with the file. She nodded a hello to me and exited.

Before he could resume his protest I said, ''I'd like you to do it while I'm here. I need to know.''

I took the file to look at while he called. I read the list of tenants and lease expirations, noting that Claudile's was indeed up at the end of the year. I could hear Bob working his way through the amenities with Ruth Durney. I paid attention when he got to the main question. There was a long pause, during which time he looked at me with his well-groomed eyebrows raised. He made notations on a pad then said, ''That's all? You're sure? Okay, Ruthie, thanks a bunch. I'll be in touch.''

''Vandenberg,'' he said, reading from the pad. ''She moved down here after separating from an Air Force guy stationed there at the air base. Nothing prior to that. On the duplex, Ruth said she took off with six months still on her lease. Furniture was all rented.''

''Got the name of the airman?'' I asked.

He handed me the page off the pad. ''It's all right here. Now, you said there was something to do with your building?''

''Keep the art gallery there. Renew at the same rent if she wants to,'' I said.

''Wait a minute, Jake,'' he said. ''I've got a top-notch tenant ready to take that space at twice the rent you're getting now.''

''No,'' I said.

''It's Smiling Jack. You know, the guy with the fancy beachwear store of the same name.''

''I prefer the art gallery,'' I said.

''He's going to be mad. I promised him,'' he whined.

''Smiling Jack mad? Tell him that's bad for his image. Thanks for the info on Carrie,'' I said on my way to the door. ''See you.''

He followed me to the outer office. ''We'll have lunch one of these days,'' he said, then added the dreaded, ''Stay sanitary.''

I barely heard him. I was thinking more about Tech Sergeant

Owen Berry at Vandenberg Air Force base than I was about Bob Claiborne.

I DIDN'T BOTHER WITH the mirror after I was clad in my Day-Glo shorts and tank top. I simply donned my Killer Loops and headed for the beach.

Claudile was lugging a painting from her car to her gallery as I bounded out of my stairway door. She was momentarily in my path and for that moment I thought crazily of trying to jump over her. It seemed important that she not see me in my psychedelic outfit. She cocked her head and smiled.

"Hello, Mr. Sands," she said holding her grin. "Off to the beach?"

"Yes, right," I said, quickly slipping off my sunglasses. "How are you today?"

"Great," she said. "You know that problem I told you about? My lease? It's all taken care of. The real estate office called to tell me that I could renew at my same rent if I wanted. I can't tell you what a load off that is."

"Terrific." I started edging my way by her.

"You were right, I guess, about them wanting to keep us," she said moving with me. "Do you know Mr. Claiborne very well?"

"Bob Claiborne? I know quite a bit about him. Why?" I asked it, but I was sure I knew the answer.

"He doesn't seem to understand that I don't want to have dinner with him. I wish there was some way I could make it clear to him without jeopardizing my lease situation here."

"Tell you what, next time he mentions it, ask him if he intends to bring his wife, Flossie. If he keeps acting like a jerk, then mention those magic words 'sexual harassment.' That should do it."

She put her head back and laughed. It was a laugh of fun and discovery. "I hadn't even thought about that. Is his wife's name really Flossie?"

"Really," I replied. I put my Killer Loops on in preparation to leave and took a few steps away.

"Your friend was by again," she said, as the space between us grew. "Night before last."

"My friend? Who do you mean?" I stopped moving away.

"I shouldn't say your friend, but the man who was here before, trying your door. Remember I mentioned him to you?" She waited for my nod. "I think it was the same man. He was in the dark back there, but his size and movement made me think it was the same man."

"At my stairway door again?"

"No, he wasn't. He seemed to be waiting for you. Your car was gone, I noticed, so I assumed he was waiting."

"Did you speak to him?" I asked.

"No. I had come back to the gallery after dinner to pick up some papers, and that's when I saw him. He was very still. He probably didn't know I saw him."

"Thanks, Claudile," I said and started my backward move away again. I was backed almost to the parking lot when she said loud enough to reach me, "Love the glasses."

"Killer Loops," I said, keeping it ambiguous in case she wasn't teasing.

When I got to the beach, I found Collin standing at the fringe of a large group watching Mako and Riggs play a team up from Zuma. I settled silently in beside him. He did a quick head turn and said, "Blue," but he kept his attention on the play.

With my more educated eye I could see the things Mako did that I had missed before. Most of the good players hit with either hand but were dominant with one or the other. Mako used his right as a feint at the ball many times before striking it with his left. I didn't see anyone else doing that. His left-handed serve put an opposite spin on the ball from what most players usually faced, which worked to his advantage. His sets were always high and close to center. He had amazing control of the ball.

"Next to me, he's the best," Collin said, reading my mind.

"You must have been quite a team," I responded.

"Yeah," he said quietly. His eyes stayed on the play.

"How about Riggs? He seems pretty good."

"He was my partner, too, awhile back."

"Did you win with him?"

"Yes," he said with a funny twist to his mouth. "He's like a rejected lover, that one."

"Meaning?"

The twist became a grin. "Meaning, watch yourself, mate, he's a jealous ex."

"Terrific," I said in the spirit of the tease, but I found myself watching Riggs with a slightly different eye.

There was a moment, between points, when Mako looked our way. It was a long look, with something communicated that I could not read. At the same time I noticed Riggs' eyes on Mako. Collin watched another point played before he said, "Next court, blue. We're about up."

It was one of the middle nets, one away from where Riggs and Mako held their supremacy. "Are we ready for it?" I asked.

"We'll know soon enough."

The day before, which I had spent on stakeout, made me eager for the exercise and the competition. We started out well and got better the more we played. We were getting used to each other, and Collin was beginning to trust me to hold up my coverage. He expected me to make the plays and was ready to follow up. We meshed as a team better than we had ever done before.

We won the court once in the midafternoon but lost it in the next game. By the end of the afternoon we had both won and lost in some very close matches. Collin seemed pleased.

"Tomorrow, blue, we take and hold," he declared. "Pismo's for a schooner?"

"I have something I have to do tonight," I said.

"She got a name, this bird you've got stashed away?"

"It's a business thing, not a girl thing," I answered.

"Sure, blue," he said. "Tomorrow, then."

I watched Collin leave in the midst of the swarm of people who were always close by. They were mostly girls, but Collin was popular with the other male players as well. It was an ongoing party to them that started at the beach and continued at Pismo's. It was summerlong, and as summer narrowed toward its end, I could see the intensity of the party growing.

I was not the only one who watched Collin's procession from the beach. Mako watched from his place at center net. He was statue still with his eyes locked on Collin. There was nothing to read in them or his face, not even when he became aware of my eyes on him. He looked back at me for a moment, openly and frankly, before giving me a comrade's wink. Riggs stood behind him, also watching Collin. His face had a more serious set to it.

Questions began to surface as I trotted up the beach toward home. Why were Mako and Collin no longer partners? Or Collin and Riggs?

VANDENBERG Air Force Base was not much like some of the desolate, ugly places I had experienced in the past. It was set on some prime California real estate, close to two small cities, Lompoc and Santa Maria, and just a little more than a stone's throw from the ocean. The fact that it was only forty-five minutes north of Santa Barbara didn't hurt much, either.

I could see right away the entry procedures into a military base hadn't changed. The guard approached my car with the stiff formality I expected. The only thing to have changed that I could detect was that he wore SP on his sleeve instead of AP. Twenty years ago they had decided to dump "Air Police" in favor of "Security Police," but the guy inside the uniform was the same type.

"I just got into town," I said, "and I'm looking for a buddy stationed here. He's an E-6 by the name of Owen Berry. Could you do a little check for me?"

He left me with a curt nod and returned a moment later with a number. He pointed me to a pay phone just outside the base and said, "Sergeant Berry is in west housing, sir. That's on base, so you'll have to call him to arrange for your entry."

"Any guesses where he might be if he's not at home?" I asked.

"You might try the Surf Mist, sir."

"What's that, a bar?"

"That's the Club, sir. It's called the Surf Mist Enlisted Club." He wrote the number on the paper with Berry's home number. I noticed that he knew the number of the Surf Mist by heart.

It was eight thirty at night, so on a hunch I tried the Surf Mist first. I had Owen paged and waited a good three minutes before a thin, slightly high-pitched voice said, "This is Owen Berry."

"Hi, Owen," I said. "My name is Jake Sands. I was wondering if you could spare me a few minutes now to talk about something rather important. I'll come there to the club if you want, or I'll be happy to buy you a drink off base. Whichever you prefer.''

"What do you mean something important?" he asked.

I had not called ahead because I didn't want to spook him or Carrie if she was with him. I did not want to mention her name until I saw him and could get a read on his reaction. I held it like an ace in the hole and hoped I wouldn't have to use it. I said, "I don't want to sound too mysterious about this, Owen, but it's something I don't want to mention on the phone. It's no trouble of any kind, so don't let that concern you. Maybe you'd be more comfortable meeting there at your club?"

"Yeah," he said after giving it a moment's thought. "Okay, you come here. I'll call your name in. What was it again?"

I told him and also mentioned what I was wearing so he would know me. The SP at the gate passed me through, giving me directions to the club. As I drove the streets of the base I was struck by its orderly sprawl. It was an impressive installation that stood as a mute testimony to the military might of the good old U.S. of A.

At the Surf Mist I felt a small tug at my military traditionalism. I wondered how the old-timers who had spent their off-duty hours in officers' clubs, NCO clubs, and enlisted clubs would have felt about renaming one of those places the Surf Mist. I wondered, too, what else was breaking down with the nomenclature.

Tech Sergeant Owen Berry met me just inside the door. He was not what I had expected. He was a short, thick man who looked as solid as a tree trunk. He had Popeye's forearms, with biceps to match straining the short sleeves of a checkered shirt. He did not have a neck, just a roundish head sitting on a slope of meaty shoulders. I followed him to a table at the back, where he sat down, granting a slight nod at another chair for me. He was drinking hard stuff with a beer chaser. I could see from the empty glasses left behind that others had been at the table.

"I hope I didn't interrupt a good time," I said.

"Nothing special," he answered in his comically high-pitched voice.

"Where's Carrie?" I asked with a look around as if I quite naturally expected her to be there.

"You know Carrie? How so?" he asked.

"We had a mutual friend, Julie Price."

He nodded in that piece of information without a change of expression. "So what is this important thing you have to tell me?" he asked.

"Not tell you, talk about," I corrected. "What I'm really doing here, Owen, is trying to find out if Carrie's all right. She left her house, her job, and as far as I know, Santa Barbara in a big hurry."

He tossed back the shot glass and slopped some beer chasing it. "I know," he said. "But I don't know where she is."

"Have you seen her or talked to her?" I asked.

He shook his head. His eyes did all the things that interrogation manuals tell you to look for to detect a subterfuge. They blinked, they shifted, they stayed very much away from direct contact with me.

"Tell me about you and Carrie?" I said.

"What are you, her new boyfriend?" He made the question a whiny sneer.

"Did she have a lot of boyfriends? Is that what happened to you two?"

For a moment I thought he was going to show me some anger. He played with the idea, I could tell, before giving up on it. Instead of anger, what came out of him was weariness.

"She grew up in Barstow," he said, as if reaching way down for it. "Do you know where Barstow is?"

He looked at me suddenly as if it was something important. "I've been through it many times," I answered.

"Yeah," he said wryly, "everybody goes through. Carrie thought she was missing out on something with everybody always going through."

"You grew up together, did you?"

"Nah, I was assigned to an air base near there. It was my first duty after I'd finished basic. Anyway, I'm ten years older than her," he said. "She worked at the Dairy Queen. That's where I sorta got to know her."

"You got married in Barstow?"

"Vegas," he said. "Her old man, stepdad really, didn't go for er marrying just after school. He wanted her to hang around and work and support him some more. We eloped. She thought she was getting some kind of security or something, and I thought I was getting the prettiest girl I'd ever gone out with.''

"How long did you last?"

"Long time," he said. "She cut out on us a year ago, but she kept saying she was coming back. We'd go see her in Santa Barbara, and she'd come see us here, but she never came back to live. That's what you want to know, isn't it? You want to know if she's here? Well, she's not."

"You said 'we' and 'us.' What did you mean?"

"Megan and me."

"Who's Megan?"

"You don't know Carrie very well, do you, mister? Megan is our girl. She's seven."

"Where is Megan tonight?" I asked.

He looked stricken. He could not think fast enough with the booze coursing through his system. He fumbled with it mentally.

"With a sitter," he said weakly.

"At your house?" I asked.

"Yeah, at the house," he answered.

"No one answered when I called there earlier."

It could have been comical, that expression on his face. Maybe if I had seen it from across the room, I might have laughed. The hard round face crinkling up around the eyes, and the chin making that hurt toddler's quiver should have been funny. But I was close enough to see the hurt.

"Is she gone?" I asked. "Did Carrie take her?"

"No," he answered firmly. "I sent her."

"You sent your daughter away? Why? To get her out of Carrie's reach?"

"It was Carrie said to do it. She was scared for her. Said someone might take her or kill her," he said, full of booze and full of pain.

"When did she say that, Owen?" I asked.

"A couple of weeks ago," he answered foggily. "Seems like more. She boozed a lot, and did other things, too, this last year she never did before, but she was sober when she came and told me to get with Megan. She didn't seem to care much for herself. That was the first time I ever saw her not put herself first. That's what convinced me.''

"And Megan is safe now?'' I asked.

He gave me a sour laugh. ''You could put a gun to my ear and I'd never tell you more. How do I know you're not the one she was afraid of? You got the look to scare somebody like Carrie.''

"If you thought I was the one, you'd never have talked this much to me,'' I answered honestly. ''That and the fact that there's a record of me and my car at the front gate here. You had that figured before you let me in.''

"Yeah,'' he admitted.

"And Carrie? Is Carrie safe?''

"I don't know,'' he answered with his head down. ''She hasn't called. I haven't heard a word since that last visit when she told me to get Megan safe.''

I wrote my name and number down on a napkin and passed it to him. ''Have her call me if you hear from her, okay, Owen?''

He raised his head enough to agree, but not enough to see me out the door.

TWENTY-TWO

I STAYED UP late after returning from Vandenberg, thinking some about my talk with Owen and some about my meeting with Willis. They seemed to be miles apart, yet they were both related to this thing I was caught up in. I again listened to the tape from Carrie's machine and spent quite a bit of time staring at the corkboard, hoping something would click into place. It was well past three in the morning before I went to bed.

I let the phone ring, knowing that it would be picked up by the machine. A blurred watch dial told me the hour was not yet seven, so I turned over and closed my eyes again. It wasn't until I heard the voice of the caller that I woke up. I reached for the phone and rubbed at my face, trying to expunge the drowsiness.

"Yes, Carl," I said. "I'm here. Now what was that you were saying?" From the other room I heard the machine voice-stamp the day and time on the message that had been abruptly ended when I picked up the phone.

"I'm no good with those things," he apologized. "I get my words all crossways. I was just trying to say that Millie come up with the name of the other friend Julie mentioned a couple of times. Angie it was. I remembered, too, after Mil thought of it."

"Angela Borne," I said. "I know her. Any men? Boyfriends?"

"Can't think of any. I just wanted to get that name to you in case it was to mean something. Does it?"

"I can't answer that yet, Carl. It helps, though, to know that Julie thought of her as a friend."

He did not speak right away. He made a sound as if to speak, then stalled out once before getting on with it. He said, "I've put a lot of hope in you, Jake. I know it's wrong of me to do that to you, to add that kind of pressure on you, but all I can think of is finding the one who did it. That's the only thing that's keeping me going."

"I think the same person may have killed three other people. I'm learning more each day," I said.

"I hope he don't come after you," he said and then added as an afterthought, "But then, from what I've seen of you, I'd doubt that he'd have a very easy time of it."

"You hang in there. I'm going to find him."

"I know it. Sorry if I bothered you this morning, but I thought we ought to tell you everything we can remember."

"Call anytime, Carl, with anything," I said. "You never know when a little piece of information might do it."

I went into the kitchen and put on coffee. I was tempted to call and wake up Jason. I badly needed to bounce some things off someone. Instead I took my coffee into my study and stared at the corkboard. I moved some of the cards around to expose the holes in the information. My eye kept coming back to Barney Gable. There was a big hole there. I thought about what I knew of him. Horses, ex-wives, and boats. Where was his boat? I wondered. It was a question that had reoccurred in my mind ever since his death. It was time I did some checking.

In sneakers and sweats I took a jog up the beach to the marina. I had several options on how to go about finding Gable's boat. I could check with the local registry or the yacht club, of which I was sure he must have been a member, or I could nose around, ask a few questions, and maybe get lucky. I chose the latter because I didn't want to make it too official and get anyone else looking just yet.

To get a feel for the place, I stopped at the little café at the edge of the marina. It was one of those places that catered to its regulars, and a new face was easy to spot. They saw me as an alien right away. I took the role and played it for an advantage. To the waitress who finally deigned to come my way I said, "Maybe you can steer me right. I had a buddy who used to keep a boat here, but for the life of me I can't remember what he called her. You ever know Barney Gable? He came in here, didn't he?"

She looked at me with an obvious impatience and answered with that in her voice. "He's dead. Drowned."

"Yeah, I know. A shame. Good guy, old Barney. Do you remember what he called that boat of his?"

"I wouldn't know. It was down there on the end with all the other big ones," she said. "You want something?"

"Coffee, if it wouldn't be too much trouble."

I left after one cup of tepid coffee without having made any new friends. I walked down in the direction she had indicated as the locale of the big ones. It was not difficult to see what she had meant. There were a couple of monsters harbored at the end, but I doubted that either had belonged to Barney Gable. I did not want to call any further attention to myself in connection with Gable's boat, so I decided to try to ferret his out by the process of elimination; that and what little I knew about the man.

I was looking for a name. I had no clue as to what sort of boat the man had owned, but I was betting that I would know it by its name. Gable had shown some sense of humor in the way he named his horse ranch. I had to think that naming a boat would bring out some of the same characteristic. I walked along the docks trying to casually read the name on the back of every boat in every slip. Some were clever, some were not, but none spoke to me of Barney Gable. I worked my way down toward the two big ones at the end. Larger boats in the yacht class were docked in that vicinity. The names were classier as well. On the smaller boats I had read names like *My Ole Gal*, whereas the larger more elegant ones bore titles like *Lady Pacifica*. The bigger ones gleamed with shiny chrome railings and varnished teakwood accents. The last slip before the dock's end was occupied by a beautiful fifty-foot motor sailer. It had the look of emptiness houses get when they've been deserted for a long time. It did not gleam, although it was a splendid vessel. It had not been recently washed and rubbed and polished, as the others next to it had been. I walked down next to it and saw the signs of careless neglect. The yacht had been docked and left with many items loose in the aft deck area. That was an invitation to extensive damage should even a small sea action occur.

I had looked it over fairly well by the time I got to the end of the dock where I could step around and see the name on the rear panel of the boat. As soon as I did I felt that little click inside my brain. The boat was called *Frankly My Dear*. I knew without question that I had found Barney Gable's boat. He had named it

as a play on the association of his name with another, more famous Gable named Clark, and Clark's portrayal of Rhett Butler,
whose line to Scarlett O'Hara, "Frankly, my dear, I don't give a
damn," was famous.

I was careful not to be too obvious in my interest in the *Frankly
My Dear*. I marked its position mentally but wandered away from
it without another conspicuous look in its direction. I left the
marina at a slow jog, making a straight run along the sand back
toward the pier. I kept my eyes alert for detail, though, for use
on my next visit to the marina, which would be at night and from
the water.

At home I went directly to my book, looked up the number,
and made a call. Her voice was businesslike but with that same
breathy quality I remembered from the last time I had seen her.

"Jake Sands, Angie. I hope I'm not calling at a bad time."

"Great minds do run in the same channels," she said in a much
more friendly tone. "All my book work is finished, and I was
about to call you for another evening at Chez Angie."

"My turn," I reminded. "We can make it tonight or tomorrow
or any other night that's better for you."

"Tonight," she answered quickly. "I have a date with Robert
Redford, but I'll break it for you."

"What a coincidence," I responded. "I was supposed to see
Kim Basinger, but I don't want to drive all that way into L.A."

"What can I bring?"

"Not a thing, but tell me what kind of food you like. I'm pretty
flexible in what I can fix."

"You terrible show-off. I did a simple little lamb, and now I
suppose you're going to do a beef Wellington or something."

"Would you like that with the traditional goose pâté, or shall
I improvise?" I teased back.

"Why am I getting the horrible feeling that you're a better
cook than I?"

"Because my line of bull has been carefully refined to fool
young damsels like you."

"I won't chide you for that redundancy because it's so flatter-
ing," she said, chiding me for the redundancy. "If you really are

flexible, then fix me a typical American meal. Or better yet, Southern. Can you do Southern, whatever that is?''

''Thank God you chose that, because that's the only kind of food I really can cook,'' I said.

''I can hardly wait,'' she said as if she meant it. ''What time?''

''Eight o'clock,'' I replied. ''It will take me that long to find the rattlesnake.''

''Don't you dare.''

I ended the repartee with, ''Just as an appetizer. Tripe looms large as an entree.''

She had a nice laugh.

During the last part of our conversation I had been staring at the answering machine next to the phone. It displayed a 1 and a blinking light, as it had done from the time Carl Price called and intercepted his message. Instead of erasing the aborted message, I hit the playback and listened to Carl's tentative voice beginning his message. The message ended abruptly, with the mechanical voice following it with date and time. The sound of the sudden interruption grabbed onto one of those dangling threads of thought that lived in the subconscious. Julie's message on Carrie's machine had stopped in just the same way. I could hear it play back from my mind as I had heard it in Carrie's house the first time. It had always bothered me in an undefined way. It had not ended right. It had not had the sound at the finish of the other messages.

It came on me like a punch to the stomach. If Carrie had picked up her phone while Julie was leaving that message, it would have cut the message off in that abrupt way. If Carrie had talked to Julie that night, it raised a whole set of different possibilities. Maybe there had been no second call by Julie that night after all.

COLLIN WAS NOT on the beach when I got there. Mako was and trotted over to me as I approached.

''Hey, man,'' he said, ''I been meaning to tell you, you're getting good with your sets. I've been watching.''

''I've noticed,'' I replied. ''Thanks for the good words.''

''You might try laying your hands back a little more. It keeps

your eyes under the ball.'' He demonstrated with the ball he wa
holding.

I laughed. "I'm lucky to get to the ball."

"You were with the Rams, I hear," he aid.

"No, never played the pro game. Not even very good at th
school level. I matured late," I responded.

He held the ball against one hip and looked at me as if for th
first time. "Really? Riggs was ready to put money down that yo
were a defensive end for the Rams. He was a receiver for th
Raiders for a couple of seasons. Thinks he knows everybody tha
ever played the game. So, what was it? Basketball?"

"A little of everything," I answered, trying to steer him of
me.

"I know, the mystery man," he said with a bent smile.

A trip line snapped. I kept my eyes level and unreactive, but
was doing some fast data recovery inside.

"Mystery man?" I punched it with a little laugh. "Where d
you get that?"

Nothing showed behind his shrug. "The girls, I guess. Every
thing comes from the girls, doesn't it?"

I held the silent question, Which girl?

Mako spotted Collin and nodded in his direction. "Gam
time."

"Trying to steal my partner?" Collin asked, kidding.

Mako and Collin exchanged a look I couldn't read. Mak
walked away without answering.

"He sees us coming, blue," Collin said with his infectious grin
"The whole beach sees us moving up."

I faced my Killer Loops to his. "Tell me, Collin, is there some
thing going on here bigger than the game?" I asked.

His eyes were hidden behind the mirrored lenses, but his fac
didn't change. "You tell me, blue."

"I'd only be guessing," I said. "But I'll tell you when
know."

He laughed. I admired his white teeth.

"Is that when I learn about you?" he asked.

"What's to learn?"

"Your history, mate."

"Boring stuff," I said.

"That should make quite a conversation when we get around to it, blue. Your history and mine," he said. His eyes were on the men tapping fists by the net. "We're up. Let's keep the court all day, what say?"

We did just that. There was something in our partnership that had meshed. We had gotten into each other's heads the way good teams always do. That day we were "zoned," as they said on the beach. There was an extra fire there as well, which our earlier words had sparked. We were each proving something to the other and using volleyball to do it.

Several times during the course of the day I was aware of Mako and Riggs watching from their court. Riggs was the more intense of the two, giving me stares usually reserved for wife stealers. Mako took the edge off with his nods of approval, but I could feel undercurrents from them both that made me curious.

Our crowd grew. The beach bunnies staked out towel space at our net, and the next-ups from other courts watched our play. I could feel what was happening. We were the contenders. Collin and his partner would soon be making their move on Riggs and Mako, was the way the beach crowd read it. It was heady stuff, all that attention. I could see it work on Collin like a mainland upper.

When we retired the court undefeated, Collin once again suggested a beer at Pismo's. "Foster's," he said. Foster's was a brand of Australian beer that was twice as potent as the American variety and came in cans twice as big as ours. It was also twice as good, if my memory served me correctly.

"Tomorrow," I said. "I've got a date tonight."

"It'll be wild tomorrow night, blue. Saturday nights always are."

"Saturday night at Pismo's sounds like just what I need," I said. "I'll buy a lottery ticket, listen to the results, and then come buy you a beer with my winnings."

The Killer Loops kept me from seeing much around the eyes. But the smile stopped. "You play the lottery, do you?" he asked in a grim way.

"Doesn't everybody? Julie did." I dangled myself out there

like a minnow in a stream. I could imagine what Jason would have to say about it.

"Did she, now?" he said and regained his composure. "Our Jule was quite a girl."

"Somebody killed our Jule, Collin. Do you ever think about that?"

"Every day, blue. Every day. See you tomorrow, mate."

"Tomorrow," I agreed.

I wondered how long I would have to chum before the sharks would strike.

TWENTY-THREE

I OPENED the front door for Angie at ten past eight, having barely made it, cleaned and dressed, at that. My hair was still slicked back, wet from the shower, and I did the last buttons on my shirt just before reaching the door. I had lost track of time in the kitchen once I had sunk into that old well of contentment.

"I hope I'm appropriately late without being rude," were her first words. "My, my, this is impressive. I've always wondered what it looked like up here."

"Want to see the rest?" I offered, leading her inside.

She did, and I showed her. She seemed to like the same things about it I did: the high ceilings, the big rooms, the views from every window, and the access to the terrace from every room.

"I'd kill for a kitchen like this," she said as we ended our tour there.

"Yes," I agreed. "I lucked out when I found this place."

She didn't ask if I owned it or leased it. I admired her restraint. We settled on the front terrace, where I had a chilled bottle of Meursault waiting. She accepted a glass, tasted it, and gave me an appreciative nod.

"You're not having any?" she asked.

"Not at the moment," I replied. "I've become addicted to these fruit-flavored waters you put me on." I lifted my glass and toasted her.

She took a look at the sweep of view. "What, no strolling violinists?" she asked. "This is the most romantic setting I've ever seen. I don't know how you can ever leave it."

"I don't all that much. The violinists are late, but if you want to pick your own musical poison, it's right there." I pointed inside to the cabinet housing the heart of the sound system. "I'll get our dinner on while you do that."

I could hear her making small comments or exclamations as she went into my collection of tapes and CDs.

"I can't find your M. C. Hammer," she called out tongue in cheek.

"It's probably in the back," I answered. "I don't play it every day."

I took our first course out to the terrace table, lit the candles, and seated her as the beginning strains of some New Age jazz surrounded us. I looked at her in surprise.

"The tuner seemed easier," she explained. "This smells divine and looks divine. Tell me what we're having."

"Soup," I answered.

"I want a complete chef's presentation of everything," she demanded.

"It's mint and cold cucumber soup," I supplied. "Made with fresh tomato juice, chicken stock, yogurt, garlic, cream, egg, shrimp, cucumbers, and mint."

"This is Southern?" she asked after she tasted it. "It's marvelous."

"It's Southern, but not country."

I cleared the bowls and brought the plates.

"Oh, this looks too beautiful to eat," she said kindly. "I want the presentation."

"Boneless skinless chicken breasts in an herb batter, fried in peanut oil. It's topped with dabs of hot jelly pepper sauce." I pointed onto my own plate at the next item. "Carrots and parsnips in tomato-lime sauce over red slaw, then next to that you have your basic basil-and-garlic grits, and on the side are your lacy corn fritters, or as you would call them, hoecakes. Whew."

"I am stunned. You really can cook," she said.

"Please hold that comment until you've tasted it."

She did, and she liked it. So did I, and the feelings that went with it of returning to an old hobby I had all but put aside.

"Lemon chess pie," I said as I put down our desserts. "It's Southern traditional."

"And you made this, too?" she asked with open astonishment.

"Anything to impress a lady."

"Oh my goodness," she said when she tasted the coffee. "What do I taste in the coffee? I mean other than the cinnamon?"

"Chicory," I replied. "You said Southern. That's Southern."

It was great fun for me. She was a perfect guest, exclaiming over all the right things, eating with real appetite and complimenting me with expressions of feigned envy. She insisted on rinsing the dishes for the dishwasher and made me wait with my coffee out on the terrace. When she finished she joined me on the chaises on the side terrace facing the city. She brought the rest of the Meursault with her.

"You even have an after-dinner change of view," she said in wonder. "You are a surprising man, Jake."

"How so?"

"You don't fit your look. Have you any idea how you look to other people?"

"Like the Beast in *Beauty and?*"

She laughed at that. "No, I'm not putting you down. You're handsome. But you're very dangerous looking, don't you know that?"

"Maybe a little beat up around the edges, but not dangerous," I argued.

"Unh unh, dangerous," she argued back. "I saw the way Buck backed off in Pismo's. I've never seen Buck do that before. Who are you, Jake?"

"Now how am I supposed to answer a question like that?"

"You mean I've finally stumped you?" she said with a laugh to lighten things. "I thought I might get some dark secret out of you, but I can see you're used to these female interrogations."

"Speaking of Pismo's, I have this question that keeps coming up in my mind. Who were Julie Price's friends? Was there anyone she talked to more than others? That sort of thing. Do you have any thoughts on that?" I said nonchalantly.

"I can't think of anyone."

"Someone she might have buddied up each time she came in? Like you, maybe. Did she always talk to you?"

She appeared to think about it. "No, I thought of her more as a customer than as a friend. We certainly weren't confidantes."

"But you tried to warn her away from Collin?"

"I've done the same for you," she reminded me.

"Touché," I said, letting the subject rest.

As she picked her wine glass up from the side table between

us, I noticed the quarter-turn rings she'd been making while we talked. She drank the rest of the Meursault while we tested each other's wits and intellect. She was quick and well informed on things in the world. She got the subtle things and planted them as well.

She looked at her watch. "Good Lord, look at the time."

I did. "It got late early," I said, not bothering to give Yogi Berra credit for the line.

She turned in her chair and leaned over facing me. "Would you be upset if I went home now?"

"No," I answered, caught completely off guard by the question.

"This may sound silly to you, but I like what we have going. I don't want to mess it up with either one of us making some moves that might be too early. Do you understand?"

I got to my feet and helped her up. "I do indeed. And what's more, I agree. I wish I had the guts to say things like that."

"I'm thinking that maybe I could know you a long time," she said.

"That's a nice thought," I said, seeing her to the door.

She turned to me, and as she had done at her own place, took my head and pulled herself to me in a kiss. As she kissed me she pressed the rest of her long, lean frame against me. It had the intended effect.

"Goodnight, Jake. My shout next time."

"Goodnight, Angie." Then just before she stepped into the elevator I said, "By the way, I'm curious about something."

She turned to me, good natured and quizzical.

"How did you know where I live?"

Her face froze in midsmile. Her eyes remained on me and seemed to fight not to change.

"You told me," she said without much conviction.

"No," I replied. "I never did say."

The inner wheels turned swiftly behind those eyes. There was a moment of sudden relaxation as the right depiction was found.

"Oh, right," she said. "Maybe you didn't, but I knew because I've always admired this place. Your name got out very fast when you moved in. You'd be surprised at the gossip level in this town. Anyway, I put the name together when we met. Simple."

"Yeah, simple," I agreed. "Goodnight, Angie."

"Night," she said. Her eyes were turned away when the doors closed between us.

I stood at the terrace railing watching Angie to her car. She walked directly to a black Mustang convertible parked next to my car. I was surprised to see her unlock it and get in. I had expected her to walk on by and go to something else. But what? After a moment of mental wrangling I summoned up the picture of a car in her driveway the night I had been there for dinner. I thought about it hard. In the first place, it had been of a light color, tan I thought, and secondly it had not been a Mustang. I seemed to remember a Toyota Celica. Had she traded cars in the interim? Further, the car that had followed me from Angie's that night down the Pacific Coast Highway was black. I found myself wondering if it had also been a Mustang.

I thought about it long after Angie and her black Mustang had vanished. I finally stuck it back there in that part of my brain that was filling with other unexplained pieces.

I checked my watch against the busy Cabrillo foot and car traffic. A glance out at the marina showed all the same signs. It was a hot end-of-summer Friday night. I did not expect it to wind down until well past midnight. I went into my bedroom, closed it down, and set my alarm for three a.m. I was asleep in minutes.

THE ALARM BROUGHT me up out of an unmemorable dream. I staggered around, clearing the fuzz while I double-checked the dive bag I had packed earlier. I had a short-sleeved wet suit top, mask, fins, snorkel, weights to counter the buoyancy created by the suit, towels, waterproofed light, and a watertight belt pack holding all the tools any good break-and-enter man would need.

I parked in a dark corner of a harbor lot midway between the marina and the pier. After I donned the wet suit I walked nonchalantly across the two hundred yards of sand to the ocean. It was a quiet night and a very quiet sea. The surf was a gentle roll that hardly made a sound that would carry beyond the shoreline.

I pulled down the mask and adjusted the snorkel as I slipped into the water. I put on the fins when I got in waist deep.

I was happy to have the wet-suit top, for even though it was a hot summer night, the Pacific can be a chilly swim. I preferred to be comfortable. As I moved away from the shore I could feel the cool water seep its way under the neoprene. Almost immediately the body heated the trapped water to the comfort level. I checked the snorkel and the mask for fit before sliding below the inky surface.

I used the fins in a slow, easy swim out and around the mouth of the harbor. Once in the marina, I lifted my head out to make visual checks from time to time. Occasionally I could hear the sound of a laugh or a raised voice from one of the slips along the way. There was at least one group out there that was not giving up the night easily.

After a few wrong turns I found the *Frankly My Dear.* I went aboard over the stern railing, crouching as low as possible to avoid making a silhouette in the night. I went directly inside the cabin through a door that should have been locked but instead stood ajar. I pulled on a pair of rubber gloves, then closed the door behind me and used my penlight to find my way around. I closed what curtains I could before settling in to my task at hand.

It was a mess. At first glance, it appeared to be bad housekeeping. I stood in the center of the main cabin to get my bearings. It was a large lush room with roomy sofas and chairs. At one end was the galley, and across from it was the interior bridge with a duplication of all the controls that were atop on the flying bridge. There were two doors, one aft and one forward, off the main room. The aft door was two steps down, and I figured it to lead to the main stateroom. The forward door most likely led to the guest stateroom or -rooms.

For the moment, I concentrated on the salon, or main room. I had to pick up details in pieces as my light focused on them. It was difficult to connect it all to a larger picture, but as I saw more of it I began to get the impression of a room that had been ransacked. The search had been thorough and rough. I noted a panel had been torn from a wall, disclosing a hidden compartment. It was empty.

A check of the galley showed the contents of the cabinets and refrigerator had been dumped unceremoniously onto the floor. The same was true with pans and dishes. All the drawers had been overturned in the search. What I found most amazing was that the entire back interior of the refrigerator had been opened to disclose still another secret compartment, empty and large.

There was a mix of smells in the place with all the foodstuffs scattered about, but one terribly sickly-sweet smell managed to stand alone. It always did. It was the smell of death. I saw some blood spatters along the wall leading to the aft door. That convinced me to try that one first.

It was as I had guessed, only more so. It was a huge, lavish stateroom, which I imagined had originally been two rooms. There was a double bath, a king-sized bed, a chaise, and a table with four chairs. There was an oversized shower in one of the bathrooms, with a steam attachment. The steam unit had been pulled out, and behind it was yet another large hidden compartment. There were two in the bedroom, one behind the bed's headboard and the other in the ceiling, both gaping open and empty.

Whoever had searched the boat had known exactly where those compartments were. Some questions began to form about who had been here looking, and for what. And why all the secret compartments? I thought I knew the answer to that one.

As I went back into the main salon, that sweet rotting smell hit me much harder than it had before. I looked across the room at the door leading to the forward compartments and dreaded what I might find there. It took all my force of will to open that door.

There was a small passageway separating two staterooms. Their doors were standing open. At the end of the passageway was another door that I assumed led to a bathroom. In both staterooms there was the same disorder as I had found before. There were also more revealed hidden compartments.

Finally I opened the door at the end of the passageway. The smell of death was heavy in the air by then. Towels had been packed around the bottom of the door, possibly to keep that smell in, but it was too strong. Once the door was opened it was almost overpowering. Rookie cops who first encountered it often became too sick to function. It was a smell a person never forgot, and it usually accompanied a sight that would forever live just behind the eyes. I decided I had better do something about the smell before it started to gag me.

I went back up the passageway until I found a floor access to the engines in the galley. I lifted the panel and went down the steps to a clean, efficient engine room. The dual Chryslers looked brand new. It was a sharp contrast to the condition of the rest of the boat. I searched the corners until I found the small utility cabinet, which held a two-gallon gasoline can kept as primer fuel. I found a rag and soaked it in the gasoline before replacing everything as I had found it.

I returned to the passageway and the door at the end, holding the gasoline-soaked rag up close to my face, inhaling its fumes. It cut the stench enough to let me continue. I pulled the door fully open and at first saw only a pile of mattresses, cushions, and apparently anything that could be crammed into the small cabin. It was only after I bent and looked closely behind the light from the flashlight that I could see something beneath the pile. I pushed back some of the cushions for a better look.

The body was wrapped in clear plastic. I could see the faint outline of a foot and leg, but the rest of the body was beneath the pile. I held the rag to my nose, burning my nostrils with the fumes of the gasoline, before I put it down long enough to move more of the cushions. With some out of the way, I was able to lift the others enough to give me access to the body. I crawled in beside it, holding the rest of the pile on my back. There was something very heavy in the pile which made movement slow and awkward. As I inched in, I shifted the light enough to see that the body was nude and badly bruised. I worked my way deeper into the limited space until I finally made it up toward the head. The weight of the pile was more difficult to manage as I became more stretched out. Eventually the entire weight was held up by my back and left arm, which was extended slightly in front of me. In my right I held the penlight.

The face was almost unrecognizable, but the hair, the hands, and the strawberry birthmark on the left shoulder did it for me. I had seen the strawberry birthmark when she dropped her robe from her shoulders as she drifted into a mental twilight there in

Julie's bedroom. I was instantly sad. Her death had been an awful thing, no doubt filled with terror, as had been Julie's. The thick plastic wrapping added to the grotesqueness. Her mouth hung slack and open, exposing broken stubs of teeth behind split, battered lips. Her eyes were frozen open in horror and pain. I could see no more of it. I backed out from beneath the pile, letting the weight fall again onto the body beneath it. I put back the cushions, replaced the towels to the space at the bottom, and retrieved my gasoline-soaked rag before closing the door and heading for the open space of the main salon.

I did not dally. I took a moment to be sure my thinking was back on track, then opened the door to the night air and stepped out on the aft deck. I breathed in that air in deep gulps to cleanse my lungs and nostrils of the reeking stench of death. I slipped silently over the rail back into the black water of the marina.

Many times on my swim back to the harborside beach I lifted my head from the water to pull off my mask and wash my mouth and nose in the water of the sea. It helped, but there was nothing I could do about that vision, which now lived with me, or about the sadness I felt.

I was back home before dawn, in bed, fighting hard to push out the images of the night. I closed down my senses, emptying my mind of memories of Carrie. It was harder not to think of how that horrible death would affect Owen and a little girl named Megan, but I couldn't let myself dwell there. I had things to do now, and I needed sleep to do them.

TWENTY-FOUR

I HAD LEFT THE DOORS onto my terrace facing Cabrillo Boulevard open, and that Saturday morning Cabrillo awoke early. I had managed to get a couple of hours of sleep, so I accepted that as a bonus and got myself up and into the shower. I stood beneath the cold water, letting it pound the top of my head and the back of my neck while I thought through a few items. Twenty minutes of it and I still had some loose mental strands dangling. Still slightly wet from the shower, I called Jason from my study.

"I knew I should have turned these things off last night," he grumbled. "You know what your problem is? You have an old-fashioned notion that people are supposed to rise with the sun. People don't rise with the sun, Jake. Civilized people, that is. All that redneck music you've been listening to has ruined you and made you one of them. Next you'll be driving a pickup truck and swilling beer from long-necked bottles."

"I found Carrie last night, beat to a pulp, wrapped in plastic, and stuffed in the forward head of Gable's boat," I said without preamble. "Been dead awhile from what I could tell."

"Oh boy," he sighed. "I guess this thing isn't just going to dry up and blow away, is it?"

"I don't know if I should tip the cops to the body just now or not." I was looking at the corkboard and the card with Carrie's name printed on it. It was pinned in the center beside Collin's card. The question mark I had put by her name no longer applied.

"What do you gain, and what do you lose?" he posed. It was his standard formula for decision making.

"I gain some freedom from the burden of the knowledge, and it gets the police involved in the solving of it. There may be prints and things. It also might connect to Gable's death in some physical way they can pick up in forensics. I lose some open-ended options."

"Yeah, those old open-ended options," he said. "Tell you the way I see it. Carrie is dead, nothing can be done to help her now. So if you need another couple of days, take them. You can always call it in after you've played it out a bit. What do you lose that way?''

"Less," I replied. "I'll do it that way. Besides, the sooner it's out in public, the sooner her little girl is going to have to deal with it. I'm in no hurry to push that button.''

"So, what's Gable's boat like?" he said, moving me to safer ground.

"Nice, elegant, and enough secret compartments to make for a few suspicions," I replied.

"What's it called?''

"Frankly My Dear."

He put it together fast and laughed. "Funny guy, wasn't he? What do you mean suspicious? How suspicious?''

"What do secret compartments on a boat mean to you?''

"It depends. Are they secret like hiding a wall safe behind a painting is secret, or are they secret like in undetectable to the structure and such?''

"I'm not sure I see the difference, but I'd choose the latter," I said.

"Smuggling, then. What do you think? Drugs?''

"Maybe so," I answered. "Look how it lines up when you consider some of the other players we know about. Kohler in San Diego. Abbot in Seattle. It's a possibility.''

"How does it figure with what happened to the girls?" he asked.

"Julie's forty million dollars makes it figure. Drug people are scumbags that go for easy money no matter how it comes. My bet is that Gable was one of the scumbags. What's yours?''

"I bet with you, amigo. So what do you do now?''

"I push it a little bit. I started with Collin yesterday. He's very cool, but I'll see what happens when I turn up the heat.''

"Anything I can do?" he asked. Jason loved action more than anyone I ever knew.

"Can you come up here today?" I asked. "We'll have some lunch at Tony's, and then you'll get to see some beach volleyball.

I think it's time you got a firsthand look at the sport of the twenty-first century.''

"Do we have to have lunch at Tony's? How about the San Ysidro Ranch?"

"Tony's," I insisted. "I have to talk to him about something anyway."

"I've got a few things to do," he said. "You meet with Tony, and I'll come up after lunch. Anything special you need?"

"Bring your Nikon with the zoom lens and give a call to Lewis or one of our buddies at the Paladin Group and see if there were ever any rumors in the mill about Parkland or Gable and drugs. Keep it in the office. If they've got something, great. If not, I don't want them doing any checking, okay?"

He did not answer for a moment, which told he me was making notes. He always made notes and I never did. It was a bone of contention between us. "Okay, see you about one," he said finally and added, "at your place, not Tony's."

I hung up the phone and sat facing my corkboard. After a moment I moved Carrie's card to the deceased side. First there was Julie, then Parkland, Gable, Kohler, and now Carrie. I sat at my desk and stared at the board, thinking how little I knew about the late Carrie Berry. I tried to imagine her last day. Had she been grabbed out of her house and taken someplace, or had she driven to meet someone she knew and trusted? In what? What would she have driven in? I had never seen a car at her place, and Julie's Wrangler was with the Prices. It was one of those things that had always bothered me from the fringe out there, slightly out of focus. It was something I needed answered.

I found the paper upon which the security police guard at Vandenberg Air Force Base had written the two numbers. I dialed the home number of Owen Berry. The thin voice I remembered as his answered.

"Hi Owen, this is Jake Sands, from Santa Barbara. Remember me?"

"Yessir. I'd like to apologize for the other night if I said anything. I was a little drunk."

"You have nothing to apologize for, Owen," I said. "You were very nice to me, considering everything. I forgot to ask you one question. I forgot to ask you if Carrie had a car. And if so, what kind?"

"Yes sir," he said. "She had a Toyota."

"Color and model?"

"It was a tan Celica," he answered.

"Thanks, Owen, I'll be in touch," I said.

I could hear him asking me if I had heard anything about Carrie as I put the phone down. I was afraid to handle that one.

A few moments of thought had me reaching for the phone book and the Toyota dealership. The service department was closed on Saturdays, but I was transferred to the in-house authority on all matters pertaining to Toyotas.

"Was that 20R motor only in pickups, or was it also in your passenger cars?" was my question.

His answer was what I was expecting. "It was in the Celicas of the same model years as the pickups."

"Did they have the same exhaust manifold problems?"

"They would, yes," he answered.

The more I learned, the more confused I became. I took the mess to breakfast with me. I went to Moby Dick's on the pier and sat by a window looking out at the sea.

AT NOON I stopped in at Tony's Beachside and got the news that Tony was not due in until the evening. I had pasta and a salad and left a message for him to call. By one I was dressed for the beach and waiting when Jason pulled into the lot.

I got into the passenger seat of the Rolls and pretended not to notice his reaction to my attire.

"What did you hear on Parkland and Gable? Anything?" I asked naturally.

"Are you kidding with this outfit? What's that on your head?"

"It's a cap," I answered straight-faced. "With the bill turned up."

"That looks about as silly as all those goofs that wear baseball caps backwards. Every time I see one of them I think it's like wearing a big sign saying, 'I'm so damn stupid I don't know front from back.'" He considered me another moment. "At least

it's facing forward. Those are the latest thing in sunglasses,
presume?''

''Killer Loops,'' I said, leaving it there.

''Of course,'' he agreed. ''What else?''

''Parkland and Gable?''

''Parkland was considered a dirty lawyer. His clients were
mostly white-collar muggers that he kept from doing any hard
time by breaking a lot of ethical barriers. No drug rumors. A
white-lady user, maybe, but that's a maybe. Gable? Yes, lots of
rumors on him. DEA had him in their sights.'' He gave his report
with an occasional glance down at a small notebook. ''Nothing
on Kohler. I ran his name by them just in case. That's it.''

'' 'White lady' as in cocaine?'' I asked.

He nodded. ''You'd think a guy that worked hard enough to
become a lawyer would have enough sense to stay away from
that stuff, but they may be the biggest customers the scumbags
have.''

''You brought your camera,'' I said, noting the case in the back
seat. ''Good. I want you to park on the street and get some good
tight shots of some of the guys I'm playing volleyball with. Especially my partner. Okay?''

''Good old Collin,'' he said. ''Yeah, okay. Then what?''

''When you're sure you've got him, clean and tight, take the
film in to the La Cumbre Plaza Mall and leave it in my name
with the one-hour place. You can't miss it. They've got a big sign
up.''

''That's it?''

''That's it,'' I affirmed.

''Okay, I'll drop the film and head back to Malibu, but if you
need me later, give a call. I'm getting the feeling you might need
somebody to watch your back.''

''I'm fine,'' I said as I unfolded from his car. I leaned back in
and said, ''Park as close as you can to the center nets down there.
That's where we'll be playing.''

''You're not riding down with me?''

''I don't think that would be too smart,'' I said. ''Thanks,
Jase.''

''You don't let anyone we know see you like that, do you?''

"I'm wearing it to Malibu next time we have lunch."

"You'd fit right in. We've got a lot of radical dudes down here," he said and started his car. He pulled away content to ave the last word.

THE ATMOSPHERE on the beach was charged with excitement and strange anticipation I had never felt before. I was either greeted r watched by most of the other players as I passed on my way the court next to center net. It was an odd feeling. It was as if hey were expecting me to do something.

There was no sign of Collin. Riggs and Mako weren't present t the center net, either. I settled in on the sideline and watched decent match play out, but all the while I could feel the heavy veight of eyes on me.

A triple-toned horn sounded from Cabrillo Boulevard. I turned see Collin waving from a red Corvette as he turned into the each parking lot. I glanced around and saw Jason's Rolls in a ood position across the street. I was sure he already had his amera working.

From the minute Collin stepped onto the sand, the day on East Beach changed. He came toward me parting a sea of people. He ooked like he was in the middle of a swarm, and he also looked ke he was enjoying it. I could hear him laughing as the people onverged upon him. It was different than it had ever been before. t had the feeling of a prize fight, and he was the fighter entering e ring.

"Blue," he called out to me. "You ready for the big day?"

"Maybe you'd better explain 'big day,'" I said.

"We're playing for it all today, mate. King of the beach stuff oes on the line. You ready for that?" He showed me the white eeth I envied so much. "I threw it down at Pismo's last night. Ve got a straight match. Two out of three games, blue, and we wn it all." He made an expansive gesture with his arms spread- g out toward all the beach.

Some extra buzz was starting from the people around us, and only took a moment to recognize Mako and Riggs making their ay toward center net.

"We're playing Mako and Riggs?" I asked.

"Who else?" he said, losing none of his smile. "Let's get
bit of a warm-up on this court first. We play center net at three."

His easy, careless manner showed me nothing. He shove
passed the ball to me and we did some pops and sets on the
sideline until the court opened up for us. We played points be
no games against several different teams. I could feel a set of
nerves beginning to build just beneath my diaphragm.

When Collin felt we were warmed up enough, he led the wa
to a spot at the sideline of the center net.

"Just one thing, blue," he said. "These guys like to set rea
close to the net. We can back them off if we win the jousts."

"Jousts?" I asked.

"That's when you and the other guy both have a shot at th
ball at net. Get your hand on it, grip it, so they can't knock it off
Let him push it a little on your way up so he gets his arm ex
tended, then you make the play on the way down when he hasn'
got any leverage. That's going to be tough, because Mako i
strong. He's going to win most of the jousts with anybody h
plays." Collin's delivery was slightly distracted. His face wa
turned toward where Mako and Riggs were standing, although h
was speaking to me.

I could see Jason's car in perfect position for the center net.
turned my back to the car and moved between it and Collin. T
Collin I said, "Let me see your glasses a minute. They're differ
ent from mine, aren't they?"

He obligingly pulled his sunglasses off and said, "Only th
color, blue. These are the best. I got you the same."

I nodded and after a quick look at them, handed them back t
him. If Jason had been paying attention he could have gotten
clean shot of Collin without the sunglasses. That was what
needed.

Collin replaced his glasses. Then he looked at me as if he ha
caught on to what I had done. I saw his head turn looking for m
accomplice. The smile again...and the teeth...and he said, "Wa
it my glasses, blue, or my sexy brown eyes you were wanting t
see?"

I was saved from answering by Mako and Riggs, who ha

come over to us while we talked. Mako settled in next to Collin and said, "Let's get it on."

Collin's smile never wavered. He said, "G'day Riggs, Make." He exaggerated the broad Australian dialect. It was the first time I had heard him call Mako Make, but it spoke to their past history as partners.

Everyone tapped everyone else's fist in the street version of a handshake. I knew Jason would have some words on that little action later. Then we took the court. It was just before three.

Play stopped at all the outer nets. The beach bunnies and the other players alike moved in to see the match. As we warmed up with Riggs and Mako, I could see the crowd around us swelling to include most of the people on East Beach that day. A girl placed a stool beside the seaward net post and stood atop it. She had a whistle on a cord around her neck that identified her as our referee. I looked at Collin and nodded to her.

"That's Sharon," he said. "It's the big time, mate, with the ref, the crowd. Won't get your nerves, will it, blue?"

"The adrenaline might help my vertical," I said, making a reference to my jumping ability.

Collin faced me with his back to the net and said, "We'll beat these guys. You play the way you've been playing. Don't try for more than that."

"What's the big deal about this match?" I asked, indicating the huge crowd around us.

"Tradition, blue," he answered. "This is Labor Day weekend. That's when the two best usually square off."

"How did we get our ranking?" I asked. "Last time I looked, we were still working our way up."

He shrugged. "It's the match everyone wanted to see."

He left it at that. I looked around at the people who were still vying for space to settle in and watch the games. If I was amazed by it, I could imagine what Jason must be thinking from his position in the car.

It was interesting to be part of something like this. As the play began, I felt the tension ease, much in the same way it happens with the first contact in a football game or the first punch taken in a boxing match. In a sense the whole thing became a blur, with some very distinct moments locked in slow motion. Amazingly enough, the first game played very close. My size helped us at the net, and Collin's agility was enough to counter most of the good shot making by Mako and Riggs. Riggs was not taking it well. He appeared to be getting angry.

"Watch the setter until he puts the ball up, then watch the striker," Collin advised after I had been faked out by a clever play at the net by Mako. "And remember, Mako is left-handed. Don't go for that right-hand feint."

The advice worked. We began to frustrate Mako at the net. I even won a joust from him using the technique suggested by Collin. We were also lucky. Balls that should have been good for them went wide or long by mere inches. I began to believe Collin. I began to believe we could win.

At game point for us Mako got a good set and went for the kill. I could see the pumping legs of Collin taking him fully across court to dig out the ball from the corner. He was fully stretched out in his dive when he got his hands under it and popped it up, saving it for me. I moved back with him and set the ball automatically forward and very high, thinking to give him time to get up from the sand and get to the set. I hit the ball too far forward. It came down on the opposite side of the net as a perfect set for Riggs. Riggs went up for it, brought his arm up to strike, and suddenly found Collin high in the air in front of him. It was too late for Riggs to change his shot, and Collin made the block at an angle away from Mako.

It took a moment for me to realize that we had won the first game. Collin leaned over, catching his breath for a moment before he stood and raised his fist to me. "That's the first one," he said, "I told you, blue. I told you." Behind him, both Riggs and Mako displayed angry faces.

We took a short breather before changing sides and starting the second game. There was an ugly set to Mako's mouth as we went to the side. I was content that it had nothing to do with me, but I wasn't so sure that held true with Riggs. He seemed to direct his glare in my direction.

"You're serving great, Jake," Collin was saying. "That spin is getting them. Try a few more down the line this game when

Riggs is back.'' He continued to talk to me, giving me detailed
pointers, until we took the courts again.

We leveled the sand with our feet and cleared the lines before
starting the second game. I looked across the street for Jason's
car, but it was gone. I hoped that meant he had gotten pictures
of Collin, Riggs, and Mako and had taken them in for processing.
I was especially hopeful about the picture of Collin without his
sunglasses.

A different Mako faced us in the second game. He was intense
and angry. He was a fierce competitor, but he was playing beyond
a level of competition. As he turned it up, so did Collin. The
game was clearly between the two of them. Riggs and I were
supporting players. Mako struck each ball with his full concentration. As he made contact he did so with the *kiai* used in martial
arts to consolidate force.

Riggs and Mako won the second game, and what I found most
interesting was the reaction of the crowd. It was very quiet about
it, in direct contrast to its reaction when Collin and I had won
the first. I put it partly to our underdog status, because of me, and
mostly to Collin's popularity. I had underestimated what a star
he was on East Beach.

We had played the second game close enough to keep the fire
lit in Mako. He had firm words for Riggs as we took our break
before the third and final game. Riggs' expression was grim.

Collin spoke close in my ear. ''Havin' fun, blue?''

''Yes,'' I answered honestly. ''I'm having a great time. You?''

''If you only knew, partner, if you only knew,'' he answered
somewhat enigmatically.

The third game started with a long point and a missed kill shot
by Riggs. Mako grabbed Riggs by the shirt and yelled at him. I
didn't hear the words, but the meaning was clear. I looked at
Collin, and he repeated his enigmatic line from before, but with
a slightly different inflection. ''If you only knew, partner.''

We held a one-point lead when they served down ten to eleven.
Collin made a spike down the line, which Riggs saved, putting a
good ball up for Mako. Mako made a set close to the net and
high into the wind. Riggs ran in hard to make the kill with the
wind moving the ball in the air. He went up and I went up. He

was high in the air and adjusting his body to the sway of the ba
in the wind. He hit it into my block and landed hard and o
balance. His knee took the landing at an awkward angle and a
parently popped on him.

Collin was up patting me on the back for the block when v
both noticed Riggs was not getting up from the sand. Mako ra
to him, yelling again. Riggs shook his head and said, "I've hu
my knee. It's bad."

"It can't be," Mako yelled. "Get up, Riggs. Walk it off."

Riggs shook his head again. "I can't put any weight on it."

Collin and I moved under the net to help him up. We carrie
him to the sideline, where he made it clear he was in a great de
of pain. "It's a ligament tear," he said as we put him dow
"Posterior cruciate. It's the second time I've done it. Damn."

Mako stood by the net alone. He held the ball and squeezed
in frustration. "I'll get Danny to sub," he said.

"No substitutes," Collin said. "You default."

"Like hell," Mako responded.

"You're a point down, and we have the side out," Collin cam
back. "You lose, Make, just like I would have lost if my mar
here had gone down."

"Then it should be a draw," Mako persisted.

"No go. You default, you lose."

Collin and Mako faced each other at a distance of perhaps fiv
feet. I expected to see that distance closed at any moment by
furious Mako. He worked hard at controlling himself, althoug
his anger was a visible thing. Collin added fuel to the flame b
grinning.

Finally Mako turned without another word to Collin and pushe
his way through the crowd. Collin watched him all the way
the parking lot. He turned back toward me and gave Riggs a funn
look.

"What did you have on this match, Collin?" I asked.

"It was just a little bet between friends," he said. Again th
strange look to Riggs. His smile turned in my direction. "Pin
slips."

"Pink slips? You were betting your cars?"

"Yeah," Collin said. "His Beamer against my 'Vette. He thought it was a sure thing."

"Beamer" translated to BMW, which translated into some pretty big bucks. I wondered just what Mako did to make that kind of money. I decided to ask. "What does Mako do for a living?"

Collin seemed surprised by my question. "A living? Mostly he gambles," he said. "He's taken an extended leave from his regular work. Like me."

It was supposed to mean something, I supposed, but I missed it. There were too many people around us to continue a conversation. I backed away from the growing circle of people who moved in on Collin and stood next to Riggs.

"Were you in on the bet?" I asked.

Riggs frowned. "How could I be? It was Mako's car against Collin's Corvette."

"But you knew about it?"

"Mako never plays without some kind of bet. Sometimes he even bets against his own side," he said. He limped a few feet away before adding, "Congratulations."

There was enough irony there to make me wonder about it, but before I could ask for clarification, Riggs had limped away. I shrugged it away and followed suit. As I left the beach Collin called out to me from the center of a squirming sea of suntanned skin. "Pismo's, blue. It's our big night."

"I'll be there," I called back. I wouldn't miss it for the world.

THE ONE-HOUR PLACE was run by a fellow named Tim who knew what he was doing around film. He quickly found the envelope with my pictures.

"I just got these finished," he said. "Four-by-sixes okay? Your friend didn't say."

"That should do it," I said, taking the pictures.

"Your friend said to tell you he was impressed," he said. "I don't know about what or anything. That's just what he asked me to tell you."

I was sure I would hear all about it later.

I waited until I was back in my car before looking at the pictures. They were in perfect focus and exposure, as I was sure they would be from Jason. There was one picture, close up, of Collin with his sunglasses off. He got more of all of us, but it was clear that he had no easy shots. Mako and Riggs were always in movement or turned away, except in the background of a couple he got of me looking his way. It was enough for my purposes.

Jason was smart, he was thorough, and he was good at everything he did. The world wasn't making men like Jason anymore. It was a shame.

Tony still wasn't in when I stopped into his restaurant. I left some of the pictures in an envelope for him with a note saying I would appreciate it if he could identify the volleyball player who was always in for lunch with Barney Gable. I put in one of the close shots of myself so he could have a laugh.

TWENTY-FIVE

PISMO'S PARKING LOT was full, as was the street on both sides in front of it. I drove a block farther up from the beach before I spotted a place barely large enough for the Porsche. I still occasionally tuned my radio to KCAW and had done so that night. The music had grown on me. It was free of any memories but reminded me of a time when things were simpler, people were kinder and somehow more honorable. The only drawback to KCAW was the announcers. They babbled and hit the country twang a bit too hard.

I listened to the Saturday night DJ as I worked my way into the slot. "Git those tickets in your hot little hands and check it out. That ol' lottery's worth seven million this week, so here she goes. Six, nine, fourteen, nineteen, forty-one, forty-five. Lordee mee, I hope one of you fine folks is a brand-spankin'-new millionaire. Yessiree, I do."

I turned off the ignition and sat in the sudden silence. That was just the way Julie had heard it, I thought. What a moment that must have been. How slowly the realization of it must have come. The doubt, the resistance to believe it true, must have created a real inner turmoil. Then to accept it, to fly with it, must have been the most intoxicating moment of her young life. I could imagine it all. I got out and locked the car, took a deep breath, and used the walk to Pismo's to refocus.

People were filling the doorway on the way in and out. I recognized most of the faces from the beach. Inside the doorway I took a moment to adjust to the sights and sounds of the Saturday night Pismo's crowd. The beat of the live music gave a heavy pulse to the place. It was steamy, and after a moment of unbalance, sensual. Half the people there were still dressed in their beachwear. They had donned tops of one sort or another because they were required, and shoes or sandals because they, too, were required, but bikini bottoms and surfer shorts were everywhere. I

could imagine these people as the ones who were afraid the fun
would end if they took the time to go home and change clothes.

I heard my name and saw Terry waving me over the heads of
people, from a table about thirty bodies away. I waved back and
he motioned for me to join them. I hesitated, since I had other
very definite reasons for being there, but moved slowly through
the crush in that direction. He edged out to usher me in the last
few feet.

"Look who's here," he announced to the table. "The new king
of East Beach."

Troy and Tom rose to offer their hands and Benny gave me a
sullen stare. I had ruined his life in some way and he wanted me
to know it. The ladies with them smiled nicely while making room
for me to join them.

Terry made a shambles of the introductions, getting my name
right, but none of the girls'. They were young enough not to care
and giggled it off. I could see the problem. There were three
empty pitchers on the table that had once held beer. Another,
which still did, was in Tom's hand.

"You were good out there," Troy said. "I was impressed."

"Yeah," Terry agreed. "That Riggs and Mako are a great
team. You were right in there holding your own. Man, did you
pick it back up fast."

"You give me the partner he had and I'd look good, too,"
Benny offered. I decided I didn't like Benny.

"Benny, get a grip," Troy said. Everyone at the table laughed
but Benny.

"No, Benny, get a life," Terry said. Everyone laughed again.

"No, Benny, get a wife," Tom said, which was enough to put
them all over the edge for some reason. But then they didn't need
a reason. They were happy and harmless and looking for that
night which would someday be a stellar memory.

The laughter stopped in Tom's eyes first, then the others followed suit. They became still and stared up at something behind
me. The girls' giggles were beginning to falter when I turned to
see for myself.

Collin stood behind me. He was dressed in slacks, sandals, and

Hawaiian-style shirt. His hair was slicked back in the style pop-
ularized by *GQ* models.

"Your shout, blue," he said to me, ignoring the rest of the
table.

I got to my feet. He made the slight tilt up to me. I said, "Do
you know everyone?"

He nodded to the table and said a barely audible, "Yeh."

The three Ts chimed a chorus of, "Hi, Collin."

The girls squirmed and straightened in ways they had certainly
not done for me. They gave him little waves, and he again nodded.

"Got a table at the back, mate," he said to me.

I nodded.

"I'll see you there," he said, and without a look at the rest of
the table, turned away and was gone.

It was awkward. He had brought something to their table that
had cast a pall upon their evening. It had been so quick and so
subtle. There was nothing I could do to change things back. I sat
down and stayed with them a short time longer before I finally
said my good nights and made my departure as gracefully as
possible.

I worked my way through the crowd to the back section. I got
a lot of waves and pats on the back en route. The table where
Collin sat with several others was in the center of the back area.
There was one empty chair, directly across from Collin and between two girls. I was sure that was no accident. He nodded to
the chair when I approached.

He introduced me to the girls, Patricia, "not Pat," and Karen.
I could feel his eyes on me as he did so. It was a given that he
was misreading my assessment of them. I was reading them, not
as individuals, but as type. As individuals they were quite something to look at, tanned, pretty, and full of an energy that gen-
erated sex appeal and displayed that attitude of "I'll try anything." The type, however, wasn't unique. The type was
everywhere there was sun, sand, wealth, and the freedom to be
slightly wild. The type was not bad. It was simply something
younger men should experience and older men should avoid. I
tended to fall toward the latter category. Also their pupils were a

little too dilated and their energy a little too hyper for my taste. I said hello to them and the rest of the table as I took my seat.

The group playing in the main room was easier to take at a distance, but the music was an active presence with us. The girls never missed an undulation with the beat. Their legs and hips were in constant motion. The only time their hands and shoulders were not involved was when they picked up the pink frothy drinks to sip through the straws.

"You play darts, blue?" Collin asked me.

Darts and table tennis were games everyone played at one time or other in his or her life. I had seen the world championships of table tennis in Tokyo, and I knew forever afterwards, if anyone asked me if I played table tennis, I had to give it a conditional answer. I did the same with darts. I said, "I have played, and I understand the basic rules of the game, but I'm not much at it."

"Let's have a game, you and me," he said.

Without waiting for my answer he was on his feet striding to the back wall and the dartboard. He plucked the darts from the board and handed off a few to me. He toed the line and expertly lofted his darts at the board. "A few practice," he said.

Collin was not bad. He used too much wrist, however, at release. I took the line and tossed my darts from memory, dredging up suggestions on the toss from long-forgotten acquaintances from long-forgotten pubs of the past. "Keep the forward foot and head in line and still, elbow forward at sighting, wrist firm at release. Aim to the high edge of the target early on and bring it down as the confidence rises." It was simple stuff, but it was enough to bring me up to a competitive level.

"Want a Foster's?" Collin asked as the waitress gave a look for orders. I shook my head and ordered one of those Canadian orange-flavored soda waters I remembered Angela had suggested when I first met her. It brought her to mind, and I took a quick reflexive look into the main room and the bar for her. She was not there, but I had not expected her to be.

He looked at my grouping, then back at me. "You can do a little bit of everything, can't you, blue? That's as good as any of these louts around here do who play it all the time."

From the moment Collin stepped to the dartboard it began to

draw a crowd. Collin made things happen, and everyone wanted to be in on it. As soon as the waitress made her delivery, he raised his Foster's to me in a sort of toast and said, "What'll we play for, mate?"

I sipped at my water and considered it. "Forty million dollars," I said. "Winner takes all."

"You got forty mil, blue?"

"Not yet," I said, "but I'm getting close."

His face relaxed completely as he looked at me. The smile was gone, as was the pose of denial. His eyes showed more interest in me than I had ever seen before. We were an island of two in the midst of all the rest gathered to see something happen. What went on between us was silent and unreadable to those around us. To us it was a reaffirmation of the things we had read in the other the first time we had met.

"Since neither of us has forty million dollars, maybe we better put a wager we can afford, eh?" His smile came back.

"Like pink slips?" I suggested.

"You're my mate, my partner, so let's make it nice. Tell you what, Jake, you leave the stakes up to me. You won't be sorry," he said. There was that gleam of challenge in his eyes I had seen before.

"So if I lose you tell me what I've lost, and if I win you'll tell me what I've won? You ever get anyone to take this kind of stupid bet with you before?" I asked.

"It's all a matter of trust, blue," he countered.

"So it is," I agreed. "All right, I accept."

He was like a child who had just gotten his way. He was gleeful as he set the rules of the game. He was in his element, competing, surrounded by admiring people, and in control.

Collin became more fascinating to me by the moment. It was something to observe, the way he dealt with those who swarmed around him. He was unquestionably the center of things. His will to win, even in the game of darts, was also worth noting. I wondered if it was simply part of that basic Australian obsessiveness with competition and sport or if it went deeper. I suspected the latter.

Collin hit a streak of good tosses that put him ahead, although he was slightly high and right on all his throws. His features took on a grim set. I kept us close with a near-perfect round of soft lobs that looked more lucky than intentional.

I glanced around as I sipped from my flavored water and was surprised to see Mako standing with the group watching. He saw my eyes catch him and gave me the thumbs-up sign. Before my next turn I saw him and Collin exchange another of their unreadable looks.

As we came to the final round, Collin became completely focused on the board. It was as if he hunkered down mentally preparing himself for a fight, but he threw no better for all his concentration. I was up last and I had only a minor deficit to make up. Collin and I both knew I had an easy win in sight.

I had always found darts to be a funny game. No one but the one tossing the dart knew how it was intended to fly. The kibitzers on the sideline could only read the result. All I needed was a decent throw to win it, but I reasoned that I had more to learn about Collin by losing. I aimed for the lower ring of the board. I was loose with the toss, because I was not trying for the win, but as it turned out, it was a lousy throw and a perfect strike. To the eye, I couldn't have made a better toss. It was dead center.

It was fleeting. It was instantaneous with the victory. It was dark and dangerous. It was Collin's look to me when the dart landed. Of course, it might have been my imagination, because in the next second he was lifting my arm in exaltation.

"My partner," he announced to all watching. To me he said, "Quite a shot that, Jake. Was that something you were holding for the end? Are you that good?"

I didn't answer. I didn't need to. There were enough other people pressing in and talking, and the moment moved on. I stood in its midst and watched with some detachment as Collin assumed stage center. It was where he belonged. It was the only place he was happy.

He led the way back to the table. As I moved along in his wake I had one of those rare moments of objective insight, or oversight, whichever the case may be. I saw myself in this group of young playful people as the interloper I was. I must have looked quite foolish to the casual observer. I must have appeared to be a man desperately trying to hold on to whatever vestiges of youth I had remaining. Oddly enough, it was probably in some part true.

My thoughts had taken me into a blank stare at the back wall, which was adorned with the large poster-sized blow-ups of pro beach volleyballers in action. Some were legendary figures in the sport who had played at East Beach. Karch Kiraly, Sinjin Smith, Kent Steffes, Randy Stoklos, names of almost mythical standing to those who followed the game. It was a sport that was growing fast and countrywide. The promoters were taking their sand, their nets, their players, and their games to the beachless Midwest and elsewhere, to swelling crowds of fans.

"Kiraly has a vertical leap of forty-one inches," Mako said from beside me. "He plays in the ozone." After a beat he added, "Like Collin."

"You're not bad yourself," I replied.

He ignored my compliment. "What's your vertical?" he asked.

"Off the sand, about one inch. Off any other surface, maybe twice that high," I said.

He grinned. I heard Collin's voice calling, "Jake. Partner, come on. You too, Make, come sit." It was not a real invitation.

Mako shook his head. His eyes held steady to Collin's, and again I had the feeling that they were communicating in a language only they could understand. "I got a date," he said to Collin. He turned back to me.

"See you on the sand," he said and put his fist toward me, knuckles out.

I tapped my fist on top of his, then he did the same back to me. I was a foreigner in a strange land who had learned the customs slowly and carefully.

As Mako glided into the mass of bodies in the main room, that feeling of being watched took up residence at the back of my neck. I turned around toward the group at the table giving the full one-eighty a careful scan. I was not surprised to discover Riggs leaning against the end of the bar staring back at me. It was not the first time I had caught him doing it. I remembered the times on the beach when that same feeling of being watched had led me either to Riggs' eyes or Mako's.

His expression, which could best be considered sullen, did not change, even when I offered him a short nod of salutation. An odd note sounded when I played the whole scene. He was leaning most of his weight upon the knee he had allegedly hurt earlier that afternoon. It would seem that he had enjoyed a remarkable recovery. I ended our visual impasse with a mix of impressions. Either Riggs was nursing a deeply set and old resentment toward someone in my part of the room or he was a very sore loser. I turned away from him, wondering how well he had known Julie Price.

The chatter at the table drifted around me without my really hearing much of it. I was putting my mental house in order, trying to find the right cubbyhole to park Riggs. Mako, too, was hard to define in normal terms. I heard my name as if said for a second or third time.

"Do you like Mexican?" Collin was saying.

It took me half a second to catch on that he was asking me about food. "Love it," I said, ever the good sport.

"Then it's Casa Tampico," he said. "You won, so I buy dinner. I owe you dinner anyway for the way you played out there today. Super, partner."

"And if I had lost?" I had to ask.

"But you don't lose, do you?"

He got to his feet and made a general farewell to everyone at the table except Patricia and Karen, to whom he gave a quick motion to join us. The girls rose, along with me, and we began to make our way through the crowd. Collin worked it like a politician. Everyone wanted to be noticed by him, and he did his best to leave tidbits of recognition in his wake. I found his technique masterful. All the way out he was casting promises of his return later in the evening. MacArthur couldn't have done it better.

Outside, Collin took Patricia by the arm and said, "Jake, you take Karen with you. We'll meet you at the Casa Tampico." He and Patricia were entering the parking lot on an angle toward the red Corvette as he added, "Coast Village Road, Montecito," just in case I didn't get out much.

Karen settled into my car, making some appreciative sounds. "Wow," she said, "What is this?"

"A Porsche," I answered and started it.

"Oh gee, I knew a guy once who had a Porsche, but it wasn't like this. This is nice. Fast too, I bet." Her face wrinkled up at the sounds coming from the radio. Her hand automatically went to the dial. "May I?" she said as an afterthought.

She was already tuning in another station by the time I was able to nod. When she found what pleased her, she pumped up the volume a notch. It was my worst fears come true. I was trapped inside my own car with a rapper slinging unintelligible street philosophy at me.

Karen danced in her seat all the way to the Casa Tampico. The metal sound that followed the rapper found her soul. She went into an orgasmic dream with it. To me it was an electronic nightmare. By the time I finally parked at the Casa Tampico I still had not been able to discern a tune.

Collin had not yet arrived, according to the hostess and a quick visual check, so we waited at a small table in the bar. The waitress had just delivered Karen's strawberry margarita when the hostess came to the table to ask, "Are you Mr. Sands?" To my nod she added, "Telephone for you."

I took it at the end of the bar. The voice at the other end said, "What say, mate? You getting on with our Karen okay?"

"Fine," I replied. "Where are you?"

"Bit of a change of plan. Patricia here wanted to make a stop," he said. "We're sort of not in the mood for food right now, if you get my drift."

"I have an active imagination," I replied.

"So we may not make it."

"I was beginning to make that assumption."

"The bill's all taken care of. I have a running tab there," he said.

"Good, I'm a big eater," was all I could think of to say.

"Take good care of Karen now," he said with heavy innuendo, and he was gone.

I thought about it as I rejoined Karen and told her. Her comment surprised me. "You mean you didn't know he'd do that? So let's eat. I'm starved."

She had fajitas and margaritas and a dessert called fried ice cream. I had the fajitas and coffee. Neither of us had much to say. I spent most of the meal trying to read the little demonstration in manipulation that Collin had managed. There were no simple explanations, no matter which way I looked at it.

Karen asked, "What now?"

"You mean you're still hungry?" I said, somewhat amazed.

"I mean with us?"

"Us? Nothing."

She smiled and asked, "I mean where are we going from here?"

"I'm dropping you wherever you want, and then I'm going home."

"That's not what Collin had in mind, you know?"

"I know," I replied.

"Okay," she said, not unhappily. "I have to visit the toi toi first."

She grabbed her bag and was up and gone before I could rise to help her with her chair. It was just as well, I thought, because with today's manners she wouldn't have known what I was doing, anyway. When she returned she was abubble with new energy, and her pupils were back to full dilation. She sniffled, too, and rubbed at her nose, afraid she had left some residue of white stuff there.

In the car I asked, "Where to?"

"Back to Pismo's, I guess," she said with a bouncy shrug.

I turned down the volume of the radio slightly before I asked, "Did you know Julie Price?"

"Sure. Everybody knew Julie. She was great."

"Were you friends with her?"

She shook her head. "No, I just knew her. She wasn't really tight with anybody except maybe Angie."

"Angie? You mean Angela Borne?"

"Yeah," she said, "I guess that's her name. Anyway that's who she always was talking to."

"She owns a bikini shop?"

"That's right. You know her?"

I nodded my head and drove in silence until we reached Pismo's. Collin's red Corvette was in the parking lot. As I pulled to a stop I said, "Karen, would you do me a favor?"

"Sure," she said in the same voice and manner Marilyn Monroe would have used.

"Do you think you could keep Collin from seeing you for fifteen minutes or so?"

"Oh sure," she said. "I'll just stay on the dance floor. He's always in the back." If she found my request odd, she didn't let it show.

"Thanks," I said. She put her hand on my arm as I helped her from the car.

"You're a really nice guy," she said. Again she sounded like Marilyn Monroe.

"Tell me something, Karen," I said. "Were you ever Collin's girl?"

"His girl?" She gave me a rueful smile. "I was with Collin, if that's what you're asking. No one is ever Collin's girl."

She looked small and sad to me as she disappeared through the doors of Pismo's. I wondered what she sought here and for how long she would seek it.

TWENTY-SIX

BREAKERS WAS lush and magical at night, the stuff old movies were made of. Palms and tropical plants of all varieties were lighted to give the impression of a fantasy paradise. The bungalows and main buildings blended in with the illusion of a world designed to be an extension of Eden.

I had already ducked two security guards by the time I was on the grounds approaching Collin's bungalow. I saw another in his golf cart making a turn in my direction. I strolled down the center of the walkway, whistling, but with my head down. He slowed long enough to say, "Good evening, sir." I looked around as if brought from some deep thought and responded, "Oh, good evening," and went back to my head down stroll. He continued on his way, to my great relief.

At Collin's bungalow I made sure I was unobserved before I set about picking the door lock. I was not too good at it if I had to rush. Manipulating the two tines to feel the locking pins was something I had never practiced but had simply done when I had to do it. As a result, I was never sure it was going to work.

I managed to get through both locks on Collin's door in a fairly short time. Nevertheless, once I was inside, I took a moment to restore my poise. The feeling that someone is coming up behind you and about to shout, "Hey, you, what are you doing there?" can frazzle even a good set of nerves.

I found the light switch and put it on. I closed down the plantation shutters before turning on all the rest of the bungalow's lighting. There were three rooms, a living room/dining room combination, a bedroom, and a bathroom. There were no cooking facilities, as such, although there was a wet bar area with a microwave off the dining room section.

I started with the bathroom. I noted his choices in toothpaste, mouthwash, soap, cologne, and all the rest. It was top-quality stuff—there wasn't a generic product to be found in his vanity cabinet—and said basically what I already knew about him. The usual bathroom hiding spots came up empty. I left there with nothing to show for my search but a hand slightly damp from feeling the inside of the toilet tank.

I checked my watch as I went into the bedroom, wanting to keep my inside time down to twenty minutes if I could. That was the outside limit to what I figured I could get if Karen kept her word to me. If she did not, well, then it was another thing entirely and not something to consider at the moment.

The bedroom was divided into a sitting area with a TV and a sleeping area with a king-sized bed. I checked the drawers in the dresser, doing a quick feel along the bottoms inside and out. There was nothing taped to the back of any of the paintings and the planters contained real plants growing in real soil. I pulled the cushions on the chaise and chair and did a visual on the underside of the table. The bed came up clean, as did the bedside tables. I went to the closet next, with time beginning to nip at my heels.

My first impression, as I looked into that closet, was that there was a lot of silk. At least twenty shirts of silk in every color were hung in perfect order. Four blazers, a tux, slacks of all types, a couple of dark suits, and some of those Hawaiian-style shirts in a very fine Pima cotton. I worked my way from one end of the closet to the other. It was the other end that gave me the surprise. Uniforms with white shirts and dark blue pants and jackets hung fresh from the cleaners. The shirts had patches sewn to the sleeves and on one a badge was already affixed to the breast pocket. That's what gave me the jolt. It was a fire department badge.

I compared the sizes of the shirts and jackets to the others at the other end of the closet and came away with a perfect match. All the clothes belonged to the same person, and that person had to be Collin Fraser. What was he doing with fire department uniforms? I put that question aside for the time being while I hastily went through all the pockets of the hanging clothes. After that wasted effort, I was very short of time.

I hurried into the living/dining room and stood for a moment gaining some perspective. First impression said, "sterile." It was well decorated in the style I thought of as Palm Springs standard, with rich fabrics on oversized furniture. I wandered around the room trying to get a feel for the manner in which Collin might use it. It was pure hotel. The daily maid service kept the place spotless. My only hope was to pick up something from the areas outside of their responsibilities.

I sat in all the chairs, feeling a little like Goldilocks and wondering how and why a man like Collin Fraser lived in a place like Breakers. It had to cost a fortune, so where did he get his money? It was not as a fireman, of that I was sure. That question began to loom larger for me the more I tried to get into his surroundings. I sat on the sofa, feeling the overstuffed pillows give enough to cradle me comfortably. I wondered if he sat there of a morning reading the paper or if he entertained in that room. I tried to imagine where he would secure a small envelope he might want to keep hidden.

I picked up the faint outlines at the other end of the glass-topped table almost by accident. I was not looking for them and noticed them only as I moved away from the sofa. When the light reflected the smudges, my first thought was that it was sloppy housekeeping. Then I reasoned that they must have been left there after the maids had been in that day. It was only when my subconscious moved me closer to the watermarks that I recognized them for what they were. They were the stuttered circles made by a glass rotated in quarter turns. Angie had done that with her coffee cup and she had done it with her wine glass at both her place and mine. It was her signature as surely as if she had written it with pen and ink.

I checked my watch and was not happy to see that I was at twenty-five minutes on the inside. There was still too much I had not had a chance to check out, but at least I was not leaving empty-handed. The fireman curve was one that would take some figuring. That and Angie. I assumed she had been a visitor sometime that afternoon. The maids probably made their rounds mid-morning or early afternoon, and she had most likely been there after they had finished their service.

I killed the lights and opened the shutters for a good look outside. It seemed quiet enough, so I eased open the door and stepped out. Immediately, I had that feeling of being watched. I looked in every direction and could detect no sign of anyone, but still I

It the eyes on me. My mind was probably starting to play tricks
 me. I had pushed the limits on it, and my paranoia was telling
e it was time to end my visit. I got to my car as quickly as I
uld and left the elegant Breakers to the more rich and famous.

It was still only eleven p.m. when I pulled away from Breakers,
 I decided it might be a good time to play a trump card. I drove
 Montecito and to the small cottage beside the railroad tracks.
er black Mustang convertible was in the deadend driveway, and
 the lights were on. I could hear music coming from inside as
approached the door and for a moment hesitated out of an old
andard of propriety deeply ingrained in me. If I was wrong, I
asoned, then somehow I would find a way to apologize. If I
as right, no apology would be necessary.

Angie opened the door after my third knock. She did not seem
rprised to see me. The fact that she was slightly drunk might
ve softened the edges of her reactions, but I had the feeling
at she saw in me the inevitable.

"Hi Angie," I said. "I took a chance that you might be home
d still awake. Am I disturbing anything?"

She was shoeless and wearing the same kind of shorts and
ose-fitting shoes she had worn on my first visit there.

"Mel Gibson couldn't make it," she said with a wry twist to
r mouth. "Come on in."

I followed her out to her veranda, where she had been sitting
inking wine. She offered me a glass and I waved it off.

"Is what I hear true?" Angie asked. "You and Collin, the
ngs of East Beach?"

"There's only one king of East Beach. That's Collin," I an-
ered.

She smiled ruefully. "All the time I was trying to warn you to
ay away from him."

"Just like with Julie?" I added.

She gave me a quizzical look then said, "Yes, just like with
lie."

"Angie, why did you lie to me about your friendship with
lie? According to what I now hear, you and Julie were pretty
od friends. 'Tight,' I believe, was the way I last heard it de-
ribed."

She looked away from me and when she came back she w angry. "Who told you that? Buck? You've got a nerve sneakin around my back asking questions. I never said she wasn't a frien I never said that."

"Angie, did you know Carrie very well?" I asked.

"Carrie?"

"Yes, Carrie Berry, the girl who shared the duplex with Juli Her car was in your drive when I came to your house for dinner.

She looked intently at me. She said, "You're mistaken."

Whatever had been going on between us, in her mind, change at that moment. It was visible as a fleeting sadness in her face

"That could be," I said. "That car, Carrie's car, is the sam car that tried to run me over, I think. I would very much like know who did that."

"You think I know something about that?"

"I think you know a lot that you haven't told me," I said. decided to take a gamble. "For instance, you didn't tell me th you and Julie were good friends, and you didn't tell me that Jul called you the night she died."

"You don't know that."

"I know many things, Angie. I know you were with Collin his place this afternoon. You and Collin, huh? That's another litt lie you told me."

She drank from her wine glass while looking over its rim me. "I liked Julie," she said. "I liked her very much. She had kindness about her that girls her age don't usually have. She w smart and pretty, and she had the greatest body on the beach, b still she was kind. Never a bad word about anybody. Always the to cheer you up and give you encouragement. If you think I'd part of anything that would hurt Julie, you're wrong. Dead wron mate." She twisted the last line with a heavy Australian accen

"Okay, Angie, then let me leave you with this," I said and g to my feet. "I'm only interested in one thing here. Forty milli dollars. I'm the fly in the ointment that's going to blow the l off if anyone tries to cash out the ticket without cutting me in.

"I don't know what you're talking about," she said witho much conviction.

"Sure you do."

"So that's what you are?" she spat out suddenly. "You're an extortionist."

"I'm worse than that, Angie. I'm the partner from hell. You pass the word."

She stayed as she was as I left the veranda. I had not gotten answers, but I felt reasonably sure I had delivered the message through the proper messenger. How she figured into it I was not sure, but I knew she was in there somewhere. There would be a time to place her puzzle piece later.

PARKED IN my usual spot and took a good look at my building. The lighting on the trees surrounding it was good. I thought it compared favorably with the landscape lighting at Breakers. It was not much for security, however, a point that Claudile had been trying to make for some time.

There was an envelope from Claudile that had been pushed through the mail slot in my stairway door. The lighting in my private stairwell was just good enough for me to be able to recognize the logo of her gallery in the upper left-hand corner. It gave me a nice little lift to see her artistic rendition of my name on the envelope. It was sealed, so I chose to hold it for a letter opener upstairs.

I looked at the security system lights to be sure that there had been no intrusion while I was away. Everything checked out well as I opened the upper level door of the stairway. I used my key to disarm the alarm system before opening the door into the penthouse. The interior trap alarms gave me another twenty seconds to key in again or punch in the number code, which I did at the central station next to the kitchen. It was a good security system, as far as security systems went.

After opening all the terrace doors and letting the hot night air circulate, I turned on lights and found some coffee in the refrigerator, which I poured over shaved ice and sugar. The message light blinked, showing two messages. I hit replay and heard Jason's voice saying to call him at any time. He would be up late, he said. Tony's message was next. He was laughing at the beginning of it. "Baby, you are some cool dude," he said. "And lemme tell you I heard the news. You knocked off the numero

unos, is that right? Jakey, you never cease to amaze your ol
paesan. Is there nothing you can't do? So, about these picture
here, yeah, I got a match. I got your boy, so take a run by an
I'll point the finger, okay? Ciao, amico."

While I listened I slit open the envelope left for me by Claudile
Her handwriting was the kind that came on fancy invitations.

"Mr. Sands," it started. "I hope you don't think I'm a nos
neighbor, but that man was back this evening lurking in the shad
ows behind the building. I had to take some things to the Dump
ster and saw him back there. He can be up to no good, and I hop
it brings you no harm. I am writing this as I close up and he i
still there. It is ten p.m. Sincerely, Claudile."

I put the note aside and retraced my steps to my entry door. I
faced on the backside of the building and in the daytime offere
a spectacular view of the mountains. At night there was a viev
as well of the city lights, but my interest was in what was at th
base of the building. I hit the high-powered lights that were in
stalled for such purposes. The entire perimeter of the buildin
was instantly illuminated. I could see every inch of what wa
below. There was no lurker to be seen down there behind th
building. The shadows that might have hidden him before wer
no longer there, and neither was he. If he ever was.

I turned off the high-intensity lamps and secured the door be
hind me. As a precautionary measure I did a quick walk-throug
of the rooms and glanced out on each terrace just to put the smal
tug of apprehension to rest.

On my way back to my iced coffee, I chose a couple of Jacki
Gleason CDs and switched on the speakers to the terrace.
thought of calling Jason then, but there were things I needed t
think out first. The fireman angle with Collin had really throw
me. Angie was a big question mark. I needed some time alone t
do some serious mulling.

I took my coffee outside and felt the air beginning to coo
slightly. It was, to the school kids and the tourists, the last week
end of summer, and I could hear the occasional laughs and shriek
of the late-night revelers. From the speakers, Hackett's trumpe
took the melody, and I leaned out over my railing, swaying my
glass with the gentle lilt of the song.

He had been more patient than I. That was my thought when he black drape fell. He also knew just where to hit me. I thought hat, too, not that it did me much good at the moment. It was like ne of those dreams I had as a kid where I was being chased and ny feet wouldn't move. Here I was suddenly helpless and losing onsciousness fast. I could feel my body being pushed and lifted, nd I knew I was going over the rail. The mix of thoughts was trange. Behind it all was Gleason playing while some character vas busy doing me in. Bobby Hackett's trumpet was my companion into the empty space on the other side of my terrace railng. The *click, click, click* of my mind measured and calculated s I felt the railing slip away from my hands in my last futile rab at life. There was an awning down there, but where? Was t left of me or right? Was it straight down? *My funny valentine. Don't change a hair for me. Not if you care for me.* I kicked hard eft as my fingers lost contact with the railing. I laid out parallel o the building and fought against the meltdown. Bobby Hackett ould play a hell of a trumpet. Jackie Gleason should have made nore music. I should have lived a longer life. The darkness inside ny brain swallowed me.

TWENTY-SEVEN

A HORN HONKED. From a faraway place a woman laughed and squealed when something evidently vile but fun happened to her. An occasional car accelerated on a street someplace nearby. There was a surf sound, and from a point far above me, music. A sweet and mellow horn sent me grabbing for a memory. Bobby Hackett.

I opened my eyes and looked up into a fuzzy darkness. I blinked to clear my focus on the distant specks of stars. My head was heavier than I could remember it ever having been before. It did not turn so easily, either. There was a thing holding on to my neck that hurt me if I tried to move it. Wasn't I supposed to have arms and legs? Didn't I come here with hands and feet? Where were they? Why couldn't I feel anything down there? To hell with it, I thought. I was too tired to deal with it then.

It might have been one minute or ten or more, I had no way of knowing. When I came to again, I had some pain and some awareness of where I was and what had happened to me. I started the body check again. Breathing was fine, eyes and ears worked and I could swallow. The pain was intense behind my head, running down my neck. The panic rose up and I fought it off. Not yet, I told myself, the panic could always come later. First, I had a few things to do. To begin, I had to bring my right hand up and flex my fingers. That did not seem to be working out quite right. I compromised. I settled for just flexing the fingers, then just moving one of the fingers. None of it was working out quite right.

None of the rest of it did, either. There was no feeling in either my arms or my legs. There was no feeling below a certain point along my shoulders. It ended just about where the pain left off. "Okay, Sands, you can panic now," I said aloud, trying to lighten my anxieties.

Strange thoughts jumped into my mind. I found myself trying to remember who it was who had written that no man is an island.

could have developed an interesting argument against that at the moment. Then I remembered Mitch Grant, a guy I hadn't thought of in years. He had lost his foot right next to me in the mud of Quang Tri province after he had stepped on a mine. He had looked up at me as I had hauled him back to the medics and said, "God, I'll miss that foot."

That reverberated in my mind along with a myriad of other thoughts as I ran through my physical checks again. My neck allowed slightly more movement of my head, so I used that to do a better visual of my surroundings. There was no sign of my ambusher, for which I felt a great relief. He must have assumed forty feet onto concrete was fatal. God bless the Rainbow Awning Company. God bless my tenants for complaining. God bless the Surf and Turf Realty. Was I forgetting anyone?

The sound coming from the street that dead-ended behind my building was easy to recognize. A car was starting up with the sound of a faulty exhaust manifold. I did not have to see it to know it was a tan Celica with a 20R engine. I automatically moved at the sound. A pain shot down my spine and made me catch my breath. It was sharp enough to cause me to arch my back against it. As it passed to a dull-throb status, I slowly became aware that I was balancing myself on numb but usable arms. I turned, sending pains shooting in every direction. My back and neck muscles were giving me hell for making them bear the brunt of the fall.

As the muscle spasms released somewhat, the feeling slowly returned to my hands and feet. I tested them carefully and finally was able to make the right hand fist and then the left. The feet and legs came around in the same way. After what was probably a very short time, but a very long mental journey, I got to my feet.

The awning was completely down. I had taken it dead center, most likely with a slight bounce, before it gave way. I stood on top of it and again God-blessed the Rainbow Awning Company. They made a fine product. I twisted and stretched a bit to make a better assessment of my physical condition. I had some trouble with a couple of ribs in my back, which only hurt when I breathed, but that seemed to be the extent of it. Two busted ribs was a pretty good trade-off in my book for what could have happened to me.

By the time I was back upstairs some other sore spots made themselves known, not the least of which was the left side of my head right behind my ear. I ignored my physical condition long enough to check out the backside railing with a high beam lamp. I found what I had not seen on my earlier cursory check. The railing on the northwest corner of the building had definitely been scarred by the modern-day version of the grappling hook. I imagined what had been used was the air-propelled magnetic attachment line that enabled a climber to set jaw clamps on steel railings several stories up.

Someone had chosen the darkest corner of the building, climbed up sometime while I was gone, and hidden around the terrace patiently until I returned. My earlier terrace check was so perfunctory it would have been easy to remain undetected. None of my realizations made me feel any smarter. In fact, it had been some time since I had felt quite so dull witted.

It got worse. As I did a hasty inspection of key areas inside I could see that on the way out my visitor had found my desk and corkboard. The desk had been swiftly searched and the drawers emptied. The corkboard had been pilfered of two cards. Under the "deceased" heading, Carrie Berry's card was missing. From the center section Collin Fraser's card was also gone. As far as I could tell, that was the extent of it: It had probably been an afterthought. The thinking might have been, even if my death was ruled an accident, that corkboard could have thrown some light on a few connections the police might not have made. Someone evidently did not want the names of Collin Fraser and Carrie Berry to be part of that linkup. I wondered what my visitor thought about seeing Carrie's name listed under the deceased heading.

I turned the spa heat up to high, threw in some mineral salts and took the telephone in with me. When the jets of hot water had finally managed to make some difference in the soreness I was feeling, I dialed Jason's number.

"I got a little careless and played it a little stupid, but I may have turned a corner in this thing," I said as a prologue to what I had to tell him.

"How bad is it?" he asked immediately and seriously.

"I took a dive off my terrace into my new awning," I said. "The Rainbow Awning Company is going to love me."

"You got thumped and dumped, or you decided you wanted to fly?"

"I've got a lump behind my left ear that was on its way up while I was on my way down," I answered. "Funny thing is, I had a warning. Claudile left me a note telling me someone was hanging around the place. Whoever it was came up over the back railing, hid out of sight on the terrace, and waited for his shot at me. I made it easy for him by leaning out onto the railing. Not too smart for all the baiting I've been doing of late."

"What baiting? No, wait a minute, I can't think on the damned phone. Get that guest suite ready for me, amigo. I'm coming up to spend the night," he said.

He was gone before I had a chance to argue. I dialed him back, but he let it ring. The last thing I wanted just then was Jason coming into harm's way. It was too late to do anything about it, though, so I leaned back into the hot water and accepted it.

I soaked some more, took a cold shower, taped my ribs, and took a forty-five-minute nap before Jason arrived. He had keys to the elevator, alarm system, and doors and was up and in just as I finished dressing again.

He poured himself a Glenlivet and we settled in on the terrace, where I brought him up to date on all that transpired since I had seen him earlier in the day.

He pondered it several moments as I listened to the waning sounds along Cabrillo. The tourists were finally running out of steam and turning in, it seemed. I inwardly smiled at the vision of my friend swirling my problems in his glass much as a seer might rub a crystal ball.

He said, "This Collin is an interesting fellow. Smart and interesting. Let's take this connection with Gable. If he was tied in with him on some gambling scam in the volleyball games, then it figures that he might have been linked with other things Gable was into."

"I'm not sure it was Collin that Tony met with Gable," I corrected.

"It doesn't matter," he said. "He was in there some way, no matter what. Gable was smuggling, of that we can be sure, and if it was dope, then your boy Collin fits in. I don't know his angle on it, but the one big problem the drug scumbags have is showing some visible means of support. Think about it. A fireman works twenty-four on and forty-eight off. Pilots and airline stewards have a similar opportunity. It's reportable income, respectable, and that lets him do everything on a cash basis and stick some in banks here and there. It's a sweet deal if he doesn't get careless."

I nodded and listened to Jason think it out. Most of it was in the realm of what I had already concluded.

"I don't want to be critical here, amigo, but I think you've made a mistake by getting too close to this Collin," he said.

"It wasn't really my move," I replied. "He's the one who made it happen. That's the part of it that's hard to understand. He's evidently known all along what I've been after, yet he pulls me into his inner circle."

"Could be that he's hung up on dangerous games. Either that or he wanted to know where you were all the time. You think he's the one who sapped you?"

I said, "It's likely, but tracing back to my thinking when I came in here tonight, I'm not so sure. Before my short visit with Angie, I had just come from Collin's place, and before that I had seen his Corvette at Pismo's. I was fairly certain I knew where he was, which is one reason I was so careless."

"But you said you heard the other car, the one that hit you?" he reminded.

"Right," I said. "There is one way I might be able to nail Collin to it. I need to pay him another little visit."

His raised eyebrows expressed his thoughts on it. He gave it a deep sigh, put aside his glass, and said, "Come on. I'll drive."

He stayed silent most of the way to Breakers. I was silent as well, as I tried to put my thoughts on Collin in some rational order.

"You got a plan?" he asked when Breakers was in sight.

"Drive through the garage first. Let's see if he's home," I said.

The garage had a card-operated security gate, but Jason fooled the card receptor with a magnetic recorder. The problem we left behind us was a confused receptor which might not accept legitimate cards anymore. We found the red Corvette on the first pass. Parked right next to it was a BMW I recognized.

"I see he collected on his bet," I said.

"What bet?"

"That BMW belonged to a fellow named Mako until this afternoon. He and Collin put up pink slips on the match. I think I mentioned that we won it," I said.

"Yes, you mentioned it," he replied. "So now Collin owns two cars and both are here. He's home, I'd say."

"Pull into an empty space and wait. I want to see what I can pick up from his bungalow."

"You're going back in there?" he asked.

"Not in, around." I exited the car before he could form his argument.

The ribs were beginning to be a real nuisance. I could feel that little grab of pain that came with each deep breath, and deep breaths seemed to be in demand. It made movement by stealth a bit more difficult, and bending down to blend in with the bush shadows brought on some real hurt. The one guard I could see working the grounds at that hour was heading away from me as I moved toward the rear of Collin's bungalow, so I was able to step in to the windows standing up. I got my breath and my bearings at about the same time. I was outside his bedroom window, which showed some slivers of light from around the closed shutters. I moved over a bit to the area of the terrace. There was music from inside, and light, but no voices. The shutters were too well made to allow any peeks inside.

I stepped up onto the terrace and got as close to the sliding terrace doors as possible. Still no sound of voices, yet for some reason, a feeling more than anything else, I was sure Collin was not alone inside. Possibly it was the fact of the music, which was too faint to be identified beyond the heavy rock beat.

I waited, listening closely for any sound from the inside. It began to seem odd to me not to hear voices or sounds of some sort beyond the music. I pressed in closer until my ear was against the glass of the sliding door. I focused my concentration on that one ear, pulling every sound possible to me from the interior on the other side. There was nothing to hear but the music.

Suddenly a light reflected off the glass. A guard was running with a flashlight in front of him from the direction of the main building. I heard the golf cart with the grounds guard approaching from the opposite direction. The two men were converging upon me at a rapid rate. I moved back into the shadows and dipped behind the potted triple-tiered cherry bush just as the guard on foot passed. He plunged on toward the other corner of the bungalow where he met the golf cart.

The two guards spoke in muted voices that carried fairly well to me. They were concerned about some guest's complaint about a loud argument in one of the bungalows. They seemed to be concentrating on a bungalow one over from Collin's, so I decided it might be a good time for me to make my departure. I gave another quick ear to the door, came up empty again, and slipped back out across the grounds in the direction of the garage.

Jason was not a happy man. He gave me something akin to a growl when I rejoined him. "Well?" he said.

"Not sure," I replied. "I think he's there all right, but I can't be sure. At first I thought he wasn't alone, but now I don't know. I couldn't hear any sounds but some rock music."

"What now?"

"Let's drive around some of the other parking areas. There's an open area by the tennis club and another visitors' lot by the main building."

We found it in the tennis club lot. The tan Celica was parked in a space not too far removed from the entrance to the guest bungalows. Jason pulled up behind it, and I got out. There was nothing in the car that could be seen from the outside. The doors were locked, and I did not see much to be gained by breaking into it and risking some security guard catching me at it.

When I got back inside the car Jason said, "That sort of clinches it, I'd say."

"Looks like it," I admitted.

"You have a hell of an advantage. He thinks he killed you and 〔h〕e's sitting in there feeling safe. How do you plan to use it?"

I thought about it along with a few dozen other things. I said, "In the daylight, with as many people around as possible. I'll see 〔h〕im at the beach. I'll play all my trumps then."

"How do you feel about bringing the police into it?" he asked.

"This doesn't belong to the police anymore."

"Am I supposed to know what that means?"

I shrugged it off. I was not sure I could put it into words. I 〔w〕as not sure my own thoughts on it were clear. I did not feel like 〔e〕xplaining about Carl Price, victims of violent crime, and the state 〔o〕f the criminal justice system in America. He let it pass and drove 〔b〕ack to my place in silence. Once he had a fresh Glenlivet in his 〔h〕and he said, "This Collin is a dangerous, unpredictable fellow. 〔Y〕ou are carrying a gun, aren't you?"

I shook my head. He gave it a big sigh and shook his head, 〔t〕oo, but in a much more exaggerated and agitated way.

"That's not smart," he said. "Look, Jake, I don't know what 〔i〕t is with you. You used to carry a gun to the market, now you 〔d〕on't wear one when you really need it. Why?"

"There are too many guns," I said.

"Do you mind if I don't buy that as an argument?" he said in 〔h〕is own sarcastic fashion. "Give me a straight answer on this 〔o〕ne, okay?"

I thought about it. It was tough to organize in a way that I 〔c〕ould explain. I said, "The last time I pulled a trigger it was close 〔r〕ange and into someone I did not want to see die. I'm not sure 〔h〕ow I feel about all of it, but I do know that there are many times 〔w〕hen I wake up from a dead sleep seeing her face at the moment 〔I〕 shot her. How many of those images can I store?"

"Good Lord, Jake, she was trying to kill you. Let me tell you 〔t〕his, old friend, if you had not pulled the trigger on her, you 〔w〕ouldn't have to worry about storing any images at all. You 〔w〕ould have been just another poor slob under a slab in that pretty 〔c〕emetery at the edge of town." He sipped at his drink and felt in 〔h〕is pocket for a cigar. "Let's move outside so I can light this 〔t〕hing. I need my pacifier."

I led us to a point on the terrace where the breeze would take

the smoke away and sat listening to the waves break below us
while Jason puffed his cigar to life. He smoked, sipped his scotch
and with occasional looks at me, considered the whole thing. Finally, he said, "You wouldn't want to have to kill Collin, would
you?"

I had never considered it just that way. The thought surprised
me. I let it settle before I responded. "No," I said, "I wouldn't."

"Even though he tried to make Humpty-Dumpty out of you?"

"That's hard for me to believe," I replied.

"Because you've bought into that whole partnership thing he's
sucked you into," Jason said, letting his exasperation show. "You
amaze me, Jake, because for all you've done in your life, all
you've lived through, you are still an innocent. You still trust
people too long. Don't be fooled by this guy. He's dangerous
and you better damn well be ready to kill him when he takes you
on next time."

"I intend to be more careful," I said, in what I knew was a
weak response.

Jason looked at the end of his cigar for a long moment before
pouring a small amount of his drink on it to extinguish it. He
said, "You know, pal, there are a few of us who would miss you
if you got too careless. You might keep that in mind the next
time you dress to go out. I'm tired. Goodnight."

"I'll remember. Goodnight, Jase," I said. I watched him wheel
himself toward the guest suite. I considered the luck in my life
that had brought me Trinia and Josh and a friend like Jason Meddler.

A short time later, I opened the locked steel cabinet in the back
of the large closet of my bedroom. From inside I took out the Sig
Sauer 9-mm and two ammunition clips loaded with hollow-point
and Teflon-coated bullets. The next time I dressed to go out, the
Sig would be in the belt against my spine.

TWENTY-EIGHT

THE PHONE WOKE ME. I looked. It was six ten in the morning.

"Hope I didn't wake you," Carl Price said from the other end of the line. "I remembered you said you were an early riser."

I did my best to clear my mind and my voice. "Right, Carl, I am. What's up?"

"The police called us about Julie's things. They think they found them in the possession of a man they took into custody yesterday," he said. "They called us last night, and I tried to reach you, but you wasn't in."

"No, I had a busy night," I replied. "What did they tell you about this guy?"

"Not very much. The detective said he had Julie's wallet and things in his car or something, I'm not quite sure on that part." He slowed as if thinking about it. "You know Mil and I gave the police a list of things, jewelry and all, and they said at the time that if it ever showed up they'd call us on it. They mentioned her ring and want that identified, because that was something taken off of her."

"You're talking about the rose ring?" I asked.

"Yeah, the signet ring that she made all her marks with," he replied.

"Did they tell you anything about the man? Was he a mugger, burglar, anything like that?"

"The detective said there was a history of arrests on drug charges. Do you think this could be the one who killed Rosie?"

I was not prepared for the question. It took me a minute to bring my thoughts on it into balance. "Why?" I asked. "Is that what the police are thinking?"

"They kinda hinted that. I'm coming down there to identify the ring and other things later on today. That's what I was calling you about, to let you know."

"Carl," I said carefully. "Did they mention finding the lottery ticket?"

"No they didn't."

"He didn't do it, Carl."

He gave a long, loud sigh. "You think he found the stuff someplace?"

"No, I think it was planted on him." I chose my words carefully. "I believe there are four others, besides Julie, that have been killed by the same person. I think that person is beginning to feel some heat and will soon make a big mistake. I intend to be around when that happens."

"You sound like you know who," he said.

"Maybe I do," I said. "I think I'll be able to answer that for you very soon. When do you get here and where will you stay?"

"I get in there this afternoon at three. I'll be taken to the station to see the things right after that, and then I'll stay overnight at the Lemon Tree Inn," he said. "I'll call when I get to the motel."

"Find out if this man they have in custody came to them by way of an anonymous tip. I'd give odds that's the case," I said. "If so, then I'm positive that he had nothing to do with Julie."

Carl's voice had an odd quiver to it. "You know, Jake, when I heard they had this man, I didn't believe it either. I believe in you, and I hope the police don't get to him first. Do you know what I mean, Jake?"

"I know, Carl."

"Do you really think you're close to finding the one who did it?" he asked with the innocence of a child.

"Yes," I answered.

"I don't have to put it into words with you, do I, Jake? You know what I need because you've been there."

"I know."

"Is there anything you want me to do when I get to Santa Barbara? Is there anything I can help you with?"

"No," I said. "You stay in your motel until you hear from me. I may or may not have news for you before you return home."

"For Millie's sake, I pray you do."

I was wide awake after my talk with Carl, but I went in and

lashed cold water on my face to complete the job. I never felt
ly up for the day until I had that small shock to my system. I
ed some warm-up calisthenics, which the sore ribs put a fast
d to, shaved, and showered before going out to put on coffee.
I was finishing a second cup before I heard Jason's door open.
e joined me with an agenda of complaints.

"That bed is too damn hard. I might as well have slept on the
or," he fired for an opener. "I just got to sleep when the phone
1g. Who'd call at the break of dawn like that?"

"Carl Price," I replied. "Coffee?"

"Yeah, I need it. What'd Price want?"

I told him about my conversation with Julie's father. He lis-
1ed while sipping his coffee. His head nodded occasionally in
reement with my conclusions.

"The police around here are too good to be fooled by a phony
1nt," he said when I had finished.

"Agreed. But if this boy they've got has some weak alibis, it
uld begin to look not so phony."

"What's your play now?"

"Collin."

"Be careful, he's a smart one," he cautioned. "You've got an
vantage as long as he thinks you're dead, but as soon as he
ows otherwise, he'll be coming after you again."

"I'm not sure he came after me the first time," I said.

"No, you want to believe that he's a nice guy who works for
e fire department and plays volleyball on the beach and writes
s mother once a week. You drop your guard again, amigo, and
u might be dead."

"That won't happen."

"I'm going to Malibu, but I'll be back up later tonight. Is the
d in that other guest room any softer?"

I shrugged, knowing my answer would make no difference.
1e bedroom, sitting room, and bath he stayed in had been done
ecifically for him. The bed was the same as he had at his own
me, and the bath had been specially equipped for his needs.
nnie, the decorator and a mutual friend, had been meticulous
all such details. I did not bother mentioning any of that. All I

said was, "You can try it if you want, but you don't need
come back up here, Jason. I'm not going to get careless agai

"I might believe you if I didn't think you had a blind s
where this guy Collin is concerned." He drank the last of
coffee and waved off an offer of more. "You're not going to
convinced about him until you take that lottery ticket out of
pocket, are you?"

"I don't know, Jase. There's something odd there, and I ca
put my finger on it."

"Try words," he suggested.

"I had a feeling last night outside Collin's place that I sho
go in. I almost did," I said. "I think I would have if those secur
guards hadn't come by."

"I'm not getting it. You mean break in, or politely knoc
What?"

"Break in, I guess. I'm not sure what vibes I was getting,
something was wrong in there. I'm almost sure of it now. I te
you about the music and no sounds other than that, but there w
another thing I was getting. Do you know that feeling of bei
watched? Well, it was as if someone was on the other side of t
glass door doing just what I was doing. I could feel them listeni
for me."

He gave me a look of appraisal before answering. "Are y
forgetting you took a forty-foot dive into a piece of canvas ov
concrete last night? I don't think your judgments could be all t
sound after that little header, do you? But let's say you we
reading it right. So what? Collin heard someone outside a
played it the way any guy who had killed five or more peo
would play it. That sure as hell doesn't mean that you go chargi
in there after him. By the way, are you carrying the Sig?"

"I will," I said. "I have to find my permit. It's in the safe
think, with my passport and other papers."

"Permit or not, you carry," he said. "This is too far along

I nodded agreement and saw him down to his car. He sa
"You probably think I'm more hindrance than help at this poi
but I don't like sitting on the sidelines, so I'll be back." I
pointed his thumb at Tony's and added, "We'll have lunch wi
our redheaded friend tomorrow."

I laughed. "Tony doesn't have red hair."

"Not on purpose," he replied and was gone. He was still smiling when he passed along Cabrillo.

THE RIBS DEMANDED some attention, so I downed some aspirin and did a tight retape over them. I did the things that would be normal for me on a Sunday morning. I made a large breakfast, retrieved my newspaper for the crossword, and lounged out on my terrace, watching the day fill up with people. It was another hot one, and the tourists who had chosen Santa Barbara for their final fling of summer were out in force.

I sat back in the shade, feeling the heat rising around me. The sun was baking the day as well as everyone who ventured out in it. Tony's Beachside opened for lunch at noon, and his lot began to fill up with patrons who scurried inside for the air-conditioning. I waited for Tony.

He was late. I saw his new Lamborghini take the corner into the lot like it was a Grand Prix pit stop. He parked just outside the back entrance of the restaurant and hopped out of his car dressed in a dark suit with the sheen of fine silk. He disappeared inside the restaurant at a quick step.

I went downstairs. Claudile was opening her gallery as I passed.

"Did you see what happened to the new awnings?" she asked.

"Wind?" I offered.

"It looks more like the work of vandals," she said. "Did you get my note?"

"Yes, I did, and thanks. It was nothing, but it's nice you keep a sharp eye," I said. "You be careful, though, in going around the back area at night. The man you saw could have been waiting for you."

"I thought about that later," she admitted. "I won't do it again. I'll call the police the next time."

"That would be the thing to do," I said as I got to the corner of the building.

The awning over the window of the rare books store was as I had left it the night before, still partially hanging from the wall at one end. The rest of it lay on the concrete-and-tile walkway.

"I guess we should notify the Surf and Turf Realty about this," I said.

"I've done it," she replied with a large smile. "By the way, want to thank you for the Flossie line. It worked like magic."

I smiled back. I would have given anything to see Bob Claiborne's face during that little exchange.

I crossed the parking lot to Tony's Beachside just in time to intercept Tony when he reappeared from the back door of the restaurant.

"Hey, paesan," he said. "I'm late to a wedding over at the San Ysidro. Wanta come?"

"No thanks," I responded. "I thought I'd get that info I wanted from you?"

"Oh, yeah," he said and seemed torn between going back inside and getting into his car. "There are a couple of other pictures of him, but in that picture of you looking at the camera, it's the guy behind you looking over your shoulder."

I tried to visualize the shot he was talking about, but all I could remember was the one picture of myself I had put in as a gag.

"Do you have the pictures here?" I asked.

"Home, sorry," he said. "Would tomorrow be okay on them?"

"Sure, and thanks."

"I'll be back here later tonight," he said. "Come have some dinner."

"Can't, but I'll be in tomorrow for lunch with Jason," I said.

He slipped into the Lamborghini and started it up. "Good," he yelled over the sound of the engine. "See you guys tomorrow."

I was not sure he looked all that pleased about it as he jumped into his car and peeled rubber out of the lot on his way to San Ysidro.

I made a hasty return upstairs and pulled the negatives from the photo packet. A magnifying glass helped me to locate and study the picture he had mentioned. It was of little help. I could see some detail of a person behind me in the shot, but it was impossible to recognize anyone from it. I needed a print on it.

I found the gun permit in the safe and added the Sig Sauer to

y belt beneath my shirt in the back before locking up and leav-
g. I made sure the security system was engaged as I closed the
ound level stairway door behind me. The heat swarmed around
e as I took a quick peek under my car for any loose wires or
usual lumps that might be in evidence. It was amazing how a
rty-foot drop could develop paranoia. I was just as careful open-
g the car door and took my time feeling around the seat before
tting in. There was a small moment of dry throat before I finally
rned the key, but it all faded into a silly sense of overreaction
hen the engine started.

I dropped the negative off with Tim at the one-hour place and
ked him for a blowup of the face in the background. Then at
st after two o'clock I headed for East Beach. It was more
owded than I had ever seen it. I cruised Cabrillo until I was
le to find a parking spot with a decent view of the volleyball
urts. The middle net was in use, but there was no sign of Collin.
tuned the radio to an oldies station and leaned my seat back to
ait in comfort.

It was a good time to do some thinking. I let the images float
ithout putting any firm holds on them. I kept seeing Carrie and
lie; Carrie as a battered corpse beneath a plastic shroud and
lie as a lively, radiant girl with dreams about to come true.

Just before four o'clock the newsbreak came. I looked over the
each through the binoculars and listened with divided attention
the news reader. Players I did not know occupied the center
et. They, as well as the people around the court, seemed to be
aiting for the day to begin. The play was halfhearted, and the
ttention of the nonplayers was of a searching nature. I had the
eling we were all waiting for the same man.

The slow penetration of what I was hearing from the radio
rought the binoculars down. The newsman was saying, "The
oast Guard said today that the fire was spotted by the crew of
service boat for one of the offshore drilling rigs. They put the
xplosion of the yacht at about four a.m. By the time the service
oat reached the wreckage, the yacht itself was sinking, but they
ere able to identify it by name. The yacht was the *Frankly My*
ear, owned by the late Barney Gable of Santa Barbara. The
pokesman for the Coast Guard said there is an investigation un-

derway as to the strange circumstances of the sinking of the Gabl
yacht.''

I turned the radio off and considered what I had heard. Some
one had deep sixed the Gable connection and Carrie's body a
at one time. I wasn't sure how much of it would stay down o
unrecovered, but I had a suspicion it was done to buy time. Some
one was feeling the heat, and someone would make a mistake
Perhaps they already had.

I started the car and drove to the La Cumbre Plaza shoppin
center. Tim gave me a thumbs-up when I entered the one-hou
photo shop with eyebrows raised asking the question.

"Just finished," he said.

I paid him, and he handed over an eight-by-ten envelope. "It'
a little soft but readable," he added.

"That's all I care about," I said. "Thanks, Tim."

"He knew he was being photographed," Tim said.

"What do you mean?" I asked quickly.

"Well, you can see you looking right at the camera, so yo
knew, right?" He waited for the nod. "Then when I cranked
up on the fellow in the background, I could see that he was fol
lowing your look. Whatever you saw, he saw. I just figured yo
could both see the camera."

And the car, I thought, visualizing the Rolls as it had bee
parked with Jason shooting from its window.

"Thanks, Tim," I said again, hurrying out the door.

"Anytime," followed me into the traffic of the mall. I mad
my way through the rush of people to the parking lot and my ca
I instinctively looked around before getting inside. I started th
car, put on the air conditioner, and opened the envelope.

The blowup was soft, as Tim had said, but there was no mis
taking the man Tony had identified as the volleyballer who
lunched and gambled with Barney Gable. I was not surprised a
I sat looking at the picture for all it meant. It supplied the nec
essary link between that man and Gable, Parkland, and Kohler.

As I sat thinking it through, I suddenly had the feeling that
had made a serious mistake the night before. I was struck with
sense of urgency. I started the car and pulled out of the parkin
lot, heading toward the 101 and Breakers. The picture lay on th

eat beside me, staring up at me from behind the wraparound
lasses. I should have gone in last night, I kept thinking. The face
ehind the sunglasses became a taunt.

I drove fast, but deep inside I knew that I was too late. I should
ave broken into Collin's place when I was there last night.

TWENTY-NINE

I PARKED IN the lot behind the tennis courts close to the tan Celica, which was still parked as it had been the night before. I too a pair of latex gloves from a rear-seat compartment and made a assurance check on the Sig in the back of my belt before leavin the Porsche. I knew my way around pretty well after all my recen visits and was able to skirt the main paths on my way to Collin' bungalow. Even so the traffic was heavy. People were comin and going between many of the bungalows, some with drinks i their hands, as if there were a massive open house. The part atmosphere was enhanced by a Mexican mariachi band playin by the pool. Evidently Breakers spared no expense to give th guests a memorable Labor Day weekend.

The bungalows around Collin's were overflowing people, an I certainly did not want to be seen fumbling with a lock by anyon who might be able to recall it later. I roamed a bit, seeking a saf way into his place without being spotted. There was simply to much light and too many people. I checked my watch, noting was close to five, and opted to wait it out until the sun had dippe behind the first skyward juts in the west. I walked close enoug to Collin's bungalow to hear the music from inside. It was th same as I had heard the night before, which only increased m sense of dread.

The lobby was quiet. Breakers was not the kind of place fellow simply drove up to and said he wanted a room. It was reservations kind of place and a concierge kind of place. The des clerk was probably sent to a special school just to learn that non communicative way of saying "Yes?"

I did not worry about that guy remembering me, because h wasn't bothering to give me much eye time. I asked for a pa phone and he sneered me into a small alcove off the lobby. looked up the number and dialed the Lemon Tree Inn. Carl Pric answered on the first ring to his room.

"Was it Julie's ring?" I asked.

"Yes," he said. "It was all Julie's things. But it was like you aid, Jake, they got the guy on an anonymous tip. The detective aid the man had a perfect alibi, too, for when Julie was killed. e was in jail at the time."

"That figures," I said. "How do you feel?"

"Okay, but a little down. It was hard to look at those things ad to know what they meant. Somebody took them from her. omebody who'd killed her."

"When are you heading back home?"

He took a beat before answering, "I told Mil it might be a ouple of days. You sounded like you was onto something."

"Yes, I am," I said. "Nothing that would hold up in a court f law, though."

His voice came back to me thick with emotion. "It's important be sure, Jake, but let me ask you a question. Suppose this fella at killed your family had plea-bargained or gone up for a few ears and some parole board turned him out on the streets again. Vould you be sleeping?"

"No, Carl, I wouldn't."

"That's why I'm staying."

"I know," I said. "When I know with absolute certainty, ou'll know. Okay?"

"I want to see him," he said with a tremor in his voice. "I've ot to."

"No one knows that better than I do, Carl. I'll be in touch with ou later. Get some food and some rest."

His voice was faint again when he said good-bye. He would ever be whole again, but he was only asking to get something ack. I had to see that he got that chance.

I ordered an espresso in the coffee shop that Breakers called a istro. It had a nice outdoor area from which I could see the rounds and watch a waterfall empty into a small lagoon that ooked like a movie set. Breakers was a kind of Disneyland for dults. It was no wonder that so many celebrities made it a home way from home. I nursed the espresso long enough to let the ast, long shadows blend into an overall pattern of dimming light. paid the tab and left fantasy world reluctantly, not exactly look- g forward to the reality I expected to be soon facing.

The people traffic had dwindled by now. There was a "Do Not

Disturb" sign on Collin's door that I pulled off while I worked on the lock. Once I had the door open, I replaced the sign and slipped inside. I stood just inside the door and closed it behind me. The lights were on and the music played from the stereo components across the living room. Without moving I said, "Collin?" There was no answer.

Then my eyes began to bring me some minor details. A soft pillow was on the floor. A large chair was turned askew. The doors of the cabinets were all ajar. There were droplets of blood on the marble entry floor.

I stepped carefully around the blood spots as I pulled on the latex gloves and followed the trail of droplets into the other rooms. In the bathroom I found the towels missing from the racks with one of them bloodsoaked on the floor. I lifted it and tried to assess the amount of blood it had absorbed. It dripped when it was raised from the floor, telling me that the amount was considerable. In checking out the rest of the bathroom I noticed the fancy shower curtain had been pulled off its hooks, except for two left holding it at one end. Someone, woozy or weak, possibly pushed, had grabbed the curtain for balance. The marble of the tub enclosure showed a smear of blood, which indicated to me that the person had continued to fall. It also hinted strongly of an open back wound.

I called out Collin's name again as I entered the bedroom. Again there was no answer, but there was strong evidence that whatever had taken place had happened here. The drawers of all the dressers were pulled out, furniture was toppled, and a small room safe was standing open and empty. The folding doors of one of the closets was broken inward. I could see the smear of blood down one of the doors. I bent at the closet to inspect the carpet, which was blood soaked; some of the blood had dried. There was a round splintered hole in one of the closet doors that went straight on through. I pulled the door back and looked inside where one of the jackets had been knocked down. I found the bullet barely lodged in the back wall of the closet.

The bullet told me the blood was probably a gunshot wound from a .357 Magnum. At least one errant bullet, I surmised, and one sure hit. Maybe two guns, maybe one. It was all guesswork at this point, but it was something. There were a couple of other towels in the bathroom, bloody but not soaked like the one in the

athroom had been. The clothes hamper in the closet was half
lled, but none of the clothes in it bore any bloodstains. Either
e victim was shirtless or took the blood-soaked shirt out of the
ungalow with him.

I stood in the center of the room letting my senses absorb. A
ilenced gun, most likely, because anything else would have been
eard. Something had been heard, I remembered. Those two
uards last night were checking out a complaint of loud voices
om one of the guests. They had it pegged as the bungalow next
› Collin's, but it had probably come from this very room. I had
robably gotten there within minutes of the shooting.

After a few moments of absorbing the scene, I let my mind do
ome imaging. Someone, possibly shirtless, stood by the closet
·hile across the room someone else threatened with a silenced
un. The victim moved to avoid the first shot but was hit in the
hest or stomach by the second round, which might have gone
irough, leaving a bad exit wound. He or she fell hard against
ie closet doors and most likely appeared to be dead. It was prob-
bly a he because of the force of the impact on the doors. My
uess was that whoever had taken the hit lay there unconscious
or several hours. His body weight compressed the wound enough
› he didn't bleed to death. He woke up, and the heavier bleeding
tarted again. He did what he could to staunch the blood flow
·ith towels.

It seemed to dead-end there. The big question that remained,
ther than who was involved, was, Where did they go? Especially
ie one who was shot. I did another visual survey of the room,
·ying to pick up on anything I might have missed the first time
irough. Something finally registered. The bedside phone had
een pulled to the edge of the table on the opposite side of the
ed. The blood on the receiver told me that whoever had been
hot had also tried to call someone.

I took a close look at the phone and felt a slight setback when
noted it was an ordinary hotel telephone. That eliminated the
hance to use a redial button. The instructions on the face of the
hone were the standardized form found in every hotel. The num-
er to dial for local calls was nine, and I noted that the nine button
·as blood smeared. So were the six, eight, two, three, and zero.
: suddenly became significant to me that the one, four, five, and
even were clean.

I sat down on the bed giving it a moment to gel, as I mulled the potential value of the information. Eight-nine-six, eight-nine-five, and eight-nine-seven were common local exchange numbers. With the five and the seven both clean, it seemed that the person called was in the eight-nine-six area. That was Montecito. I took the other numbers, the two, the three, and the zero, and tried to imagine how many combinations I would have to dial to get it. It was a daunting task.

I started dialing combinations doubling the zero: 896-0023, 896-2003, 896-0203, 896-2300, and on until I determined the zero had been used only once. Next I tried doubling the two. As I dialed, I knew there were other possibilities. It could have been long distance or even one of the numbers that did not answer. Those who answered claimed not to know a Collin Fraser, and there was always the chance that one of them had lied. The odds seemed great as I continued the tedious dialing of the nine for the outside line and then the adjusted version of the numbers. Keeping track of what I had already dialed was growing difficult and I was looking around for a pad and pencil when the number I had just dialed was picked up by a machine. I had already forgotten which combination of numbers I last used when I recognized a voice. It said, "You have reached 896-2032. I cannot take your call at the moment, but if you care to leave a message, please wait for the tone. G'day." It was Angie's voice.

I hung up before the tone sounded. I gave myself a second or two to get my thinking in order before I made my way carefully out of Collin's bungalow. I made sure the "Do Not Disturb" sign was on the door and the latex gloves were back in my pocket when I left.

How nice it would be, I thought, to wander poolside among the rich and famous, drink margaritas and tequila sunrises, and listen to the music of the mariachis. Maybe take some time to flirt with some sleek lady in an Armani suit flashing diamonds the size of walnuts. Or maybe just blend anonymously and forget that all of life was not so beautiful, and that even for the young and starry-eyed it could end in terror.

THE COTTAGE SAT small and isolated among the tall eucalyptus trees, as if hiding there in the dark. I pulled into the driveway not trying to secrete my approach. It was beyond the time for that.

There was a light inside the house from a lamp in the living room. I could also see the figure slouched in the chair across the room and behind the lamp. The door stood slightly ajar so I pushed it open and walked in.

Collin pulled himself more upright upon seeing me. His eyes held a mixture of surprise and amusement. "Hello, blue," he said.

"Surprised to see me alive?"

"A bit," he answered.

"But not as much as someone else will be, right?"

He gave me that smile. "An understatement, mate. For my part I didn't really believe you'd be that easy to take out."

He moved slightly, and his face twisted up in an expression of pain. The towel he held to his lower chest was red with blood. I sat in the chair next to his.

"How does it feel to be king of East Beach? Lot of sheilas for the taking now, mate." He almost pulled off one of his great smiles.

"Tell me about Riggs."

He looked at me for a moment for what I meant, found it, and said, "Yeh, Riggs quit, but he didn't throw it. He knew they'd lose, and he couldn't stand that moment. He's not the kind you want watching your backside."

"I take it Mako has been dumping him on bets?"

"Lotta money changes hands on the sand, blue."

"Why are you here?" I asked.

"Why are you?" he asked back.

"You. Tell me about Angie."

He stared at me as if trying to decide whether to answer me or not. Finally, he sighed out much of his energy and in a tired voice answered, "Someone I knew from my time down under."

"Time? You make it sound like a jail sentence."

He started something that was supposed to be a laugh but became more of a spasm of pain. "Australia was a bit of that for me, blue. I was sent there by me mom when I was but a lad," he said in an exaggerated Aussie dialect. "I am one of those rare birds with two citizenships...American mother and Aussie father. Not really wanted by either, so when I got to be a handful for one, off I went to the other. Sad story, eh mate?"

"And Angie?"

"A bird. A sheila. A fine specimen of the opposite sex, wouldn't you say?" The devil danced in his eyes momentarily. "She was mine until an Adelaide judge sent me away for stomping in a bloke's face. You'd have done the same to that one, I know you. We're something alike, you and me. We make a good team."

"And Angie?" I persisted.

"Ah, yes, always wanted to be where the movie stars lived. She made it, I'll say that for her. She came on over here, sort of immigrated, you might say. She wrote me in jail, mind you, and kept me up on her adventures. Even after I got out, she wrote. Very loyal, our Ange." There was a certain delirium creeping in as he talked.

"So you came over here and happened to run into her again, or what?"

"I got into a bit of trouble again, in Sydney, and had to skip the country. Naturally, I came to this land of milk and honey, which is after all my homeland too. Angie had a boyfriend living in, so rather than be a bad sport about it, I became his partner in the transport business. Very decent of me, don't you think?"

"Moving drugs? Decent isn't the word I would choose."

"You know a lot, don't you, mate?"

"How deep were you in?"

"I'm small potatoes. All I did was courier the stuff. Sometimes I made pickups at the airport in L.A., but most of the time I made deliveries to places like Bakersfield and San Luis Obispo. I did, at least, until our golden goose dried up. It was a risky business, blue, worth every penny I got for it."

"And that was a lot, wasn't it? All paid in cash. That why you got the job as a fireman to cover all the money you were getting? Am I on the right track?"

"Like you read my bio, blue."

Lights flashed across the windows as a car turned in to the driveway. I took a look and saw Angie pull her Mustang to a stop a good car length behind my car. I doubted that she was real happy to see it there.

"Is he still her boyfriend?" I asked, putting my attention back on Collin.

His eyes seemed to have trouble focusing on me. He moved

his head from side to side to clear them. "Still? That's a toughie. Yes and no. She got a bit unhappy about some of his behavior, but then we're all kind of tied into some business together, so it muddies the water."

"You mean behavior like the thing he had going with Carrie Berry?" I asked.

"You know about that as well?" He shook his head. "I knew you were special, blue. What else do you know?"

"I know the business you have together is tied to Julie's forty-million-dollar lottery ticket," I said flatly.

"Yeh, you sent us that message loud and clear. That's what made him try to kill you. I wasn't in on that. He told me after he thought you were dead."

"And how about Carrie? Were you in on that?"

"What about Carrie? She split," he said almost as a question.

"No, Collin, she was killed and stuffed in the forward cabin of Gable's boat," I said. "I saw her before your partner blew up all the evidence."

"He killed Carrie, too?" he said in a voice that did not sound like him.

"Tell me about Julie," I said finally.

"I'll tell you," Angie's voice said from behind us. I turned to see her standing just inside the door. She came in and knelt beside Collin at the chair. "How is it, Col?" she asked.

His head went back, and his eyes closed with a short nod. Life was draining out of him through the red towel he held against his chest. She looked at me. I kept my eyes as blank as possible.

"You caused this," she said, as if making a simple statement of fact to me. "Why wouldn't you leave it alone?"

"You were going to tell me about Julie," I reminded.

"She was my friend," she said sadly. "She used to visit me, and sometimes she would bring her housemate, Carrie. That's how he met her. I don't know how the rest happened, but I know that he got her hooked."

"Carrie's dead, Ange," Collin said, as if it was hard to believe. "I heard."

"Hooked, you said?" I prompted.

"The white lady," Collin said with his eyes still closed. "She loved it. According to him she became a pure junkie for it. More like a slave, I guess you'd say. We sent her for the dicier pickups at the airport in L.A. We'd watch from the parking lot across the street to see if she made it out with the bag without a tail. We even used her car for transport. We never worried about being stopped and searched in her old Celica. Sweet deal.''

"You knew he killed Julie?" I asked.

Angie's jaw clinched tightly. "He was there the night Julie called for help with her car. She was leaving a message on the machine when Carrie picked up the phone, and Julie told her about having the winning numbers in the lottery. She was so excited that night. I know because she called me, too, at Pismo's.''

"Yes," I said, "I heard the message she left on Carrie's machine. Why did she call you?"

"Just to say that she had some incredible news to tell me. She said Carrie was coming to take her to a gas station and she wanted me to wait for her at Pismo's. I'd never heard her anything like she sounded that night.'' She stopped as if remembering it. She looked at me, shaking her head in some sort of soundless misery.

"Only it wasn't Carrie who showed up," I said. "He did. Go on, Angie, tell me the rest of it. And tell me how you and Collin wound up trying to grab a piece of the forty million for yourselves. That should be very interesting.''

"Julie was already dead," she said defensively. "There wasn't anything we could do to bring her back.''

"He killed her, took the ticket, and then what?" I asked, trying to keep my contempt for them in check.

Angie's emotions were close to a breaking point. I could hear it in her voice when she answered me. "He didn't get the ticket right away. Julie didn't have it with her. It was Carrie who found it for him in Julie's house.''

She looked for help from Collin. His eyes were on me. His grin was sardonic. He said, "You know who you're after now, eh?"

"I know," I said.

The grin turned to grimace. He said, "I knew you'd get onto him. I knew from the first time I met you that you could be big trouble. Do you remember when we met?"

"I remember. It was the day of Julie's death."

"Of course," he said, his voice very tired. "She was great, our Jule. I miss her.'' He drifted again, his energy spent.

'Sure, you miss her so much you got in on the action with her
er.''

'She was long dead, blue, by that time.''

'Why did he shoot you, Collin?''

'He's cleaning house, and he blamed me for bringing you into
gs. Which I did, of course. I wanted you to have him, mate.
never rat on a partner, never give him up by name, but he
uldn't have killed Julie. That's something he never should
e done. So I brought you in close where you would be a bother
im. It was great sport, like watching a cobra and a mongoose.
ich are you, Jake?''

heard a sound from the street I recognized.

'I take it he's the one who tried to run me down on Cabrillo?''
aited while he nodded. ''A warning or the real thing?''

'He doesn't give warnings.''

'You still haven't told me how you got cut in on the lottery
et,'' I said.

'He gave it to Angie to hold in her safe at the store. She
ognized Julie's mark on the back of it. It wasn't all that hard
ut together.'' There was only a hint of what had earlier been
mile. ''I guess you might say we blackmailed him, blue.''

'And he went to Gable to get a quick payday on the ticket, is
it? Gable was the drug connection here?''

'Nah, just a transporter, like us. We drove the stuff and picked
money on the other end. He did the same by boat.''

'What went wrong with Gable?''

'He promised five million for the ticket but couldn't raise it
tried to run with it. I think he owed the Colombians a bundle
saw it as his way out.''

'Did you know he was killed?''

'Not at the time. I was told later.''

'And tonight you came here to do what?''

'To warn Angie,'' he said. ''To give her some chance.''

Angie said to Collin, ''The safe in the store was open. He's
n there already and taken the ticket. That's all he wanted,
llin.''

Collin tried for one of his sardonic laughs. It sounded like a
gh. ''And when he finds out it's a fake? He'll come here to
you, Ange. He's out to kill everybody who knows about that
ody ticket.''

"He's already here," I said. "I heard the Celica pass by."

Angie jumped. "We have to get out of here," she said.

I put a hand on her arm and pulled her back down. "Do have a gun in the house?"

She shook her head frantically. "No," she said. "That's w I went to the store for. There was one in the safe, but he ha now."

I took her shoulders and looked at her square in the face. " gie, answer me straight. No games," I said. "The night I here, he was hidden somewhere watching. Where?"

She gulped back her pretenses and said, "There's an area hind the back hedge, at the top of the embankment above railroad tracks. He was there."

"How did he get there?"

"There are spaces in the hedge," she said, her voice ris with the panic. "Or he could climb up from the railroad track

I said, "I'm going to give you a gun, Angie. Do you kn how to shoot?"

"No," she said. "Collin, you can use the gun."

Collin's weak shake of his head told me more than word leaned in toward him and said, "You could have been so m more, Collin."

His answer was very soft. "That's what I always thought, b but it just never worked out for me." His gaze was slightly fi as he moved his eyes to me. "We're still mates, you and You do it for me, okay? Fair dinkum, blue."

I got up and pulled the Sig 9-mm handgun from the small my back. I took it off safety and pumped a shell into the cham before handing it over to Angie. "All you have to do is pull trigger. Turn off that lamp as soon as I'm out the door. Do turn on a light, no matter what, until you get an 'all clear' fr me. Shoot at any sound coming in the house. If it's me, I'll telling you, so don't worry about that."

As I got to the door, Collin's faint voice followed me "Take care, blue. I'll see you on the other side."

THIRTY

EFT THE HOUSE at a dogtrot following the same direction I had
ard the Celica take. A half block away I turned onto an inter-
ting street that led down toward the railroad tracks and the
ach. The closest houses to Angie's cottage were on the beach
e of the railroad tracks. The undeveloped lots next to her ap-
ared to be overgrown with tight thickets of trees and shrubs. I
t fairly certain no one would be passing through those fields,
I kept a sharp eye on the street in front of me. My night eyes
re not what they once were, but I still trusted them to read the
apes and forms around me. I found the Celica parked off the
d, partially hidden by bushes, just before the railroad crossing.
had not passed me, so I figured he had taken the back route.
tepped into the center of the tracks and adjusted my steps to
spacing of the ties while I tried to assess the distance to the
ck of Angie's house.

f anything, it was even darker on the tracks, which dropped
o a ravinelike passageway with a tall embankment on one side
d a stand of eucalyptus trees on the other. It made my imagi-
tion work overtime in trying to calculate the possibilities ahead
me. There was always the chance that he had stopped at some
and I had made and was waiting in the darkness. My pace
wed to accommodate my night vision and my concept of po-
tial ambush.

At a point I figured to be about the same half block I had taken
m Angie's to the side street, I left the tracks to find a way up
embankment. It was much steeper than I had counted on and
nsiderably higher. I felt my way in both directions until I found
at appeared to be some semblance of a path up. It was slow
ing, groping in the darkness for hand- and footholds. It took
too long to work my way up, and I began to feel I was losing
race with time.

Once I was on the top of the embankment, I stopped to listen.

There were the usual night sounds, creature sounds that I had never been able to identify, but nothing seemed not to belong. I felt about the new terrain, aware that I was ten or twelve feet above the tracks behind me. With what I could see and what I could feel, I gained a fair impression of the area. There was an uneven table of perhaps eight feet from the shrubbery to the edge of the embankment. Some high grass or weeds were underfoot that created the possibility of tripping. I moved cautiously and as quietly as possible to the hedge line, looking for the spaces Angie had said were there.

Too much time, I was thinking as I groped for the opening through the hedge. Then with the sound of my own Sig Sauer blasting from some point in the darkness in front of me, I knew that what I had sought to prevent was already happening. I thrashed my way through the hedges toward the sound of the gun.

The gun fired again, which caused me to stay low as I reached the level grass inside the hedging. I stayed down against the cool, slightly damp lawn while I listened for any new sounds. Patience, I told myself, making myself remain still for the eternity it might take. I worked to slow my breathing while I focused my eyes on the house. I picked at it for any unusual movement or form I could detect.

Suddenly a light came on from inside the house. It seemed so bright and came on so unexpectedly that I shrank from it before I realized what it meant. Angie was not patient. She was scared and turned on the lamp to see if she had hit the sound she fired at. She had not.

The silhouette of a man rose up between me and my view of Collin and Angie. He sighted and fired before I could move any closer. There was almost no sound at all, but I knew the spits I heard were deadly ones. I saw Angie crumple from her standing position next to Collin. Then two more spits and Collin's face jerked and fell to the side. I was too late for them. All I could do was wait and watch.

The silhouette moved into the room with Angie and Collin and took a closer look at his handiwork. He dipped down from my view and came up holding Angie's purse. He rummaged in it for a moment before tossing it away. As an afterthought he gave a violent kick to Angie's lifeless body. Without further ado, he turned and strode from the house.

Before I was ready for him, he was outside and coming fast in
y direction. I sidestepped away from his path deeper into the
otective darkness of the shrubs. I made sure the light from in-
de the house was not catching me before I spoke.

"Stop where you are, Mako, and drop the gun," I said. "Then
ck it away from you."

He froze at the sound of my voice. It was clear he was con-
dering his chances as he held the gun a second longer than I
anted.

"Now," I said, giving it as hard an edge as I knew how.

It was hard enough. He bent slightly at the knees and waist to
op the gun in the manner of one who knew about firearms. He
shed it with his foot as far as he could. When he stood straight
ain I moved farther around to get the light at my back. He
rned with the sound of my movement. I stopped when he was
cing the light.

"Recognize my voice, Mako?" I asked.

He shook his head. His eyes were not discernible, but I could
el their intensity as they searched into the partial shadow that
ll hid me. Then I saw him get it. His body seemed to stiffen.
s voice was harsh but low. "Sands."

It was the same voice that had left the message on Carrie's
achine, "Answer, bitch!"

"You've been a busy boy. Killed a lot of people," I said. "But
e, you slipped up on. That was a big mistake."

He did not try to answer. He watched the darkness where I
ood. I was sure his mind was working over his options. I was
eling a strong desire to have the Sig back in my hand.

His body language changed. He leaned to one side in a more
sual stance and said, "Now you kill me, is that it?"

"Only if you go stupid on me," I said. "I'm interested in the
rty million."

I could see his grin even in the dim light.

"Are you saying you want to make some sort of deal?" he
ked.

"Could be. If I get some straight answers from you."

He started walking toward the back veranda. "Why don't we
 down," he said. I let him go. He sat in one of the porch chairs
d leaned back looking in my direction. He was in enough light
 I could see his eyes more clearly.

I stepped out of the darkness and sat on the porch swing. ▌
showed no surprise that I was unarmed.

"Good bluff," he said. "I bought it all the way."

"I don't think so, Mako. I think you knew right away."▐
leaned back on the swing, making my pose as casual as his. "T▐
me about Julie."

"She made me mad. I asked her to show me the ticket and s▐
kept saying she didn't have it. I thought she was lying, so▐
punched her around a little. I dragged her out of the car at t▐
Pelican Point place to give her a lesson. She shouldn't have ▌
up a fight. That really got me mad."

"You killed her because you were mad?"

"No, no. I killed her for the ticket. I made pulp out of ▐
because I was mad." He gave it a small laugh for emphas▐
"What were you to her, a sugar daddy? I bet she was a nice lit▐
piece, wasn't she? I thought of taking some of that myself on▐
or twice. I should've done it that night before I made such a me▐
out of her."

Mako no longer gave any pretense to being under my contr▐
He openly taunted me with his words and his eyes.

"And Carrie?" I asked.

"She made me mad, too."

"She found the ticket for you in Julie's house, didn't she?"▐

"She told me where to find it, yeah." He looked around at t▐
darkness. "You know a lot, don't you? Collin and me, we thoug▐
you were some kind of cop at first. He couldn't leave it alon▐
Collin couldn't. He thought it was funny to pull you in close▐
us."

"You killed Carrie because she knew you had killed Julie?"▐

"I was able to control the bitch with nose candy until you can▐
along and muddied up things." He glared across the space b▐
tween us. "She got crazy. She got so she didn't even want t▐
coke anymore. I couldn't afford to let her stay on the loose."

"She had a kid, you know? A little girl named Megan."

"Yeah, I know. And I know more than you. I know that s▐
was a tramp running around on her old man there in Lomp▐
while he was on duty at the air base. That's how I met her. I us▐
to make a delivery at Lompoc to a fellow who introduced me▐
Carrie. I'm the one who talked her into moving down here. B▐
you didn't know that, did you?"

"But she finally made you mad?" I goaded him with it.

"She needed a lesson, and I gave it to her. My hands were ... e for a day after I finished with her."

"And Collin made you mad?" I waited while he stared at me ...thout answering. "But you were afraid to take Collin on with... t a gun, weren't you? It's only the women you beat up on, isn't ... sport?"

Mako's head was moving in a short, rhythmic nod. His mouth ...s pinched into a tight line. The eyes were angry.

"And Angie made you mad too, didn't she? I saw that little ...ck you gave her after you'd already killed her. What was that ...out?" I wanted to control his thinking as long as I could.

"She and Collin pulled a switch on me. They had another ticket ...th the same numbers but a different date on it in the safe in ...ce of this one." He patted his left breast pocket. "I wouldn't ...ve come here tonight if she hadn't done that. I didn't want to ... her."

"But she made you mad," I said.

"Yes, she made me mad." He spat the words at me.

"Am I making you mad, sport?"

"It doesn't make any difference whether you make me mad or ...t, Sands. I've got to kill you either way." He took a more ...right position in his chair. "You don't know who you've been ...essing with, man."

I laughed. I made it derisive and contemptuous.

"You mean I don't know that you're a jailbird?" I threw in ...other sarcastic chuckle. "Sure I know that. You've got the ...ne jungle marks as your friend Collin. And why else would ...u be afraid to step up and claim that forty million in your own ...me? You're on a parole violation someplace, right, sport?"

He was still and wide eyed.

"The system didn't keep us safe from you, did it, Mako? But ...at else is new, huh?" I fought to keep the smirk on my face. ...was getting to him fast. "What else am I messing with? You ...nt to tell me?"

He was quick to his feet. I kept my casual pose, although I ...ve a small inner flinch. I made myself laugh. His anger was ...iling over.

I saw his set. He put one foot back with his weight on his back ...ot before making his move. His turn was quick and the round-

house kick was well executed into the porch swing. I was alrea[d]
on the lawn when it landed. My anticipation made me see[m]
quicker than I was.

I kept moving to the gun he had dropped earlier. I dippe[d]
picking it up by the barrel and throwing it out onto the railro[ad]
tracks below. I turned back in time to take a defensive stan[ce]
against his rush. I parried two fist strikes and blocked a low ki[ck]
before he backed off to reset and reconsider.

"I get it," he said as he took another step back, increasing t[he]
neutral zone between us. "You think you know some stuff[,]
that it? Man, you don't know anything. Some martial arts scho[ol]
has taken your money, and I'm going to show you what the[y]
didn't teach you. You really don't know what you're messi[ng]
with."

"That goes both ways, sport," I said.

The fact was I did know what I was messing with. I had se[en]
him. I had watched from a window on State Street while [he]
worked on his moves against a training partner. I had a go[od]
mental picture of those moves, and I also made myself rememb[er]
that he was left-handed.

On the other hand, he did not have a clue about me. He ha[s]
never even heard of the concrete cell with the early morning dri[ll]
done in the dark on rocks mysteriously placed on the concre[te]
floor overnight. He could not know about the hours of practi[ce]
done in blindfold to get the feel and sound of an opponent. [He]
would have to find out the hard way how much he did not kno[w]
about me.

His first moves were predictable. I simply blocked, letting hi[m]
try things until I got a range and rhythm from him. I backed [in]
a circle away from his left, letting him follow and initiate t[he]
contact. I could see that he liked to use his feet. His kicks we[re]
good and his combinations smart ones, but he needed more e[x]
perience in the dark. It was time to make that point.

I stepped back where the light was shadowed and let him com[e]
into me. As I expected, he brought his left knee high for a sna[p]
kick to my face. I dipped slightly to my left and drove the edg[e]
of my right foot into his planted leg at the knee. It gave, and [he]
went down. To his credit he rolled out quickly and jumped ba[ck]
up to his feet, but I was already there. I tried a little snap kick [at]

ny own into his midsection before putting him down again with
heel of the hand to his nose.

This time he was slow to rise. He shook his head as if to clear
t while I blended into the darkness just out of reach.

"Did you kill Parkland and Gable and Kohler?" I asked.

He did not answer. Instead he charged the sound of my voice.
Ie drove forward with kicks and punches delivered with force
nd energy and accompanied by loud *kiais*. His speed was im-
ressive, and it fooled me momentarily. One of his side kicks got
hrough and landed as I turned slightly away. It caught the ribs I
ad taped from the night before. I let out a loud grunt, and he
new he had finally scored a hit. A good one.

"What do you think you're going to do with all these answers?
Look, man, you're not going to be alive much longer. Don't you
et it?" He bounced about much as a boxer does upon entering
ring prior to a fight. "Parkland, yes, Gable, yes, Kohler, too,"
e said. "They tried to screw me over, man, really bad. They
lidn't think there was anything I could do, but I guess they were
vrong about that, weren't they?"

"They made you mad?"

"Yeah, man, they made me mad. You like that, huh? That
gives you some kind of laugh? Well, they're not laughing. And
ou won't be laughing."

He kicked again, and I went at his knee again. He yelled out
is pain as he went down and rolled back. His anger seemed to
vell up inside him. He roared at me, screaming things I couldn't
nderstand as he changed. He was all hands this time, keeping
is weight tilted onto his left leg. I backed through one of the
paces in the hedges onto the uneven topography at the top of the
mbankment. The weeds and grass captured one of my feet long
nough for him to lunge onto me.

I popped my cupped hands over his ears and moved him back.
Ie came at me again, and I took two soft punches to deliver one
ery hard one to his cheek. He staggered back, then seemed to
ounce off the hedge with his head down, coming full bore at
ne. I put my hands up to intercept him, and once I had my hands
n his arms, I dropped seat first to the ground. I held him and
ulled him with me as I rolled backwards onto my shoulders,
utting my foot into his stomach. When his head was just above
nine, I extended my arms and pushed hard with my foot, sending

him in a high arc out over my head. His face was to the black
sky as he sailed away from me out over the edge of the embankment. He screamed until the sound of his body landing on the
tracks below ended it.

It took me a few moments to find the path down the embankment. I could hear Mako's weak moans even before I got to the
tracks. He lay sprawled spread-eagle, halfway across a track. I
leaned down on one knee next to him and checked his pulse and
breathing. The pulse was strong, the breathing tortured. While I
was down there I took the plastic-encased lottery ticket from his
pocket.

"Can't move," he said in a choked, desperate voice.

I knew the feeling. I remembered well how the panic began to
well up inside me when I lay at the bottom of my own building
unable to move my arms or legs. I also remembered it was Mako
who had pushed me over the railing. I did not bother sharing that
with him; I was sure he wouldn't appreciate the irony of it.

"Hang in there," I said from the embankment.

"Get doctor," he cried, grabbing at me with his voice.

"I'll be back." I scrambled up the steep pathway to the shelf
on top. I took one short look back, but the shadows of the ravine
hid the tracks. I could hear him, though. He was calling my name
between loud moans.

When I entered the house I took a small towel from the kitchen.
I checked Collin and Angie for any life signs before retrieving
my Sig and then wiping the few surfaces I had touched earlier
clean of prints.

I stopped at the back porch for a moment and looked at the
swing, trying to remember the sequence of my first evening at
Angie's house. We had been on the porch swing after dinner
when the train came by. I made my calculations and figured if
the train kept to the same schedule I had about forty-five minutes.

Then I called Carl Price at the Lemon Tree Inn.

THIRTY-ONE

HE WAS smoking a cigarette and pacing in front of the motel when I turned in to the parking lot. He was obviously thinking deep thoughts, because I had to tap my horn to get his attention. He turned as if awakening from a dream, looking old and feeble. He pulled himself together, killed the butt with his toe, and jogged the short distance to my car.

"Hi Jake," he said as he settled into the seat and fastened the belt.

I nodded my reply and got back into traffic as quickly as possible. He looked at the passing lights of the ordinary citizens doing ordinary things and must have felt, as I, that we were in another dimension. This night would be extraordinary for both of us for the rest of our lives. It was something we both knew and shared.

"You really found him, Jake? You're sure?"

"Yes, Carl, I'm sure," I said without taking my eyes off the traffic I was speeding through. "You can satisfy that for yourself, though, if you want."

He took several deep breaths. "I don't know how I feel right now. I'm sort of light-headed about it. I don't know what I'll do when I see him."

"He told me he killed Julie because she made him mad. Same with Carrie. He killed Carrie, too, the same way he killed Julie. He beat them both to death with his fists. I can imagine, Carl, that they both had a lot of pain and terror before they died. He said his hands hurt for a day after he killed Carrie." I took a short glance over at him. "Did you know that Carrie had a little girl? Her name is Megan."

"What kind of animal is he?" His smoker's voice was shaky. "Tell me about him."

"He's what you read about in the papers and see on the evening news every day. He's a product of a society that's thrown away its values." I gave myself a moment to cool down. "I'll let you find that out for yourself, Carl."

He cleared his throat and looked straight ahead at the traffic. He began to speak again, but I was uncertain that he was speaking to me. His words were said in monotone, almost a recitation.

"It was on one of those shows like *Sixty Minutes,* and Mil and me watched it together. It was Texas, I think it was, where this fella from this little town there had killed a teenage girl that he'd raped. He was given the death penalty. I think it was sometime in the early seventies, but anyhow, the Supreme Court come along and made all the death penalties illegal."

He looked over at me suddenly as if to ask if I had ever heard of such a thing. I nodded to let him know I knew what he was talking about.

He continued. "Well, they gave him a life term then, and in seven years or something like that the parole board set him free. Can you imagine that? He went right on back to that little town where he'd done the killing before. They was all scared about it, but nobody could do anything. Anyhow, to make a long story short, that fellow has killed and tortured a bunch more young girls, and they've got him back again. And you know the worst of it is that some lawyers are pulling all kinds of legal shenanigans to keep that fellow free. Where's the reason gone?"

I recognized a rhetorical question when I heard one. I stayed out of it and let him do whatever he was doing to think his way through the morass that was to be his conscience for all his remaining years.

I turned off at Montecito and took the unlit street leading to Angie's cottage. The sudden dark of our new surroundings caused him to lean forward as if trying to peer through it.

"I've dreamed of getting this man," he said. "You're sure he's the one?"

"You decide for yourself, Carl," I replied. "We're almost there."

I parked next to the Celica and took two heavy-duty flashlights from the back before we left the car. I checked my watch and did a new calculation.

"Follow me, Carl. We'll be walking down a railroad track here for a couple of hundred yards. Take this flashlight and watch your footing. It's a little uneven."

"No trains?" he asked.

"One is due here in about twenty minutes," I said. "If it comes early and we have to bail off there's plenty of room to the right side. A tall embankment is to the left. Got it?"

"I got it. Mind telling me why we're on a track?"

"Because that's where he is."

He was out of questions. The only sign I had of his presence from that point on was the beam of his flashlight.

Mako shouted out at the light as soon as he saw it. When he did I took the flashlight from Carl and motioned for him to stay behind me.

"Help. Right here. I need help."

"It's me, Mako," I said from a short distance away. To Carl I whispered, "Stay quiet until I tell you."

"I can't move," Mako said. "I've got no feeling in my arms or legs. Hey, man, you've been gone a long time. I was afraid a train would come."

His voice was back and he was completely lucid. I put the light on him and could see he was drenched in sweat.

"A train is going to come in just a few minutes. Be sure you don't waste any of our time. Now tell me about Julie. Tell me all of it from the beginning," I said.

He looked into the light, eyes wide with fright. "Get me off the tracks, Sands. I've told you already."

"No," I said, "I want you to tell me all of it from where Julie called Carrie and was leaving the message. Don't leave out a thing."

He began to talk. While he did I moved one of the lights around a bit, looking for his gun. I had a fair idea of where it might have landed and found it without any trouble. He told it all, from the moment that Carrie picked up the line right through the moment where he finally dumped Julie's body in the bushes at Pelican Point. It was an amazing recitation. His voice, turned slightly crazy, betrayed the pleasure he had gotten from the killing. About halfway through I slipped a light into Carl's hand, turned off my own, and edged back into the darkness behind, where I picked up Mako's .357 Magnum.

When Mako was finished I said from my shadowed retreat, "Mako, meet Mr. Carl Price. He's the one standing here with you holding the light. He's Julie's father."

Mako looked around frantically for me. "Is this some kind of joke, Sands? We have a deal. Fifty-fifty on the ticket. You and me. We'll cut in your friend here, too, if you want."

I did not bother answering him. I spoke to Carl. "You've got about fifteen minutes. It's up to you what you want to do. If you want to leave him, leave him. If you want to drag him off the track, that's your choice." I used my shirttail to wipe my prints from the barrel of the gun and dropped it close to where Mako lay. "Don't leave any prints around here, Carl. I'll wait for you at the car."

The night was hot and uncomfortable. I waited, leaning against the car, trying not to think. The sound of the train came at me as suddenly as it had that first night with Angie. I jumped as I had done that night, and I remembered the way Angie had laughed. "It's a train," she had said. It had been a nice moment, a real one. Then, as my thoughts of Angie softened, I remembered something else. That night she had already known how Julie died. She was already a partner with Julie's killer, and he had been watching us from the darkness.

The sound of the train trailed away into the distance. The heat and the silence returned in its wake as the suffocating agents of the darkness. I forced myself not to look at my watch. I forced myself not to think or imagine things. I waited.

It was another quarter of an hour before Carl Price rejoined me at the car. He came without words of comment or explanation. I asked for none. We rode into town in a silent separation as if we were strangers sharing a ride together.

I stopped the car at the Lemon Tree and finally shut off the engine when Carl made no move to open his door. I waited again. It was a very long time before Carl rejoined me.

"Do you want to know?" he finally asked.

"I don't need to know. Do you need to tell me?"

He shook his head.

I handed him the clear plastic sheath with the lottery ticket in it. It was turned over so the back side of the ticket showed. He saw the rose imprint and turned his sad eyes to me.

"I guess I can mourn my little girl now," he said. "My Rosie."

I looked away from the tears that welled up in his eyes.

"I guess so," I said to the passing cars.

"I want you to take this." He offered the ticket back to me.

"No," I said.

"But Mil and me don't have any use for this kind of money. We got no kid to leave it on to now, and our needs are small. We owe you, Jake, more than I'll ever be able to repay."

"Maybe you could get to know a little girl named Megan," I said.

"I'll make sure we do," he said.

We shook hands and said good-bye. I watched him into the hotel before I left. He would mourn now, he and Milna, and then they could put a part of it to rest. There might even come a time when he could think about his Rosie, as she had been, and smile.

THIRTY-TWO

SUMMER WAS OVER. The heat and the sun and the crowds of tourists belied the fact on such a Saturday afternoon, but I had seen the beaches during the week. They were almost empty. They said summer was over. Soon the cooler days would come, and no more daylight savings time, and the shorter days, and then everyone would accept that summer was finally ended.

I looked out the window of Tony's Beachside at the crush of people who wandered about with that look of innocent exploration on their faces. Some seemed overwhelmed, some disappointed, and some simply exhausted. I wondered what they sought, what they expected, and what they got for the fortunes they spent on planes and hotels to come here.

"Daydreaming, paesan?" Tony asked.

He and Jason were returning to the table from a tour of the kitchen.

"I was just wondering where the recession is," I replied.

"It's in Akron, Tulsa, Trenton, and Seattle," Jason said. "It's everywhere and will be as long as we've got a tax-and-spend government."

"What did you think of Tony's kitchen?"

"Not bad."

Tony and I both knew that was the same as an accolade from Jason. Tony accepted it with a grin as he turned away to wave good-bye to a customer. Jason scowled at the room.

"You always this full?"

Tony sat and beamed. "Jase, you wouldn't believe my book. I got a two-month lead."

Inwardly, I cringed. There were a few things Jason couldn't abide. There was a whole lexicon of words such as "tasty" that drove him up a wall, but what really bothered him in casual conversation was too much slang. He was not one for the short form. If Tony said "book" meaning "reservation book," then "res ervation book'' was what Jason wanted to hear. He did not like to decode a conversation. But what he hated most of all was someone taking liberties with his name. He was called Jason by all but a very few and select number who called him Jase. Tony was not in that number.

On the other side of it, Tony was a blithe spirit and seemed not to notice his missteps. On the whole it made for a rather entertaining lunch hour for me.

Tony moved in to a conspiratorial hunch and lowered his voice. 'Hey, Jakey, I'm not askin' now, but you know that goomba I fingered for you? I mean he turns up poppin' two people and one of them happens to be your ex-partner in the beach game, you get me? Not to mention the goomba turns up to be slightly dead himself. I'm not askin', but you can imagine that I'm maybe a little curious.''

Jason made a snorting sound. I was sure it was in reaction to Tony calling me Jakey. I smiled and said, ''If you were asking, what would it be that you'd want to know?''

He held up his hands and showed both Jason and me his look of innocence. ''Oh, well, if I were askin', which I'm not, I might want to know how it all came down, you know?''

''I thought the paper covered it pretty well. One of those drug partnerships that went sour.'' I matched his innocent look with one of my own.

He nodded his head, accepting it as a closed subject. Jason and I both sipped at our espressos while Tony did some mental tap dancing. He hated silence and I figured he was trying to come up with a new topic of conversation.

I was relieved when he and Jason started talking about the restaurant business. I mentally withdrew from them to think about Carl and Mil Price. I was feeling very good about them, because when I had last seen them they had both been smiling. They had been holding Megan Berry, making a public announcement, and smiling.

They had asked me to come to Lodi, where they were holding a press conference. I went and stood in the background while they told the audience of reporters that Megan Berry was to share equally in the forty-million-dollar lottery prize. Hers would all go into a trust, and they would see to her education in the interim out of their share. They mentioned the tragic death of Carrie in

a boating accident, and the fact that she was their own deceased
daughter's closest friend.

What they did not say could be seen clearly. The way they
looked at Megan and the way she responded to them told the rest
of the story. Owen Berry stood next to them smiling his gratitude
and hugging his daughter. It was a fine family portrait. Megan
was a fortunate little girl and was going to be a very rich young
lady when she reached twenty-one.

Just before I boarded my return flight to Santa Barbara, Milna
Price stepped over to me and handed me a small neatly wrapped
package.

"Mr. Sands, there is nothing in the world we could give you
that would express our gratitude the way we feel it. This is a
token of that, because it meant something to Rosie; and because
of the way she used it, it means a great deal to us. It's the only
thing we could think of."

I was drawn back to the moment at hand by Jason making the
sounds of departure. He was pushing back his chair and saying,
"Thanks for lunch, Tony. You have a fine place here."

"Glad you liked it and glad you finally made it in."

I stood and placed some bills beneath my plate for the waiter.
"Thanks for another good meal, Tony."

"Anytime, paesan," he said. "And, Jason, you're my guest
too, whenever you're in town."

"Same goes for you, Tony, when you're down in Malibu."

Tony saw us to the door and held it open as we moved on
past him. I saw Jason looking up at Tony's hair and held my
breath. Jason cocked his head as if thinking something over.

"Tony," he said, "I admire that haircut."

Tony's hand went to his hair. "Yeah, I got a stylist down on
State Street does it," he said.

I relaxed.

"A stylist," Jason said, managing to make it sound as if he
were changing his whole opinion of Tony around that one word.

I got tense again.

"Yeah, you know, like a barber," he explained.

"Oh," Jason said with a fresh, understanding smile. "For a
minute there I thought you were talking about one of those places
that cuts, dyes, and poofs. Hair salons, I think they're called."

should know that's not your style. Well, you come see me, Tony, anytime."

Tony stood with one hand on the door and the other on his hair. "I'll do that," he said weakly. He managed to give me a small wave and said, "Ciao, amico." His heart wasn't in it.

I followed Jason to his car and helped him in with his chair. He looked out at me from behind the wheel of the Rolls and said, "Well, hell, it's not like I asked him if he dyes his hair."

"No."

He made some unintelligible grumbles while he settled himself into a driving position. He started the car before he said, "Those Prices did a fine thing."

"They're good people."

"You up to some chess anytime soon?"

"Sure," I said. "I'll stop by next week when I'm down there to see Willis. I need to let him know it's safe for him to move back into the Marina Tower, and I can't do that over the phone." I put my hand on his shoulder as he was starting to put the car in gear. "Jase, I think I'm about ready to go back to work."

He looked at me with genuine surprise. "You mean it? Want me to make some calls? Tim Brandt and some of the others?"

"No, I want to study it for a while. It'll be different from what I was doing anyway."

"Count me in."

"I already have."

"The Paladin Group might be willing to talk a special deal with us."

"We'll see."

"I guess this means I won't have anything to carp at you about," he said as he slipped the car into gear. "See ya, amigo."

"Adios."

I stepped back and watched him go. I passed Claudile's and saw her working on some papers at her desk. I was opening my hallway door when I had a sudden thought and retraced my steps.

I knocked on the open door to get her attention. She raised her pretty face to me and shook back an independent lock of hair. I stood looking at her as if seeing her for the first time. She smiled a wonderful welcome.

"Claudile," I said. "Do you go to movies?"

"Sometimes."

"Will you go to one with me tonight?"

"Does it include dinner?" she asked with her great smile.

"You bet."

"What time?"

"Eight," I said. "You'll have to pick because I wouldn't know good from bad. I haven't seen anything for at least five years."

"You haven't missed a thing."

Surprisingly enough, she seemed to be as happy about my asking as I was about her accepting.

Upstairs I spent some time straightening my office and doing some odds and ends that needed doing. At my desk I opened the middle drawer and took out the small box given to me by Milna Price. I opened it and took out the gold signet ring. The rose still held traces of the flamingo pink color. I pressed it against my desk blotter and studied the delicate shape of the flower it left. It reminded me that I still had something left to do. I looked for a number I had tracked down earlier in the week.

José Escobar was in Miami when I reached him, beginning the retirement he had so long dreamed about. I gave his wife my name, but when he took the phone he clearly did not know me.

"Sí, this is José."

"I wanted you to know La Rosa is at peace," I said.

It was cryptic enough to take him a moment. I could almost hear the thought process through the phone line. When he got it he made his sound, which made me smile.

"*Ayeee,* señor. You remembered me. Gracias. La Rosa is always in my prayers."

"And how is life for you, José?"

"I am in heaven," he said. "Soon I shall return to Cuba, I am sure."

"I hope it is as you remember it."

"I, too, but I do not hold out much hope for that. But, señor, how did you find me?" He stopped, laughed, and made his sound. "*Ayeee,* of course, you are El Cazador."

"Yes, El Cazador."

"Gracias, señor, muchas gracias."

"Por nada. Buena suerte, José."

"And to you, señor. Good luck."

I put the ring with the flamingo rose away and gave som

ought to exercise. I had a lot of pent-up energy that needed
release. I needed a good long run.

Without thinking much about it I donned a pair of the long
shorts and a tank top. I slipped on the Killer Loops and faced
myself in the mirror. I instantly felt the pangs of something lost
or missing. I stepped out my lanai doors into the heat that was
holding on to the afternoon and heard the light clamor rising from
Cabrillo. I held the cap with the long upturned bill Collin had
given me and remembered the day he had tossed me the bag from
Smiling Jack's. In many ways it seemed a thing that had happened
ages ago. Yet the memories were very fresh.

I would probably not go back to the nets of East Beach. Not
to play. But I would run there. I would run there often and probably stop and watch some good teams play and see another player
become the king of the beach. Maybe Riggs, now that Collin and
Tako were out of his way.

I suddenly lost my need to run. The energy had drained out of
me. There were still some bits and pieces in there to think out
and put to rest for good. It was a good day for that, picture-
postcard perfect. The tourist bureau must have been happy with
it. It was winding down with the kind of sea, sand, sky, and palm
trees they promised in the brochures. I leaned onto my terrace
railing to finish my thoughts and to watch it end.

Just another lousy day in paradise.